TOMORRO

Connie Monk is the
novels published in
which, *Jessica*, was runner-up to the Romantic
Novel of the Year Award.

She comes from a family of generations of
musicians, is married and lives in Devon.

by the same author

SEASON OF CHANGE
JESSICA
FORTUNE'S DAUGHTER
HANNAH'S WHARF
RACHEL'S WAY
REACH FOR THE DREAM

CONNIE MONK

Tomorrow's Memories

Fontana
An Imprint of HarperCollins*Publishers*

Fontana
An Imprint of HarperCollins*Publishers*
77–85 Fulham Palace Road,
Hammersmith, London W6 8JB

Published by Fontana 1992
9 8 7 6 5 4 3 2 1

First published in Great Britain by
Piatkus Books 1991

ISBN 0 00 647095 5

Set in Palatino

Printed in Great Britain by
HarperCollinsManufacturing Glasgow

AUTHOR'S NOTE

This is a story where fact is interwoven with fiction. To the best of my knowledge there are no such villages as Shelcoombe or East Rimford; these are fictitious as are the characters who inhabit them. Spanning a period from September 1939 to June 1945, the Second World War is fact, as also is the little known evacuation of six entire parishes of the South Hams in Devon at the end of 1943, the area taken over for the training of American troops prior to D-Day.

CHAPTER ONE

The scene was so familiar that on any ordinary day Jane would hardly have noticed it at all.

'Thanks for the lift, Mum.' Liz took the food hamper from the back seat then slammed the car door. Then off she went, carefully closing the five bar gate behind her and skirting Folly's Meadow to come to the shady patch under the elms where the workers would eat their dinner.

Often enough at harvest time Jane had brought food out to the fields, great hunks of bread and cheese, wedges of fruit cake, cider. Now she climbed out of the car, went to lean against the gate; she wanted to absorb the sight and smell of the morning, capture and hold on to it. What was it Mrs Sid had said to her as she'd come down from making sure the bedrooms were ready for the unknown evacuees who had to be collected? 'Ought to be down on our knees saying thank you . . .'

Jane head the distant purr of an engine as Tim brought the tractor pulling the wain through the top gate. Today Sid Collyer was riding aloft. Half gardener and half general help about the place, Sid – and 'Mrs Sid' – had been part of the Denby Farm even before Tim had brought Jane there as his bride eighteen years ago. A day like today stirred happy memories. Where had all those eighteen years melted away to? Newly married, the Gowers of Denby, they'd been so proud, so sure of all that lay ahead. And how kind the years had been to them. Her mind had no room for memories of hard times – the struggle to meet the bills, the uphill battle to send the children away to school when the time had come.

Today she looked across the field, and what she saw was to her the embodiment of all they were. Tim, as

7

unchanging as the days of the week, as certain as the sun that ripened the harvest; Richard, Liz's twin; less than a month and they'd be sixteen; Hartley, as dear as if he'd been one of the family. She watched the boys, with Charlie, one of the farm lads, turning the stooks with their two-pronged forks; she must have seen it all countless times before, but never with this clarity. Oh, but she did say thank you! And as if to be extra certain she crossed her fingers tightly as she said it. 'I know how lucky we are. Thank you that Tim's a farmer, thank you that the boys are too young to have to be part of war if it comes, thank you that they're here in dear, safe Devon.'

Tim stopped the tractor then climbed down and went to supervise the boys; he must be sure the corn was dry enough to be lifted. This year it had been slow to ripen. By the time reaping was finished, the heavy mists of the mornings had meant that often they couldn't start carrying until afternoons. Now he noticed Jane, and waved. He didn't stop what he was doing, neither did she expect him to. And from that distance he couldn't know that her fingers were still crossed as she returned his wave.

'Just look at it! No business driving on a tyre like that. There'll be nothing I can do with it, except get you a new one.'

'I was about halfway here when I felt it go flat. After that I only crawled along, but I had to keep going. I've got to collect children from the Village Hall. You *can* change the wheel for me while I'm picking them up, can't you, Ted? If they've got masses of luggage we can't walk all that way.'

'You got to take some o' these 'vacuees, have you? The wife told Jo Biggs when he called round checking out what space we had that if trouble starts then she has to have room for our Mary and her two. Lives in Southampton now, you know. Southampton . . . now that's a place Jerry'll have in his sights – can't leave our Mary there. These youngsters the Billeting Officer was on about – that's what Jo Biggs calls himself these days, did you know that? – they're all out of London, I believe.'

'You'll do the tyre straight away, won't you, Ted? I shan't be long getting them.' For urgency wasn't a word Ted Maddiford understood.

'I'll see to it, never fear. But it'll cost Mr Gower a new tyre, arr, tyre and innards too.'

Jane pulled a face. Then she nodded as she climbed out. 'Oh, well, can't be helped. I had to get here.'

Ted Maddiford, owner of the local garage, smiled. Who could help it? In a world full of gloom like today's was, Jane Gower was a ray of sunshine. Always ready with a smile and a cheery word. Pretty as a picture, too, in her dungarees and a shirt that, from the size of it, he reckoned she'd borrowed from her husband's drawer. Still looked no more than a slip of a girl for all she'd got a family taller than she was herself. The years seemed to rub off her without leaving a stain. There wasn't another like her round these parts. Just imagine the cut some of them would look if they decked themselves out in the things she wore.

She started down the hill to the Village Hall, calling: 'Thanks, Ted,' over her shoulder and not giving him a chance to do more than wave goodbye in reply. A tank full of petrol could take a good five minutes at Edward Maddiford's Garage; usually there was little to hurry for in Shelcoombe. But there was nothing usual about today, not in this sleepy village, not anywhere. The very difference of this Saturday seemed to Jane to be accentuated by the sameness of her familiar surroundings. The church standing at the summit of the sloping graveyard; the cob and wattle cottages opening straight on to the narrow pavementless lane; a terrace of stone houses; Madge Tozer's grocery shop; Oswald Peatty's butchers with its swinging sign proclaiming his sausages to be 'the best in the west'; then, added at the turn of this century, the school and the Village Hall. From Harold Batty's Bakery came the smell of newly baked bread, a smell that lingered on the air long after the crisp loaves were taken off in his cart for daily delivery. Hardly realizing she did so, Jane slowed her pace, then finally stopped. Nothing changed in Shelcoombe. Seeing it today was like seeing it all those years ago for the first time. Then she'd come to it as a stranger; now it was so much part of her life that it took something like the threat that hung over them to make her see it all. She remembered the sombre tones of the announcer as he read the BBC's hourly news bulletins on the wireless; the stark headline of the morning paper: 'Will it be War?' But what had this corner of the South Hams to do with the atrocities that were happening in Europe? Nothing. Standing quite still she opened her mind to the scene around her just as she had as she'd watched Tim and the children getting in the harvest: the breathless quiet of the late summer afternoon; at the far end of the street the Village Hall and the school. All of it unchanging as the years went by, unmarked by the passing of time. Yet was it? On a railed-off patch of grass in front of the hall stood a reminder of the scar left on Shelcoombe by that other war, the stone memorial bearing the names of those who had never come back, boys who must have gone proudly to their 'new school' when first it had been built, men and boys from these cottages . . . In the warm sunshine she felt a touch of chill.

Just inside the hall were the officials, some wearing the green of the Women's Volunteer Service; others she imagined must have travelled from London, or perhaps Totnes where the children had got off the train. At a table sat Jo Biggs. Until this summer he'd been a temporary clerk, getting work where he could. The Billeting Officer! It was up to him to rule whether a house was fully occupied or whether room could be found for a child from a danger zone. People who'd ignored his existence now found time to wish him 'Good-day' as he pedalled on his way. It might prove worthwhile to keep on the right side of Jo!

Today he sat in state, pen poised, a list of names before him.

'Ah, Mrs Gower, I believe, from Denby Farm.' With newfound condescension he waved her in front of his table.

Jane had the impression that the children had been made to put their best foot forward for their journey. Some were wearing what she took to be their 'tidy' clothes, others clearly had been bought something new to come away in, shorts and skirts that allowed for growing. The one thing they had in common was that on string around their necks hung cardboard boxes in which they carried their gas masks.

'I'm taking two,' she told Jo Biggs.

'Madam, I have my list, I know exactly who you're taking.'

At the end of the line of waiting children was one little girl who'd missed out on the sprucing up, Sunday best and new clothes alike. The cleanest thing about her appeared to be her gas mask box. A few of the others carried their luggage in attaché cases, most had carrier bags; this child had neither. All her worldly goods were in a pillowcase that had long ago forgotten it had ever been white. From this distance Jane couldn't tell whether her floral cotton dress was dirty or merely faded. Either way it was too short. She wore no socks, just lace-up boots. And on her head was a dark green beret. Lots of children wore berets – but this one was pulled down almost to her eyebrows, her short, straight hair just showing at the back. Next to her was a skinny boy, pale-faced, looking swamped in shorts and pullover, clearly new and bought to last.

As Jane's gaze moved along the line of waiting children, Jo Biggs boomed: 'You two at the end of the row. The girl with bare legs – yes, you, child! – and the boy, step forward. Come along, step up here.' Authority had spoken. Then, presumably to Jane: 'Two children, unrelated, different sex. Where possible families are kept together; unrelated children of the same sex may share a room. You have space for unrelated children of different sexes. Sign here for receipt of them, also for your

11

Allowance Books. Three and six a week, each child, from the Post Office. That's all. You may take them.'

The children had come to stand by the table, neither of them quite looking at anyone.

'Hello, I'm Mrs Gower and I'm going to take you home to stay with me. Is there anyone you want to say goodbye to?'

Two heads were shaken.

One of the helpers came forward, presumably a teacher.

'I didn't hear either of you say "How do you do?" to this lady. What is she going to think of London manners if you can't do better than that?' Her tone was kinder than her words but Jane noticed how the corners of the little girl's mouth wobbled. The day had been enough to bring tears very near the surface. Still they didn't speak.

'Do they know their addresses? I'll want to write to their people.'

'Parents will be notified officially, madam,' little Hitler cut in from his place behind the desk. 'You people have no conception of the machinery of organization behind this project.'

Turning her back on him, Jane ushered her new 'family' outside into the late afternoon sunshine, resolved that whatever officialdom did she would write her own letters.

'I've told you my name, so now you tell me yours.'

'I'm Greta.' From below the rim of the green beret big brown eyes looked at Jane, 'and he's Eddie. I'm seven – well, going on seven. Eddie's eight.' She must have only recently lost her front two top teeth. One of the new ones was just breaking through the gum; of the other there was no sign yet.

'And you're special friends?'

'Well, y'see – ' Eddie started. But it seemed Greta had made herself spokeswoman.

'We live just by each other in Digbury Mansions. He's older 'n what I am but he couldn't go to school when the

12

other kids went 'cos he's been poorly in the hospital. So his ma used to leave Ed at my place while she went out working.'

'But you're at school now, Eddie?'

'Yes, Missus. I got behind with m' learning, started when Greta did even though I'm older.'

'Eddie's ever so clever though, Missus,' Greta was proud to boast on his account. 'Quick as anything he got into the next class.'

But clearly his rise in the academic world hadn't come between them.

'Now I'll tell you about us and where you're coming to stay, shall I? I'm Mrs Gower, I told you that before. My husband's a farmer, so we live in the country, at a place called Denby Farm. We've got two children, Elizabeth and Richard – we call her Liz. They're twins, a lot older than you, they'll be sixteen in a week or two. When term starts they go away to boarding school, but they're home now for holidays. Then there's Hartley.'

'Is that a boy or a girl, Missus?' It seemed to Greta a silly sort of a name.

'A boy. He and Richard are at school together. He's almost like family. His parents moved abroad and he's been coming to stay with us most holidays since he was about your age. He's older than the other two, he was seventeen last week.'

She realized her mistake when she saw the quick look that passed between the children. Came when he was about their age! Still there and he's seventeen!

'Then there's Mr and Mrs Sid. They don't actually live in the house with us, they have a cottage just across the yard. He looks after the kitchen garden, grows the vegetables, sometimes he works in the fields; she helps in the house. The chickens are really my job, but when the children come home in the school holidays they help. Once you've settled there, perhaps you will too.'

She felt their owl-like stare. Neither of them made any comment. Perhaps she'd gone too fast, overwhelmed them with the thought of strange people and places?

In fact what put them out of their depth was that she was so unlike any of the mums or aunts of their experience; she was different from the teachers too. What funny clothes she was wearing, like the workmen who dug up the roads. And this place, it was so quiet. At home there was always something to hear: buses, motor car horns, bicycle bells, the man with his newspapers on the corner of the street, sometimes even a barrel organ; here there was nothing but quiet. Digbury Mansions seemed a very long way away. It hurt even to remember the feel of home.

By the time they got to the garage, Ted Maddiford was winding the jack and lowering the car to stand squarely on its four wheels.

'Only just that second done. Had a bit of an interruption,' he added, nodding his head towards his cubbyhole of an office. 'Gone now, she is, but I took her in and made her a cup o' tea, that's what delayed me. Looked as though she needed it too. She's all the way from London. Not with today's lot; today the trains were full up shifting the children. No, she's not what you'd call an official evacuee, but come for shelter for all that. Trained down yesterday, got herself bed and breakfast in Totnes. Looking for a place to bring the child and made up her mind it has to be Shelcoombe.'

'Is she a relative? Is that why she came to you?'

'Never clapped eyes on her, not 'til now. No, it seems she stayed here as a child. Thought I'd have my ear to the ground, what with having the garage and all. But folk are cagey about what space they've got, frightened word'll get back to Jo Biggs –' He left his sentence unfinished but Jane suspected that Eddie and Greta were smart enough to put two and two together. 'That's it then, Mrs Gower, four good wheels'll get you home safe. I'll get the other one done for you in a day or two for a spare. Tell Mr Gower he'd best leave it 'til about Tuesday.

'And what sort of a state will the country be in by then, eh? Mr Chamberlain's given 'im one last chance. What's the hope of Hitler deciding to behave himself, though, that's what I'd like to know? Land us all fair and square in the cart if he don't, and no mistake.'

Jane opened the back door of the car for Greta and Eddie to clamber in.

'You've got yourselves a good billet 'long there at Denby Farm,' Ted shouted, his face close to the window.

Then he swung the starting handle and they were on their way.

The drive home gave the newcomers their first lesson in country living. They were about a mile outside the village, bumping their way along the rutted lane, when towards them, piled precariously high and taking up the full width from hedge to hedge, lumbered a horse-drawn wagon.

'Look out, Missus!' Eddie sat upright on the edge of the seat; in fact he was nearly thrown off it altogether when she rammed on her brake.

'Steam always gives way to sail,' Jane laughed, quite unperturbed, turning to look through the rear window, ready to reverse.

The children didn't understand what she meant. It was just one more thing to come between this place and Digbury Mansions. Jane took her foot off the clutch and back the car leapt until they reached a gateway where they could pull off the lane and leave room for the cart to get by.

'Thank 'ee, Mrs Gower.' Reining in his horse, the elderly farmhand drew the wagon to a halt as he came level with them. 'Not many minutes behind me young Mike Brewer's following up – he's got another load same as this. Best you let the car stop where 'tiz 'til he's gone by. Else it'll be back and forth for 'ee. Jus' the two of us, then road'll be clear. He's bringing the last load. That'll see Mr Carlisle's harvest safely home. 'bout the only bit o' good news for our hearing today. Danged wars!'

'I'll wait here, George. Thanks for the warning. We're catching up now at Denby too after all the rain.' Then, to Greta and Eddie as the cart started forward again: 'That's Devon for you!' Clearly it was the way she liked things. The children glanced at each other, a guarded look, giving no hint of what was going on in their minds.

After a minute or two the second wain went swaying by, then they were on their way again. The next time they stopped would be because they'd come to journey's end, or so the children thought. It seemed they were wrong.

'This is the beginning of Denby Farm,' Jane told them as once again she came to a standstill. To the pair from Digbury Mansions, one field looked much the same as another, but it seemed polite to nod their heads and try to appear interested. 'You see those cows just coming out into the lane? They're ours. I'll wait and let Clem get them along to that other gate. He has to drive them across that field to the farm buildings, do you see?'

'They ain't 'arf big, Missus. What d'you mean, "they're ours"? You mean, we got to live with animals as 'uge as that?'

'Not live with them, Greta.' In the driving mirror Jane could see the little girl's worried expression, her brows almost disappearing under the tight rim of her beret. 'They belong to the farm, that's what I meant. Clem's driving them over to the sheds. It's time for their afternoon milking.'

Determined to show herself in a less frightened light, Greta sat straight, her hands clasped in her grubby lap. Grown-up conversation seemed to be called for.

'I suppose living out here you don't get the milkman come calling? We do, o'course. We get our milk left on the doorstep back at Digbury Mansions. All clean and white it is.'

'I seen cows before.' Eddie aired his superior know-

16

ledge. 'My mum took me on the charrie to see her Aunt Flo. I seen cows in the fields then.'

'I know. You told me about it. But you never said what dirty buggers they are. Bet the milk we get at 'ome don't come out o' cows covered with muck and filth like what they are.'

'The milk's pure and clean, Greta.' Jane saw their cattle from a new viewpoint. 'If you like, we'll stop and see Clem start the milking.'

Eyes like organ stops, Greta shook her head. Eddie remembered his manners and his 'No thank you, Missus' answered for them both. So, this time, as soon as the lane was clear, Jane made straight for home.

'Thought you would have been here before this. Kept you waiting, did they? Liz came back with the empty hamper, and brought a message from Mr G. Says, can you take them a bite more of something? They'll not be done 'til dark. They're on with the threshing. She went back on her bike this time. Mr G thought these two might like to have a ride out to see what they're up to.'

'That's a good idea. This is Mrs Sid – remember I told you about Mr and Mrs Sid? This is Greta and Eddie.'

Mrs Sid sniffed. 'Well, best you come inside. Careful of those puddles, and mind you wipe your feet.' No effusive welcome, but nothing in her tone to suggest there was anything unusual in two strangers being taken in, nor yet that Greta's footwear was less than normal. Her manner earned their respect. They skirted the mud and wiped their feet with vigour. Jane even fancied there was a hint of relief in the glance they exchanged as they were ushered into the kitchen.

'Cor!' Greta breathed. 'Look, Ed.'

And Jane looked too, looked and really saw. The enormous kitchen with its flag-stone floor, white-washed walls, the red and white checked curtains (for during the day they pulled the new thick black ones right back out of the way), the old well-scrubbed

17

wooden table, the wheelback chairs. Almost the whole of one wall was covered by a huge built-in dresser, shelves nearly to the ceiling housing the everyday china, drawers and cupboards below. It was more than just the sight of the room that Jane felt, it was its atmosphere. The heart of the house had always been this room.

'Cor!' It wasn't quite a sound, any more than the look she cast on Jane as their glances met was quite a smile. But there was no doubt, Greta had heard the heart beat.

'When you've had your tea, you can come with me to see where Mr Gower and the others are working. Remember we saw the wagons with corn being carried?'

'They must scrub some of that train dirt off before they touch my cakes. I'll see to them while you pack up the food. Don't forget they've got a big meal waiting for when they do finally get home. No use filling themselves up on bread and goodness knows what.' Then, having disposed of Jane: 'Upstairs with you, you two. I want those hands given a good scrub. Bring your luggage and I'll show you what's to be your rooms. Now, I expect rooms kept tidy, dirty clothes put in the basket, beds made. We all have our jobs to do in this house, and you'll have yours.' Her voice grew fainter as she marched ahead of them up the stairs.

Behind her back Eddie pointed at her and mouthed silently: 'All right?'

Greta nodded. And this time there was no doubting the smile. With Mrs Sid, they felt safe.

'Now then – Greta? Is that what she said your name is? – let's see what you look like without that blessed hat. I can quite see you have to bring it, of course, weather might turn and it'll be just what you'd need. But not in this sunshine. Take it off and let's see if you've got some hair hidden away there.'

Ah, and judging by the rest of you, you'll have some visitors in it too. Just look at them, poor little creatures! Not that he looks so neglected, but I'll have both of them in that tub before they're a couple of hours older. Sauce

18

for the goose is sauce for the gander. Wouldn't want her
to think they weren't both getting the same treatment.
Silently she planned their evening.

It was partly Mrs Sid's wrap-around overall that put
the children at their ease. They'd seen plenty of women
dressed like that at home. They liked her hands too,
hands that had never been afraid of hard work. The top
joint of the first finger of her left hand was crooked, a
legacy of a wood chopping accident when she'd been no
older than Eddie was now. A tiny woman, and years
ago a delightfully pretty one. Even now there was a hint
of her former beauty in her rare smile, and she never
gave up the battle. As wrinkled as a prune, yet every
night without fail she rubbed cold cream into her face
just as every night she wound up her long, thin hair in
twenty-five separate rags. In the morning each strand of
crimped hair was pinned on top of her head, then the
whole covered in a net she liked to think of as invisible.
Then one thing more: Mrs Sid would never dream of
starting the day without her gold studs in her pierced
ears. Sometimes, on special occasions, she'd add a
touch of colour to her lips and a dab of rouge. But today
wasn't as special as that.

Jane noticed a dish of little cakes had been conjured
up while she'd been out, each one topped with icing.
Not the usual fare for the ravenous appetites that came
to the table at Denby. You're an old softie, Mrs Sid, she
laughed to herself as she made the tea, but it would
never do for me to let you know I thought so!

They were coming back down the stairs.

'I've made the tea. We'll have a cup with the children
shall we? Then you must go home, Mrs Sid. You've
been here the whole of the day.'

'Ah, well, today's no ordinary day, what with one
thing and another. No use pretending that it is, not for
any of us. Don't you worry about me. Now, these two
have been telling me they've seen some of the farm
already. If you ask me, that'll do them for the first day.

19

Better if they stay home with me and get their luggage unpacked and settled in their rooms. They're going to give me a hand here, isn't that so?'

Greta nodded, her mouth far too full of iced cake to speak. It was Eddie who looked at Jane with a worried frown.

'If you say we got to come, then we will, Missus.' Then, remembering what his mother had told him about its being rude not to give a person a name, 'Mrs Gower.'

But Jane didn't say it.

With a sense of freedom she took her basket of food to the workers, her foot hard down on the accelerator. Not that there was any need to rush. She knew very well Mrs Sid hadn't got a roaring fire in the kitchen range for nothing. Her sights were on a steaming bath-tub; better to leave her to get on with it!

There was no sign of anyone in Folly's Meadow. The corn was lifted and the last cart load carried off to the barn. So along the track she went, almost taking off over the bumps.

'You lot don't look very busy. Are you on strike 'til you've been fed?' she called, seeing them standing gazing at the idle threshing machine.

'A cog's just sheared right off,' Tim told her.

'Can you do it? Or will you have to ask your dad to send a man?'

'No, I can fix it. But I'll have to drive over and collect the key of the stores from Dad so that I can get a new cogwheel. I don't want to have to wait until Monday.'

This was where Tim had an advantage over the average farmer. When his father had opened his first store and workshop in East Rimford, Tim had been a schoolboy. 'Herbert Gower and Son, Agricultural Engineers' had proved to be wishful thinking; Tim was determined to farm. The business had flourished, the name had never been changed.

'Fancy it happening now!' Jane mustn't let herself believe it was an omen. 'It would have been good to get it finished before morning.'

20

As far as she was concerned, Tim was always something of a thought reader. She felt his finger ruffling the short curls at the nape of her neck.

'It's cut and carried. That's what we were aiming for. We're not beat, lady, don't you think it. What have you done with the kids, then? Didn't they turn up?'

'They wanted to stay at home with Mrs Sid.'

If, at that moment, they could have looked in on the scene in the steamy bathroom at the farmhouse they might have found the children less sure. Eddie was at the tap end of the tub, Greta the other. (The very idea of it would have horrified Jo Biggs. Two children, unrelated!) The air was full of the smell of carbolic as those work-worn hands got busy. Not an inch, not a nook or cranny, escaped her and if any uninvited livestock had found their way in they certainly wouldn't have outlived Mrs Sid's ministrations. Quiet and chastened, the children subjected themselves. Presently, clad in their nightwear (Eddie's pyjamas covering hands and feet; Greta's outgrown nightgown with no buttons), blankets around their shoulders and each with a mug of cocoa, the sting to their pride was fading. Although whoever heard of anyone being ready for bed when it was still daylight. Wouldn't the kids at home laugh? Like a couple of babies!

That Saturday was drawing to a close. The second of September 1939, a day like no other. The end of an era, or a day that had served as the mirror of all that one's life held? Whichever it was, everyone knew as the sun went down that the last hours had been special.

The evacuees went to bed in their unfamiliar rooms. To think about home gave them a horrid aching feeling inside. Saturday night at home. . . no, think about Mrs Sid. That water was so hot it made a red ring round you. Felt nice afterwards though, all smooth.

''ere, Eddie,' Greta hissed. No reply. She climbed stealthily out of bed and crept to the room across the corridor. 'Eddie, you ain't going' to sleep, not this time o' day?' Still her whisper was hardly audible.

''course I'm not! Better come and sit on the bed. Don't want Mrs Sid hearing and coming after us.'

'What d'you reckon to it?'

'Reckon I'd rather be back 'ome.' His voice croaked.

She bit her lip. Eddie was almost crying; he never cried. It was up to her to make him feel better.

'Bet we soon will be too. Hey, Ed, that Mrs Sid – she's not so bad, is she?'

'Neither's the other one – Mrs Gower 'erself. Just got to get used to the queer sort of things she wears, then she's all right I 'spect.'

And having both made a valiant effort to cheer each other, their eyes met and each read the fear in the other.

'What d'you reckon they're doing at home?' Eddie gave in. It was no use pretending that wasn't where their thoughts were. ''spect your dad will have gone in to my place. Bet you anything they're all talking about us, trying to picture what we're doing. They'll be missing us like anything.'

Greta nodded. Thinking about home made her tummy hurt.

'Do you reckon we'll have to go and see those horrid great cows tomorrow?'

'Dunno. Here, you'd better hop back to yer own room. There's people talking in the yard. They must have come bacc from wherever it was Missus was going to take us.'

As Greta crept back across the landing, Mrs Sid opened the kitchen door to listen. They hadn't looked much like sleep when she'd marched them off up the stairs; she'd just give an ear to them, didn't want any tears on the first night. A scuttle of footsteps, then Greta's door closed. Satisfied that they'd found their own salvation, she put on her coat ready to go home. Politicians! Got themselves into Parliament, couldn't run a fish and chip shop some of them, making a mess

22

of the world so that poor children had to be sent off from their homes. Not that some of them wouldn't be better off. That little Greta, sore in all the cracks she was. Doubt if she'd ever had a good bath like that in all her life. And those poor bits of clothes she'd brought in her pillowcase!

Back in bed in their separate rooms the children heard something familiar. A gramophone record, 'I'm in a Dancing Mood', a song they knew; why, back at Digbury Mansions Eddie's mother had that record. The voice of Jack Buchanan was like the voice of a friend.

Richard had never had any time for dancing. On the school holiday when first Liz had wanted to share her new ballroom prowess with Hartley and him, his talents had gone no further than the waltz; so he'd put himself in charge of the gramophone. To please Liz, Hartley had followed her instructions. That had been four years ago, and still Richard's job was to choose the records and give the handle the occasional few turns if the tempo slowed.

For Hartley and Liz dancing had taken on a new meaning. Hardly moving her head, she peeped in the long mirror on the end wall. If only some of her friends could look in on them now . . . she imagined their envy, so sure that none of them could have a boyfriend with looks to compare with Hartley. It was only recently she'd even considered him as anything other than an 'almost brother'. That, even as a child, he'd been beautiful had meant nothing to her. Now, at seventeen, he was enough to stir any eager young heart: dark hair, not wavy and yet not quite straight, dark brown eyes fringed with long lashes, white even teeth, features perfectly symmetrical. Through the long summer holiday Hartley had worked on the farm every bit as hard as Richard, yet his hands showed no sign of it. Richard's complexion had weathered; Hartley's had tanned.

Richard sorted through the pile of records; behind his back Hartley held Liz closer. She even thought she felt his lips touch her hair – or did she imagine it?

'What about this next? Arthur Askey's "Bee Song". You two don't want just dancing stuff, do you?'

They did. How else could they move around the room locked so closely? But even with each other they didn't share the secret of first love. Frightened of not being taken seriously perhaps? Even more frightened that what the other felt was no more than the friendship of childhood? So they agreed to have Arthur Askey and after that they settled for a game of Monopoly.

Tim had gone to borrow the key of the store and collect the replacement cogwheel.

At Denby the kitchen was a study in black and white now, windows and doors shrouded in thick blackout curtains, walls a stark white. Night had come. The day was over.

But it wasn't finished with them yet.

The key returned to his father, Tim set out for home. Night driving was made difficult by the new blackout regulations, the headlights covered except for a narrow strip. Not much more than a mile to go and he would be in the village. The ground was becoming more familiar.

What was that? Someone cowered by the trees at the side of the lane! He was level before he realized anyone was there. Surely it was a woman, carrying something. He pulled to a stop, then reversed back to her.

'Are you in trouble? Have you broken down? Perhaps I can get it going for you.'

'No, it's not that. I'm on my way – we're on our way – to Totnes.'

He saw now that held tight against her she had a child, sound asleep with its head flopped on her shoulder. Her right arm was around it and in her left hand she had a suitcase.

24

'Totnes? But that's miles.'

'Once I can get on to the main road, I may be able to get a bus.'

He couldn't see her clearly, but he was attracted by her voice, soft and low-pitched. Certainly she wasn't a local. Tim realized he wanted her to speak again.

'You have to get to Totnes?'

'That's right. If there's no bus I'm sure I'll get a lift once I'm on the proper road.'

'There's a gate a few yards further on. I'll turn the car then I'll run you there. You've got your arms full.' Not waiting for a reply he let out the clutch and moved forward.

'There, Ben,' she whispered into the sleeping child's ear, putting her case down and easing him on to the other shoulder, 'it's going to be all right. This is the beginning of things getting better.' His only answer was a sound-asleep snort.

Leaving the engine running, Tim got out and lifted her case to share the back seat with the new cogwheel, then he opened the door for her to sit next to him in the front.

'Have you been visiting Shelcoombe? Couldn't someone have found you a lift?'

'Shelcoombe's where I've been. But I don't know anyone there.' In the dark she glanced sideways at her rescuer. Not that she could actually see him. He smelt nice, she decided, obviously a pipe smoker. 'I ought to have made enquiries first. It was stupid of me to think I could just arrive out of the blue and find everything as – as perfect as I remember. Anyway, childhood memories are probably painted in prettier colours than reality.'

'Most memories are, I expect, if we're honest. You've been here before, then?' By this time he'd turned out of the lane on to the Totnes road. 'Were you looking someone up? Perhaps I can help you? I live a mile or two the other side of Shelcoombe. In a district like this you get to know pretty well everyone.'

'I expect the whole idea was crazy. It began with one of my earliest memories. When I was small we used to come to a cottage – I don't even know where it was, just that it was somewhere near Shelcoombe. I feel I'd remember it but perhaps the truth is I'd not even recognize it now, only in memory. I don't know how many times we came – my father used to rent it, I suppose. Probably only for a few weeks each year, but when I look back at summers when I was small it's always Shelcoombe. Perhaps I won't even find it, but I remember the sunshine, the smell of the country, the feel of the gritty sand moving under my feet on the edge of the shore. And like a fool I expected it would all be waiting for Benny and me.' She found herself telling him, not just about those memories of childhood, but about leaving London, about being so sure that this was where she had to bring Ben, about the bed and breakfast house in Totnes where she'd stayed last night and where she was sure there would be room for them again tonight. Finally she told him about the hours she'd spent knocking on doors and being turned away; sometimes the space had already been commandeered for evacuees, other times it was 'I have to keep a bed for my daughter' or 'for my sister and her family.' In the dark she couldn't see Tim's expression as he listened.

By the time her story came to this point, Meg Hayward realized they must be well on their way back to town.

'You're going miles out of your way. I'll be perfectly all right if you drop me somewhere along here. My arm's ready for the case again.'

He slowed the car. She wasn't feeling nearly as strong and brave as she made herself sound, and felt a sense of isolation as he pulled up. He was going to drop her off here on this empty road.

'Now, I'll tell you what I suggest . . .' As he spoke he took his pipe from his pocket, put it in his mouth, then struck a match. For the first time she saw him. A man somewhere in his forties – 'middle-aged' was how her twenty-year-old mind termed it – a good face, clean shaven, weathered, his brown hair thick and wavy, strong-looking in keeping with his general appearance. That feeling of being alone disappeared. The match burnt down and he threw it out of the window, then lit another. He'd liked her voice and now as he drew on his pipe he studied her, thinking that what he saw suited what he'd heard. Smooth dark hair, worn to her shoulders in the page-boy bob favoured by fashion, eyes that looked at him with the directness he'd expected, arms holding the sleeping child. What a hell of a mess they'd all got themselves into that youngsters like this had to break up their lives together. Where was her husband? Soldier? Sailor? As if aware by contrast of the good life he and Jane had built.

'This is what I suggest.' Satisfied that the tobacco was alight, Tim discarded the spent match. 'I'll turn the car round and we'll go back to Shelcoombe. You can't find what you're looking for in just a few hours, especially with a baby to care for. Have a few days with Jane and me. She'll find a corner for you.'

'You haven't had to take evacuees?'

'Two. Jane brought them home this afternoon.'

'But if the Billeting Officer has said you've room for two, are you sure you can take us in? And it's not everyone wants a baby in the house.'

This time he laughed. 'You don't know Jane!'

He turned the car and set off back towards the wooded lane where he'd found her, and on into Shelcoombe. In the dark they passed Edward Maddiford's Garage, passed Oswald Peatty's sign telling them his sausages were the best in the west, passed the school and the Village Hall. Then to the country, high hedges on either side of the narrow lane. She couldn't imagine what shape her future would take but for tonight she and Ben had found a refuge and kindness, and with the confidence of youth her flagging spirits were on the way up again.

CHAPTER TWO

Coming in from the darkness outside, the kitchen seemed dazzlingly bright. A blue and white checked cloth covered the table, set for a meal for five, a meal that smelt good.

'Jane,' Tim ushered the strangers in, then re-pulled the heavy curtains across the door. 'I've brought us two visitors – Meg and Benny. We can find them somewhere for a night or two, can't we?'

Greta's 'Cor!' wasn't in Meg Hayward's vocabulary, but silently she said its more up-market counterpart as she took in the scene, the warmth – and above all the woman who turned to welcome her.

'Of course we can. It won't be the Ritz, but Denby is very elastic.' Jane asked no questions.

In those first seconds the two women sized each other up. 'You don't know Jane!' Tim had said and, from his words, Meg had created a picture of someone homely, probably plump and motherly. In Ted Maddiford's opinion, the years had rolled off her and not left a mark. Slightly built, even at this time of evening she was still wearing her old dungarees and a check shirt with the too-long sleeves rolled back. Her hair was cut short, it curled naturally and went the way it wanted with no heed for fashion; at one time it had been pure gold, now it had faded to pale honey. Her eyes were striking, a clear light blue and fringed with long lashes. All that Meg took in at a glance, with a sense of surprise that it didn't match the pre-formed image. It wasn't what Jane looked like that mattered, though, it was the natural, easy warmth of her welcome. 'Denby is very elastic.'

And Jane? What did she make of the stranger arriving at this hour?

'I was on my way back to Totnes, I must have tried every house in the village. By daylight it'll seem easier. Perhaps out of the village, away from the school, the Billeting Officer has let something through his net.'

Every syllable was clear, not clipped and harsh like some of the announcers on the wireless, but soft, almost husky. Around them on the farm Tim and Jane were used to the broad West Country speech; they had no strong dialect themselves, their children certainly hadn't, elocution trained at school. Even if Meg had been a plain woman her voice would have over-shadowed any shortcomings, but she was good looking with her shining dark hair, neat features, clear hazel eyes, well-cut clothes.

'We'll think about tomorrow when it comes,' Jane told her. 'More important right now is Ben. He'll need some supper, won't he?'

'No. There was one person in the village who asked us in. It must have been after six o'clock. She'd got a house full of children, her own and evacuees, but she gave Ben some gruel and a rusk and I changed him. So unless he wakes I'll just leave him to sleep with his clothes on.'

'He looks well away.' Jane was playing for time while her mind explored every avenue in the hope of coming up with an idea of what to do with a baby. 'Keep him in here in the warm while I sort something out, so that he'll be safe while you have your supper. I'm afraid for tonight you'll have to have him in your bed, but he can't be left up there until you go or he might crawl out.' She guessed him to be at about the crawling stage.

The den, that would be the best place for them.

'We're starving, Mum.' Richard looked up from the game of Monopoly as she went in. 'Isn't Dad back yet? When can we have supper?'

'You're always starving, my lad. Yes, he's home. He's brought a visitor, a young woman with a baby and no

30

place to sleep. While Meg – that's her name – has her supper she'll need to lay Ben down somewhere safe. I was thinking, if we turn the sofa in here round to face the wall and make a nest of cushions on it, that'll do him.'

'Gosh, we're bursting at the seams, aren't we?' Liz was caught up in the excitement of a house full of strangers.

'Can you see to it for him while I get their bed ready in the old nursery? A night or two, that's what Tim suggested. We'll see.' She frowned. 'Can you imagine, looking for a bed with nowhere to go?'

Three of them, all relinquishing their Monopoly willingly, yet she recognized exactly what it was that spurred each one of them. For Richard, it was the knowledge that the sooner it was done, the sooner supper would be ready; for Liz it was eagerness to play a part in setting the scene for a changing world; it was Hartley she looked to to be sure a comfortable nest was made for the child.

'In the morning we'll get one of the cots down from the loft,' Jane said to Tim when they finally found themselves alone. Bursting at the seams it might be, but at last the house was quiet, only the two of them still up. 'The boys will climb up for it while you're out getting the thresher ready.'

'Is that what you want, Jane? You've got two extra already. I only suggested she should come for a few days to give her time to look around.'

'If she finds somewhere, then fine. But, Tim, she's not likely to. People who've wriggled out of Jo Biggs' net aren't going to admit to having room for anyone.' She'd banked the fire up in the range. Now she closed the damper to make sure it burnt slowly and stayed in all night. 'This morning I was remembering all sorts of things, Tim.' Her job done she sat on the edge of the wooden table, her legs dangling. 'How it was before we met . . . all that time when Mother was ill . . . my stepfather . . . that dreadful scrapyard. The way I always knew when he'd been drinking from the way he drove the cart . . . oh, I was remembering lots of things that for years I'd tried to forget.' She seemed to be weighing up whether or not to go on. He waited. In the way he did, he knew she was building up to the real point. Then, her eyes meeting his: 'I couldn't see why we had to be drawn into things that don't concern us – now, I mean, not then – half of me still can't. Germany, Poland – even London – what have we got to do with any of them?'

What she'd said had stirred his own memories too. It had been the day of her mother's funeral. Pushing his broken down motor bike along an isolated Exmoor lane, he'd noticed the lights of a house; perhaps they had a barn, somewhere with a lamp where he could work? A cottage and a scrap merchant's yard was what he'd found – and a young girl, her black dress accentuating the paleness of her face. In the barn she'd sat on an upturned box watching him work. Watching him and talking to him too. She'd loved her mother, had nursed her through a long illness; now grief had been mixed with excitement that at last she'd be free of the man she could never understand her mother marrying. In the light of the lantern her blue eyes had sparkled into life as she'd sat on an upturned box and watched him at work on his motor bike, the girl who from that first evening he'd not been able to get out of his mind. He looked at the woman she was today, happy and secure.

'That was this morning, Janie. And now?' he prompted.

She answered honestly: 'It's a bit like wanting to get the harvest in while everything's still normal. Mrs Sid says we should go down on our knees and say thank you that we're safe and lucky. It seems to me we've got to be a bit more constructive than that, we've got to show our gratitude, like saying "If we share what we've got, then we earn the right to it".'

'So you want Meg and Ben to stay? Did she tell you where her husband is?'

Jane shook her head. 'Didn't mention him. But I'm right, aren't I, Tim? We've got to take her in.'

He took her small, suntanned hand and held it against his cheek. 'I thought much the same thing, out there in Folly's Meadow,' he told her. 'The world and its problems seemed a million miles away.'

'But they're not. They're here, our windows frightened to let out a chink of light.' Then her thoughts going off at a tangent, she giggled. 'Dirty buggers, that's what Greta thinks of your Guernseys.'

He smiled, but all he said was: 'You're right, it's not much of an effort for us to make to help the war along.'

'War! It hasn't even happened!'

'Say it again, Janie, make the most of it while you can. There's no doubt of what we shall hear in the morning.'

He lifted her down from the table. She leant against him, feeling the caress of his chin against her ruffled curls. In his basket Mufti, their terrier of no fixed breed, let out a stifled yelp as he dreamed, just loud enough to rouse Simpkins the tabby cat from her sleep on the wooden fireside chair. She stood up, turned round two or three times and clawed at the cushion before she re-settled herself, tucking her tail round her. Another moment to leave an indelible impression on Jane, probably on both of them.

'Time we were in bed, my lady.' If the pressure of his chin was a caress, so was his voice. The night was as special as the day that had preceded it. She raised her head as her mouth sought his. Tightly she clung to him. This was her world. Nothing, not even war, could take this away from her.

In their years together lovemaking had never lost its wonder; still it was a silent communion, a reavowal of their need of each other. But tonight it was more even than that. As they moved ever closer, practice and instinct their guide so that at the same moment they would gain the climax they reached towards, it was as if into this act of love they put everything their years together had been. Yesterday and tomorrow, past and future; as long as they had each other they had everything.

The next morning by a quarter past eleven Tim was home from repairing the threshing machine, the wireless was turned on and they all gathered around it.

'I am speaking to you from the Cabinet Room at 10 Downing Street . . .' Mr Chamberlain's voice was sombre. Even before he told them, they knew. The war had come. An hour ago, half an hour ago, there had been hope. Now there was none. Silently they listened, standing around the wireless, a silence that held as the National Anthem was played. Then Tim switched the set off.

'That's it, then.' It was Sid who spoke, knocking out his pipe on the bars of the range. 'Didn't you say you wanted to get that threshing finished with? I'll give you a hand, Mr G. Sunday or no, we'll all be happier when it's done.'

His 'That's it, then' was the nearest any of them came to talking about what they'd heard.

'Come on, you two, let's go on over,' Richard said, and gladly Liz and Hartley followed. They didn't want to listen to what the grown-ups had to say. Suddenly they felt that they were part of the world that mattered. War! And who would shape the future that came out of it? They would! Only by themselves could they talk about it, hear the swagger in their voices.

Eddie and Greta stood small and silent, watching and waiting, uncertain what the next move would be; to them 'war' meant gas masks, London being blown up, them having to be here in this place they didn't know and with people who were strangers; 'war' meant something dreadful for the people back at Digbury Mansions, and they'd been pushed out so they wouldn't be part of it; 'war' meant . . . ? They didn't know what it meant. They didn't look at each other, neither wanted to see how frightened the other one was.

Like them, Meg had no experience of war. As the wireless was switched off she needed to fill the silence. Yet she couldn't, there was something about the other four that stopped her. Jane, Tim, Sid, Mrs Sid . . . none of them quite looked at anyone. 'That's it, then' – then sheltering behind the work that waited. Twenty-four hours ago they'd acknowledged there was no reasonable hope of avoiding war, they'd been able to talk about it. But twenty-four hours ago it hadn't actually happened. Meg saw them as untouched. How different it would be this morning in the London she'd left behind.

'I'll see we're back for dinner at half-past one, lady. Will that do?' Tim said, and for answer Jane nodded. He picked up his hat from where he'd thrown it down on the table. Just for a second their glances met; neither spoke. But Meg didn't miss the silent message. She'd never been more aware of just how alone she was.

'I'm off to see to a few things at home, but first, Mrs G., let's turn this the other way round. This side feels like toast.' Mrs Sid put her hand to the mattress that was propped against the nursery fireguard in front of the kitchen range. This morning the boys had climbed into the loft and brought down the long disused cot.

'I'll help.' Meg reached to take one end of it.

'That's it. You and Greta see to that end, Eddie and I can do this.' Mrs Sid put herself in charge. This morning her cheeks were rosier than nature intended and her mouth had a touch of lipstick. Ordinarily her 'bit of war paint', as she termed it, didn't come into use until, Sunday dinner cleared away, she put on her best dress for the afternoon; there was nothing ordinary about this Sunday – and if Mr Chamberlain told them they were at war, she wasn't going to be caught not looking her best.

Tim waited until the mattress was propped back against the guard, then he said to the children: 'Come on, you two. If we're to be back in time for half-past one dinner there's plenty of jobs you can give me a hand with.'

'You mean with them cows?' Greta's eyes were wide.

'No, there are no animals where we're working today. You know how the corn grows in the fields, don't you? I expect you've seen pictures. We've finished cutting it, but after that it has to be threshed.'

'You mean given a whacking?' In this place nothing was beyond belief!

'In a way. That's how it used to have to be done. You see, we have to get all the ears of corn off the long stalks they grow on. These days we do it with a machine. It gets carried up on a moving belt. The ears of corn are blown free of the stalks – they come out through something like a chimney except instead of sticking straight up into the air it bends – then they're blown out into a big heap. Then they have to be bagged.'

'Cor!' This time it was Eddie. 'And we can help, Mister?' Then, remembering just in time, he added: '. . . Gower.'

'Yes, there's plenty to do. Make sure you're not wearing anything that matters, it's dirty work.'

'I'll put on m' old dress. Wait for me, Ed.'

If what they'd seen already was her best, whatever could her old one be like!

'We'll wait. Quick as you can.'

A minute or two later Jane watched them drive out of the yard, Tim and Sid in the front, the small helpers in the back. She couldn't know what went on in an eight-year-old mind, or in a going on seven one either, but she'd seen the way they'd looked as Mr Chamberlain had made his announcement. Tim must have noticed it too.

'Mrs Gower,' Meg's voice cut into her thoughts, 'all this – the cot and everything – you and Mr Gower have been so good to me. Looking back to last night, it was like a miracle when he picked us up. But I must find somewhere where I can work.'

'Don't rush into anything, Meg. Everyone's life is at sixes and sevens at the moment. And, you know, because we're so lucky here, I'm glad we're all being shuffled up together. There's you on your own with your baby, then there's Greta and Eddie – sharing our home with you all makes me feel we're earning the right to be here, safe and away from it all. Some people would call it superstition, but to me it seems like logic.' She was surprised to hear herself letting Meg, almost a stranger, into her secret bargaining with providence.

But Meg seemed not to have been listening. 'You wonder about my husband. More likely you've guessed. It's always the same – women who've had everything easy are the first to jump to conclusions and to condemn. Well, you're quite right. I haven't a husband. I never have had one. If the authorities thought I couldn't look after Ben properly, some interfering busybody might say he'd be better away from me.' She turned round, her eyes full of fear. 'I *must* find work, show that I'm capable of earning a living.' She looked cornered, hostile. 'I wasn't going to tell anyone. You won't say anything, Mrs Gower! Promise me. I simply have to find a place, don't you see?'

'I'm Jane, not Mrs Gower. I shall tell Tim, but no one else. We're your friends, you know that. That sounds like Ben awake. Shall we go and put the cot together before you bring him downstairs?' There were still so many unanswered questions. She was sure there was far more to Meg's story than she'd been told. Her voice, her clothes, her whole bearing, suggested that Ben's father might have been the cause of the rift between Meg and her past.

Together they took the cot parts and went upstairs.

'If you really mean what you said, then I'll send for

the rest of our things. I could only carry the one case, you see.' There was a smile in Meg's voice.

Denby was drawing the newcomers unto itself, just as it had with Hartley all those years before.

Attached to one end of the Dutch barn was a shed, grandly known as 'Tim's office'. Coming from the mushroom shed Jane crossed the yard towards it, not for anything in particular. It was a habit of the years. If she saw the door open and knew he was in there, what more natural than she should join him? Coming towards the door she recognized Meg's voice inside.

'Oh, it's you!' If she was surprised to find her here with Tim, she was even more so at her own reaction. In the house she'd accepted Meg, just as she had Greta and Eddie. But Tim's office belonged to him – to him and to her.

'Don't worry, I'm going,' Meg said it pleasantly enough, then turned to Tim with: 'Thank you. Just talking about it helps, you know.'

Talking about what? Jane frowned. Then Meg went out, leaving her with Tim. Just as she usually did, she hoisted herself up to sit on the sloping counter where he kept his books and records.

'Has she told you – about Ben's father, I mean?'

'No. Someone with a wife, I imagine,' Tim answered. 'She's only a kid herself, even now. Can't think what in the world her own family must be thinking of. Surely there's someone who cares about her?'

'Anyway, she seems to have lost the urge to rush away. She and Ben manage quite well in the old nursery.' Despite the unexpected disgruntled feeling that niggled at her, thinking of Ben she smiled. 'He's a poppet, Tim. He belts around on all fours, knees straight, arms and legs stiff. Follows Mrs Sid everywhere. I left him on the kitchen floor surrounded by the entire contents of the saucepan cupboard. Getting the feel of the place, that's what Mrs Sid called it!'

'It's Meg I'm concerned about. It's not just what she says, it's the feeling I get from her. She's alone, she's frightened, and living here she's not got enough to fill her time. Idleness is a lonely state, Jane. She's an intelligent girl, she needs responsibility. I was thinking – you've got more than enough to do. Why don't you train her to look after the mushroom sheds, take them off your hands? You'd be glad to have more time in the house now there are four extra to look after.'

Jane frowned. 'Living here she's not got enough to fill her time! If she's so intelligent, I wonder she needs to be pointed towards something. She needn't be idle.'

He heard the pout in her voice, and laughed. 'That doesn't sound like my Jane!'

There was no answering laugh as she told him: 'The mushrooms are *my* baby, Tim, they always have been. And she's never offered to help anyway.'

'Umph, well, it could be that she doesn't want you to feel she's pushing in. We'll have to think something out, see what we can do to make things better for her.' Then, changing the subject: 'Here, lady, move your behind an inch. You're sitting on a pamphlet I've had from the War Agricultural Executive Committee.'

'Sorry.' Jane wriggled along the bench, her usual good humour immediately restored as she took the circular he held out to her. Extra home production of food was essential, she read. The Ministry of Agriculture was asking for a million and a half extra acres of land throughout the country to be turned over to the growing of crops. 'We don't waste any space, Tim. We use every square foot we've got. Sid was even talking about digging up the lawn at the side of the house.' Her eyes were alight with laughter. 'Do you reckon that'll keep them happy?'

'He's a good old lad. Seriously though, Jane, there are more efficient ways of feeding a country than land being given over to grazing. How much extra arable acreage they want in Devon they don't say, but one thing's sure

– every farm will be putting more under the plough this autumn.'

'Sounds like being a boost for Dad's business. Which reminds me, I went East Rimford way to town this morning and popped in to say hello to him. Your talk of ploughing made me remember. He had a Land Army Girl there, the first I'd seen. Brand new and smart in her jodhpurs and green jumper. Made me feel a real scruff.'

'If it's compliments the lady's after, ask me later when I've time on my hands. Down you get, you're sitting on the milk returns now.' As he spoke he lifted her from the bench, an easy, natural action; just as it was for her to buffet her head against his shoulder.

'I shall leave you to your labours and see how the children are getting on packing their trunks.' But still she hovered. 'I hate the end of the summer holiday, Tim. After having them home for nine weeks, the house seems so empty when they go.'

'Umph.' He dropped a kiss on the tip of her nose. 'No chance of it being empty this year. At least our Cockney sparrows seem to be settling – and Ben. I suppose it's easier for children.' She knew his mind was back with the problem of Meg.

On that first Sunday, the fateful 3rd September, Jane had written two letters, one to Eddie's parents, one to Greta's father.

'It's just Dad an' me. Ain't got a mum, not now. Used to have one, o'course, but I can't remember about her. 'spect Dad's missing me. Normal times, I look after things.'

When the letters had been ready both the children had wanted to drive with her to the village to post them. They'd taken the envelopes and dropped them carefully into the pillar box then turned to her with what had been their first proper smile. Perhaps Digbury Mansions wasn't so far away after all!

After that they started to write their own letters. Six

going on seven could do little more than draw pictures and write underneath them what they were: 'Me on kart', 'The dog. I lik im', 'Ed and me wurkin in feeld'. Greta looked at Eddie's pictures with admiration, but if he offered his help she always refused. 'No, I gotta do it meself.' All their pictures were of their new life.

It was about a week after Jane had found Meg talking to Tim in his office that he came into the house during the morning. It was something he often did. 'Hears the coffee cups rattle,' was Mrs Sid's opinion.

'You know, I could do with another pair of hands out there,' he said, biting into a wedge of cold bread pudding.

Liz and the boys had gone back to school. This was Jane's least favourite time of year.

'I could give you a couple of hours after dinner each day,' she offered, never doubting that was what he'd had in mind, 'just as long as I get to the school in time to pick Eddie and Greta up.'

'It was Meg I had in mind. You say you're wanting to get a job, Meg, so I thought, where better than Denby? I don't know whether you like the idea of helping us out there in the fields, but if you do, I'd be glad to have you.'

'Oh, yes, I do want to work, and to feel I'm able to repay you for being so kind to Benny and me.' How white the whites of her eyes were as she turned to him gratefully.

'Good. That's settled then. Not a full day, because of the boy. Two or three hours though. Enough to make yourself useful, I promise you that.' He smiled his pleasure at what he saw as the answer to her problems. Then, to Jane: 'Ben'll be all right here, won't he? That's all right with you, lady?' But not for a second did he doubt it.

'Ben's quite at home,' Jane answered. She felt ugly, ugly in her soul. That the clear skin and bright eyes of a

41

girl of twenty could do this to her shamed her – and that very shame withered her spirit further. She held her chin high and forced a smile.

Jane told herself she ought to be ashamed, she who had so much. Less than three weeks ago it had been she who'd persuaded Meg to stay. A baby, a suitcase carrying their few belongings . . . she'd seen it as a pointer to what this war expected of her.

Meg had told her that she'd sent for her luggage and even when the trunk had arrived containing clothes that bore the clear hallmark of quality, Jane's welcome had still been as warm. In her heart she knew exactly what it was she resented: Tim's concern.

The day after his suggestion found Meg clad in well-cut jodhpurs, ready for her first morning of work.

'He shouldn't be any trouble.' She nodded her head in Ben's direction, but he was much too interested in his favourite saucepan cupboard to notice that he was being talked about. 'I'll just slip out without telling him I'm going. If you think he should go down for a sleep, well, I leave it to you.' She ran her hands down her hips, glancing at the trim fit of her breeches. 'Ages since I wore these.' Clearly she was excited.

'Bit of a horsewoman, were you?' Mrs Sid sniffed.

'I used to ride a lot. And they still fit. Wonderful feeling when you put on something you haven't worn since before a baby and it fits. Can you remember, Jane?' There was nothing but friendliness in the look she turned on Jane . . . and yet . . . and yet . . . the word 'remember' seemed to make a back-number of her.

'Mrs G. never put on an ounce. Better figure to this day than many I could mention half her age.' Tact had never been Mrs Sid's strong point. Thinking she was defending Jane, she seemed to push her firmly towards middle age. 'Well, you'd better get along, or the morning'll be old before you get out there. Won't have time to be a hap'porth of use to anyone, dressed for the part or no.'

Left alone with Mrs Sid, Jane tried not to let it show that she watched Meg cross the yard to collect Elizabeth's bicycle.

'That young madam needs watching. Not the sort to be without a man paying attention to her. Sid's got her sized up. Anyone's for tuppence, that's his opinion, and he's not usually wrong. Men see the signs, don't need it spelled out, they get the feel. And since he said that to me, I've been keeping my eyes open. Oh, I've seen the way she talks to the men out there in the yard – Miss La-di-dah with her fine talk, but that don't mean anything when it comes down to brass tacks. That young minx means trouble. Feel it in my bones. Me and Sid too.'

'I expect we shall find she'll work as hard as any lad and Sid'll change his mind.' Yet even while Jane defended their visitor, in her imagination she was following her across to the field where Tim would be waiting. 'She thinks the world of Ben,' she went on, as if to prove Meg's good points to herself. At the sound of his name the young man crashed two tins together like a pair of cymbals, shrieking with glee at his cleverness.

'Oh, yes, I'll give her credit for that. Brings him up in a regular routine; keen to be seen as the perfect mother. And she'll work well enough on the farm too. She'll win their admiration, of course she will. Not everyone's as uncomplicated as you and me. There are plenty who find it important to be admired, to give a good impression. Good with the boy – ah, and likes us all to take note of it.'

Jane told herself it was laughable that old Sid should harbour thoughts like he did. She'd put it out of her mind. So easy to say and so difficult to do. Each morning, as soon as Ben's breakfast was over, off Meg would go. Sometimes Tim would look in and collect her, sometimes she'd ride Elizabeth's bicycle to whatever part of the farm they were working. She was always willing, always cheerful – no wonder the men on the farm looked forward to the hours she worked.

September gave way to October. As week followed week, a daily routine established itself.

'You're not sending Meg to help Clem with the milking?' Jane put a smile in her voice as she asked Tim.

'No, she couldn't manage that. The mornings are too early for her and teatime she has Ben to look after. But, Jane, I'm glad I thought of putting her to work. She seems to enjoy it and she works hard, doesn't expect any favours. She handles the horses as well as any man. With Master and Fury in harness, she drove the seed drill as if she'd grown up to it. And you must have noticed how keen she is? Likes to talk about what we're doing.'

Oh yes, Jane had noticed! She wished she hadn't asked.

It was about a fortnight after that when, one morning, Tim came into the mushroom shed where she was filling the baskets ready to take to town. Casually he mentioned that he'd spoken to Meg about learning to drive the car. It was a reasonable suggestion; often there were things to collect from his father's stores or from the merchants in the Cattle Market.

'Do you want me to teach her?' she offered.

'No, that's all right, lady, you've got enough to do. Anyway, the gears on your car are different. Better for her to learn on the one she's likely to use.'

Jane didn't answer.

Silently he watched her picking mushrooms and laying them carefully in their baskets. Something wasn't right. He'd felt it for days, yet hadn't been able to put a finger on it.

'Jane, you worry me. Everyone feels tension I suppose, the future's so uncertain. Then you've got the children to worry about. Are you doing too much? You look tired. Or is it the heat, the airlessness, in these sheds?'

'I'm not tired.' It was true, but she heard the irritable note in her voice.

44

He took the basket out of her hand and put it on the ground, then turned her face up to his. 'There's nothing wrong? If you weren't well, you wouldn't hide anything from me?'

''course I'm well. I'm never ill.' Her laughter was brittle, she wanted to turn the knife in her own wound. 'You were telling me about Meg learning to drive. Yes, a good idea. So you're going to take her out in the Morris?'

'The Morris, that's right. Better for her to get used to that. But me give her lessons? I haven't time to waste on that. It was Ralph's idea she ought to learn; he's offered to teach her.'

'Does she know it won't be you?'

'Shouldn't think it occurred to her that I'd teach her.' He frowned. She couldn't follow his train of thought. 'I think our Meg is looking for a bit of romantic dalliance.'

'And you?' How flat her voice sounded.

'Me?' He seemed not to understand what she was suggesting. 'You're not serious?' But she was, he could tell it by the way the corners of her mouth trembled.

They'd accepted each other almost without thought or question for so long. Only in the act of making love did their bodies and minds fuse and bring them moments of awareness. 'You *are* serious. Janie, what are you thinking?' Her chin in his hand, he tilted her head, willing her to look at him. 'Darling, you're crying.' And she was held close in his arms. Familiarity and acceptance can dim the vision. With sudden clarity they could see. Nearness had nothing to do with his hold on her, nothing to do with the habits of day to day living.

She gulped, wiping her eyes and nose against his shoulder.

'Suppose it's because I look at her – and I see that I'm not young any more. I'd never thought about it before, then suddenly she was there with you, and I . . . I . . . old . . .'

'Old? You?' His soft laugh chased away all her fears.

45

'Janie, you could never be old. Twenty or eighty, you're my Lady Jane. What's age got to do with us, eh? We're us, the Gowers of Denby. Remember when we were first married how cocky we were to call ourselves that? Seems sort of silly still to be saying I love you; how proud I am – '

'Don't, Tim, you make me ashamed. It was just that I felt as if the lights had all gone out. I felt lost. I ought to have known.'

'Yes, lady, you ought to have.' His gaze held hers. 'I may not be bright, but I'm not that much of a fool. Do you imagine I'd ever look at anyone else when I'm married to the prettiest woman in the district?' He shut his eye in a half wink. Through her tears she laughed. They needed to cling to normality. 'I'll drive in with you to take the mushrooms. Are they ready?'

She nodded. 'Thanks. You take them into the shops for me. I'm not fit to be seen.'

'I've just told you how fit to be seen you are. You've had your share of compliments for one day. Come on, lady, damn the petrol, we'll go down and look at the sea before we go into Kingsbridge. We owe ourselves.'

They turned out the light and left the shed in darkness then went into the morning sunshine. Suddenly the world was new again, none of the depressing things they read in the newspaper could hurt them. She carried the two baskets of mushrooms, Tim had his arm lightly around her shoulder.

From the window Mrs Sid watched them load the baskets into Jane's car. She sniffed, this time with satisfaction.

Meg's driving lessons had to be combined with essential journeys. With petrol already rationed, there was none to spare for joy riding.

'Wouldn't like to say who's doing the teaching,' was Mrs Sid's opinion. 'If you ask me, young Ralph'll be learning a thing or two.'

46

But now her words couldn't hurt. Jane said cheerfully enough: 'She must be doing well. Tim said she drove the tractor yesterday.'

'I dare say she works as well as the next. Seems a capable sort of girl, have to give her her due there. Look at this sunshine. Never think we were into December, would you?'

'It's just the weather they want. You know they've ploughed Long Meadow. Tim wants to get it seeded with winter oats.'

'Time's getting on.'

'The ground's just right as long as the weather holds out like this. Tim wants me to collect half a dozen ploughshares from the stores on my way to Kingsbridge. Is there anything we especially need in town?'

'If you've got time, can you pick me up a pattern and some four ply wool? A pretty pale green, I thought. I want to make young Greta a cardigan. You choose a pattern. Not too plain. The child would like to have something a mite fancy if I'm not mistaken.'

'You've got a soft spot for your friend Greta, haven't you?'

'Soft spot nothing! What do you want me to do with the dark winter evenings? Waste my time reading twaddling stories? Better keep your hands busy. And I'm not seeing a child coming out of this house looking the cut she would if we didn't try and fit her out a bit decent.'

The ploughshares stowed away on the floor of the back of the car, Jane went into her father-in-law's office. There was an easy friendship between them, something she'd never achieved with Tim's mother. Often she'd take the longer route to town, through East Rimford, and call and see him.

'Thought I'd waste ten minutes of your morning,' she greeted him now. 'Throw me out if you don't want me.'

'Was just thinking about you, my dear.'

'Oh? Thanks.' She took the cigarette he offered and

perched herself on his desk. 'Why's that? What were you thinking?'

'Oh, nothing in particular. Had a letter from young Richard this morning. I suppose that's what set me off.' And ready to waste that ten minutes, he held his lighter to her cigarette, then to his own, and settled in his chair. 'Busy at Denby, I suppose? Like everyone else, Tim'll be putting all he can under the plough.'

'Yes, he is. And it's all going to make for extra work. Fine as long as the men don't run off and join up. I hear that John Carlisle has lost two, and I have the feeling our Clem is getting itchy feet. That's the trouble, Dad, they all know each other. One goes and it unsettles another. Only two more terms after this one and Richard will have left school. That'll be a relief in more ways than one.'

'The fees, you mean?'

'That's one thing, but it'll be great for Tim to have him there.'

Herbert Gower studied the tip of his cigarette with exaggerated interest.

'Don't push the lad, Janie. We can't make our children do what we think is right for them. They have to make up their own minds.' Then, looking at her over the top of his half-moon spectacles: 'I should know! Would never have done to have stood in young Tim's way. Yet when he was a boy I never doubted for a second that he'd come and work with me here.'

'But, Dad, it's different with Richard. Every holiday he spends most of his time on the farm. He takes it as a matter of course that when he's home he works outside. They both do, Richard and Hartley too. And think how lucky we are. Richard will be in a reserved occupation. There's plenty for Hartley to do too – but he's taking his Higher School Certificate this year, I imagine he'll go on to university. Hartley always was brainy.'

'Of course Richard works when he's home. He's an active sort of boy. But a job in the school holidays is one thing; turning him into a turnip basher is another.'

'Turnip basher indeed! Tim's no turnip basher!' she laughed, looking at him affectionately. What he'd said this morning was the nearest he'd ever come to admitting how disappointed he'd been when Tim had had ideas of his own. 'Actually,' she changed the subject, 'just at present he's turning into a toy manufacturer. I'd forgotten how clever he was at it. He's been making a wooden rocking horse – just a tiny one – for Ben. It's his first birthday at the end of next week.'

So they talked of other things. Richard's future was forgotten. The ten minutes wasted, the cigarettes smoked, she dropped a light kiss on the top of Herbert's balding head as he sat at his desk, and stood up to leave.

'Me and my mushrooms must go on our way.'

After she'd gone Herbert picked up the threads of what he'd been doing when she'd arrived. But he couldn't put the conversation out of his mind.

CHAPTER THREE

Jane didn't hurry. Her mushrooms delivered, she bought a few stocking fillers to put by for Christmas for Greta and Eddie. Even though it was a long time since the twins and Hartley had given up the pretence of believing in Father Christmas, this year she was very tempted to fill socks for them too. It would all add to the fun of the festival. Having children in the house gave that touch of magic. Even Ben would surely sense that there was something special in the air.

Next came the knitting wool. She took note of her instructions and found a pattern 'a mite fancy', with a panel of blackberry stitch on either side of the buttons and a stand-up collar. That should keep Mrs Sid out of mischief these dark evenings! Her shopping completed, she got back in the car and headed towards Shelcoombe. Even then she had nothing to rush for, and as her petrol coupons were in her handbag she decided to fill up at Ted Maddiford's as she went through the village.

When, the pump handle idle in his hand, Ted asked: 'And how's those little Londoners settling?' she knew he was pining for someone to talk to. And why not? For a man of his disposition it was a lonely life these days; no petrol for joy riding, less motoring miles resulting in less cars to repair. This was one of those autumn mornings when, looking upwards, she felt she could see forever, the pale blue sky clear and high. It would be a poor thing on such a day if she couldn't spare ten minutes to gossip with her old friend.

'Reckon old Mrs Harnett must have been taken off to the hospital,' he told her, giving the handle of the pump a couple of turns as he spoke just to show willing. 'I did hear that the doctor had been called out to her last night.

Older than she looks, you know. I've been here not far short of thirty years and to my way of thinking she'd forgotten what it was like to be young even then.' And it seemed he'd forgotten now that to pump petrol from the storage tank he needed to turn the handle. 'Well, I dare say she'll be better off in hospital. That daughter of hers is one short of a dozen, always has been.'

'Who told you she'd been taken in, Ted?' Jane showed the interest expected of her.

'No one. Just summized it, you might say, knowing about Dr Hookins having to see her last night. Saw the ambulance go by. Was a while picking her up – well, she's not the sort to go without a bit of a battle,' he chuckled, 'not Edith Harnett. Saw them come back again, hell for leather they were going too. I laughed to myself. Bet she was letting them have the sharp edge of her tongue, rattling her about like they must have been, racing along the way they were.'

Another minute or two with Ted, then on down to Harold Batty's Bakery. She'd take the children some jam doughnuts for their tea. So another five minutes went by. Such was shopping in Shelcoombe. From there she drove straight home, looking forward to seeing Mrs Sid's delight at the knitting pattern.

Even before she could turn into the yard, Mrs Sid appeared, her hands clasped, her fingers tightly knotted together.

'At last! Thought you'd never get here.' Her wrinkled face contorted, '. . . taken him . . .'

'Taken who? Ben?'

'No! It's Mr G. Didn't know where to get hold of you . . . Sid, he telephoned to old Mr Gower, thought you might be there. You'd already left.'

'Taken Tim! Who? Taken him where?' Already she was reversing out of the yard, looking neither to right nor left. And already, even before she was told what had happened, she knew just where the ambulance had been coming when it had passed Ted's garage and why it had gone back 'hell for leather'. If John Carlisle had been a driver of the same ilk as she was herself, then it might soon have been making a second journey! Fortunately he jammed his brakes on just in time, then carefully drove around her to park in the yard of Denby.

'I'll drive you,' he told her without preamble. 'I was with Tim's father when the call came. He's gone straight to the hospital.'

'But why? What's the matter with Tim?'

'Slide along the seat. She'll be all right, Mrs Collyer, I'll see she isn't alone.'

Mrs Sid nodded, wiping her face with the hem of her overall.

'Mrs Sid! Answer me, can't you? What's the matter with him?' Jane's heart was hammering into her throat.

'It was the harrow, the tines of the harrow . . . Sid heard him cry out, rushed straight up there. Never seen Sid so upset. When he got across the field to where it happened –'

'I'll tell her as we go.' John's voice was quiet but firm. 'Sid spoke to Mr Gower. I was there. I'll bring her safely back, I don't know when. Try not to worry.'

Jane heard it all. It was as if they were talking about someone else. And here she was, sliding across the seat so that John Carlisle could take the wheel.

'Up in the top of Long Meadow, that's where it was.' Mrs Sid's words tumbled out before he slammed the door shut and, crying as she was, they made very little sense. 'There I was, stirring the puddings for Christmas, and up there at the top of Long Meadow –'

'I don't know how he fell!' Meg appeared from the kitchen. Her voice was full of fear, her face white. '. . . didn't know until I heard him scream – ' Her voice cracked.

'That's enough!' This time Mrs Sid was clear enough. 'Just you pull yourself together!'

John didn't wait to hear any more.

Later Jane would realize just how thankful she was to

have him with her as they followed the route the ambulance had taken; now she seemed to have tunnel vision, seeing only that Tim was waiting for her.

John Carlisle had been at Keyhaven all his life, his father had farmed it before him and his grandfather before that. A bachelor, his lifestyle had been very different from the Gowers'. Even now, after eighteen years of marriage, thrift was in-built into their design for living. There had been no easy fortune to be made from farming in the twenties nor yet in the thirties; often they'd had a struggle to make ends meet. But one only had to look at John to know that he had none of the anxieties so familiar to them. When first they'd met him, he'd been consciously good looking: fair hair and moustache, clear blue eyes. Now, in middle age, his locks were thinning, the parting becoming ever lower so that the hair could be swept across to hide the bald patch that threatened; his complexion had coarsened. But his elegance never changed. The quality of his tweeds, the cut of his suits, the leather of his tall boots – polished and boned – were clear evidence that he was no working farmer. Keyhaven was probably the largest holding in the district, the granite house under its roof of local slate run by an efficient housekeeper. Had John been married with a family, the school fees would have presented no problem. But he had no one but himself; he couldn't know the glow of satisfaction Tim and Jane felt when once again the cheques were posted at the start of each term.

As he drove he cast a glance at her, sitting by his side and staring straight ahead. He wasn't sure how much she'd been told before he'd arrived.

'He fell between the tractor and the harrow. The ground was soft, it was the tines of the harrow . . . it's bad, Jane.' It was his gentle tone as much as what he said that frightened her.

Almost aggressively she answered him: 'Things always look bad when they happen. Meg's still quite new to tractor driving. She was scared, that's why she was so upset.'

53

'Yes, I dare say. But it was Sid who telephoned Tim's father, not the Land Girl. I don't want to panic you – but, Jane, he's been badly injured. Sid isn't a man to be easily upset. It's better to brace yourself for it before we get there, try and be ready for whatever damage there is. Sid says they couldn't stem the bleeding.' Another look at her.

'Of course they couldn't! Sid and Meg, how could they? He's in the hospital by now. The doctors will know what to do.' Brace yourself, he told her. The streak of superstition in her wouldn't listen to him. Tim was strong, he was healthy. The doctors would look after him. She told herself it was for Tim's sake she wouldn't listen to John's warning. But in her heart she knew it was for her own sake too; she daren't give rein to her imagination. The tines of a harrow! Tim being dragged along, the tines cutting into him . . . her own arms felt like lead, her hands tingled right to the tips of her fingers. She wanted to tell John to hurry, but it was easier to sit here. If she spoke, he'd answer, she'd have to concentrate.

Up the village street they sped. Ted Maddiford recognizing her car and waving as he stood outside waiting to catch any passr-by with five minutes to spare for a chat. Could it have been only half an hour ago that she'd stopped for petrol? The sky was still as high, still as blue. She shivered.

'I can't understand how it could have happened.' Mrs Sid glowered at Meg as she said it. Maybe she couldn't understand, but there was no doubt where she put the blame. 'Hark now, there's Ben calling out, awake from his nap. About time you took hold of yourself and saw about mashing up some food for him. No good expecting me to wait on you, I'm busy with the puddings. If I don't get them on the boil we shall be up half the night waiting for them. Never in all our years here have I made the puddings for Christmas and not had Mr and Mrs G. give them a stir. Not that I'm superstitious, wouldn't be so wicked. Doesn't seem right though, like asking for trouble. Here, Sid, you give them an extra stir up. We'll have to make do with that.'

'And you, Meg? Have you made your wish on them?' He had many a reservation about Meg, but it wasn't in Sid's nature to be unkind.

So she stirred. With her eyes closed, she wished.

'No use you wishing you'd been more careful,' Mrs Sid sniffed. 'That's what we'd all be wishing if it'd do a hap'porth of good.'

'I'm going up to get Ben.' Meg escaped. She sounded composed. The old couple might have been surprised if they could have seen her sitting on the edge of the bed, holding him against her, her face buried against his warm chest. His podgy hands pulled at her hair. He gurgled his pleasure at the unexpected fun.

'Benny. Oh, Benny boy, what've I done?' Ben obviously thought this a great game. He wriggled against her, chuckling with delight at her show of attention.

Downstairs Mrs Sid transferred the mixture into six buttered basins.

'Here, Sid, don't sit there doing nothing. Just put your finger on the knots while I tied on my covers.' Then, as one by one the white cloth covers were tied over the basins: 'Can you understand it? How a man can get himself hurt like that, after all the years he's worked in the fields? There, that's the last one tied up. Now, into the copper with them and they can boil till bedtime. Just tell me – how could it have happened?'

'As near as I can tell, there were two tines broken on the harrow. He took new ones out to the field and fitted them there, all done to save a bit of time. Must have got the job done, then he'll have stood up. Meg'll have been waiting the word to move off, looking straight ahead you may be sure, not wanting to lose the straight line of the furrow she was breaking down with the harrow. How he slipped, I don't know. My guess'd be he stepped on a clod of earth and twisted his ankle, got taken unawares and fell forward. Probably let out a curse to himself as he tripped, just like anyone would. And Meg, she'll have heard him say something, mistaken it for the word to start up, then probably wanting him to see how quick she could be to act, she'll have roared away. He must have fallen against the back of the tractor, got caught between that and the harrow. The ground is softish, fresh ploughed, soft enough that he got half under the damned thing.' Sitting with his elbows on the kitchen table Sid buried his face in his hands.

'Hark! Here's that Meg coming down. Sit up straight, Sid, do. We're not going to let her see us buckled under.'

Except for five rows of wooden chairs, the hospital waiting room was bare of furniture. The windows were set so high in the brown-painted walls that, even with the blackout curtains pulled right back, the sunshine had no chance of filtering on to the isolated groups of people who waited. At the sound of footsteps every head turned. A nurse? News? No, it wasn't a nurse, it was a man and woman . . . hope and expectancy died as quickly as it had been born. The silent wait went on.

'What a long time you've taken getting here!' Usually Emily Gower managed to disguise her resentment of her only son's wife. Today she was too upset for pretence. 'Father phoned me as soon as he'd seen how things were here.' Herbert was never anything but 'Father', no matter whether she spoke to Tim, Jane or even the children. 'I've had the time to call a taxi to bring me and still get here before you. Fancy, out there frittering your morning as if you've nothing better to do, and our poor Tim . . .'

'Where is he?' Ignoring the greeting, Jane turned to Herbert. 'Have you seen him, Dad?'

'No, my dear. They wouldn't let me see him. He's still in the operating theatre.'

'But they must have told you *something*?'

'Come and sit down. We've a long wa t before he'll be able to see anyone.'

'But I must know what they're doing to him! Isn't there a nurse? A sister or anyone?'

'Wait until they bring him out of the theatre. Until then, they won't be able to tell you anything.'

'Just sit down and be quiet.' Emily leant towards her. 'Now that you have finally got here, don't let's have an exhibition.'

'Now, Emmie, you're upset, we all are. We must just hang on to what patience we can. It won't be long before they come to tell us he's coming round again.' Herbert had had years of experience of smoothing ruffled feathers.

Footsteps. This time it *was* a nurse. But not for them. The wait went on. Seconds ticked to minutes, to an hour, an hour and a half. Each time a nurse approached every head was raised.

'Mrs Gower.' At last Jane heard her name and jumped to her feet as a plump young nurse came towards her. 'Your husband has been brought back from the theatre. Would you like to come into the office for a moment? Sister would like to speak to you.'

For a fleeting moment Jane felt sympathy for her mother-in-law, saw the way she looked up at the sound of the name which was hers too. As Jane stood up to follow the nurse, her mother-in-law watched the uniformed figure lead the way, her eyes full of hurt.

'I'll tell you everything she says,' Jane whispered, offering an olive branch.

'Humph.' Which could be interpreted any way she liked.

'Come in, Mrs Gower. Do sit down.' She liked the firm way the sister spoke. Somehow the tone of her voice drove out some of the devils that had found a way into her mind during that long wait.

'The nurse said you wanted to talk to me? About Tim. She said he's back from the theatre. Can I see him, sister? I don't even know how badly he's been hurt.' She heard herself firing the sentences, each one a question.

'It was a very nasty accident, Mrs Gower. Mr

Humphreys attended to him himself – he's the senior surgeon. He managed to save his arm – at first he feared he might have had to amputate.'

'Oh, no . . .' Hardly even a whisper.

'I'm afraid the nerves are torn. It's impossible to say at this stage whether he'll have any use in it. But before that, Mrs Gower, he has a very long way to go. His other injuries, internal injuries, were severe. He farms, I understand?'

'Yes, he does. But we'll all have to work that bit harder until he's better.'

'It's too early to know how he'll be. With broken bones one can give a fairly accurate assessment of how long it'll take. Injuries like this are quite different, no two cases are alike. It's certain, though, that he'll need a great deal of support. Particularly in his type of work. At this stage, it's hard to imagine that he'll be fit for manual work of any sort. He may prove us wrong, but you must be prepared for that possibility. I'm sorry. I wish the prognosis were happier.'

'He's very fit, very strong. Won't that help?' She pictured him, only hours ago, walking across the yard, setting out for his day in the fields. '. . . hard to imagine he'll be fit for manual work . . .'

'A healthy constitution must help.' The sister was sizing her up, assessing whether she had the stamina for the truth. 'But,' she decided, 'I imagine you're a woman who'd rather face things squarely. It'll make it easier for him, you know, if you're already prepared, if you've had a chance to come to terms before he has to face whatever hurdles are ahead. You say you'll all have to do a bit more to help. Well and good. But that may not be enough. Farming may be physically beyond him.'

With her mind Jane understood what the sister was saying, but her heart wouldn't, couldn't, believe. It was Tim she was talking about, Tim who never had a day's illness, Tim who'd had plenty of hurdles through the years and never been tripped by one of them. And neither would he by this. She'd back him, she'd help him, she'd protect him.

'Thank you for being honest with me, sister. He's very tough, even germs don't settle on Tim.' She heard herself talking, felt her face crease into a smile. Tim would be well, Tim must be well! On the way to the hospital, when John had warned her, she'd resisted the doubts; she still did. 'When can I see him?'

'Once he comes out of the recovery room you may see him, just for a moment. It'll be tomorrow before anyone else is allowed in – and tomorrow before he's talking.'

Back in the waiting room she told them something of what she'd heard, told it in her own words, painted a picture she could accept: it had been feared that he might have had to lose his arm, but the surgeon had saved it; his injuries would take some time to mend and he'd need all the help they could give him before he was well enough to do all he'd been used to doing. To put those other warnings into words would have been like losing faith, like tempting fate.

Years of experience had been Herbert's teacher. He knew how best to take Emily home without her feeling that she held second place to Jane.

'Can we visit tomorrow, did she say?' he asked as Jane came to the end of her version of the interview.

'Yes. It's going to be that long until he comes to and he can talk to us.'

'Then Emmie, my dear, you and I will go home. Thank you, John, for looking after Jane. By tomorrow I dare say she'll be independent again, now we all know the worst is over.' And, like a lamb, Emily let herself be taken home, expecting the others were doing the same. Neither of them imagined that one hour, two hours, nearly three hours later, Jane and John would still be waiting.

'Mrs Gower, you may see your husband for just a moment. Don't try and make him talk. If he just sees you, he may settle. He's asking for you.'

Jane nodded. Her feet wanted to run as the nurse led the

way through a long ward and into a side room which held only one bed. She'd imagined him lying there, pale and tired, the sort of image everyone was used to from the cinema; she'd imagined him holding his hand to her, saying nothing, happy just to know she was there. She'd not imagined him looking like this!

'Tim...' She bit her lip. Shock at what she saw seemed to have turned her to jelly. Then reason took over. How could anyone go through what he had and not be battered? Any part of him that was unbandaged and visible was covered with iodine. His head was swathed in dressings, his body too; only his left arm appeared free of them. His face was grazed and swollen. But that's nothing, she told herself. A few days and he'll look like himself again. Already she was pulling herself out of the shock of her first sight of him.

'Only a few moments, Mrs Gower, we mustn't tire him. We want him to have a good night's sleep. He won't be so restless once he's been allowed to see you. I'll be back in a little while.'

Jane crossed the room that was no more than a cubicle and leant over her husband.

'Tim,' she whispered, 'it's all over, Tim. You'll soon be better.'

His eyes opened – or more accurately one eye opened, the right one was much too swollen.

'Better...' he breathed. 'Home...' The eye closed. She could tell it hurt him to breathe, yet with all the fight that was in him he was making an effort. Perspiration broke on his face. She wiped it with her handkerchief.

'Don't talk, darling. I'll just sit here. Try and sleep.'

'Mus'... talk,' he panted. 'Ah... ha...' Every breath was a battle. 'Th' far'.' The farm! Did he know? Did he realize they'd warned her that his farming days might be over? But of course he didn't. How could he? Anyway, she didn't believe them. It was nonsense. It had to be nonsense.

'Don't worry about the farm, Tim. Not now. Get better

first.' Bending over him, she spoke quietly, rapidly. Time seemed to their enemy. The nurse would only leave her for a minute or so and in that time she had to reassure him, she had to make him understand. 'I'll see things go on. I'll get everything done, truly I will. Sid'll help more this time of year – and John'll help, John Carlisle. He's waiting outside. He's said he'll do anything until you're on your feet again. In the holidays the boys are here. Don't worry. Don't even think about it. Honestly, I can keep Denby going – and when you come home, I'll help you. I'll do more until you're quite fit again. You're going to be all right, that's the main thing. It'd take more than this to get the Gowers of Denby down.'

'Th' farm . . .' The breath was catching in his throat. He coughed, a small wet cough. The sound of it frightened her yet she didn't know why. She'd nursed her mother, she'd been with her when she'd died, the rattle of her breathing was something she would always remember. This cough was quite different; it must be an aftermath from the anaesthetic.

'Tim, the farm's all right. And soon Richard will be home with us.'

'Jane –' There was something he was desperately trying to say.

'I promise you –'

She took his hand in hers. Gently she touched his grazed cheek with her lips.

'Jane –' He tried to clear his throat, something seemed to be choking him. Her instinct was to sit him up. How could they hope he'd sleep if he couldn't even breathe?

Not two minutes ago she'd come in wanting just to be left alone with him, hoping the nurse would forget them and give them time. Now, turning away from him, she opened the door into the ward.

'Nurse!' She heard the panic in her voice.

It was the sister who came. One look at Tim, at the trickle of blood that escaped from the corner of his mouth, and Jane was bundled out of the room.

Her long wait wasn't over yet.

Usually by this time 'the Sids' would be in their own home. This evening, with Meg, they waited, listening for the sound of the car. Nine o'clock . . . ten . . . eleven. The puddings were taken up, rich and dark; Mrs Sid took the cloths off them and the steam gushed into the room, filling it with the smell of Christmas.

It was Mufti who heard the engine. He sat up in his basket, head on one side, ears cocked.

'That dog's heard something. Hark!' Mrs Sid's head was on one side too and her ears as near to being cocked as she could make them. 'That tyke's never wrong! That's a car coming. Is it them, do you think?'

It was. The car turned into the yard. Then silence. Seconds dragged to minutes.

'Dratted blackout! Can't so much as take a peek at what's holding them up. Go out with a torch, Sid. Perhaps they've brought him home. They'll be wanting a light and an extra hand.'

'If they were, she'd give us a shout.' But he did as she said just the same.

Car doors slammed, first one, then a second. Voices. Was John Carlisle coming in with them? No, that was his car starting up now. Watching the curtained door, Meg and Mrs Sid waited. To and fro swung the pendulum of the clock on the wall, the steady sound of it something that normally no one even noticed. Mufti whimpered. He seemed to know things weren't all they should be.

Then they came in, Jane first with some parcels in her hand, Sid just behind her.

'Take it steady, m'dear, just come close to the fire.' He led her forward to the wooden armchair by the range. Still clutching her shopping, she sat down.

The other two waited, neither of them able to ask the question that suddenly didn't need asking. Good news didn't come this way. No use pretending, the boy must be poorly. Mrs Sid took the packages and put them on the table, then she bent over Jane, taking her hands and starting to chafe them in her own.

'You're cold as ice, child. Get her a drop of brandy, Meg. It's in the sideboard cupboard.' And to Sid: 'Did Mr Carlisle tell you anything?' Easier to ask him than Jane. Poor Mrs G., she looked really done in. 'How were things?'

Sid shook his head helplessly. Come on, man, speak up. Hour after hour waiting here, then not being told how bad things are.

'Here, I've poured it.' Meg came back.

She pressed the glass into Jane's hands. Meg! At the back of the mists of Jane's mind was the echo of a warning voice: 'That young madam means trouble.' Meg! It was as if the whole thing were a nightmare. Get Meg out of it and it would be gone. Jane swallowed the brandy at a gulp. The fiery liquid made her eyes water; it brought her face to face with reality. There was no escape. She looked around the room: the white walls, the stark black curtains, Mufti by her side watching her, one ear up and one down, sensing something was wrong.

'Is he bad? How long before they'll let him home? Did they give you any idea? Is he much harmed? Whyever can't one of you –?' Mrs Sid looked at her husband as she asked, but it was Jane who told them, hearing her own voice as if it belonged to someone else.

'Never coming home. Tim's never coming home.'

'No! You mean . . . ? I don't believe . . .'

'Presently,' Sid intervened, 'I'll tell you. Just look to her now. It's her we've got to look after.'

Jane listened to them, she heard the kindness and concern in their voices. 'Look to her now . . .' And she was the *her*.

'Some nice warm soup. You'll feel better with some food inside you.' Mrs Sid helped in the only way she knew, and Jane found herself steered to the table and a spoon put in her hand. She swallowed the vegetable soup; it was easier to do as they said. Holding her tail high, Simpkins lapped milk from her bowl. The room was steamy with the rich smell of Christmas puddings. It was Mufti who broke the cocoon that shock had wrapped around his mistress. He stood on his hind legs, his front paws on her chair, then gently tapped her.

Something in her snapped. She wanted just to escape.

'I'll come up with you,' Meg offered, putting a hand on her arm.

Jane recoiled from the touch. 'Don't! Don't touch me!'

Climbing the stairs, she was running away from the Sids' protecting love . . . how smooth the wood of the shining bannister was under her palm . . . running away . . . to what? There was nowhere to run. *Their* room, his and hers, gone; Tim gone . . . she mustn't think, wouldn't think . . .

The next morning it was John Carlisle who telephoned both the schools and arranged for the family to come home. And as if she were standing outside herself, looking at some nightmare, the day before Tim's funeral Jane met their trains. She could feel their need of her; she knew she was failing them. The truth was, to give them the warmth they needed would have brought life into her own numbed mind.

It was that same evening that crossing the hall she saw the door of the den half open. They would be in there, the three of them. She ought to go and talk to them. But in the doorway she stopped, ashamed at her own relief. Only the twins were there. Sitting on the sofa, Richard was holding Liz in his arms, cradling her to him, her head against his chest. Neither of them heard her, they turned to each other just as they always had. And, thankfully, Jane stepped back before they noticed her.

Next day the sun shone from a clear sky. Stony-faced she sat between Richard and Elizabeth in the undertaker's limousine, with Hartley in front next to the driver. Slowly they turned out of the yard, Denby with its curtains closed as if the old house couldn't bear to see him go. Slowly along the narrow lane they knew so well, past the school where a game of rounders was in progress, up the village street, past cottages where the blinds were lowered. Slowly, up the slope of the graveyard to the door of the church. Elizabeth was crying, Richard staring ahead of him, his chin up. 'Richard – the man of the family – ' No, she pulled her thoughts away from that avenue. Just follow through the familiar doorway, follow, don't think.

So many people! The whole of Shelcoombe must be here. Tim had been everybody's friend – no, she pulled away from that avenue too. Hear the words, such beautiful words . . . Then outside again to where she could smell the newly dug earth of a grave. She knew a moment's panic that Meg might be amongst the group who waited; followed by relief that there was no sign of her; followed by unreasonable anger that she could have gone walking with Ben as if today were no different from any other. They assembled around the grave, everyone quiet. The sudden sound that shattered the stillness came from further down the village street: a youthful burst of cheering from children in the school playground. It found a crack in the cocoon that protected her. It was the sound of life.

'. . . we commit this body to the ground; earth to earth, ashes to ashes, dust to dust . . .'

Jane raised her head, stared upwards at the clear pale wintry sky. Across the open chasm she saw Liz was crying, saw Richard holding tight to her hand. And just as she had been last night, she was relieved that they turned to each other and not to her. There was nothing of her to give. Then the rattle of dirt being thrown on to the lowered coffin. Another cheer from the playground. Friday afternoon, games afternoon. Last Friday she and Tim had collected Greta and Eddie as they'd passed the school on their way back from the cattle market. 'Cor, look, Ed! Uncle Tim's come for us.' Last week . . . a day just like today. She closed her eyes. So clearly she could see him, his eyes smiling into hers. 'We're us, the Gowers of Denby' . . . 'All right, lady?' With her eyes closed, she nodded her head. There was something like a smile

65

playing at the corners of her mouth. If anyone watched her, they probably made allowances.

That one brief moment of communion, her spirit with his, and then it was gone. The day was once again just so many hours to be got through. But at last it was over. Tim's parents had driven away; 'the Sids' gone to their cottage; Eddie and Greta, out of their depth, frightened by the finality of death and not knowing how to deal with an emotion they didn't understand, were in bed; Benny was in his cot and Meg upstairs with him; Mufti had had his last sniff round the yard and come back to his basket; Simpkins was curled up on the wooden armchair ready for the night.

The twins and Hartley had come home yesterday. For their sakes as well as her own she'd be glad to see them off back to school on Sunday. She supposed now they must all be together in the den. Were they able to talk to each other? Was it her fault that they seemed to avoid being alone with her? Or was she imagining it? Was it she who was running away?

Mufti touched her leg with his paw, his head on one side, one ear up and one down.

'Good boy.' She knelt down, glad to feel his paws on her shoulders, rubbing her face against that velvety patch by the side of his mouth. Silently they communed. 'Shall we go out, boy?' He'd already paid his last respects to the yard for the night, but he never missed the magic ring of 'out'. His bushy tail thumped the ground. And for Jane, anything must be preferable to the long, lonely night that awaited her.

Once out in the yard her canine friend forgot his concern for her. He sniffed at all the familiar stopping places, then went to scratch the door of Tim's office.

'Mufti! Here, Mufti!' In an exaggerated whisper she called him back, scared that if she shouted one of the Sids would know she was here and come after her. She felt imprisoned by their care of her; every moment they seemed to watch her.

66

But still Mufti scratched the door. She's not had the courage to go into the shed where Tim had always done his paperwork; his things were still on the bench just as he'd left them. Soon she knew she must come to grips with what had to be done. Soon, but not now. Yet tonight, standing in the dark yard, the black sky alight with stars, she couldn't turn away. Almost daily she'd looked in there to speak to Tim; sometimes no more than calling a message, more often climbing to sit on the sloping bench he'd used for a desk, watching him, talking to him. It was almost possible to believe that in there she'd find a way to him. Reason would have told her there was no sense hoping for anything so unlikely – but reason couldn't reach through the misery that held her.

She followed Mufti, familiarity leading her to avoid every rut and puddle and telling her, even in the blackout of a moonless night, just where to find the handle of the door. Inside it would be dark, but she wouldn't need light to find his spirit. Her heart was thumping. Turning the handle, she realized her hand was shaking. She didn't even try to stifle the dry sobs that seemed to choke her. They would be a relief. Here in his room he'd be near her; for him and with him she would share the anguish she'd been fighting to hide.

Catching her breath, she was halted in her tracks. The lamp was burning, a thick blanket over the window shielding its rays from the yard.

'Hartley! What in the world are you doing in here?' she rasped. Finding him here had snatched from her the solace she'd so nearly found.

'Aunt Jane – I'm sorry. I came here yesterday when I got home. I'm sorry.'

'Yesterday?' she repeated stupidly. All these days she'd been frightened to come here, to the place that had straightaway called to Hartley.

He nodded. Then he turned his face away from her. He was kneeling on the floor, the lamp close by him at his side, and she saw that when she'd disturbed him he'd been working, finishing off painting the wooden rocking horse that Tim had made for Ben's birthday. Only she had known about the present. Often she'd sat on the bench watching him. It was a simple toy. Years ago he'd made one like it for the twins, but unlike the highchair and the cot it hadn't stood the test of time. A sketch of a horse drawn on a stout piece of wood; the wood cut to shape, the edges rubbed smooth; then, made from an old wooden wheel, two parallel rockers on to which the horse was fixed. Next a saddle-like seat and a bar for the child to grip.

'What are you doing, touching it?'

'He must have meant it for Ben.'

She nodded. '. . . for his birthday.'

Hartley turned round to face her. 'We can't not have it ready. He'd been working on it . . .'

Jane had come here seeking Tim's presence, longing for the relief of being able to cry without someone watching, worrying, trying to cheer her. Now, looking at Hartley, she slipped to her knees at his side as he knelt by the almost finished horse. It was too late for him to hold on to the manhood he was striving for. He'd come to her with his troubles since he was eight years old, but he'd never had anything knock him off balance as this had.

'Just doesn't seem true,' he gulped, the last of his control gone. 'He's here all the time Aunt Jane, everywhere! I expect him to walk in from the yard. If you listen you think you can hear him talking to the chaps.' Like a child he cried. Tonight his handsome face was pale, his eyes reddened, the lids puffy.

'I know . . . I know . . .' And just as if he were a child she cradled him close, trying to soothe him.

'I know I'm not proper family, but I loved him like – as if he –'

'I know, Hartley. It was like that with him too. With both of us. You're the same as a son to us.' She'd tried to hide her misery from all of them. But not now. Tonight she cried for Tim, for herself, and for Hartley, the little boy almost grown to be a man, the child who'd never know the love of his real parents.

He sniffed. 'Oh, Aunt Jane, I'm sorry,' he pulled away from her and took out his handkerchief. 'Now I've made you cry – didn't mean to –'

She shook her head. 'I came here to run away from everyone. They watch me – making sure I'm all right. I came here to cry. I'm glad you were here.' She sniffed, trying to smile at him. 'Sounds silly, but I'm glad, Hartley. Now we don't have to pretend to each other, do we?'

'The horse, Aunt Jane. I'm sorry if you didn't want anyone to touch it. I ought to have asked. But, you see, if I finish the painting, it's like doing something – for him. He'd started – all the paint was here ready.'

'He'd be pleased, Hartley. I bet he *is* pleased. Ben's birthday is next week. You'll be back at school.'

The following Thursday her words came back to her. It was Ben's first birthday. In the kitchen they all gathered to see his reaction to his present: 'Ben's Bronco' as Jane had heard Tim refer to it as he'd worked.

The perfect mother on this morning, Meg knelt by the side of it as she lifted her son on, then gently started to rock it.

'Cor, it's a real beauty. Cor, Ben, ride 'em cowboy!' In the best tradition of the Saturday morning pictures, Greta whooped. And nothing is more infectious to a small boy who feels himself to be the centre of attention than a gleeful whoop. He cooed, he shrieked with excitement, he rocked his body backwards and forwards, surprised and delighted at the effect of his efforts on his steed.

Turning away, Jane looked out of the window across the yard and to the fields beyond, the fields that had been Tim's. Behind her she could hear Meg's soft laugh as she rocked the horse. Damn her! Damn her! If she'd never come, he would still be here. I'll tell her to go, that's what I'll do. They must find somewhere else . . . They? But how can I turn Ben out? Oh, damn her! Why did she come?

Then, without warning, the words she'd spoken to

Hartley that night in the shed echoed in her memory: 'I bet he *is* pleased!' So unexpectedly she knew that Tim was close. She stood quite still, almost afraid to breathe. But just as momentarily as his spirit touched hers, so it was gone again. The winter earth of the fields was bare and desolate.

And into her mind came another picture as if in contrast to the bleak scene. Again she was leaning against the gate looking up the slope of Folly's Meadow; she seemed to hear the distant hum of the tractor engine and to smell the ripened corn.

Hours of hard work in the cold winter air, then at the end of the day a hot water bottle to cuddle; sheer exaustion was the only road to oblivion. On this December night she was woken by the sound of something in the yard. She listened. The wind had strengthened, the curtain was flapping into the room. Yes, there was the noise again. Someone must have left a bucket where the wind had caught it, it was being rolled across the ground. Nothing to get alarmed about – but enough to pull her firmly back to consciousness. It couldn't be very late, her rubber bottle was still warm. Hugging it to her she shut her eyes. Sleep was a million miles away. It wasn't sleep she craved. Tim . . . here in the night surely nothing could hold him from her? Her hands were warm, her body was warm. Her hands . . .? His hands . . .? Her body . . .? His . . .? Surely this way she would find him?

In the weeks she'd been alone she'd been too stricken by shock and grief to have room in her mind for the longing that gripped her now. With her eyes tight shut she strained towards the supreme moment. He'd be with her, he'd be close, closer, yes . . . Tim . . . Her head thrashed from side to side, she clenched her teeth to stop herself crying out as she felt drawn nearer and nearer to him.

Her eyes opened to the emptiness of the night. A flapping curtain, a bucket rolling across the yard, hands that were a mockery. Just as a moment ago she'd risen to the heights, so now the depths were deeper. What lay ahead of her all the more empty and futile. Tim was gone. When her wretched body clamoured for love, Tim was gone. Yet, even now, with nowhere to hide from stark reality, she knew that what she'd done tonight would become part of the new pattern she had to make of her life. A way of finding Tim, she told herself. A way of learning to live without him, she knew was nearer the truth.

It was when she was cleaning out the henhouse that a car drove into the yard. Seeing John Carlisle get out of it, she propped her stiff broom against the wire mesh of the run and came to meet him, the hens scurrying around her feet as she crossed the yard.

'You look busy. Have I come at a bad time, Jane?'

'The hens won't mind waiting for their new straw. It's nice to see you.' Superficial pleasantries, they made no demands.

'I wanted us to talk. Can we go somewhere? Into the office?'

Ah, now, that touched a raw nerve. But she gave no sign of it.

'I've not had the stove on, it'll be cold.'

'Never mind.' They turned into Tim's shed. 'Jane, I don't want to push you, but the land doesn't give one time to stand still. Have you thought what you're going to do?'

'Do? On the farm? The men are working. Even Sid. What do you mean, what I'm going to do?' He read fear in her eyes, the fear of someone who's cornered and has no way to turn.

'Denby and Keyhaven run side by side here. I don't want to push you, Jane, but land doesn't wait. Especially today with the WARAG breathing down our necks. I'd treat you fairly, you know that. Have it valued by Meredith and Brindley, put it on the market in the normal way. But, Jane, give me first refusal. Will you do that?'

'Get rid of Denby! John, I don't understand you. You mean, you've come here to talk about me getting rid of

Denby?' The Gowers of Denby – how cocky we were . . .
Tim's words echoed unbearably.

'I've come here to say, when you do, then let it be to me,
to Keyhaven.'

'I've never heard anything as crazy. This is Tim's farm,
our farm!'

She took a cigarette from the case he passed her. On the
farm most of the men rolled their own. It was an economy
that even she and Tim and practised, although mostly
he'd been a pipe man. Never John Carlisle. She drew on
the smooth, tightly packed 'Passing Cloud', so typical of
him . . . Fancy, at a moment like this, her mind going off at
such a tangent!

'I've never thought of you as a farmer, Jane.' She
recognized that his words were meant as a compliment. 'If
you change your mind, you'll tell me, won't you?'

'I shan't change my mind, John.' But he was right. She
wasn't a farmer, she never would be. To her, the farm had
meant Tim. She'd loved it because it was his, because it
was the background of their world. But she'd given her
word: 'I'll keep Denby going', and soon Richard would be
here with her. As she spoke she fingered the papers on the
bench. 'Anyway, I'm not so removed from it all as you
probably imagine. Tim and I always . . . always . . .'

'I'm sorry.' His voice was gentle. 'I shouldn't barge in
here worrying you. I didn't know what your plans were.'
He noticed how her hand was shaking as she put the
cigarette to her lips, the way she drew hard on it in a fight
for control. Then, surprising even himself: 'So, what
about this for an idea? Just for the time being, until you tell
me to push off, what about if I take over some of your
winter work in the fields? Maybe I'll use your men, maybe
Keyhaven's. It just depends how things fit in. Your top
fields ought to be planted out, the ground will soon be too
cold.' He tapped the WARAG circular. 'We're not masters
of our own souls any longer, you know.' An exaggeration
and they both knew it, but it made it easier for her to accept
the offer.

72

'I'm grateful to you, John. Tim would be grateful, too. And I'm glad you've given me the kick in the pants I needed.'

He laughed. 'Hardly that, Jane.' The very thought of him behaving in so ungallant a fashion brought her the nearest she'd been to a smile.

'You see, next summer Richard leaves school. I know he's only a boy, but he's not just *any* boy – he belongs. Once he's working here, things'll get easier all the time.'

But in the meanwhile, as John had said, the land wouldn't wait. Things don't just happen on a farm; crops don't grow if they're not planted; seeds can't be planted if the ground isn't prepared; calves aren't born if the bull isn't brought in to serve the cows. Milk quotas must be met, corn quotas must be met. Tomorrow's profit depends on today's planning. His metaphorical kick in the pants seemed to have brought life back into her numbed mind.

CHAPTER FOUR

Liz was determined to make a celebration of Christmas; to imagine the alternative was frightening.

'It'll be different this year, Mum,' she said to Jane on the first day of her school holiday, adding quickly, 'because of Greta and Eddie, it's bound to be. We've got to make it happy for them – we have, haven't we? We've never had children in the house, stockings to fill, all that sort of thing.'

'Oh, but we have, three of them . . . yours, Richard's and Hartley's. Down here on the kitchen table is where we used to fill them after you were asleep, then creep up to your rooms to take away the empty ones and hang up the full ones. We've done it all before.'

But all Jane said was: 'I've bought a few things. I'll give them to you. You youngsters can be Father Christmas.'

And because that's the way Elizabeth wanted it, Hartley backed her. Somehow they put magic into the children's Christmas, away from Digbury Mansions for the first time. Jane kept her heart firmly in its place, she held a smile on her face as she watched Liz handing out the presents from around the tree. Her misery couldn't be shared, so it must be hidden. Resolutely she joined in the games.

One thing was quite beyond her, and that was to accept Meg's presence amongst them. These days Meg was quiet. After the accident she'd never gone back to work in the fields. Each day she'd take Ben out in his pram and walk for miles. Sometimes Jane knew she was watching her, but she couldn't meet her gaze. And if she had, then Meg would have looked away. Between them always was Tim, the accident, the blame, Meg's mistaken judgement. And so through those days of Christmas the smile Jane fixed so firmly on her face never turned towards Meg. She'd meant to tell her to go before this. But how could she? How could she have turned her away to find a fresh place for Ben just before Christmas? Afterwards I'll tell her. She's got to go! Every time I look at her, I picture it happening. She did it! And somehow the days of Christmas passed.

Richard watched Liz and Hartley's every move. He was silent and brooding, his blue eyes full of hurt. If Jane hadn't been so blinkered by her own unhappiness, she would have seen.

'Liz and I thought we'd go for an all day walk,' Hartley said one morning at breakfast. 'Coming, Richard?'

He hesitated. It was Liz he was looking at, waiting for her to give some sign. Clearly she didn't notice.

'What about you two?' She spoke to Greta and Eddie. 'You'd need to wrap up warm. I shall pack our food. A winter picnic. Would you like to come too?'

'Walking all day? A proper hike?' Eddie was impressed. 'Let's go with them, Greta.'

'She's only six, Liz.' Jane frowned. 'Look at the length of her legs, then at yours.'

'I'm good as seven! Bet my legs are just as long now as they're going to be week after next when I'm seven, Aunt Jane.'

'What our Greta lacks in length of leg, she makes up for in stoutness of heart, don't you, Greta?' Hartley backed her. 'Don't worry, Aunt Jane, I promise she'll be all right. We'll walk to Slapton, to the Leys. How's that?'

'What are they like, these lays? Are they some sort of chicken or what?' Greta liked to get her facts straight.

'No, not those sort of Leys. It's a lake, right down there by the sea, but not sea water. There are fresh water fish in it – but we shan't have time to fish. There are ducks, moorhens, all sorts of other birds – we'll point them out to you. Better have your wellies with you, it'll be muddy.'

Jane listened to them. The children planning an outing,

75

just as they had every holiday. Richard growing out of the circle, the young ones growing into it. Ben, strapped into a highchair (something else brought down from the loft), was looking from one to the other, almost as if he was waiting for his turn to take part in the fun. It was too far for Greta, too far for Eddie too. But with Hartley to take care of them, she didn't worry.

'Be home before dark,' she told them. Then went off to wrestle with another day's work. At the back of her mind she had an uneasy feeling about Richard. But he was luckier than the others. He wasn't a child any more, looking for pleasure-filled days of holiday. His future was here; he could sink himself, unhappiness and all, into working on the land. Today and every day that he was here was building towards his future. For him she did what she did each day, for him and because she'd promised Tim.

By half-past nine the walkers were ready.

'Out of the yard we turn right, then just keep going. The lane gets rough after a while. Are your shoes comfortable?' The children liked the way Hartley talked to them, as if they were as grown up as he was himself.

'Aunt Jane said we got to carry our wellies. She said they weren't good to hike in. We got them in these bags.' With only one and a bit front teeth, 'bags' came out as 'bagth'.

'Good chaps.' Hartley nodded, and rather than be affronted by the change in sex, Greta puffed out her chest with pride. 'And I've got the paster, just in case of blisters.'

So they set out, the younger ones leading the way, striding manfully.

'They're good kids, Liz.'

'Yes, they're all right. I hope they don't spoil the day, though. On our own we –'

'On our own we might have got further, but the day's just as long.'

'I wish today could go on and on. Home's different, you can feel it. Dad was out more than he was ever in the house – but nothing's the same . . .' Her voice was tight. He could tell how rigidly she was holding her chin. His hand gripped hers.

By now they'd left the farm buildings behind them and were walking between the high hedges of the lane. If they thought about Richard at all, they supposed him to be working somewhere in the fields. But they were only half right. In the fields, yes. Working, no. He'd heard them arranging to go to Slapton; he'd thought of the dozens of times the three of them had been there together, he and Liz – and Hartley with them. He could have gone today, probably walked with the kids. But some devil in him turned the knife. That same devil made it impossible for him to be with them, and impossible for him to forget them. So, yes, he was in the field, just the other side of the high hedge, knowing they'd walk by on the way towards the sea. He heard them coming, he stood very still, listened, not knowing what it was he expected to hear. They passed by. They didn't suspect he'd gone to the gate, was leaning over watching them. This time he turned the knife himself. Of course they didn't suspect! They didn't give him a thought, so wrapped up in each other. Hartley, taking hold of Liz's hand. Slowing their pace, turning to each other. Liz, turning to Hartley . . . Damn him! Damn and blast him! Liz was *his*, she always had been *his*!

With all his might he kicked the iron post of the field gate, his face contorted. Physical pain was something he could understand, but what gripped him was far worse. His insides were knotted up with misery, and as the walkers disappeared round a bend in the lane his face contorted and he cried. Loudly and uncontrollably he sobbed, with his head buried against his arms on the top of the gate: for the sister who was more than a sister, was part of himself; for the father who was lost. Emotion he'd kept pent up found release. But there was no healing in his tears. When at last he raised his head and wiped the palms of his hands across his face, his gaze fell on the fields. Season would follow season, year follow year . . . A sob caught in his throat.

It was that same day that Meg followed Jane into the dimly lit mushroom sheds.

'Jane, can I come and talk to you? It's more private in here.'

She felt trapped.

'If you're coming in, do it quickly and close the door. The air's cold.' Her words held no welcome and, hearing them, Jane realized this was probably the first direct communication they'd had in all these weeks. This would be her opportunity, her chance to tell Meg she must find somewhere else.

'I'm going away. You – you and Tim – I'll never forget how good you've been to Ben and me. Even now, you've never said the things to me that you must be feeling. *I* did it! I wanted him to see how quickly I could start up the tractor. It was my fault.' All this time they'd avoided talking about it, yet now Meg could no more have stopped the words that spilled out than Jane could have answered them.

'You must hate us every time you look at us. Tim brought Ben and me here, both of you took us into your home – you must remember all the time how he picked me up that night. If he hadn't, if he'd left me to find my way to Totnes, he'd be here now.' In the near darkness Meg could say things she could never have said in the house, even without Mrs Sid's listening ears.

The seconds ticked by, the silence lengthened. Those same accusations had hammered at Jane's mind. Yet now, hearing Meg voice them, she wasn't prepared. So easily she could agree, get rid of Meg and so try and erase the whole nightmare from her mind. But was it so simple? Turning her back, she closed her eyes. The humid atmosphere, the stillness, the familiar musty smell of the compost, these things wrapped around her; and with them came the memory of another occasion, standing here just as she was now. How eaten up with misery and jealousy she'd been! Tim, taking her into his arms . . . 'Twenty or eighty, you're my Lady Jane.'

'Nothing is that simple,' she said at last. 'If I could hate you and feel better for it, how easy it would all be.'

'Every time I look at a ploughed field, I can hear it –'

'You say you want to go away. Have you found somewhere? Where are you going?'

'There's nothing happening in London, no raids. The paper refers to it as a phoney war. People are going back. That's what Ben and I will do. I used to work in a place that grandly called itself a Home for Retired Gentlefolk. I dare say I could get my job back. There are nurseries these days where they look after babies –'

'But Ben's settled here, he's one of us.'

'Every time I hear the tractor, I remember!'

'Of course you do.' It seemed to Jane that hers was only the voice; it was for Tim that she spoke. 'But running away isn't going to make it any easier. If Tim were here –'

'If Tim were here, I wouldn't feel like it.'

'Just listen a minute. I don't mean if it had never happened. I mean if he could speak to us now, hear what we're saying – and perhaps he can – you know what he'd want?'

'I should think he'd want me gone.'

'Tim never had much time for quitters. He'd want you to put on your working clothes and get on with the job. Drive the tractor, make friends with your memories.'

'How can I make friends with that?'

'There were other times too. You were happy enough working there, you can't tell me you weren't. Remember the good things.' She turned away and started picking mushrooms. 'Here, if you want to be useful while we're talking, take one of these baskets and fill it. Cut them gently and lay them in carefully, pink side downwards.' She didn't say that what seemed like years ago it had been Tim's suggestion that Meg should learn to take over the mushrooms. Now, silently, the two of them worked.

'Well done, lady.' A smile touched her mouth. But the light was too dim for Meg to know and wonder about it.

'So you don't mind having us here?' the girl said presently.

'For me to mind would be like you running away – it would be letting him down. Anyway, you and Ben are part of the establishment these days. That looks about right for that basket. We'll do one more each, then I must take them into town.'

In the winter dusk Jane saw the walkers return. Liz came first, the haversack strapped to her back, Eddie striding manfully at her side; behind them was Hartley, Greta riding pick-a-back. She saw the little girl bend forward and whisper something in his ear. He nodded, then he put her down. Grinning from ear to ear, it was she who led the way into the kitchen.

'We done it, Aunt Jane! We done it, Mrs Sid! Been and seen them Leys. 'fore we go to bed, I'm going to do a picture for Dad. Let's do that, shall we, Ed?'

Hartley helped Liz take off the haversack. There was no need; she could easily have slipped it off her shoulders. That was one thing Jane noticed. Another was the way she looked at him as she turned round, her eyes speaking to him alone in a way that, older and more sophisticated, she'd learn to hide. Between the two of them was a shared secret. And why not? At their ages falling in love was part of growing up. They didn't guess as they rushed headlong into their first romance just how hurt they could be. It wasn't for Liz she feared; it had more to do with the look in Hartley's eyes. Yet why should she fear for Hartley? With his looks, he'd never be short of a girlfriend. At seventeen he wasn't quite six foot tall, but he probably would be by the time he finished growing. On the sports field, as in the classroom, he shone; it seemed his future was assured. So why did it hurt Jane to see the look he turned on Liz?

*

January was nearly over when a letter came from Eddie's mother. There was to be a 'See the Children' special train, a help because they came for cheaper fares. 'George Blake, Greta's father, is coming with us. He doesn't take to letter writing, but I said I'd get you to tell Greta. We know you have been kind to them, we can tell from the pictures and letters they send, but I can't wait to see my Ed. A lot of the kids are back home again already.'

Reading that gave Jane a hint of what was ahead. The first fear of imminent air-raids had been lost, swept under a carpet of apathy. She knew how she'd feel if her children had been sent to live with strangers; at the first chance she would have brought them home. She felt herself in sympathy with Louise Clegg, Eddie's mother. It was Greta's father she'd taken an instinctive dislike to even before she met him. Sometimes Eddie had a letter from home. The nearest Greta ever got to it was a message to 'tell Greta her dad sends his love.'

On the day of the visit she used precious petrol to take the children to the station to meet their parents.

'There 'e is! There's Dad!' In all these months Jane had not heard such a screech of excitement from Greta as she raced down the platform to throw herself into the arms of this little man she held on such a pinnacle. Small, a sad face that could nevertheless light up with laughter, his tweed jacket and trousers were none too clean, ill fitting, and even in their young day had never been a match. Around his neck he wore a muffler and on his head a cap. Jane felt he lived up to her expectations – or down to them. Then, as he came towards her, Greta clinging proudly to his hand and skipping with happiness, her eyes met his and she knew she'd done him an injustice. Louise and Albert Clegg were much as she'd expected. Both had put their best foot forward for the day out. They were clean and quiet, minding their manners.

'Well, 'ere we are then.' George greeted her with a

grin, 'and you'll be Mrs Gower. I'd know you from the pictures our Greta draws. You done her real proud, and no mistake. Looks like a million dollars, does my little princess.'

Mrs Sid had insisted on coming in, Sunday or no, and prepared a good dinner, to 'let them see we know how to live here in the country'. Then the children took their parents for a walk, showing off their knowledge of the farm, while Jane spent an hour on her milk returns. Seeing them back in the yard, she opened the door.

'Cor! You got a stove same as us, eh, Greta?' Without waiting to be invited, George craned his neck to see inside. 'Smells like home, that does. No getting away from the stink of the old oil stove.'

'Mrs Gower,' this time it was Louise, 'another hour or so and we'll have to think of making tracks for the station. Could we have a word?'

'Of course. You mustn't think you're expected to wander about all the afternoon. The children must show you their rooms, take you round the house. You'll want to see everything so that you can picture where they are.'

'That's just it, you see. They did take us upstairs. That young lady in the house, she said it was all right for us to look. But "picture where they are", you say . . . That's just it. A lot of the kids are back home already. I told you that in my letter. It's not that we're not grateful. You've been kind to Ed, I know. But there don't seem no point in keeping him out of London. Quiet as anything, it is. Isn't that so, Alb?'

''sright.'

'Home?' This time it was Greta, her huge dark eyes suddenly with lamps lit in them. 'You mean we're coming home, Dad?'

'Wasn't me what said it. It's Ed, here. They're collecting up Ed's bits and taking him back.'

'What d'you mean? You saying you don't want to take me too?'

'Not that I don't want to, you know that as well as I do!' George turned helplessly to Jane. 'I'm going in the Army. Different for old Alb here, he's working on munitions. That's why I wanted to come down, see for myself that things were all right for her, make sure that you – well, you've got kids. You must understand what I'm trying to say.' His face puckered as he struggled to express himself without giving offence. 'So now I've seen. Now I know she's better off down 'ere than ever she'd be back in the Mansions.' Then to Greta: 'What about that then? Put in for m'pair of boots and m'rifle. Old Adolf better watch out, eh, princess?' His sad face forced itself into a smile. Jane could have cried to look at them.

A couple of hours later she and Greta stood on the platform waving the train out of sight. It was only then that the little girl gave way, her body shaken by rasping sobs. Her faithful Eddie was gone, full of excitement to be returning to Digbury Mansions; and worse, far worse, her dad was going off into a world she knew nothing about, a world she couldn't even begin to imagine.

That night she didn't want her cocoa, nor even a piece of cake. Pale and quiet she went up to bed when she was told. When Jane looked in to see, she was tucked up warm, her eyes closed. It was later and Jane was in bed when she thought she heard a sound from Greta's room. She crept along the dark corridor to listen.

'Hush, Greta love, don't cry.' She knelt by the side of the bed. Greta let herself be pulled into Jane's arms, yet there was no way of coming near to the unhappiness that consumed her.

'Just that I don't feel well. Don't want to go to school tomorrow. Tummy ache.'

'Forget tomorrow, love. What about if you come back to my room, cuddle in with me for tonight? Sometimes if you don't feel well it's nice to be near someone.'

Greta didn't answer, but she got out of bed and, in

83

the dark, put her hand in Jane's, making for the corridor.

'Shan't know where he is. He's going to belong to the war.' By now they were lying side by side.

'He'll still belong to you, Greta. It's happening to people everywhere, in this country, in other countries, people they love going away. But you know, there is one way you can help him.'

'Don't see how. Don't see there's anything. It's like not being part of things.' Her voice was gruff, hardly above a whisper. Jane knew that anything more and the tears she was fighting would win their battle.

'Oh, Greta, you're part of things all right. For your dad, you're right in the centre of things. You can help him if you let him feel you're happy. Like you did at the station, not letting him see how sad you felt. You're his princess. You never told me that.'

'Why should I say? That's just me and Dad knows that.'

'There, you see! And think of all the months you've been here, he didn't really know what it was like. I know you wrote to him, but he'd not seen, not met me, not seen Mrs Sid, or Ben, or Mufti; not seen where you go to school or the bed you slept in. None of that ever came between you. You both knew you were his princess.' Was it too deep for a seven-year-old understanding?

Silence. Greta wriggled closer. A still longer silence. She was turning it over in her mind, Jane could almost hear her.

''nother thing you didn't say, Aunt Jane. I got my new teeth, my two top teeth, since I been here. He'd never seen me with 'em 'till today. I look different, but he knew things was just like before.'

Jane put her arm around her.

'That's right, Greta. You can stay with a person you love without being able to see them.' To her it made sense and, there in the dark, she was pretty sure it did to Greta too.

Tomorrow morning it would be school without Eddie, but Greta was no coward.

Each week the twins wrote home; at their schools an hour was set aside for letter writing on Saturday morning. Elizabeth's letters this term were shorter than they used to be; Jane suspected a longer epistle went to Hartley. Richard's never varied; not more than a side and a half of the paper, seldom less. There was something comfortingly reliable about the unchanging quality of Richard's weekly missive.

Then came a Monday when the bulky envelope, the scrawl of his writing, told her something was up. Putting the letter in her pocket, she took it to the privacy of Tim's office.

'Jane! Can I come in? Mrs Sid said I'd find you here.'

At the sound of Herbert Gower's voice, Jane pushed her letter under a pile of papers.

'A nice surprise, Dad. Yes, of course, come in.' She forced a note of welcome into her voice. And why not? Of course it was a nice surprise. It was just that now, at this very moment, she was frightened her manner might give him some hint that the chocks that had supported the frail structure she'd been trying to build had been knocked from under her.

'What brings you out on a Monday morning? Are you like us, losing your staff? Having to do your own deliveries?' She heard how over-bright she sounded. 'Ralph wants to join the Army. He told me on Saturday. I'm going to apply for a couple of Land Army Girls, Dad. Don't you think that's the best thing? Take a lad on, and likely as not he'd want to spread his wings . . .' There was a rasp in her voice.

'No, I'm not delivering. I've come to waste ten minutes of your day.' He used her own expression as he drew up a second stool. 'Have you heard from the children? Are they getting along all right. Letter day, Monday, isn't it?'

She nodded.

He tried again. 'We've talked about it before, Jane, my dear. About Richard. I had a note from him this morning, too. Says he's plucked up his courage to tell you.'

Again she nodded.

'It had to come, my dear. I've seen it, I've told you. We can't plan for our children, we have no right.'

'It's the war. It's this damned, damned war! Can't you just imagine them all at school, their heads filled with their OTC training? "And what are you going to join when you leave?" "I'm going home to work with my mother on the farm!" Sounds grand, doesn't it? Would make him feel a real hero! Damned, cursed war!' When did she start crying? '. . . can read it if you like.' She pulled the letter from its hiding place and held it out to him.

The seconds ticked by as Herbert read. Jane wiped her face and blew her nose, the storm seemingly over.

'Poor lad.' He passed the scrawled sheets back to her. 'It wasn't easy for him to tell you, Jane. He's talked to me about it, you know. I've tried to hint to you. It's not just the war – although I dare say that's put a bit of urgency into it. You'd not have kept him here on the farm. I'm sorry, my dear. I know what it feels like, remember?'

'How can you? It never made any difference to you that Tim preferred farming. The business was *your* baby. You created it, you saw it grow.'

'I think, Jane, we have to face this squarely, be honest with ourselves. If Tim had still been here, would this have mattered so much to you?'

She shook her head. 'You say it's like Tim leaving you, starting on his own. If you'd been killed,' she spat the word, glared at him as she said it, 'would he have walked out on his mother?'

'I don't know, Jane. No, I doubt if he would. Times were so different then. You're a brave woman, and a capable one. My theory is that Richard believes you're strong enough to manage without him. He's hardly more than a child, my dear. It would be madness for you to pin your hopes on him taking his father's place, even if right now he saw no other life for himself. But he does. The world's a big and tempting place when you're sixteen years old.'

'Anyway,' she sniffed, striving to sound calm now, 'it'll be summer before he leaves school. He's not seventeen until September. He won't be able to go to sea straight away. The war might be over. When he gets home, away from his friends and all their heroic talk, he might forget all about his wild ideas. He'll help with harvest just like he always has, he'll see how much he's needed . . .'

'No, Jane. You mustn't do it to him. Give him his freedom to fly and he'll always come home to you. Tie him here, feeling you depend on him, and – God forbid – he might live to hate you for it.'

He took his pipe and tobacco pouch out of his pocket, then felt deeper and produced a packet of twenty Players which he put on the desk in front of her.

'Present for you. I can't smoke alone.' Poor lass, he thought, watching her tear the packet open and pull out a cigarette. 'You could always consider getting a chap in to manage the place. If Ralph goes, you'll have a cottage empty.'

She frowned. John Carlisle's words came back to her. 'A farm needs someone to look ahead and plan.' But a stranger making the decisions for Denby?

'I'll think about it, Dad. I don't know about a manager.' This time she smiled at him, her eyes redder, even her nose brighter than it should be. 'I don't reckon I'm making such a bad fist of things. I'll see how it all goes.'

So they put the question of Richard and his future out of the way as they smoked in easy companionship. Only later, after he'd gone, did it come back to her. And with it came John's proposition. Sell Denby? She imagined moving out, the home she and Tim had built stacked into the remover's pantechnicon and trundling away up the narrow lane; the fields they knew every foot of belonging to John Carlisle; this make-shift they'd grandly called 'the office' with John's hat on the hook Tim had screwed into the wooden wall. No! Denby belonged to them, the Gowers. She lit another cigarette then read Richard's letter again. You had to take whatever life saw fit to dish out to you. You might not like it, but you had to take it, then knock it into shape! She might have no stomach for the way ahead, but she'd not let it beat her!

CHAPTER FIVE

Often John would drive into the yard, the sound of his car bringing her out from wherever she was — henhouses, mushroom sheds, dairy, or even the house. He seldom came indoors. The office was small, it was bare of all comforts, but one thing it never lacked was warmth. To John the smell of a paraffin stove would always be a reminder of that winter when, in trying to give Jane the support she needed, he first came to know her for herself, not simply as Tim's wife. Before long she became used to these informal visits; she even began to look forward to them.

With John she didn't pretend. When there were things she wasn't sure about she asked him. Somehow he made it easy for her, made her feel less out of her depth. She'd haul herself to sit in her favourite position on the sloping desk top, her knees drawn up and her feet planted on one tall stool while he sat on the other.

She threw herself into the challenge of doing a job of work that demanded everything she could give. Every few days he came, sometimes for no more than five minutes, sometimes for an hour. He made no demands on her, their talk was always about the farm. He guided her into making her claim for payment for the acreage that had been tilled for the first time at the WARAG's request; he guided her on what feed supplements her cattle needed; but he never pushed advice on her, nor yet seemed surprised at the things she was uncertain about. And perhaps most important of all, he gave the impression that he had time to spare.

It was the day after she had received Richard's letter. From where she worked in the mushroom shed she heard the familiar sound of John's car stopping in the yard.

Opening the door, she called out to him: 'I'm in here, John. I've nearly finished.'

He joined her in the humid, dimly lit shed, closing the door without being told.

'Do you have to drive into town with those?'

'Yes. I always get them there on Tuesday mornings.'

'That's what I thought. I was wondering – how about if we go in together? We might have a steak lunch at the Red Lion.' There was something almost boyishly shy in his invitation.

'That sounds like a treat. I'll have to tidy my scruffy self up a bit first.' Dungarees and an old sweater of Tim's was not attire for lunch, even at the Red Lion, the pub frequented by most of the farmers visiting the Cattle Market. 'There, that's the last basket. Come into the house, John. Talk to Mrs Sid in the kitchen while I get tidy. Shall we go in your car or mine?' The surprise outing had shaken her out of herself; she found she was unexpectedly excited at the prospect. And there was something else: today with Richard's letter still at the forefront of her mind, she had no heart for their usual tête-à-tête in the office . . . her lesson in how to run the farm.

For weeks she'd not dressed in anything but work clothes for the farm. Now she put on a blue skirt and jumper, court shoes, her camel coat; her hair was always the same, the curls sprang naturally where they willed, but she decided her face could be improved on and did her best with it. In all these preparations she hardly gave a thought to John. She was dressed, she was going out, somewhere outside Denby the world was still there, waiting. Finally she looked in the long mirror on the wardrobe door. Suddenly, without warning, it was as if she saw her reflection not with her own eyes but Tim's. 'You look nice, lady.'

She bit her lip. The woman in the mirror looked

back at her. In each other's eyes they read the loneliness.

It's twenty to twelve already. The mushrooms should be there by now. Pull yourself together, they told each other.

How strange it was that when John said those same words to her as they drove out of the yard: 'You look nice', there was no echo of Tim.

'I've almost forgotten what it feels like to wear a skirt,' she laughed.

'Perhaps we might do this more often.' Then, wary in case he'd said the wrong thing: 'When we both have to go to the Market. Humph?'

'You're very kind, John. I think putting on proper clothes, coming out into the big world, makes me see just how kind. I seem to have taken you dreadfully for granted. I'm sorry if I've let you think that. I don't know how I would have got through these last weeks without you.'

'Then I'm glad I was there.'

It was later, the waitress at the Red Lion had just put their food in front of them, when she couldn't hold back any longer from saying what was at the front of her mind: 'I had a letter from Richard yesterday. Just a boy's dreams of glory, that's what I tried to believe. Dad says I'm wrong, that he's serious . . .'

John understood everything she hadn't said. Choosing his words carefully, he told her: 'It's true, Jane. He's not cut out to be a farmer.'

'How can you say that? You mean Richard's talked to you?'

'Eat your food,' he prompted, for she was making no effort to begin, sitting with knife and fork poised. 'Yes, he's talked about joining the Merchant Navy. If things had been different, if Tim had still been here, he wouldn't have felt so guilt-ridden about it.'

'That's what Dad says, more or less.' The Red Lion had a reputation for serving the best steaks in the district. She chewed automatically, the meal wasted on her. 'I was so sure, John. I never doubted. He's always enjoyed helping.'

'That's one thing. Turning himself into a farmer, born and bred, to spend the rest of his life on the same few acres, is quite another.' He gave a boyish grin. 'Hear the voice of one who knows!'

What a moment for her to be struck by the thought that even middle-aged and battling to disguise his thinning hair, John was still a handsome man. If there were such a thing as a tailors' fashion book for well-suited farmers, then surely he could grace its cover. For was ever a working farmer so elegantly turned out, with such well-manicured nails, such highly polished boots?

'You've never regretted staying there?' She turned her mind back to Keyhaven.

He laughed. 'Me? Oh, I'm a lazy sort of fellow. I like life to be comfortable, always have. And I've been lucky. It's never fallen to me to get up at five o'clock for the morning milking nor yet to hose out the yard. I'm a bit of a fraud, Jane, a desk bound farmer. "All front and no back", that was my mother's expression for the likes of me.' Fraud he might be, but clearly he wasn't put out by it.

'Well, I'm afraid at Denby Richard would have to take the rough with the smooth – like Tim did – like I have to. Ralph's joining up and I get the feeling Clem is restless to go too.'

He didn't answer her. Silently they concentrated on their meal. John had never had any inclination to marry, but there'd been nothing of the celibate about him. Good looking, comfortably off, and certainly with an air about him that set him apart from most of the farming fraternity (all front and no back or no!), he'd never been short of female company when he'd felt the need of it. He'd known Jane at least superficially since Tim had introduced him to the pretty little girl he'd married. How long ago? Seventeen years? Eighteen? He looked at her now, comparing the attractive woman of today with that young girl.

'Jane, I've never mentioned it again, I know that's what we agreed, but this idea of Richard's may put a different complexion on your wanting to carry on at Denby.'

'No!' She was frightened by what he was suggesting, frightened that she might weaken. Denby belonged to the Gowers. 'Anyway, you've got a lovely home, what would you want with Denby as well? It's not as though you're wanting to put a manager in.'

'No, the house doesn't interest me. But the land does. Let me buy the land. Think about it.'

'I can't sell Denby. I've answered Richard's letter, told him I understand. But, John, it comes from talk amongst the boys at school. He'll get over it once he's home. Anyway, he's too young. It'll be another year, the war may be over . . .' She talked fast, the same arguments that she'd used to Herbert, clutching at straws but not saying what was in her heart: I've lost Tim, I *won't* lose his farm too. Then another straw came within reach, a safer one. 'I know you mean to be kind, but there's no practical sense in what you suggest, John. Keyhaven's about the largest farm around. What do you want more land for?' Then, quickly, in case he misunderstood and thought she was wavering: 'Not that Denby's for sale. Even a desk bound farmer like you say you are must have more than enough to do with all the papers and forms the WARAG are dreaming up.'

'What about a sweet?' He changed the subject. 'They do a very presentable apple pie and, war or no war, they still give us more cream than is good for us.'

'No thanks. But my lunch was lovely,' she added like a well taught child.

The gold cigarette case was passed and she took a Passing Cloud.

'You asked me what I want with more land. I'll tell you. Farming is on an upward trend. It must be. It doesn't take a great brain to see that food production is in the front line. The government is starting to realize it – and about time too. I may not be the sort of farmer to get dung on his boots, but I'm a planner. I know what should be done, and I make sure it gets done – ' the way he laughed took the arrogance out of his words ' – done by someone else, be sure of that.'

'So? That doesn't answer my question. Keyhaven is enough for anyone, surely?'

'If this war lasts any time at all – and the way things are going we're not heading towards victory at the moment – more and more will have to come out of the land. Mechanization must be the answer – the days of horse drawn machines, horse drawn wagons, they'll be gone before much longer. The number of tractors will double, quadruple. Even in the small farms, hand milking will go. Harvesting will be mechanized. It all adds up to efficiency and prosperity. So why do I want more land? I mean to invest in machinery. The time spent per acre will be reduced, vastly reduced; the return per acre will be increased. More land, machinery put to fuller use, greater efficiency – and the outcome of all that? Increased profit.'

'I see.' But she frowned. Did she see? One thing John Carlisle had never lacked was money.

'It's not just money for money's sake, although that's not something to be scorned,' he read her thoughts. 'Perhaps it stems from what I said about spending my life on the same few acres where I was born and bred. This war is giving me a challenge. Or, to borrow the unladylike expression that you used to me some time back, it's giving me the kick in the pants I needed.'

'Anyway, to get back to Richard. It'll be a year before he's old enough to enlist and I'm just not going to look ahead. It's a fool's game to think we can plan for the future.'

There was no answer to that.

94

That was the first of many 'working' outings with John.

At Easter the twins and Hartley were home from school. This would be their last holiday. Next term would see Liz and Richard taking their School Certificate and Hartley his Higher. All three of them stood at the threshold of what they believed would be 'life'.

'Hartley and I are going cycling, Mum. That's all right, isn't it?'

'Of course it's all right. But aren't you all going? Why not you, Richard? Go on, enjoy your freedom. Your last long break, my lad!' Her voice was jollier than the situation merited, she heard it as forced. 'You persuade him, Liz.'

'Come if you want, of course you can.'

'I don't want. I've already said.'

Liz coloured. She met his gaze, blue eyes looking straight at blue eyes, the only resemblance between the twins. Jane frowned. What in the world was the matter with them? Nothing ever came between them, nothing ever could. Liz was a true mixture of Jane and Tim: Jane's curly hair, pure gold at her age and cut short; Jane's clear light blue eyes; Tim's smile; Tim's tall build and straight back. Richard was like neither of them – average height, straight brown hair; one only had to look at him to know he possessed physical strength, and courage too. So different in appearance, yet in spirit nothing ever divided them.

Greta looked from one to the other. Like Jane, she knew something was going on that she didn't understand.

'Come on, Greta.' Jane put a hand on her shoulder. 'You and I have work to do. We'll start with the henhouses. Can you fetch the stiff broom while I get the straw?'

These days, with her father learning to be a soldier, with so many of the London children returning home,

Greta's world was built on shifting sand. Jane was determined to give her the security she needed, but giving is a two-way thing. Between them the bond was strengthening, growing out of shared 'jobs' as Greta manfully helped, and growing out of a void they both felt but neither of them talked about.

'Okay, Aunt Jane.' Ready and willing Greta made for the door. 'You go on to the chickens, I'll get the things. I know what we'll want.' Her two well grown and very white teeth showed in a beam of pleasure as she ran off to the barn.

Soon, Liz and Hartley set off up the lane on their bicycles.

It was April, a season to expect sunshine, showers, rainbows. So when an hour or so later needles of rain danced in the yard no one expected the sudden clap of thunder.

'Let's hope those children don't take shelter under the trees, young Ben,' Mrs Sid voiced her thoughts. 'Not in thunder. Wonder where they've got to? They'll come back like a pair of drowned rats, you see if they don't.'

Ben slapped his ball of flour paste on the table, delighted by the doughy feel of it between his fingers. Then, in a moment of generosity, he leant from his highchair to offer a piece to Mufti.

And all the while the young couple in question were safe and dry in an old barn, sitting on a pile of straw. They hadn't come for shelter; they'd been there long before the rain had started. Listening to Hartley's plans, Liz's clear eyes were shining. She pictured how handsome he'd look in his Air Force uniform. By Christmas he expected to have finished the OCTU course, he would have his commission and be learning to fly.

'I'll come home every chance I have, Liz, come home to see you.'

'I shan't be long at Shelcoombe. Until I can start nursing training properly, I'm sure I'll get work of some sort in a hospital somewhere. It'll all be good experience.'

It sounded very grand in her own ears. At the back of her mind, reason told her that the hospital she'd work at while she was waiting would be local. But this morning she wanted to ride as high as Hartley, to put shape to a future that was still uncertain.

'You won't be here?' For a moment he forgot he was tomorrow's hero. Instead he was a disappointed boy. But only for a moment. 'Then, wherever you are, Liz, that's where I shall come.'

'And wherever I am, I shall be waiting for you.' It sounded just like something from the movies, so grand and romantic. But if that was what excited her she honestly didn't know it. With parted lips and stars in her eyes, she turned to him.

They'd held hands, he'd even kissed her hair as they'd danced (although she'd never been quite certain she hadn't imagined it), he'd held his arm around her when he'd helped her on or off with her coat. But now her mouth was only inches from his, closer; he could feel the warmth of her breath.

'Liz, Liz, my beautiful darling, my sweetheart.' His mouth nearly on hers, he whispered. If most boys were to speak like it the words would sound affected, rather stupid. But not Hartley, and not to Liz. Her mind was reeling under the wonder of what was happening to them. Laying back on her bed of straw she held her arms to him, felt his mouth on hers. In her imagination she saw him, handsome, dashing, a hero in Air Force blue. She saw herself, crisply starched, tending the wounded . . . she took his hand and guided it under her blouse.

'Liz, you're so beautiful . . . dream of you . . .' There was something akin to reverence in the touch of his hand.

Early in May the Conservative Government gave place to a National Coalition under Winston Churchill. New fire was breathed into the apathy that had grown out of the 'phoney war'. The Emergency Powers Act laid down that people everywhere must be prepared to place themselves and their property at the Government's disposal if necessary to the defence of the Realm; mentally the nation girded itself for the battle that lay between them and victory. The people of Shelcoombe listened to the stirring words – yet it all seemed far removed from the life they knew here in the peaceful South Hams. Then, only four days later, came an announcement by the War Secretary, Anthony Eden: large numbers of men between the ages of seventeen and sixty-five were being asked to offer their services to a new Force to be called the 'Local Defence Volunteers'.

Now, here was something they understood. Here in Shelcoombe, and in towns and villages up and down the country, the war became part of their lives. Initially, there were no uniforms for these part-time soldiers, no weapons either in the first days. But one thing they never lacked was enthusiasm.

'They're like a lot of schoolboys, keen as mustard to be out there drilling. Sid bolts his tea and he's gone like a short.' Mrs Sid talked as she folded a pile of washing she'd just brought in. 'I said to him, "Don't know what you think you'd be able to do if that Hitler saw fit to drop a load of his parachuters down amongst us." But you can't tell Sid! Likely they're as barmy as each other. "I'd soon give the blighters something to think about, never you doubt that," he said, "a two pronged hayfork'd stop them in their tracks." Nothing as mad as an Englishman. I tell you they're like a lot of schoolboys.'

Jane wasn't deaf to the ring of pride in her voice.

'And he's right, Mrs Sid. If we got faced with it we'd use whatever we could lay our hands on.' The Local Defence Volunteers . . . playing at soldiers, some people scoffed. But the war was stretching its tentacles. Nowhere was untouched. All those men, young and old alike, bolting their tea just like Sid did to be off to practise warfare. To think she'd been so sure that here in Devon, working on the farm, nothing could change their lives! The Low Countries had fallen; every hour they expected to hear that France had capitulated; British troops were cut off, being pushed nearer and nearer to the beaches. Oswald Peatty, the butcher, had a son out there; Clem's brother was in France, they'd not heard from him for weeks. Only months now and Hartley would be gone.

There was no one in the stores, so Jane found the three new hayforks she'd come for, loaded them in the back of the car, then went in search of someone to book them out to her. The office was a room at the back of the sheds, a room with little daylight. Today it was in darkness. Perhaps the girl was away ill? Everyone must be busy. She'd leave a note saying what she'd taken.

'Dad! What's happened to the lights? Is there a power cut?' Herbert was behind his desk, sitting idle in the near darkness.

'No, no. Better switch it on. Can't sit here wasting my day.'

'That's not like you, Dad. Is something the matter?'

'Nothing to worry about, just thought I'd let them think I wasn't in for a while.'

'Playing hookey – and along I come and spoil it!' But she was more worried than she let him think. 'Come on, Dad,' she perched on his desk, 'I tell you my troubles, you'd say if anything was bothering you, wouldn't you?'

'Bothering me? Nonsense! Hookey – isn't that what you called it? Put the switch on, no good sulking in here doing nothing.' And just as he always did he got out his cigarettes and his lighter and they settled for a companionable ten minutes. 'What brings you over? Not a breakdown?'

'Hayforks. I've taken three, that's why I came into the office, to leave a note. Mind you, I'm not sure whether they're to be used on the hay or on what Mrs Sid calls "Hitler's parachuters". You sure you're all right, Dad?'

'Tell you the truth, Jane – but don't say a word to Emily if you see her, I don't want her worrying – but I think the real trouble is I've got so tired. But how can I complain of

99

that when – just look at these time sheets here – Bert, he's the head mechanic, seventy hours he put in last week; Jim Cutler, sixty-seven; Ted Hiles – sixty-eight. You can go through the lot. There's not one who gets a full day off in a week. So who am I to grumble? The lad from the stores has gone . . . '

'You're not grumbling, Dad, you're just telling the truth. What about getting a woman in the stores?'

'I've asked at the Labour Exchange. They sent me one yesterday, came cycling into the yard dressed up in her high heels, a great flower on the front of her hat. Wouldn't know a nut from a bolt. No good to me. And even in the office, trying to get someone to do the book work is like asking for the moon. Plenty of work to be had in town these days, what woman wants to come out here? And the youngsters would rather get themselves into uniform.'

Jane was worried. She knew he was exaggerating and that in itself showed just how out of sorts with life he felt. He'd lost his only son . . . had she ever stopped to think what that must mean?

'I'll write the hayforks in the Day Book, Dad.' She'd been in and out here so often she knew just how the simple sales books were kept. If only she had more time she could help him. The books, the stores . . . after years on the farm it was a trade she understood. But her days were full from morning till night. She flicked through the used pages of the Day Book. It was weeks since the entries had been transferred into the Sales Ledger, so the accounts couldn't be going out . . .

'Dad, spare me another cigarette. I want to talk to you. I have a theory: when life hurls something at us that we don't like, then it's up to us to bash it into shape.' She hoisted herself back on to her perch on his desk.

Nothing was settled, but driving home she couldn't ignore the bubble of excitement. It turned the corners of her mouth up in a smile; it put a brightness into the colours of the countryside that she hadn't seen for so long. Almost back at Denby she saw Greta ahead; running home wouldn't have been much fun, but with her skipping rope it was great sport.

'Do you want a lift,' Jane drew up alongside her, 'or are you beating your own record?'

'No, I'll come with you. I did a hundred and forty-one times over the rope, didn't kick it once. Then I got it caught up in a tree and had to start again,' she panted. 'So I'll ride with you. Look, there's a car outside. Whose car is it?'

'It's the hire car from Totnes, usually meets the trains.'

Mrs Sid had heard them turn into the yard and came scurrying to meet them.

'It's that Meg. Got some visitor in the sitting room.'

'Who? Her husband?' Not a hint of Meg's secret.

'No use asking me who! This knock came on the front door and it was Meg who went to answer it. I heard voices, I expected she'd be bringing whoever it was through. But, no. Into the sitting room she went and shut the door. Just crept along the passage, thought I'd get some idea what sort of a person it was she'd got in there. But Benny, he followed, not a hope of listening quietly – so I had to stay back.'

'Man or woman?'

'Oh, it's a man all right. A man with a great voice like a fog horn. Not a rough man, don't misunderstand me. Voice that booms like a cannon. For all its loudness, though, the funny thing was I couldn't get the gist of what the pother was all about.'

'Pother? You mean he's shouting?'

'Well, if he's not shouting, it's time someone told him to turn the volume knob down.'

'Before you go outside, Greta, put your play clothes on, won't you? Then can you take these hayforks to the barn for me before you collect up the eggs from the yard. You know where to stand them, don't you?'

''course I do.' Greta was already to the foot of the stairs. 'I'll take Ben, shall I?'

'What, picking up the eggs! Keep a good eye on him then.'

'Well, buck up anyway,' Mrs Sid had the last word. 'If you want to be in time to hear your Children's Hour while you have tea, you'll have to be slippy getting your jobs done first.'

Greta would 'buck up' as she was told, but watching her go off up the stairs Jane seemed to hear the echo of: 'Race you getting dressed, Ed.'

She never said how much she missed him. But then, Greta wasn't the sort to parade her feelings.

From the sitting room came the sound of voices. Voices? Just one voice, for anything Meg might be saying was swamped.

'I'm going to see who it is.'

'That's it, you do. Coming marching in here without a by your leave. And that little madam! You'd think the place belonged to her the way she took him off and shut the door. You let them see who's mistress, Mrs G.'

But it wasn't that that took Jane to the closed door of the sitting room. It was the threat in the authoritative tone. Over the months Meg's fear that Ben would be taken away from her seemed to have vanished. Now, after all this time, had her past caught up with her? The voice must belong to Ben's natural father . . . yet it wasn't a young voice. How could she have fallen in love with someone who sounded like that? Whatever sort of man Jane had expected, it certainly wasn't this.

'. . . thank us for it.' His voice reverberated as she went into the room.

'A visitor, Meg? How nice. You should have let her know you were coming. She could have driven in to the stores instead of me, then gone on to meet you.' She heard her sugary tone and wondered whether it sounded as false to the stranger as it did to herself.

'Jane, you're home!' There was no mistaking the relief

102

in Meg's voice. 'This is my uncle. Reverend Hayward.'

He held out his hand to Jane, but the look he threw at his niece took away any warmth in his greeting.

'You note the name? A gold ring from Woolworth's can't disguise the name!'

'You're trying to tell me that Meg isn't married?' She smiled gently. No one could guess how her heart was hammering. 'Oh, but I knew that. She told my husband and me about that from the first. And I'm sure,' with a meaningful pause, '*you* more than most of us must always be conscious that there isn't one of us who goes through life without fault.'

'Madam, er – Mrs, er – ah yes, Mrs Gower.' (She could see her sweet tone had unsettled him from his high perch and inwardly she laughed.) 'Waywardness – that's what brought it about, make no mistake. My wife and I took her into our home.' Once started he seemed set for a long speech. They could tell it by the way he stood, head up, gesticulating as though he held the centre of a stage.

'Since she's confided so much in you and your husband, you'll know then how my brother met his death, the circumstances in which I found myself her guardian. Guardian, yes, and provider too. But we didn't shirk our duty. We taught her the difference between right and wrong. Has she told you that, I wonder? Or did she let you imagine she'd had no moral guidance? Was that the excuse she made for her wanton behaviour? She was twelve years old when she came into my household. From that time she had a good Christian training. But the seed was sown, inherited from her father. My own brother – but nothing alike about us. A womanizer, no staying power, no sense of responsibility. It's in her blood. We gave her a chance. And if she didn't know that what she'd done was a sin, why do you suppose she hid herself away from us? Shame, that's why, for the way she misused the care we gave her.'

'Caring for her as you do, these years must have been an anxious time for you, Reverend Hayward. You must have been worried for her happiness. That's what you want for her, of course you do. You'll be able to take home a good report to your wife.' Again that gentle smile. Meg watched her performance, unsure which side of the fence she was on.

'Mrs Gower, it's not a *report* I intend to take home. It's my niece.'

Meg took a step backwards, out of her uncle's range of vision, shaking her head violently.

'You want to take them home with you; I want them to stay here. We shall have to leave Meg to decide what they do.'

'She'll decide nothing! She is under age. She will do as I say. If it's the child you have such concern for, then there is no need. I have been to a great deal of trouble to find a family to take him in – outside my own diocese, of course, I took a colleague of long standing into my confidence. Imagine the shame I felt! He was able to recommend this family to me. They are good, God-fearing people. Sad to say there will be many children reared without fathers as an outcome of the immorality bred by this wicked war. But one thing is sure: this child – Benjamin – will be brought up to know right from wrong. None of them will be given a better start.'

Jane saw terror and pleading in Meg's eyes. She was shaken by the intensity of her anger that anyone could assume the right to try and take a child from his mother. In that moment her own mind was made up: Meg belonged here at Denby.

'And you call yourself a man of God!' she scoffed.

'Madam, how dare you speak to me in that tone?'

'You expect to hand a child over as though he were a parcel of groceries! If you intend to drag Meg home with you, to take Ben, then you'll have to do it through the Courts. Have you ever asked yourself why she left you in the first place? You may have brought her up to recognize sin, but did she know happiness, did she know love?'

'I'll remind you, madam, I'm not some oaf from your cowsheds.'

'You're a man, no more and no less.' Then for good measure: 'Less than most, less than my "oafs" on the farm, as you call them. They'd have more care for other people.' She wished she could have thought of a clever and cutting retort, but anger made her speak first and think after.

'Talking to you only convinces me I'm right. What am I to gather of the place she's come to? You and your husband know of her wanton behaviour, know of it and very likely encourage her to carry on down the same road.' But perhaps her words had resolved him to let himself be seen in a better light. His mouth twisted into a smile even though his eyes didn't get the message. 'Try and imagine what it has been like, not knowing where she was.'

Meg couldn't stay quiet any longer. 'How did you find out? Who knows where I am?'

'Ah, I'll tell you.' And so he did, his voice loud and clear so that outside in the yard, searching in all the usual hiding places for the eggs, Greta listened, fascinated by the ring of it even though she couldn't hear the words. It appeared that he'd stayed with his brother-in-law in Cheshire and whilst there had visited a home for the elderly evacuated from London. Nothing unusual in the name Hayward. Surely fate must have had a hand in the reaction of one of the less able of the old ladies whose mind was given to rambling. 'Hayward, such a lovely child, Meg Hayward.' The memory of the pretty girl who used to help look after her made her shed a tear. 'And little Benny. Do you know my Meg? Pretty girl. Hayward same as you . . .' Her mind was that of a child, but she'd enough for the Reverend Edgar Hayward to have a lead to grasp at. It seemed other residents remembered Meg, they'd even had a letter saying where she'd gone.

'Mrs Gower, you know enough of the world, the attitude of people to an unmarried woman and her bastard. Meg may not be strong enough to put the child first. We have to give her the willpower to do what is right for him.'

'Of course we do. There we're all three of us agreed. You think it's better for him to be sent away to strangers; I think it's better for him to stay here where he has a good home and is surrounded by love. Reverend Hayward, I expect I sounded aggressive just now, threatening the Courts. Much better we work it all out between us in a friendly fashion, then you'll be able to reassure your wife. After all, she must have been dreadfully worried.'

He's nibbling at the bait, any minute we'll land him. Send him on his way feeling able to wash his hands of them just as he'd like, and without his conscience bothering him. If her aunt is like this, no wonder Meg found herself a way of escape! The gentle smile didn't leave Jane's face.

Edgar Hayward looked from one to the other. He was a short man, probably somewhere in his fifties. His Roman nose and jutting chin prompted those of his parishioners who looked on him with awe to say of him: 'There is a strength about the man', and his enemies: 'Looks like Punch and has just about as much humility!'

'She's under age, you seem to forget. She's in my jurisdiction until she is twenty-one.' Clearly if he went down, he meant to be seen to be fighting.

'Of course. And if she wants to hand Ben over to strangers, and to come back with you to live at the vicarage, then I can't keep her – although we'd hate to see them go. I can understand you want to have her back with you. But, if she chooses to stay and carry on here as we'd planned, then, Reverend Hayward, even if a Court could be persuaded that she should give up her work here, be taken away from people who love Ben – and we all know that's not likely – by that time, she wouldn't be a minor any longer.' She laughed, consciously she made the sound a ring of pure pleasure at how well things had worked out to everyone's satisfaction, looking at him with such a lack of guile, innocently waiting for him to show his own pleasure at the happy solution. 'But what a good thing it is that she's so well settled here and you don't have to feel responsible any longer. Off you go home to your wife and tell her her mind can be easy, Meg and Ben are fine.' So might she have dismissed a child, its problems solved.

His face flooded with colour, a vein stood out on his temple. Rarely had he been so angry. Little chit of a woman, how dare she tell him what to do!

'Don't dare use that tone to me!' He shook his finger only inches from her face.

Jane suppressed a laugh. She hadn't enjoyed herself so much for a long time. Her patently guileless expression threw him off balance more surely than any argument.

'You're upset, and I can understand it. You must be so disappointed not to have her back with you again. But even so, you must be thankful that while you've been worried for her, your prayers for her have been answered. And now you've seen for yourself that she and Ben are in safe hands.'

The Reverend Hayward raised a clenched fist, opened his mouth, closed it again saying nothing, then turned and picked up his hat from the sofa.

'Shall I go and bring Ben in so that you can tell his great aunt what a lovely boy he is?'

'I've no time for that. The car's waiting. Good day to you, Mrs er – er – yes, well, good day. And you, Meg, never say I shirked my duty! All the trouble I've been to to find a place for the child, then journeying down here. Yes, and I would even have put up with having you back in the house again until you're of age. A man of duty – and never you say otherwise. Well, now I wash my hands of the whole miserable affair. My conscience is clear. You've made your bed, your aunt and I will leave you to lie in it.' Leaning towards her, he screwed up his eyes. 'Just be careful who you share it with. This once we would have taken you back. Now, I've finished. Done!'

With a flourish of his arm he made it clear he meant to see himself out. At heart there was much of the dramatist in him.

As the front door slammed, Jane and Meg started to laugh.

'Pompous old ass!' In her relief, Meg giggled, 'Jane, you were wonderful.'

'What a man! And today I was just in the mood for him!' It was a long time since she had felt so light-hearted. Her eyes dancing, she shook her finger in Meg's face, her voice a poor imitation of their departed visitor's: "Remember my position! Don't dare take that tone to me!" If you saw him in a play, you'd think he was exaggerated.'

'His opinion of himself *is* exaggerated! You know, I'd almost forgotten what it was like being with him. Jane, how I hated him!'

'I can understand that! Anyway, he won't be troubling us any more.'

'He didn't want me back anyway. I bet he'll stop at the phone box to ring home and tell Aunt Cynthia they can breathe easy again, I'm not coming. They never did want me, even when I was a child. I suppose his conscience prods him occasionally. My father was younger than him, and so different. He was – oh, he was fun. He might not have made a study of sin like Uncle Edgar did, but he knew all about hope. With him everything had the excitement of an adventure.' Even talking about him put a sparkle into her voice. Then she paused. The next part wasn't so easy. 'After my mother died – I was ten then – he got into financial trouble, tried to put things right by speculating more than he could afford and things got worse. Anyway, in the end he was drowned. It was a sailing accident in Cornwall. A dreadful day to have taken a boat out, but when he was worried he loved to sail. I suppose it cleared his mind. It wasn't suicide.' Her glare defied Jane to believe otherwise. 'My saintly uncle used to tell me it *was*; he never missed an opportunity to talk about suicide, about the evilness of taking your own life. But Father wouldn't have done that, I know he wouldn't. However bad things were, he wouldn't have thrown me on to Uncle Edgar. He hated him.'

'And having met the little charmer, I'm not surprised.' Jane was determinedly cheerful, sensing the black memories that the visit had stirred up.

'He's gone then? Whoever the visitor was?' Mrs Sid came in. Something was afoot. Things were going on she knew nothing about. 'And good riddance, with a great voice like that! Make a fine town crier, whoever he was. Coming into a person's home carrying on like it – some people seem to have no sense of how to behave.'

Let Meg answer her, Jane decided; tell her as little or as much as she wanted. She went into the hall and lifted the telephone receiver. As she waited for the operator she heard Meg's retort, in that voice she kept especially for Mrs Sid, 'I expect you managed to hear what was going on?'

'I'm not interested in what your callers want, don't you think I am, young lady,' came the sharp reply – and in the voice kept especially for Meg.

But as Jane asked the operator for 'Shelcoombe 216' she noticed they both stopped speaking. Did they recognize John's number?

That was on the first Monday in June, the 3rd of June 1940. For Jane the date was to hold a special significance, she'd realized it that afternoon as she'd made her decision. But more than that, the 3rd of June was a day that saw the writing of the opening lines of a page of history special to an island race. From their moorings and harbours a fleet of 'little ships' was setting off. From the south coast, from Kent and Essex, from the Thames and London's gateway to the sea they came. Pleasure boats, fishing boats – what sort of craft didn't matter. Each was brought willingly, each crewed by volunteers. For on the other side of the narrow neck of the English Channel, all that was left of the British Expeditionary Force was cornered, battered and defenceless, being pushed back on to the beaches of Dunkirk. Perhaps the time would come when history books would tell of the retreat as a defeat, but never by those who remembered it!

Three days later when Winston Churchill spoke, the voice that already the nation was beginning to recognize reaching every home as people gathered round their wireless sets, he didn't try to dress up the truth. That was never his way. Many of them wounded, all of them weary, those that remained of our army in France had been brought home. Now the war for survival had truly begun. He knew and understood the spirit of the English people. The phoney war had begotten apathy. Dunkirk, refusal to be conquered . . . these were the things that put steel into their hearts. And what could be more characteristic than the fact that in their minds Dunkirk became a victory? The army had been brought home by a fleet of volunteers, ordinary men in little boats. This wasn't the act of a nation who would ever know the meaning of the word 'defeat'.

On that Monday evening Jane pedalled in the direction of Keyhaven. Her mind was on the call she'd heard for rescue craft. Today of all days – the war at its lowest ebb, and out of it would have to come new strategies, a fresh approach before they reached the final victory. Today, when into her own life had come a sudden pointer to the way she meant to go. A new beginning . . . And just as she never doubted the ultimate end the war would have, so she never doubted that she would make something of her own way ahead.

'Do you always eat in here, or is it because you have a visitor?' Their meal over, Jane let her gaze wander round the dining room at Keyhaven, the highly polished walnut furniture, the glass-fronted cabinet housing delicate ornaments, the gleaming parquet flooring almost covered by a huge Persian rug.

John laughed. Just as surely as she was taking in the picture so was he – the picture of Jane here in his familiar surroundings, facing him across the dining table.

'In the summer I usually have an evening meal in here, if I'm at home. In the winter I often eat in the study – my contribution to the war effort, only one fire. To be truthful most evenings these days I'm out with the platoon – your Sid amongst them.'

'You said "eat first, talk after".' She poured his coffee from the silver coffee pot Mrs Wainwright, his house-keeper, had put in front of her. 'We've eaten. John, did you mean it – what you said about wanting the Denby land but not the house?'

'I meant I want the land. Jane, if you've changed your mind, if you've decided you want to get rid of the house too, then I still want first refusal. But it's the land I need.'

'That's what I thought. I'm still worried. Supposing after the war Richard's had enough of the sea? Have I any right not to have the farm waiting for him?' It was a question, but John made no answer. She didn't expect one. 'All these months I've been taking one day at a time. Each morning presented its hurdles, each day I managed to get over them. But there was no feeling of satisfaction. The future had no shape.'

'You were doing it for Richard?'

'I promised Tim . . . that's what I find so hard. I know what I've decided is right. But I promised Tim. You see, we were both so sure about Richard –'

'No, Jane, that's not true. Richard has told me himself. Before he went back to school last summer, the war was only a week or two old but he talked to Tim about his future.'

'He couldn't have! Tim would have told me.'

'Who was to say then that the war would go the way it has? People hung on to the hope that it would soon be over. The might of the French Army – the impenetrable Maginot Line. Richard was only just sixteen. It was all far into the future and Tim told him not to say anything to you, apparently. I dare say he hoped peace would have come by the time Richard was old enough. Then you wouldn't have minded if he'd chosen a life at sea instead of on the land.'

Was that what Tim had been trying to tell her? Had he known in those last minutes that he was leaving her truly alone?

John waited. When Jane had phoned him saying she wanted to talk to him, he'd known it was about something important. 'Eat first, talk after' he'd insisted when she'd arrived, rather as a child might save his favourite sweet until last. Now what she'd suggested gave him hope. She was moving in the right direction; he must let her go at her own pace. So for a minute neither of them spoke, each lost down the avenue of their own thoughts.

'I won't part with Denby, not with the house. But the land – John, I'm not a farmer. I hate getting rid of a single acre of it. Yet I know I must because I can't stand still all my life, I must move on.'

'Move on? But you want to keep Denby?'

'Oh, me,' she tapped her chest, '*this* me, I shall be there. But life can't stand still, I can't live yesterday.'

'Jane, there's no need for you to part with a single acre.'

'I don't see how.' And she truly didn't. During these months they'd grown to be such good friends; she'd looked no further. But then, she'd been surrounded by a thick mist. Hadn't she just told him how she'd taken each day as it came and seen nothing beyond?

'Marry me, Jane.' There! He'd said it. Words he'd never expected to say to any woman – or never until lately, and even then he'd not expected to say them so soon. Words that seemed to hang in the air between them as if they didn't quite belong.

Marry John! He was her friend, he'd been her greatest support . . .

'John, you don't mean it! You've not a marrying man.' She tried to laugh it away. 'We're friends, you and me.'

112

'And aren't people who marry supposed to be friends? Jane, I wouldn't have said anything yet, I didn't want you to feel I was pushing you. But hear me out before you jump in with a "no". Think of Richard and his future. You still hope that one day he may realize he wants to farm after all. All right, if I rent the land at Denby then I'd relinquish it if that was ever what you wanted, you know that. But how much better for him if what was waiting for him was Denby and Keyhaven too.'

'No, John. You're making it sound like a business proposition. And doesn't that show what a real bachelor you are?'

'I'm making it sound like something you may be prepared, at this stage, to consider. Heavens, I know well enough you're not in love with me – to use the language of the romance writers.' It was language that didn't come comfortably from John; he looked almost apologetic as he gave a boyish grin. 'But you said yourself, we're good friends. There's a lot of sense in what I suggest. Jane, why go on battling? The children will soon go off, do whatever they want to do. You have a life of your own.' Leaning across the table he took hold of her hand, something he'd never done before. Inwardly she recoiled.

It took no longer than the seconds she felt the pressure of his hands on hers for her to see him with new eyes. A handsome man, but that was something she'd always accepted; a charming escort, courteous and thoughtful, nothing new in realizing that; ah, but here was where her thoughts took her into strange territory. As a lover, someone to share her bed with . . . she seemed to stand back and look at him afresh. And just as she had a new vision of John, so she did of herself. The need she'd known during the months she'd been alone, the unfulfilled frustration. Tim, always it had been the longing to be one again with Tim. And what was ahead? Years and years of nothing and no one. In those seconds she was frightened, frightened of the loneliness and even more frightened of running away from it.

'John, I can't marry you.' She spoke quickly, closing her mind to what she wouldn't acknowledge. 'I was Tim's wife for too long to rush next door and make a life. I'm fond of you, truly I am.'

Almost she imagined there was relief in the way his eyes smiled into hers.

'Keep it in mind, Jane, promise me you'll do that. You know I'm not going to pester you.'

He'd not pestered her about the farm either, yet here they were discussing whether he should rent or buy the land at Denby.

'Aren't you going to ask me, John, what's brought me round to my decision – about the land?'

'We got sidetracked.' Still his eyes smiled. She was beginning to relax. 'I'm asking. What brought it about?'

'This afternoon I went to get some hayforks – I've got a feeling they're wanted in readiness for invasion. Sid had a gleam in his eye when he asked me to collect them. Anyway, I was at the store with Dad. They're up to their eyes in work – partly it's the time of year, of course, but he's short of staff. These days there's work to be had without cycling out of town to find it.' There was a new air of decisiveness about her. 'It suddenly seemed so obvious. I'm not a farmer but I do know the nuts and bolts of the trade – the implements, the spare parts. I can help him with the books and the bills. It's not just that I *can*, but it's something I really want to do. It's a job that's worth doing, there's a purpose behind it. And, it sounds silly, I suppose, but me, Tim's wife, and him, Tim's Dad – it sort of holds the link firm. I can't really explain.'

'You're a nice woman, Jane.'

'Probably a selfish one. It's something I really want to do, and do well. Isn't it funny? All those years ago Dad hoped Tim would want to work there. Now he gets me. Not much of a substitute. John, it's coming up to nine o'clock. Can we put the wireless on, see if there's any news?'

'Yes, we must. I understand the Matthews brothers

114

have taken their fishing boat. Went off at first light.'

He turned the wireless on. 'This is the BBC Home Service. Here is the Nine O'Clock News and this is Joseph McLeod reading it.' The idea of the announcers being known by name, their voices recognized, was new; a constant reminder of the threat of invasion and the danger of the radio network being taken over by an enemy. Silently, John and Jane listened.

'If you're renting the farm to John Carlisle, that'll put me out of a job,' Meg said to Jane later that same evening. 'It seems back to front, you going to work and me staying here with Mrs Sid. But it's difficult with a baby. If it weren't that I'd have to leave you others to look after him, I could help out instead of you.'

'I'm looking forward to it. I'm doing it because I want to. We shall still need to fill the mushroom orders each week though. The mushroom money is worth having.'

'Don't worry. I can pick those and take them in on Tuesdays. You'll miss your Tuesday trips with John Carlisle.'

'Umph.' It might have meant anything. The remark had set her thoughts in motion. That's why she didn't notice that Meg, too, had other things on her mind.

'Jane, that cottage where Ralph was? It's bigger than the Sids', isn't it? How many rooms has it?'

'One reasonable bedroom, two small ones, another that's about as big as the broom cupboard. Then downstairs there's the kitchen, a scullery, and a living room. Quite a good living room for a cottage. Why?'

'Suppose I picked up some second hand furniture? I could live there with Ben. If only it weren't wartime, I could take visitors.'

Mufti let out a muffled bark. In his dreams he must have been chasing one of the farm cats.

'The war isn't going to end in a hurry, we can't kid ourselves any longer. But people will always need holidays.'

115

'The way things look now, the war may end quicker than any of us want. Who'd have thought a few months ago we would have been saying that!'

Who'd have thought any of this a few months ago? But if that's what her heart was saying, Jane gave no sign of it.

'And we're not saying it now! Oh, Meg, of course it won't happen. Think of Ben – and Greta – Liz, Richard, Hartley. Think of those men going off in their little boats today – from what you told me this afternoon, I bet your father would have been one of them if he'd been here. Think of him and of Tim. But it's not going to be over in a hurry and it's up to us to make something of our lives. Furniture, you say. Let's think what we have we could spare.'

CHAPTER SIX

Jane felt pleased with herself as she pedalled along the lane home from East Rimford. Her first day helping in the stores had been busy, the hours had disappeared without her realizing; she'd been useful and she'd enjoyed herself. The June evening was warm, the slanting rays of the sun touching the scene with magic.

Rounding the final bend she came in sight of home and, there outside the gate of Denby, was Greta.

'Mr Sid said there wasn't anything to do about the chickens. He said he's looking after them now. Even the eggs were all picked up, Aunt Jane.' All that was part of the new plan, that and Meg taking the mushrooms to town. 'I could do any other jobs?'

In Jane's enthusiasm to help Herbert, she'd not considered what being put out of work would do to her erstwhile 'partner'.

'As soon as you break up from school you can come with me in the mornings if you like. There's plenty of work for you there.' That was the difference between being an employee and one of the family! If Greta was bored, or if she got under people's feet, she'd have to come home. But Jane couldn't just break off their partnership.

Over the next few weeks No. 1 Farm Cottage was made ready for visitors.

The threat of invasion had never been more serious; to look at any map was to see how vulnerable the country was, only that narrow strip of channel between the south-east corner of England and poor conquered France where Hitler was mustering his forces. Nevertheless Jane took time away from her cash books and coils of barbed wire to attend a large auction sale in a house in

Kingsbridge. Meg spent hours with a whitewash brush. It was early in July that the last curtain was hung, and on that very same day the fighter planes were scrambled from the airfields of Kent to intercept bombers approaching Dover.

'ARP Find peace and tranquillity in the beautiful South Hams of Devon. Every care and comfort in former farm cottage. Mrs Gower, Denby House, Shelcoombe. Tel: Shelcoombe 223.'

'There's the letterbox, the teatime post's come. Go and pick it up, let's see if there's anyone else writing to Mrs G., wanting a holiday.'

They were well into July. Less than a week and Greta would have broken up, term over. Already Meg was playing host to a bank manager and his wife, with a school teacher booked in to arrive at the end of the week.

'There's one letter for Aunt Jane. And look, Mrs Sid, I got one for me too.'

'Is that Eddie writing to you again, duckie?'

'No, that's Dad's writing. Look, see, he always writes like that.'

Mrs Sid glanced at the envelope and sniffed disparagingly. But it was lost on Greta who was slitting the envelope open carefully with a knife, treating it will all the respect it deserved.

'What's your dad got to say for himself then? Not often he puts pen to paper, I must say.'

'Oh, look, Mrs Sid! That's him, that's Dad. See, he's drawn a picture of himself for me.' She chuckled with delight.

'Drawn one, you say?' But even Mrs Sid smiled as she looked at the caricature of the soldier, his hair standing up in short spikes like new mown grass, his small frame swamped in a sloppy Army uniform and his feet looking twice the size they should in huge boots. The strange thing was that the face with its cheeky grin really did look remarkably like George Blake's. 'Fancy him being able to draw like that! Never think it to look at the lettering on the envelope.'

'Dad always writes big and clear. He doesn't like people writing joined up, Mrs Sid, he always does block. I do too when I write to him.'

'That's it, ducky. If that's the way he likes it.' Fancy that! It must be that he couldn't write what Greta called 'joined-up'.

'You can read his letter if you like. Then when Aunt Jane gets in we'll show it to her too.' Carefully she smoothed out the sheet with its large block letters and passed it to Mrs Sid.

'DEER PRINCESS, I HOPE YOU ARE WELL, I AM GETTING ON OK BEING A SOLDURE. SOON I WILL HAVE SOME LEVE. I WILL TRY AND GET DOWN TO SEE YOU THEN. ARST MRS GOWER IF THATS OK. GOD BLESS YOU. LOVE FROM YOUR DAD.'

'That's a real nice letter, Greta. You put it somewhere safe and take care of it.' Mrs Sid surprised herself. When she'd seen the envelope she'd not expected its contents would bring a lump to her throat.

Only yesterday Richard and Hartley had arrived, exams over, their final term at school behind them. Tomorrow Elizabeth would be home too. Proudly Greta showed the boys her picture. It was Richard who stuck it to the kitchen wall. He did it to please Greta and, at the time, so it did. Looking at it she could imagine what his leave would be like . . . probably he'd have a whole seven days or even more with her. She knew it would be soon, while she was on holiday from school.

Each day she went off with Jane – each day when they came home she looked to see if the post lady had brought her a letter saying how soon he was coming. They'd been partners in the henhouse and she was determined she and Jane would be partners in the stores at Herbert Gower and Son. She learnt to sort out cubbyholes of nuts, cogwheels, brackets, all the paraphernalia of the machinery used on the farms; each spare part had a number on it, they mustn't be muddled. Greta was quick to learn – and she was one of the world's workers. If the Labour Exchange had sent anyone with half her tenacity Herbert would have been pleased to take them. So she filled the days as she waited.

It was the end of August when the looked-for letter at last arrived. 'DEAR PRINCESS, I GOT MY LEAVE. I SHALL TRAIN DOWN TO LONDON, STAY THE NITE ON SUNDAY 8TH WITH ED AND HIS MUM AND DAD, THEN TRAIN ON DOWN TO YOU ON MONDAY 9TH. GOT 14 DAYS PRINCESS. THANK MRS GOWER FOR SAYING I CAN COME. GOD BLESS YOU. YOUR LOVING DAD.'

A long letter, worth every day of the waiting. Having delivered his messages, Greta folded the letter carefully back in its envelope and put it with the other few he'd written to her, then went back downstairs to count off on the calendar the eleven days until he'd arrive.

Hartley was expecting his papers telling him where and when he had to report for his medical; Elizabeth had written to a training hospital, resigned to the prospect that any experience she got while she waited would have to be in the local hospital. Richard was the problem; he seemed resigned to nothing. Glance at him when he wasn't aware and his expression was sullen.

'Richard,' Jane called out to him when she saw him collecting his bicycle from the barn, 'here a second before you go out.'

'What's up, Mum? Want me to do something for you?'

She shook her head. 'Nothing's up, not with me. It's you. Is anything the matter? If it's because of the farm –'

'Mum, I told you. I don't want to spend my life farming.'

'But something's the matter. It's hard without Tim, I know it is, for all of us –'

'I'm quite all right. You're imagining things, Mum. Look, if you don't want me for anything, I'm off.'

'Aren't you going out with the others?'

But she knew very well he wasn't. He was doing what he did most days: cycling the three miles or so to East Rimford and Herbert's business. Later on she would be driving over with Greta, but he liked to be in time to go out

120

with the men, either delivering in the lorry, or helping on a repair.

'Couldn't say what anyone else is doing.' His answer was exaggeratedly unconcerned. 'I'm going in the lorry with Ted Hiles. I say, Mum –' He hesitated, wondering how best to broach the subject '– I wanted to talk to you but there's never a chance without the others being there. It's this. Gran suggested that it might be a good idea if I stayed with Grandad and her. It would cut out my biking if I went in with Grandad.'

'If you don't want to cycle, you could come with me.'

'Oh, that's no good, Mum. As Gran says, by the time you get there it'd be too late for me to be any use. It's different for you – you're just lending a hand, not doing a proper job. Grandad would put me on the pay roll until I go off.'

At least outwardly ignoring her mother-in-law's jibe, Jane told him: 'You know you can get there just as early as you want, even from here.'

'If I move over to Gran's, I'd have Dad's old room. That's what she wants. I think it means a lot to her, Mum. You wouldn't mind, would you?'

'It's not just me. What about Liz? How's she going to feel if you clear off?'

'Oh, she won't care. I know you and Gran aren't exactly buddies –'

'Who said that?'

'Oh, come on, Mum, I'm not that blind! But, as she says, they've got a big house, as big as Denby, and only two of them in it. She actually suggested that Liz and I might both like to stay there. No, don't look like that! She meant to be helpful. She said that now you've let the farm go and are taking visitors in the cottage, if we both went to stay with her it would give you space for lodgers in the house as well. She said –'

'What a damned cheek!'

'Oh, you needn't worry. Nothing would drag Liz away.' His expression wasn't pretty. 'Anyway, Gran didn't mean it to be a cheek. After all, she *is* Dad's mother. I think she's afraid that because you and she don't hit it off, she might lose us too. Not that she would, of course. We're all she's got left, that's how she feels.'

'What rot! She's got a husband, hasn't she!'

'Anyway, it's all right with you if I pack a few things and park myself on the grandparents, isn't it? If I spend a bit of time there, well, maybe later on I'll come back.'

'You must do as you want. But never mind her! I'm honestly glad you're wanting to help your grandad. Tim would be too.'

Richard hovered. He still seemed to want to say something but didn't know how.

'Poor old Mum . . .' was all he managed. Was it that, or was it what he'd said just now about her not doing a proper job that dampened her high spirits?

'It's come, Aunt Jane!' Hartley waved a piece of paper at her as she went back indoors. 'My medical's on the 9th, that's Monday week. By the end of the month I bet I'll be training.' Jane heard the pride in Hartley's voice. Liz heard it too and, watching him, her eyes shone; she made no attempt to hide her feelings. Looking from one to the other of them, Jane felt a sudden loneliness. In her mind she tried to call up Tim's spirit; she needed to feel that he was here with her, watching the children so keen to grow up. But spirits come of their own volition or not at all.

'The 9th seems a special day all round! You go off to show the Air Force how lucky it is to get you – and Greta's father gets his leave.' She managed to put all the enthusiasm into her voice that was expected.

'Dad comes here on the Monday, but he's staying with Ed for the weekend, remember?' Greta liked to keep the record straight. 'His leave will have started. By the end of the month, when you say you'll be an Air Force man, Hartley, he'll be gone back. He'll be a soldier again.'

And if any other reminder were needed of the perpetual motion of life, of how short the span of the role any of them might play in it, it came from Ben riding his horse. Ben's

Bronco, made by Tim, finished by Hartley, given to him when he'd been so small that he'd had to be lifted on, gently rocked. Now, working his tough little body backwards and forwards, he shrieked with glee, enjoyment turning momentarily to fright as gusto overcame prudence and he was almost thrown.

To Jane, each day that Hartley had been kept waiting for that buff envelope bringing him his instructions had been something to be thankful for. For so long he'd been like a son to her. When she'd first known his parents they'd been living in Shelcoombe village, both of them doctors with a surgery in town. She remembered him as a young child, a living-in housekeeper-cum-nursemaid looking after him. Often she'd brought him back to the farm to play with the twins. As soon as he'd been old enough, he'd been sent to board at a local prep school and it was then that Gerald and Suzanne Ladell had made their decision: they were going to sell their practice, to follow their hearts and take their skills and their preaching to Central Africa. 'Just for a year or so' they had said, and willingly Tim and Jane had agreed that Hartley should come to them for his school holidays; but it had soon proved evident that concern for humanity in general was the driving force in their lives. They'd become ever more deeply immersed in their work. When Gerald had died of a tropical fever, his widow had doubled her own commitment. Sometimes Jane wondered whether it concerned her at all that her son was old enough to become part of the war.

Hitler was preparing for invasion. Over this last month each news bulletin had brought another instalment: 'Today German planes were intercepted by fighters of the Royal Air Force as they approached the Kent coast. Thirty enemy planes were accounted for; twenty British planes failed to return . . .' 'It has been reported that German planes today dropped bombs on an area to the south of London. The number of civilians killed or wounded is not yet known . . .' 'Today the Royal Air Force brought down a record number . . .'

It had started in July. Throughout August the pressure had intensified. On the 17th bombs had fallen on south London; on the 18th another massive attack followed. The bulletins were brief, facts so bare that here in Devon no one could know how near to success the Germans were coming as they attacked the seven sector-stations round the perimeter of London. Figures quoted in the expressionless tones of the news readers conjured up no picture of the human suffering. To Jane, above all else, air battles meant one thing; Hartley.

'It's sickening. Ours . . . theirs . . . oh, Mrs Sid, what if it were Hartley?'

'Just say, please God it won't be! Seems a poor bit of help to give a boy, but there's no more for us to do.'

'He's not gone yet. Fighting like this can't go on and on. Perhaps it'll be over . . .' A hope that must have been in so many hearts.

The wireless was their link with what was going on and it was from its loudspeaker, on a day with crackly reception heralding a storm, that they heard Winston Churchill pay respect to the gallant boys of the Royal Air Force. Every heart swelled with pride at his words that 'never in the field of human conflict had so much been owed by so many to so few'.

But look at it from any way one might, there was no sign of victory lurking round the corner.

The 9th of September arrived. Hartley refused Jane's offer to take him to the station; he'd ride his bike and leave it there for the homeward journey. After an early breakfast he was off, the family waving him on his way as if he were already setting out to win the war.

George Blake was no letter writer, they all knew that, so no one was surprised when he didn't let them know what time to expect his train. There was a telephone kiosk outside the station – perhaps he'd phone when he got there. Only on Tuesdays and Fridays did the rural bus come to Shelcoombe.

'If he phones from the station, let me know,' Jane said as she left for East Rimford. 'I'll go straight over and get him.'

Now that there were only a few hours to go, it seemed to Greta that the hands on the kitchen clock hardly moved. The excitement was almost more than she could bear. He was coming, and this time not just for an hour or two, but for almost two weeks. Sid had said she could show him how she could clean the henhouses; she'd teach him to find the new eggs that the hens laid in such unexpected places, and how to pick them up without hurting them. Hartley had promised to lend his bicycle. She could take him to the Leys and tell him what the birds were – she remembered their names, and if she wasn't quite sure which was which she wasn't going to admit it.

To Liz, too, the day seemed endless. In the afternoon she decided to cut the front hedge. It gave her a chance to watch for her returning hero without making it too obvious – or so she imagined! Greta had her own hero to wait for and she didn't care who saw how excited she was. She'd been told she could wear her best frock, her hair had been washed specially and this morning she'd brushed it a hundred times.

She had been bought a second hand bicycle. First in the yard and later in the lane, Hartley had run by her side holding the saddle until finally she went her first wobbly few yards solo. Now, although the ruts in the ground meant she had to perform the dual feat of avoiding potholes and at the same time keeping her eyes on a point straight ahead as Hartley had told her, she was allowed out alone.

'I won't go far, Liz,' she said, wheeling her bicycle out of the yard, 'just up the lane as far as the crossroads.' Then, with a mischievous twinkle: 'If I see Hartley coming, I'll tell him you're watching out, shall I?'

Liz was in no mood for teasing. 'Don't talk rot! With him

joining up and Richard cleared off, someone has to cut the hedge.'

'When Dad gets here, I expect he'll help.' Her two front teeth bit into her bottom lip. 'Do you reckon his train's in yet, Liz?'

'I shouldn't wonder. Watch out he doesn't pass you in the station taxi. He won't expect to see you on a bike.'

Greta nodded. In all her life she'd never had such a red letter day as this. Looking straight ahead as she'd been taught, she started off up the lane. That was at about three o'clock. At four they were still out there, Liz with the makings of blisters on the palms of her hands, Greta ploughing backwards and forwards the half mile or so to the crossroads. She wouldn't let herself feel those nudges of disappointment, she wouldn't own that she'd expected he would have been here before this.

In the hall at Denby, Meg answered the 'phone. Liz stopped work, shears poised, and waited, even though reason told her it couldn't be Hartley.

Jane saw her waiting at the crossroads, perched on the saddle of her bike, balancing with one foot on the raised grass verge of the lane. Concentrating just on watching for her visitor, Greta didn't notice anyone approaching from behind. She sat as still as a statue, the skirt of her best dress spread carefully around her. Jane had pedalled as hard as she could, she'd had only one thought, to get here . . . Now, at the sight of the little girl, she slowed her furious pace. Suddenly she didn't know how to tell her.

Then Greta heard her and turned.

'Has he come? Have you come to get me home? How did he get there and me not see?' No eyes had the right to reflect such trust and happiness. Already she was turning her bike, ready for the homeward ride.

'No, he's not come, love.' Oh, help me, give me the words, help me, help her . . . 'Greta, there was a telephone call.'

What hurt most was to see the change in Greta's

126

expression. Expression? No, that was it; suddenly her face was a mask. She looked at some point on the ground just ahead of her. It was as if in her heart she'd always known it was only a dream, something too wonderful to happen.

'You mean, he's not got his leave? They stopped 'im coming?'

'He got his leave . . . he went to Eddie's people . . .'

'Aunt Jane!' This time Greta did look up, her eyes wide and questioning. 'You're crying, Aunt Jane. Never seen you cry.' The much loved bike fell to the ground; Jane pushed hers against the hedge. 'What's up with Dad? Why hasn't he come? Aunt Jane, why're you crying?'

Jane sniffed. What use was she to Greta if she behaved like this? But it wasn't fair, her heart cried out, a child who had so little, it wasn't fair!

'Didn't mean to cry, Greta. Suppose it's because what I've got to tell you is going to hurt. Because I love you, and I've got to hurt you.'

'He can't come. That's it, isn't it?' But still she couldn't understand. 'He phoned you up to say he's not coming? But he wouldn't, Aunt Jane, Dad wouldn't do that, not if he's got his leave –'

'No, your Dad would never do that, Greta. He was excited about coming to stay with you, just like you were. But he's not coming.' Tightly she held the little girl's hands. 'Last night there was an air raid. Bombs fell on London, on Digbury Mansions.'

'You mean, Dad got hurt? Is he in some hospital? Is that it?'

'I think it happened too quickly for him to have known. It was Ed's mother who phoned. Your dad was a very brave man, Greta. Do you remember someone called Mrs Crawley?'

Greta nodded. 'Old Mother Crawley, that's what us kids called her.' Jane knew very well that what the children had called the old woman wasn't important, not to her, not to Greta. The child was putting off the moment, frightened of what she was going to be told.

'Mrs Crawley was trapped in her flat after the bombs fell. Your dad went in to try and pull her free.'

'What d'you mean?' She had to ask. Unless she heard it in words, she wouldn't let herself imagine it could be true.

'The wall fell – Greta, they said it was too quick for him to have known.'

She was only seven – seven going on eight, she liked to think. This wasn't the first time she'd faced the finality of death, but when Tim had died she'd been on the outside.

She didn't cry. Jane wished she would.

'Never been round the lanes,' her voice was hardly more than a growl, 'was going to take him rides, show him the fields, and the Leys – all that. Won't never do it now.'

Jane knelt on the summer-hard ground. She wanted to meet Greta on her own level. It was one of those rare moments. Between Greta and her there was a plane where their spirits met. She'd known it once before, on that night Eddie had gone back to London. But it had never been as important as now. Was she expecting too much of seven going on eight?

'He'll know. He'll see all the things you want to show him.'

The huge brown eyes looked at her unblinkingly. Had she kept up with what Jane was trying to say?

'When he was in London, or when he was in the Army, he could only know what you wrote and told him. Now, Greta, he's near you every time you open your heart to him. There's no time or distance to come between you.'

She waited. Silence except for the call of a blackbird. Had she said enough? Too much, perhaps?

'You mean, people aren't dead at all?'

'I think if you love someone very much – and if they love you very much, like your dad and you – then he'll always be near you because your heart, your love and your thoughts, will hold on to the part of him that was yours.'

Seconds ticked by. Jane wondered whether in trying to simplify her own beliefs she'd given Greta anything at all to hang on to.

Greta fixed her gaze on her; it was an unfathomable look.

'Let's ride our bikes for a while, Greta, shall we? We don't want to go home yet.'

Cycling would need Greta's concentration. And even more important, Hartley might be home at any time. The last thing Jane wanted was for him to come bounding along, full of the excitement of his own day. So they took the lane to the left, in the direction of East Rimford, neither of them talking as they rode. A mile or so on, they stopped, propping their bikes by the side of a five bar gate. Jane looked at Greta, so pale and composed. If only she'd let go – cry.

'Aunt Jane, how do I know he can see it all? All that – what you told me – how do I know? How can I make it be like that?'

Jane steadied her while she climbed to sit on the gate, then hoisted herself to her side. She didn't answer immediately. While she sought in her heart for the right words, she could feel Greta waiting.

'I don't think you can force it to happen, Greta. I think it comes of its own accord, probably when you're not trying at all. When you ride round the lanes or when you clean out the henhouses – any of the things that are part of your life – suddenly and without your even trying, one day you'll hear his voice. Only in your head. But so clearly it'll be as if you could see him with your eyes as well as with your heart.'

Another silence. She knew that Greta was weighing up every word she'd said.

'Like being his princess, you mean? Didn't make no difference that I didn't see him, I knew I was still his princess.'

'That's just what it's like. Something just the two of you share. And you always will, when you're seven or when you're grown up. You'll remember the feeling of being with him, of being part of him, knowing that you're his princess. The love in your heart for him won't ever alter any more than his for you will.'

129

How was it that, even though Greta turned her head away, Jane sensed that at last she was crying? There on the top of the gate she cradled her in her arms. She smelt the fresh scent of the shampoo she'd used for the special hair wash in preparation for this big day; she saw the new white socks; she felt her own neck wet with the little girl's hot tears. And she was shaken by the realization of just how much she'd grown to love her since that day she'd collected her from the Village Hall, the least cared for of Shelcoombe's consignment of evacuees.

'. . . wanted 'im to come . . .' Greta sobbed. '. . . being a proper baby . . .'

Tears can't go on forever. Presently she was quiet. She even sat up and looked around her, the occasional convulsive sniff all that was left of the storm of tears.

'We'll go home this way, Greta, on a bit further then turn left again. That'll take us back past the bottom fields of Keyhaven.'

'At home, do they all know? Don't want them all talking about him not coming.'

'Yes, they know. Everyone has to know, love.'

''spect they'll be talking about Hartley.'

'I'll tell you what we'll do – we'll dump our bikes in the yard and get the car. We'll go out for supper, just you and me?'

'Honest?' Another sniff. But this time there was the hint of a smile. It wasn't so much the thought of going out to supper, as not having them looking at her all dressed up in her best, looking at her and knowing about her dad.

Sid was in the yard when they reached Denby.

'Tell the others Greta and I won't be in to supper, Sid. We've just come back to get the car.'

'Ah, I'll tell them. Liz has promised to put Ben to bed this evening. It seems Meg is off kicking her heels up somewhere too. If you're going to town, you may run into her.'

'On her own?'

'What, our Meg? Not likely! The young chap she's got

staying there with his parents. Seems they're pleased enough to put up with a quick meal, knowing their lad's making the most of his leave. I'll tell the others that you two won't be in. Are you going to be warm enough, Greta ducky? Gets chilly when the dark comes.'

'You're probably right. Hop in the car, Greta. I've got to run upstairs and get my purse or we can't buy any supper, so I'll bring you your green woollie.' She knew tonight Greta wanted to avoid meeting the others. Nothing was ever so difficult by morning light.

Soon they were bumping and jolting along the rutted lane on their way to town. Up the village street, then towards the wood and the shaded road where Tim had found Meg. They'd already plumbed their souls, said as much as Greta could digest; yet tonight was far too important for anything less. So as they drove along they were quiet. Once in town, Jane drew up by the kerbside and turned to her small companion.

'We'll splash out if you like and go to the hotel – or there's a restaurant I know up the hill there? You say. What would you prefer.'

'Honest? What I'd really like? Me and Dad used to get fish and chips sometimes for a treat, usually if Mr Huggins had sent for him to do a bit of driving with the taxi. He'd come home jingling his money in his pocket.' Such pride in her voice. 'Fish and chips, that was our favourite. I don't mean I don't like the fish what Mrs Sid cooks, that's nice all right. But from the shop it's – well, it's just not like the same thing. Do you like it, Aunt Jane?'

'Yes, rather. And don't often get it. Living where we do, it'd be too far to come. Let's leave the car here and walk. There's a shop up the road. What sort do you want?'

'Can I choose any kind I like? Then the sort I got once – it's dearer, Dad told me, is that all right? I'll have cod if you think it's too dear – but once he bought me fish called plaice. Always remember it . . . plaice and a penn'orth of chips. With salt and vinegar. Then it's all ready to eat when we get outside, see?'

'I'll have the same.'

She felt Greta's hand slipped into hers. She knew she'd made a good move in bringing her out to supper. And she knew too that no hotel could have matched up to the child's idea of an outing as much as a newspaper package of fish and chips. It was a meal that helped bridge yesterday with tomorrow.

'Are you warm enough to sit by the river to eat, or shall we take our supper back to the car?'

By now it was nearly dark. Jane could feel rather than see the way Greta was considering the question.

'Don't know about eating them in the car, Aunt Jane. Be nice, cosy, all shut in. But might leave a rotten stink afterwards.'

'We'll worry about that tomorrow. Come on, let's get snug and enjoy our feast.'

With her own children Jane had never had this sort of relationship. It wasn't that with Greta she tried to behave as if she were younger than her years, rather it was that age had no part in it.

'No, not like that! Don't unwrap it!' Greta's voice cut in. 'Look, do it this way. You tear a hole in the newspaper down one side, just big enough to get at it, see, pull bits off. Keeps lovely and hot that way. Cor, don't it smell scrumptious?' On her own packet she showed the way, then 'pulled off the first bit' and pushed it into her mouth. Jane followed suit.

Scrumptious though it was, Greta was soon chewing – and chewing – the joy had gone. Manfully, she was trying to show how pleased she was with her feast.

'Aunt Jane,' her eyes used to the faded light, Jane could just see her worried expression, 'you didn't tell me about Ed. You said Digbury Mansions got hit with bombs, but you never told me about Ed.'

'It was Liz who spoke to Eddie's mother. She asked about him, she thought they might want to send him back here to us. But it seems that most of the children from the Mansions had been evacuated again during the last few

132

weeks. Eddie's gone to a place in Norfolk, he's quite safe. You'd have liked him to come back here, wouldn't you? I ought to have written to his people and suggested it.'

'It's funny, but I don't really mind him not coming to us at home, just so long as he's been sent somewhere good.'

'Us' 'home'. Jane reached out her hand and touched Greta's hair, so lightly that the girl didn't notice.

The munching went on. The exchange seemed to have put new heart into Greta's appetite.

There was a pathetic dignity about Greta's acceptance of her loss as the days of what should have been her father's leave went by. She never flagged as she sorted, counted and tidied in the stores.

It was a Tuesday morning in October when Hartley finally heard – he was to go in six days' time.

Now it was Meg who took the mushrooms to town on Tuesday mornings. But for John and Jane, the habit of lunch together continued. Instead of driving her to Kingsbridge and Totnes delivering, now he collected her from East Rimford. The end result was the same: lunch in the Red Lion near the Cattle Market. True to his word he'd never again raised the question of marriage; it hadn't left a scar on their friendship. On this October day when he arrived to collect her, he found her talking to Richard who'd just got back from helping one of the mechanics on a job.

'Richard, busy or no, you will promise to get home for his last evening, won't you? I want us to have a celebration supper, something he'll remember.'

'Doubt if that's what he has in mind for his last evening. More likely he'll want to take Liz out to a slap-up dinner at the "George".'

'On his last night home? Oh, Richard, don't be such a grouch.' She tried to laugh his remark away. 'Come on, promise me. You can't make work an excuse, it'll be Sunday. He's off on Monday. Don't know when he'll get home again – perhaps not 'til after he's been passed out and got his commission.'

At that Richard's expression became positively sulky. He grunted something to the effect that he'd cycle over, but if Hartley had other plans for his last evening they weren't to be altered on his account. She wondered whether his ill-humour was because John had come to collect her for lunch. But clearly she was wrong. Turning his back on her – and on the arrangements for Hartley's send-off – Richard's greeting to their neighbour showed no sign of the moroseness that lately she'd seen so often.

On Sunday evening he came. Perhaps he'd been right and the best thing would have been for Hartley and Liz to go to the 'George', have dinner in the hotel dining room, feeling themselves part of the grown-up world that awaited them. As it was they all ate in the big kitchen of Denby, a festive meal of Keyhaven pheasants and Denby vegetables, followed by apple pie and Keyhaven cream. If afterwards Jane remembered Hartley's last civilian meal it would be for the tensions, the love lorn looks between him and Liz, the hang dog expression on Richard's face, the puzzlement on Greta's.

A week later Elizabeth started work at the hospital in town; she was to be an auxiliary nurse until she was old enough to go away and commence training. Now, well into autumn, bookings for No. 1 Farm Cottage were few. Even a war wasn't going to send those wanting a holiday to seek it in the murky mists of a Devon winter. The leaves were nearly all down, lying wet and slippery underfoot. The short days were made to seem even shorter by the blackout, heavy curtains shielding the windows by mid-afternoon. Now, too, Herbert was less busy. Often Jane was home by the time Greta arrived back from school. Today, her oil stove alight, she'd been working at Tim's bench, sorting out the figures for her mushroom sales.

For more than a week there had been no rain, yet the carpet of mud in the yard didn't lessen. The mist didn't turn to fog, yet neither did it lift. It was getting too dark to see what she was doing without lighting the lamp and that would mean fixing the thick blanket across the window. So in the gloaming she sat, her chin cupped in her palm, her elbows on the desk as she gazed through the window at the gathering dusk. A year had passed since Tim's accident. A year . . . A kaleidoscope of memories crowded her mind. She gave herself a mental shake, then closed her book. It was no use sitting out here.

'I'm home, Aunt Jane.' The shout came as Greta hopped off her bike and wheeled it to the barn. Like an instant tonic, the sound of it lifted Jane's spirits.

'And I've just finished in here,' she opened the door and called back, 'I'm coming in now.'

'Oh, have you done?' Clearly Greta was disappointed. She liked the 'office'. 'I hurried home, I thought you'd still be in here.'

Jane laughed. 'So I am. But it's too dark to do anything.'

'It's nice with just the light of the stove. Look up at the roof, Aunt Jane, see the pattern. When the lamp's on you can't see it. Nice smell too.'

What was it George Blake had said? Something about having a stove like it at home?

'I've got some hard homework to do. Long division sums. Me and three others in the class have been put on to long division.' Her voice rang with pride.

'Just four of you? My word, that's good, Greta.' And, habit dying hard, Jane pulled herself up to perch on the wooden bench, planting her feet on one stool while Greta sat on the other.

'Tell you what, Aunt Jane, I made up my mind about it. I'm going to get to be top of the class.'

'It's a good goal to have.' A goal, wasn't that what she'd been thinking about herself? It's what every life should have.

'Would you be proud, Aunt Jane, if I got to be top of the class?'

'That I would. But I'd be proud even if you didn't, just as

135

long as you worked as hard as you could. Everyone can't be top, Greta, but everyone can try.'

Greta sniffed. 'Yes, but it's not much good trying and not getting there, is it? That means you should try a bit harder, seems to me. Shall I tell you why – about me, I mean, why I've made m' mind up to be top? You won't go telling anyone, will you?'

'No. Cross my heart. I'll not say a word.'

'Well, it was back in London. One night when I was just a kid – oh, about six or not even six. Dad and I went down the market like we used to sometimes. It was a good time to do the shopping there in the market, end of the day. That's what Dad used to say. Good fun it was. Sometimes we came home with some of that yellow fish, 'addock or some such name, isn't it? Anyway, I was telling you. It was a night when we hadn't got much from the market, Dad was looking sort of sad. There was a new moon. As we came out of the alley by the Mansions we bowed to the new moon like we always did. I said, "Don't forget to make a wish" and d'you know what Dad said to me – and this is why I've made up my mind about being top at school – he said, "I wish you could grow up to be clever, get a good education, get a good job." That's what Dad said to me, Aunt Jane. I was only a kid, like I said, didn't mean much to me then. Suddenly at school today, when Miss Turnbull picked out the four of us to start long divisions ahead of the rest–' She hesitated, up to this point she'd talked fast, now she almost didn't finish what she'd been saying. Feeling her way, she went on: 'Remember you said it would come all unexpected? There, in the middle of the class, I felt like I heard Dad saying it to me, about wishing I could grow up to be clever, get a good education and all that.'

By now it was almost dark in the little office, the dim light of the oil stove casting flickering shadows, with its pattern of triangles of light on the wooden roof.

'So you're going to do your best to please your Dad? I bet he's pleased already, Greta, knowing that you remember that evening, and that for him you want to try.'

136

'That's what I thought.'

Jane started to slide down from her perch. But it seemed there was more to come.

'I been thinking . . .'

'What about?' She wriggled back into position. From the diffident tone she suspected the problem would take some sorting.

'I've been thinking about Dad not being at Digbury Mansions any more. I mean – well – I been thinking about when I came here, that man in the Hall and all that. Lots of the kids have gone already and, anyway, I don't expect the war will last 'til I'm grown old enough to go to work. Aunt Jane, when that man comes to take me away from here, where will he send me? Now that Dad's not there?' Her voice melted into silence. But as she'd spoken, Jane had been ready with her answer.

'I've been thinking about it, too, Greta. Not just today but for some time. I didn't want to talk to you before you were ready to look that far ahead.' This time she did slide down from the bench, to sit on the stool by Greta's side. It seemed important that they were at the same level. 'I hate to think that one day you'd leave here. This is your home, Greta.'

'You mean like it's Hartley's, even if he's not really yours?'

'Yes, something like that. But Hartley has a mother, she lives in Africa. So although we always loved him, there was never any thought of adopting him.'

'How d'you mean? What's that?'

'Adopting? It means to make a person – a child – your own. It has to be done legally. I feel that you belong here already, but that's not good enough. If I adopted you legally, like I want to, then you'd really be my little girl, another daughter.'

'But what about Dad? I know he's dead, same as my mum is, but I can't just be taken away from him. I can't have him feel I'm not his any more.'

'You'll never be taken away from him. You're his

princess, you're Greta Blake. But it would mean that always, as long as we live, we are family – you, me, Richard, Liz.'

'Cor!' she breathed.

Later that evening the first homework of long division sums proved a battle; but it wasn't the first time Greta had shown herself to be a fighter. Liz was with her at the kitchen table; a little private tuition never went amiss and this love business seemed to have given her a new patience.

Coming back from taking Mufti on his evening excursion along the lane, Jane opened the door leading in from the yard no more than a few inches, shut it quickly and re-pulled the black curtain. An Air Raid Warden never strayed as far from town to check the cracks in the blackout, but even in the country everyone was conscious of the need of it. As if to remind her, there on the table lay the morning paper: 'Spirit of Coventry Unbroken' read the headlines. The picture showed the devastated cathedral. Unbroken? Hell doesn't rain down from the skies without bringing death and injury with its destruction. No figures were given, probably none were even known yet.

'I got the hang of the long divisions all right, Aunt Jane. They'll be easy as pie now I got the hang of how they work. I know all my tables right up to twelve times, so unless I do something real stupid I got to get them right.'

The yard door opened just far enough for Meg to slip in, and appear from round the black curtain.

'Ben's in bed,' she announced. 'You did say you'd listen for him this evening while I'm out, didn't you, Liz? I've banked the fire up, it's nice and warm for you. Will it be okay if I borrow your bike?'

''course you can,' Liz agreed. 'I was going to ask you, Meg, what about us going to the Gaumont later in the week? "The Lion has Wings" is on. I'm off duty at six all this week.'

'Yes, I'd like to. If I meet Liz when she comes off duty, would you see to Ben for me, Jane?'

A good deal of 'looking after Ben' fell Jane and Greta's way, but she agreed willingly enough.

'Sure you've got an evening free in your engagement book?' Liz teased Meg laughingly.

Meg chuckled. Life really had taken an upward turn over these last few months. The cottage gave her freedom; it also put money into her pocket, her share of the profit they made from the visitors. The batch of Canadians recently arrived in the area offered plenty of opportunity for fun and there was always one or other at Denby happy to listen out for Ben.

Now she went back to the cottage to get ready, saying she'd bang on the window on the way out so that Liz would take up her post. Soon Greta went to bed, feeling six foot tall with tonight's hurdle overcome.

'It was nice today, Mum,' Liz told her mother in the few minutes they had alone waiting for Meg's bang on the window, 'Richard picked me up at lunch time, and we went to the Milk Bar. He's been so grumpy lately, but today he was himself again.'

'Yes. I though he seems happier again.' Jane had tried to understand his moods, but she'd been at a loss.

As well perhaps. For there are some things better not known.

CHAPTER SEVEN

During that winter Jane occasionally put out the newspaper advertisement and each time a few bookings resulted. One thing the war was doing was making people realize that they had to snatch their happiness when they could. No more was 'holiday' to mean a week, a fortnight or even a month, according to circumstances – by the seaside in the summer. Seventy-two hours leave for a man based at Plymouth could mean reunion with his wife in the green peace of Devon. And if, during the winter, 'green peace' became 'grey murk' it did nothing to mar the sudden oasis in their arid lives. Coventry, Birmingham, Southampton, Manchester, Portsmouth – no one area was freer from air attack than another as that winter went on, the fire blitz reaching to ports and cities everywhere. But not to the South Hams.

Yet even in havens like Shelcoombe there was a new feeling of involvement. Men and boys of what had started as the Local Defence Volunteers hurried home from work to don their new khaki uniforms and take up their rifles. No more preparing for the invasion armed with two-pronged forks! It was Churchill, with his unerring gift for finding the right words for the occasion who had named them the Home Guard. Since then they'd been integrated into the Army, had a structure of officers and NCOs. Jane was never sure how selection for officers was made, but she suspected that the men's social position in the area played a part. John Carlisle had seen no more than six months' service in 1918; in 1941 he must surely have been the best turned out Captain in the Home Guard! Sid was neither officer nor NCO, but what he lacked in rank he made up for in enthusiasm. Whether Home Guard, Fire Watcher, Air Raid Warden, Women's

Volunteer Service, the 'home front' had its own force. A spirit of unity was abroad, reaching to the smallest hamlet. And if the newspapers disguised stark reality, enlarging on acts of heroism, encouraging pride in an endurance that would never knuckle under, this was the very medicine the nation needed as the meaning of war was brought home.

Pilot Officer Hartley Ladell was handsome enough to turn any young girl's heart – and most young girls' heads for a second glance.

'You're early for visiting,' the hall porter greeted him as he presented himself in the front vestibule of the hospital. 'We don't allow anyone in 'til two o'clock.'

'It's not a patient I want to see. It's one of the nurses.'

Even to his own ears it sounded very grand, 'one of the nurses.'

'Which ward?'

'She's an auxiliary, Elizabeth Gower is her name. I don't know where she's working. I've just arrived, you see – my first leave.' He might hold the King's Commission, but there was still much of the boy in Hartley; he couldn't keep his face from smiling as he said the words.

This particular porter had earned a reputation for being the least helpful on the front desk. He surprised even himself when he said he'd go and make some enquiries.

He came back with the message that she'd gone out in her lunch break. 'Bellmay's Milk Bar, that's where they say she is. Meeting her brother.'

'Great! Thanks for your trouble.'

The door porter settled back to his crossword puzzle; but for some reason he didn't settle back to his customary grey mood. Hartley's visit had been brief, but he'd left his mark.

They were sitting by the window of Bellmay's Milk Bar, Liz with her white cap left behind in the hospital and her old school overcoat covering her uniform.

'Blimey O'Reilly!' An expression Richard had picked up in the workshop. 'See the conquering hero comes!'

141

'Where? You mean Hartley?' Liz was much too excited even to notice his tone. Sitting with her back to the window, she turned, jumped up, rapped on the glass. Hartley! Even Liz took a few seconds to adjust to the uniformed figure. Of the three of them, he was the only one not conscious of it.

'You look smashing! Doesn't he, Richard?'

'Yes, he looks good.' Yet there was no smile in Richard's voice. 'What leave have you got, Hartley?'

'Fourteen days. Then I'm off to do my pilot training. What time are you due back at the hospital, Liz?'

'Quarter to two on the ward.'

Richard stood up. 'Well, now that you've come to keep Liz company, I'll be off. We're up to our eyes in work. I want to get back.'

'Right-o,' Hartley answered, while Liz hardly seemed to notice. 'You're still staying with your grandparents, are you?'

'Most of the time. Sometimes I come over for the weekends to Denby if we haven't got a rush of work on – but I doubt if I will this week.'

'I'll ride over to East Rimford. See you then.'

Striding back to the yard Richard went over the brief meeting, each word, each glance that he'd noted between the other two. And what hurt most of all was that neither of them had felt the undercurrent, neither had cared enough to see that he'd cut short his lunch break or to wonder why. Always he and Liz had read each other's minds. Oh, yes, today he'd read her mind all right. She'd wanted just to have him gone so that she and Hartley – Hartley the hero, the great warrior, set apart from the rest of them in his Air Force blue – would be able to be by themselves for what remained of her lunch break. And this evening – and tomorrow – and for fourteen long days.

'East Rimford 21,' Jane answered the ring of the telephone bell, 'Herbert Gower and Son.'

'Jane, it's John. Something's come up. I find I have to

drive to Plymouth this afternoon – well, almost Plymouth. How about keeping me company? I'm going to see some cattle in the Ivybridge area. Then I thought we might go on into the city, find somewhere decent for a meal. Play hookey, have an afternoon off. What do you say?'

'It sounds gloriously extravagant and peacetime-ish. I'll have to go home first to get ready. Have you the petrol for a jaunt like that?'

'I can log the miles for the Ivybridge trip, and the remainder will get lost in a month's essential use.' It was a language that not so long ago would have meant nothing to them. Now that she no longer ran the farm her own petrol ration had been cut but she still had enough to keep a car on the road, and of course Meg taking the mushrooms to town each week was essential use. For John the situation was different. His allowance depended on valid agricultural needs and each month he made up a log of journeys, adding the amount used for the running of farm machinery. As he said, the extra journey from Ivybridge to Plymouth would be camouflaged out of existence.

It was early in March. The sun shone brilliantly as they set off. Today the sunroof was closed. Inside the car they could almost believe it was spring.

'Any news of where they've sent Hartley for his training?'

'You'll never guess! This is why we've had to wait such an age before a letter came. He's in Canada! Fancy sending our airmen all that way to learn to fly.'

'Plenty of sky over Canada,' John laughed. 'Great experience for him. Or is he stuck in the middle of the prairies? Flat earth and open sky, is that why they send them there?'

'No, he's in Alberta. I've looked at the map. The town he mentions is Lethbridge, a hick town he calls it, but says the people are wonderful, so friendly, and he's having a great time. When he wrote he'd not seen much except the long journey from the east – all that prairie you talked about. But of course there's all the petrol you can use there.

He won't waste his free time, you may be certain!'

'Lucky lad. Richard must feel his life is very tame by comparison.'

She shrugged her shoulders. 'Isn't that part of being seventeen, waiting to climb every mountain, being sure that the other side of the river has all the lush fields? We're all caught up in our own particular circumstances, aren't we? I dare say Hartley has other things he'd rather be doing with his life too.'

'And you? When you were seventeen, what were the mountains you wanted to climb?'

'Oh, freedom – simply because freedom was impossible as things were in my life then. But that's when I met Tim.'

'And he was your mountains?'

'He taught me one thing – freedom is nothing to do with wandering footloose, it's to do with looking around you and knowing that you are where you want to be.'

'It's to do with more than that, I fear, Jane. You're still there, you still look around you at the same things. But have you the same feeling of freedom, or are you restricted by what you call your own "particular circumstances"?'

He thought she wasn't going to answer, she was quiet for so long.

'Yes, you're right. I saw it all differently because I saw it with his eyes, too. I suppose. Oh, what's the matter with us, John Carlisle? A lovely day like this, we ought to be looking around us and appreciating every second of it.'

'I am.'

This time she didn't answer.

At Ivybridge she went with him to inspect the cattle he was interested in buying, then back to the car. With the sun already sinking, they headed on towards Plymouth. Had petrol been plentiful then the outing couldn't have had the same excitement. Stolen fruit is always sweeter. Not that either of them cheated over the rations – not as a rule – that's what gave today's small cheat that touch of spice.

The last of the sun's rays were casting a golden light on

the water as they walked on the Hoe where the larger than life statue of Sir Francis Drake stood guard. Somehow the sight of it put today's troubles into perspective. Good times, bad times; war, peace. It all rolled on, today, tomorrow and for ever. And this particular day was one that would live in their memories, they both knew it. Yet why? What had they said that had drawn them closer? Neither knew, yet both were aware of it. Perhaps the golden promise of another spring, the banks of daffodils they'd passed, had something to do with it.

He took her for dinner at a hotel only a short walk down the slope from the Hoe.

'Jane, earlier on you said something about looking around us, appreciating every second of the day.'

She nodded, all unsuspecting.

'Why should we be lonely, Jane? Two separate people, we get on well, we could make a good life together. Tell me something truthfully . . .'

'Yes?'

'Are you one of those women who need no one? Are you content to look to the future and see yourself getting stronger, more capable, more mistress of yourself –'

'Don't, John. I don't want the truth. I don't want to hear myself telling you I'm lonely.'

'Of course you're lonely, lonely for Tim. That I know. But more than that. Truthfully, Jane are you cut out to live a life alone? Marry me. We could make a good home for the youngsters – your young Greta too.' He held her gaze. 'Perhaps we'd have children of our own. We're neither of us over the hill. We've a lot of living ahead. In all my life I've never wanted any woman for my wife but you.'

'John, I can't. I'm fond of you, I think I even love you. But marriage – no, I can't marry you.'

The band struck up from its position on a dais where a few years ago the nightly trio had entertained. A double bass, a set of drums, two saxophones, a guitar, a piano, and waiting at the side, a crooner.

'At any rate you can dance with me,' that schoolboy

145

smile put her at her ease again, 'and for the moment I'll settle for that.' Guiding her to the small space set aside for dancing in the centre of the room, he held her firmly and led her into a waltz. She'd never thought of John as a dancing man, but he acquitted himself well; she tried not to let her mind go beyond that as she turned and twisted in his arms. She didn't want to listen to the words so softly crooned:

> 'When I grow too old to dream,
> Your love will live in my heart.'

How long it was since she'd danced, and then with Tim, always with Tim. John held her close. Once before she'd recoiled at the touch of his hand holding hers; now she leant against him. He was warm, he was real. The song ended but he didn't release her. They waited to move as the slow foxtrot started. 'Have you ever been lonely?' came the throbbing question. The little dance floor was crowded. They were almost moving on one spot, the steady rhythm of the drum like a pulse beat that grew stronger with every movement. Oh, yes, but she was lonely, lonely for the life that was gone, lonely for love. And feeling John's chin caressing her curls, the strength of his grip, his own desire as heightened as her own, she was frightened. Not frightened of him but of herself.

Somewhere outside the wail of the siren filled the night. The band didn't stop, the dancers still moved in their almost motionless progress. Wait and see what happened. If the searchlights picked up any planes, or if any trouble was reported, then they'd have to go down to the cellars. Jane and John had heard sirens occasionally but 'trouble' was something one only read about, raids that happened to other places.

Almost as they thought it, and before the music came to an end, they felt the floor shake.

Afterwards they might like to believe the evacuation to the

cellars had been an orderly affair. In fact, if it wasn't quite every man for himself, it certainly was a case of each group, each family, each couple, pushing and elbowing a way through the crush. No one shouted; silently they jostled for position. John had an arm around Jane's shoulders. In this mêlée it would have been easy to have become separated.

It seemed like a long trek from the dining room, through the foyer, along a carpeted corridor, then into a passageway with linoleum underfoot, through a door and straight onto the stone stairway leading to the cellars. Below ground level it smelt damp. The cellars were cold and lit only by a hurricane lamp. Wooden benches had been set in rows, ready for just such an occasion, and though they looked uninviting they were the best there was, so everyone sat down. And once seated, above all else what must have struck every one of them was the stillness. How quiet it was. Were the guns firing? Were bombs falling? Surely if there was a raid in progress they would have heard something of it? No one knew what to expect. But their first reaction was relief; they were below ground, they were safe.

'It isn't a proper shelter.' A peroxide blonde was the first to break the silence, her voice unnaturally shrill. 'To be safe you should be away from buildings. At home we've got an Anderson shelter in the garden. That's safe. It's dug into the ground in the middle of the lawn.' A creation of powder and warpaint, she was one of a foursome, the other girl far more homely, their escorts both in the khaki of the Canadian Army.

'We've got one like that too.' No trace of hysteria in the second girl's voice. 'We've only had to use it once. Like sitting all squashed up in a bicycle shed, except that the ground was all puddles and it smelt like rotting earth. Cheer up, Marcia, this'll stand up to anything an Anderson would. A direct hit and you'd have had your chips in that too.'

Marcia of the plastered face wasn't looking for

reassurance from a girlfriend. Moving closer to Canadian No. 1 she rubbed her face against his shoulder (quite unaware of John's quick frown at the sight of the mark left by her make-up on the khaki uniform), and wrapped one of her legs across one of his. Her fright was genuine enough, only instinct told her she wasn't having her opportunities for the evening wrecked by it. Wide-eyed, she looked up at her companion.

'Is it safe? You'll see it's safe, won't you?'

'Sure, honey, sure I will.'

'I know you must think me awful,' everyone was watching the performance, there was nowhere else to look, 'I'm not a coward, truly I'm not. I've always been the same. It's the penalty for having such an over developed imagination . . .'

'Sure, honey, sure,' her Canadian friend whispered obligingly. Her imagination wasn't the only thing that was over developed! Quite a handful was Marcia and, like her, he wasn't going to waste his evening. The single hurricane lamp cast more shadows than light, but with his arm around her his hand moved unerringly to its goal. He said something but whatever it was was lost on everyone except his 'Honey', for at that second the guitarist from the band struck up a chord. It was a relief to everyone.

The scene, the moment, made an indelible mark on Jane's mind. Whitewashed stone walls, the dank smell of a cellar, the pressure of John's hand still around her shoulders and, above all, fright that was a physical thing. Not just hers, everyone's, she was sure of that. Her mouth was dry, her groin ached, her chest ached. The bald-headed guitarist, a man of about fifty, had found the courage to defy fear. If he could, so could she, so could they all! Jane was no great singer, but someone had to start them off:

'We're going to hang out our washing on the Siegfried Line.
Have you any dirty washing, Mother dear?'

148

Before she'd finished the second line the chorus was loud and clear. The fact that the battle for the Siegfried Line had been abandoned when the remnants of the Expeditionary Force had been ferried home from Dunkirk counted for nothing. As Mrs Sid would have said: They 'weren't going to give that dratted Adolf the pleasure of thinking he'd got them scared.'

> 'Run rabbit, run rabbit, run, run, run,
> Don't give the farmer his fun, fun, fun'

Was it because they were underground that they heard nothing from outside? Had it been just a stray bomb dropped as the planes went on their way towards a target somewhere else – or a last one before they crossed the coast on the way home, 'Use it, don't waste it'?

Chorus followed chorus. The air grew thick with cigarette smoke as one after another they sought to steady themselves with tobacco. John noticed how Jane's hand shook as she held the Passing Cloud to her lips while he lit it.

'All Clear . . . the All Clear's sounding . . .' At last the shout came down the cellar stairs. Still John kept his arm around her.

Already people were pushing their way back up the stairway, the Canadians and their partners well to the front of the crush. John and Jane stood back, letting the crowd go first.

'All over, Jane. We'll be home before they have time to worry.'

She nodded. 'An evening we shan't forget. Perhaps it was just a scare? Perhaps everyone was as lucky as us.'

'No, we won't forget it. Something we've shared, eh, Jane? Probably both of us more frightened than we've ever been – and we shared it.'

She'd never liked him more than at that moment. Now that the All Clear had gone it took a big person to admit to having been scared. All around them people were elbowing a passageway to the stairs. There was a fever of excitement in the smoke-filled air. 'Come on, we've wasted enough time. Let's go back to the dancing.' 'Bet my soup's cold!' 'No need to have cleared the floor, we could have been dancing all this time.' How brave they made themselves sound now the danger had passed.

'Do you want to stay and dance?' he asked her as, back upstairs and in the bright lights of the dining room, they saw the band once more taking its place.

'No. It wouldn't be the same. Let's go and find the car. I'm not even sure where you parked it, but we had quite a walk to the Hoe.' She laughed. 'I hope you know your way around Plymouth in the dark better than I do, otherwise we're in trouble.'

'Turn left at the door then left again.' It sounded so easy.

Once outside they realized that everyone hadn't been as lucky as they. While they'd been down below ground, singing their choruses, the war had been leaving its mark on Plymouth; by the standards of the weeks to come the mark was small, but coming out into the moonlit night they had no way of knowing that. A year or two ago mention of a full moon would have conjured up thoughts of romance; now in this world gone mad it meant a threat of danger. To their right as they walked they could see the glow of fires still burning.

'Can't let you along this way, mister. Road's blocked,' a Special Constable halted them. 'Where are you heading?'

John named the street where he'd left his car.

'Far as I know it's all right that end. Try working round to it that way,' he pointed, 'take the next turning.'

They did. But it seemed their Special Constable friend hadn't known what had gone on outside his own patch.

Broken glass, bits of rubble, fires that were out now but still left the acrid smell of smoke on the night air. Further along the road firefighters played their hose on the upper storey of one of the terraced houses where the loft still smouldered. There were no bright lights to help in the rescue work; fire engine, ambulance, a Women's

Volunteer Service van, were shapes looming out of the gloom as John and Jane shuffled their way along. Compared with the road they'd meant to take, the damage here was slight. 'But how can any of it be slight when it's your home? What if this were Denby? The Sids' cottage, Meg and Ben's cottage . . .'

'Here, someone, here!' One of the rescue team shouted from inside a house that, from the outside and seen just by the light of the moon, appeared not to have been damaged. Drawing nearer they heard the scrunch of broken glass underfoot. The windows had been shattered, the door blasted open. The walls and roof gave it the false impression of having weathered the storm. Not so. The row of terraced houses were old, held together by love and will power.

Just for a second, John hesitated.

'Here . . . can someone carry this kid out?'

Pushing the front door further open they were straight into what must have been the parlour. By the light of the man's torch they could see that the plaster ceiling had been brought down, the sideboard been thrown forward against a table which, miraculously, had taken the strain. The Air Raid Warden had discovered the small boy, unconscious, his body covered with chunks of plaster, a chair thrown on top of him. He must have been about two years old. He'd been thrown to land with his head, fortunately, just under the table.

'Ah, good,' was the Warden's greeting. 'Can you see to young Jim, here? Get the rubble off him and lift him, easy as you can, then get him along to the ambulance. His mother's got to be in the house somewhere, I'll try in the back room. Millie Beckwith lives here, you know' (as if they might), 'she never went out and left young Jim. She's bound to be in the place somewhere.'

Combined with the official rescue teams, firefighters, ambulance crews and the Women's Volunteer Service who'd arrived with a van and were doling out tea and sandwiches, was the feeling that here were neighbours helping each other, Air Raid Wardens working on their own patch, helping people who were part of their daily lives.

Very carefully John lifted the tiny body and carried him to the ambulance.

'They think his mother's still in the house. They're trying to find her.' Jane was frightened mother and baby might get parted.

'Ah, so she will be.' A man wearing a Warden's steel helmet looked over from where he stood by the WVS van. 'That's Jim Beckwith. His Dad only went off leave this afternoon. What a sodding thing to happen! Yes, Millie must be home right enough. I'll go on down and give a hand. Never mind that tea I was going to have.' Then to Jane: 'Here, ma'am, expect you could use a drink of tea? You take it. I'll get mine later when we've seen to Millie.'

At first glance Jane had thought it a scene of desolation; but as she and John drank their mugs of steaming tea she looked closer. No, desolation conjured up images of hopelessness. Not with these people! Working together, helping each other, the links that bound them being forged in the fire of shared adversity.

As they drove home she was aware of something else. The evening had forged more links than those that bound the neighbours in the streets of Plymouth. She remembered the hypnotic rhythm of the dance band, the unexpectedness of finding John such an accomplished dancer, the sudden cruel awareness of her loneliness and probably of his too. A dank cellar, strange shadows on stone wall, fear – all of it shared; the sound of the rescue sirens, the smell of charred wood, the dust that stuck to your mouth and teeth, the sight of a little boy lying unconscious – all of it shared.

'Why don't you come in and have a nightcap?' Her thoughts drove her to put their relationship back on to the old familiar paths. With the family around her, and in the bright light, she'd be safe.

With one finger, he touched her cheek.

'No, our day ends here. Goodnight, Jane – my dear.' John never used endearments; his words meant exactly what they said.

That same evening, without warning, Richard had arrived driving the truck with 'Herbert Gower and Son' in bold letters on the door. Learning to drive had been important to him. The very day he'd been old enough, his grandfather had bought him his licence. The driving test had been abandoned for the duration but that hadn't meant Richard had taken short cuts. Each day, either with the lorry driver or with one of the mechanics, he'd had a lesson and before long was deemed safe to go solo. Tonight was the first time he'd taken the van without a valid business reason, and it was done with his grandfather's consent.

There was no van in the yard now as Jane went in. Mrs Sid was knitting by the kitchen fire as she waited.

'I didn't mean to be so late, Mrs Sid.'

'Just look at your face, child! What have you been up to? Not an accident in that motor car?'

'Didn't you get the sirens here?'

'An air raid! You mean you've been in an air raid! And all the while I've had the wireless on and been having a laugh with "Bandwagon". No, I didn't hear any siren. Wind's from the wrong quarter, I suppose. But never mind that – it's you that matters. You're not hurt, child?'

Briefly Jane told her and, just as she expected, Mrs Sid said what she'd do if she could get her hands on that dratted Adolf. But there was something else on her mind.

'Richard has come home for the night. Drove up as clever as you like in the van, all by himself. And in the dark too! He's gone to meet Liz, she's off duty at midnight. They'll put her bike on the truck.' If words could be said to hang in the air, hers did. Zipping up her knitting bag, she seemed ready to go across the yard to her cottage. Yet what she'd said hung between them. There was something Jane hadn't been told.

'What made him come?' she prompted. Yet already she felt she knew the answer.

'How they grow up! Seems no time ago they were two little mites out there in the yard with their scooter. "The scoot", that's what they called it, remember?'

'He's heard from Seatrack Shipping? Is that why he came?'

'Don't know if I do right to tell you. Yes, he's off on the 25th. He's cock-a-hoop as you please. But, dear, oh dear, he's no more than a child. Came in with such a swagger to tell us. Can see them now: "My turn now with the scoot".' A tear trickled down the prune-like face. 'If only we could turn back the clock, hold on to yesterday . . . silly old fool, I am.'

'If only, Mrs Sid.' Jane touched the wrinkled cheek with her lips. And neither of them cared that she left a grubby mark behind.

'I say, isn't this great?' Elizabeth clambered lightly into the high cabin of the lorry, her bike safely stowed aboard. 'How is it Grandad's let you bring the lorry home?'

'I'll tell you in a minute. Let's get away from town first.'

Even then it wasn't plain sailing. A quarter past midnight, who could be out on legitimate business at this hour? In front of the lorry they saw a figure moving to the centre of the road, a dimmed torch swinging towards the ground was a signal for Richard to stop.

'Out late tonight, aren't you, sir?' The helmeted head of a policeman appeared at the window. 'I'll just take a look at your identity card, and yours too, Miss. What keeps you out as late as this?'

'I've just come off duty at the hospital. My brother's taking me home.' Liz passed her identity card across for him to inspect.

'And you, sir. I'll look at your card too.' They could tell from his tone that he didn't expect them to bear the same surname.

Gower. He shone his torch and read the name on the

van. It seemed he had to believe them. But you couldn't be too careful. In his job you had to be on the look-out for spies and Fifth Columnists.

'Working a bit late, weren't you, sir?'

'No, I'll be working a bit early to tell you the truth. I've brought the van over tonight instead of waiting until morning. I'm spending the night with my sister so that I can make an early start. I have a cultivator to collect and take in to the workshops for repair in the morning – from Keyhaven Farm. I doubt if you know it. It's next door to where the family live, the other side of Shelcoombe.'

Richard was enjoying himself, all this 'cloak and dagger' stuff adding a spark of excitement to his first solo drive at night.

'Sorry to have troubled you, sir, and you, miss. Can't be too careful. I've got my job to do. Can't take anyone at face value these days. Never know what disguise trouble might take. Copped a bit of trouble over Plymouth way, so I'm told.'

'That's all right, Constable, we've all got our jobs to do.'

Richard let in the clutch and they were off. Isolated in the cabin of the lorry, yet aware that these were the things of their world, identity cards to be checked, a 'bit of trouble' away in Plymouth; they felt that they swam in the pool of life. In truth they'd barely dabbled their toes.

First they'd drive out of town, then he'd pull in, give his whole attention to his announcement. It wasn't the sort of news one could casually drop, not when driving took so much concentration. Had she realized, she might have waited, let him speak first. But how could she realize? She was just pleased that he'd met her, that he was here to share what she had to tell him.

'I've heard from Hartley. A letter came this morning. Mum had a note too. Richard, no wonder we've been so long without a letter. He's in Canada! Can you believe it, Hartley in Canada! He says it's going to be an intensive course of flying training. He's in a place called Lethbridge, in Alberta. I had to look at the atlas to remember where

155

Alberta was. He'll go to the Rocky Mountains, he'll see the prairies. And of course they've got plenty of petrol over there, so on his time off he'll go all over the place.'

'What are the birds like? Did he say?'

'Birds? Oh, you mean the girls? He says the people are great.'

'Better watch out, Liz.'

She didn't like his tone.

'Richard, why are you always so beastly about Hartley these days?' In the dark he could imagine how her eyes would be sparking fire, he could hear it in her voice. 'He's no different, it's you who've got so mean minded.'

'Thanks very much!'

'You're just plain jealous because he's an officer in the Air Force and you're too young to be any use. It's stupid. And it just proves you're too young, that you can be so childish. I'm proud of Hartley and I should have thought you would be too.'

'If anyone's different it's you! I suppose when he comes back, the conquering hero with his wings on his chest, you'll be wanting to get engaged to him?'

'I don't know what I'll be doing. I do know I shall be doing whatever I want. Anyway, I'm going to train to be a nurse, you know that. Do you expect me never to get engaged, is that it?'

Driving against a background of small talk he could manage; this, he couldn't. He drew to the side of the road and stopped.

'All right, I'm jealous. Jealous of Hartley, or of any other chap who has his eye on you. Liz – you don't know what it's been like these last months! We've never been like an ordinary brother and sister – '

Hearing him, a thousand pictures crowded into her mind. If she were to dig really deep she could recall how they used to sit face to face in a twin push chair; and certainly this evening the spirit of the two who used to vie for turns with 'the scoot' must have been abroad, for small as she'd been she remembered it just as Mrs Sid had; one each end of the big enamelled bath, Richard ever the gentleman taking the end with the geyser because it used to drip; their beds side by side, their ears straining for the jingle of Father Christmas's sleigh bells. And staying just as close as they'd grown into the next stage, their physical changes as familiar to each other as to themselves. Her memory baulked at just one occasion: they must have been thirteen, perhaps fourteen. He'd promised to wake her early one morning so that they could ride to Slapton to swim. Looking back now she realized that all three of them would have been going, Hartley as well. But in her memory Hartley played no part. It was Richard she'd waited for, feigning sleep. The morning had been wet – yet still Richard had come to wake her just as she'd known he would. So why had she pretended to be asleep, lying naked, covered only with a sheet? As he'd gently pulled back the sheet why hadn't she spoken? She'd not opened her eyes, she'd not said a word, yet as eager and curious as he had been himself, she'd responded; his exploring hand, his probing fingers had excited her. Neither of them had ever referred to that morning. Purposely, even while she'd turned on to her back, making what he did easier, she'd kept her eyes closed, made sure her breathing was deep and even. Had he realized she'd been awake? She'd believed he had. Had he guessed that, only minutes before, when she'd heard him moving about in the next room, she'd torn off her nightdress and draped herself with the sheet? 'I'll give you an early call,' he'd said the night before; and even then both of them had known.

That morning had been part of growing up, she told herself. But was that the whole truth? She remembered how on that same morning they'd met face to face at breakfast. Neither of them had referred to what had happened, yet neither had they shied away from each other. Those moments of discovery had been just another link in the chain that bound them.

Hartley had been at the breakfast table too, she could picture him there. At the time he hadn't been important but now it was because of him that she wished none of it had happened.

'. . . never been like ordinary brother and sister –'

'We're not just an ordinary brother and sister.' Her voice gave no hint of where her memories had carried her. 'We're twins, that makes us different. But that doesn't mean we're not like other people. We fall in love – you will too.'

'So you *are* in love with him. You're only a kid. It's damned silly.'

Elizabeth frowned. 'I don't understand. Richard, why don't you like Hartley any more?'

'Don't talk daft. Nothing wrong with Hartley.' The night, even the shadows as the clouds rushed in front of the full moon, set Richard's pent up emotions free. If Elizabeth's shift had finished at noon instead of midnight he could never have spoken as he did now. 'It's you, Liz. He'll touch you, his hands'll maul you – you! And you'll want him to do it, that's worst of all.'

'Shut up, Richard. Mind your own business.'

'Has he done it already? Has he – you know – has he?'

'No.'

Richard flopped back in his seat. 'If he tried that, I'd kill him.'

'Anyway,' now it was her turn to hit out at him, 'I'll do what I like with my life. If I choose to sleep with him, that's my affair. We may be twins, but you're not my keeper.' He didn't answe. Seconds ticked by. She thought the 'bad' moment was over and, hoping to put it firmly behind them, went on: 'He'll get his wings before he comes home, and by then he'll probably get promoted to Flying Officer.'

'Hip bloody hooray!' He switched on the engine and headed for home. It wasn't until they were out of the lorry and crossing the yard that he said: 'I shall only be a humble merchant seaman, but I go on the 25th.'

Once he'd gone to sea letters took a long time to come through, and post to him had to be sent through Seatrack

Shipping Company, the firm he sailed for. It was October when, docking on the eastern seaboard of America, the men lined up to collect the waiting mail. Richard was well remembered. Glancing through the bundle he recognized the handwriting on the envelopes: three from Mum; two from Grandad; Mrs Sid; Hartley – and no longer with a Canadian stamp . . . ah, this was the one he was looking for – Liz.

Pushing the others into his pocket, it was hers he slit open, the eagerness dying from his face as he read.

'What's up, old son?' Like so many of the crew, the man who asked had spent years at sea. He knew just how helpless one felt when bad news came from home.

'Nothing's up, Frank. Just a letter from my sister.'

'Sorry, didn't mean to poke my nose in. Funny thing, letters from home. Like a lot of alcoholics waiting for the pub to open, we all look for the mail. But the truth of it is, reading it we feel a bloody sight further away from them all than when we're waiting. Cheer up, ol' son, you get used to it.'

Alone again, Richard read her letter once more then folded it and tore it into little pieces.

CHAPTER EIGHT

The smart efficiency of the commercial world wasn't for Jane, yet climbing up a ladder to find a flywheel from its place in the great store shed, counting out cultivator tines for farmers with mud on their boots, then, the sale done, remembering to book it and see the account was sent – here was a job with a meaning. When Herbert said something of the sort to Emily he was answered with a disdainful sniff and a tart: 'Not to be wondered at. Wasn't she living in some scrap yard when Tim picked her up!'

But Jane worried as the busy summer months went by. More than once she'd chanced on Herbert believing himself alone and been struck by how frail he looked, tired and aged. Losing Tim must have hurt him more than he'd ever acknowledged. It was as if a fire in him had gone out.

It was one morning in August when she arrived at the yard to find he hadn't come in.

She went across to the workshop. 'Harold,' she called to one of the men working a piece of metal at the anvil. 'I have to go out and Mr Gower isn't here. Can you see someone keeps an eye on the store? Anything that's sold just write in the book on the desk – make sure you get the name and address right. I'll be back as quickly as I can.'

'Right y'are. Reckon we can find most things. Don't you worry.'

It was seldom she went to her in-laws' house. Even in the days when Emily had known that her welcome – or lack of it – could be tittle-tattled back to Tim, there had been nothing more than lukewarm cordiality in her reception. This morning it would probably be frostier than ever, looked on as an intrusion that Jane should chase Herbert because he didn't show up in the yard.

'It's Father. That's what's brought you.'

'I was worried.'

'And so I should think! Even you must have noticed he's not well. Well, today I put my foot down. Sent for Dr Timberlake.'

'I know he's looked very tired, he's had no sparkle. But always he says he's well – just missing Richard about the place, that's what he tells me.'

'We both miss him. And of course it meant a lot to Father to have him there in the business. If, all those years ago, Tim had done as he should, things might have been very different now. He would still have been here.'

'Has the doctor seen Dad?'

'Oh, yes, he came straight away. He's making an appointment for him to have some X-rays.'

'But what's the matter with him?'

'Stupid questions you do ask! If he knew that he wouldn't be arranging X-rays.'

'You know what I mean.'

'Something not as it should be with his insides. I don't think it's your place to go into details.' Her manner implied that Jane had been indelicate to mention anything so personal.

'Poor Dad. Can I go up and see him, or would he rather be quiet?'

Before Emily could think of a good reason why he couldn't have visitors, they heard him call: 'Is that you, Jane? Come up.'

Emily sniffed. 'Better do as he says.' She led the way.

For weeks Jane had thought he'd looked tired. Today, propped against the snowy white pillows in his blue and white striped pyjamas, she was struck by just how fragile he'd become, how old. His neck was scraggy, but the change in him was brought home most tellingly by his hands lying idle on the counterpane. A few months ago he would have been helping load machinery, taking delivery of great carboys of disinfectant or half hundredweight bales of twine, handling them as easily as any of the men

161

could have done. Perhaps it was the huge mahogany furniture, the brass bedstead, that augmented his appearance of frailty.

'What's all this, then, Dad?' She sat on the edge of his bed – despite Emily's look of disapproval – and bent forward to kiss his brow.

'Jane,' he reached for her hand, 'so glad you've come. What about a cup of coffee for Janie, eh, Emily?'

'If I go and make one, will you let me warm you some milk? You wouldn't have anything at breakfast time with me. I dare say you'll take something now with her?'

Jane could feel the resentment.

'All right, my dear, I'll try.' And off went Emily. 'Jane, there are things I was doing in the yard. If I'd known last night I'd got one of these turns coming, I'd have brought the ledgers home.'

'Have you had them often, Dad?' She remembered that day when she'd found him sitting in the dark.

'These last months – never mind me. Jane, drive back to the office and get the books for me. Will you do that? Next week they have to go to the auditor. Nowhere near ready. So much to do. You've kept the sales side together – what I'd have done without you, I don't know. Used to see to it all. Can't seem to get on, can't settle. The Bought Ledgers are months behind.' His eyes closed, not relaxed but tight, as if to shut out something he couldn't face. His hand gripped hers hard, she could feel his nails. Only a few seconds, then his hold slackened.

'Is it bad, Dad?'

'Like a lot of rats gnawing my guts. Poor Em.'

She didn't understand, but this wasn't the moment to question.

'You'll fetch the books for me, two Bought Ledgers, two Stock ones. Got so behindhand . . . other years I've had everything ready. Just haven't seemed able –' He shifted his position but clearly it gave him no more comfort. 'My own fault. Worrying, brooding. Got to have X-rays, did you know that?' She nodded. 'Jane, listen to me. I can't tell

162

Em, poor Em. But I must tell someone . . .' She listened. Herbert knew very well what was the matter with him and, after listening to what he told her, so did she. He was the only father she'd known. She'd loved him at first because Tim was his son, but for so long now she'd loved him for himself.

Whyever didn't you go to a doctor straight away? But only silently she asked it. Worrying . . . brooding . . . carrying his burden all alone.

'Thank goodness you're not keeping it to yourself any longer. Now they'll be able to do something for you, Dad.'

'Perhaps they will. But the books – I must see they're ready.'

'That's nonsense! Are the figures so confidential, is there any reason I shouldn't do them? I've learnt a lot since I've been with you, Dad. I can sort it out. I'll bring the Bought Ledgers up to date. I'm not as silly as I might look, you know.' She said it lightly, almost teasing him.

'You'd do that?' It was proof if she'd needed it of just how low he was. His voice broke on the edge of tears. 'Afterwards, Janie – by and by when I'm not here, I mean – the business would have gone to Tim. Not the house, not Em's home. He'd have looked after things for her –'

'Dad, that's enough. And stop worrying. I promise I'll keep things going for you.' What a moment for the words to echo back at her, spoken in a cubicle at the hospital nearly two years ago.

'Here's your coffee,' Emily came in carrying a tray, 'and I want to see you get this nice hot milk inside you, Father.'

'What a nagger the woman is,' he tried to joke. 'Just put it on the side, Em. When it cools a bit I'll have it. Now listen, what do you think of this? Janie is going to get those ledgers ready for the auditor. All the invoices are downstairs on my desk, I was trying to work during the weekend. What do you think of that, Em?' His voice might not be robust, but he spoke like a man who'd produced a rabbit from a hat.

'Very kind.' With the sniff that so often accompanied

163

her remarks to Jane. 'Just as long as you're capable. Very different thing from serving in the stores or booking up the few bits you sell. Still, make a start on whatever has to be done, then in a day or two Father will feel up to going over what you've done. He'll be able to put right any bloomers.'

Between Jane and Herbert a silent look passed, not a wink, not even a nod, but it spoke volumes: it was a shared joke, it was an avowal on her part that he could depend on her not to make 'bloomers'. She wished she were doing it for him for any reason other than this one, but unaccountably the prospect of the job excited her. Whatever her life lacked, it certainly wasn't work. Every day was busy, so why was she so eager to take on anything extra, work she'd certainly not have time for in the hours she spent at the stores? She didn't ask herself, she only knew that she was proud to be the one he trusted.

On the way out Emily gave her files full of invoices – accompanied by a suspicious look. Just because Tim had seen fit to marry the girl, why should that give her the right to poke into their business affairs? Father always had been soft as far as Jane was concerned!

Emily had a lot to learn. And the first lesson came when Herbert had his X-rays, followed within days by an operation. The second took longer, months during which he made a slow and slight recovery. There was now no talk of his having the books to check what Jane had been doing, of 'putting right any bloomers' she might have made.

Working on the ledgers ready for their annual audit was just the beginning. It opened the door and Jane saw what these months had been leading to, clearly she saw the way ahead. Working each day with Herbert had filled her time; she'd done a job she'd enjoyed and felt to be worth doing. But a business, just like a farm, must have a skipper at the helm. She knew she was that skipper. It put into her life the challenge she needed.

It was autumn when Richard came home on leave. There had always been a toughness about him. Now he seemed harder, his boyishness gone.

'You'll go up to Oxford to see Liz? She'll be dreadfully disappointed if you don't. And there's Hartley, too. You know he's stationed quite near her.'

'No. With Grandad ill, I'll stay here.' Then, his grin turning him suddenly into the boy he used to be: 'I'll come and give what you're up to the once over. You're quite a clever old stick, aren't you.'

Seeing him go back this time was even harder than the first, for by now she had no illusions. Richard was part of that desperate fight to bring supplies across the Atlantic. One day she came upon a pile of leaflets in the Post Office, one of the advertisements put out by the Ministry of Food; she brought one home and pinned it on the kitchen wall at Denby:

> Because of the pail, the scraps are saved,
> Because of the scraps, the pigs are saved,
> Because of the pigs, the rations are saved,
> Because of the rations, the ships are saved,
> Because of the ships, the island is saved,
> Because of the island, the Empire is saved,
> And all because of the housewife's pail.

Mrs Sid needed no reminding. Every potato peeling, every bit of waste, went into the pail to be collected by the pigman from Keyhaven. It wasn't really for Mrs Sid's benefit that Jane pinned it up; it was because having it there seemed to hold Richard as part of their lives.

In the first weeks after Herbert's operation, when they clung to the hope that he was making progress, Jane drove him to the yard three or four times. He wasn't well enough to do more than sit in the office and watch, but they talked, they looked ahead to what should be ordered for the winter and the spring. Farm machinery was becoming as much in short supply as anything else, there were more urgent uses for steel. She asked for more than she expected to get, more ploughs, more harrows, more cultivators; she took orders from the farmers, put their names on the waiting list, then allocated the implements as they became available. Sometimes she thought her job wasn't so very different from Oswald Beatty's in the village, letting his registered customers have two sausages against each ration book – when he was able to make them.

'She's a good girl, Em.' It was spring again. Even Emily couldn't hide from the truth any longer. Herbert's voice was weak, she had to lean over to hear him. 'When I'm – after I'm – Em, trust Jane, she'll see you right.'

'Enough of that talk, Father.' She was so much more frightened than he was himself.

'Trust her, Em love, let her see . . .'

Emily promised, of course she did. But it takes more than words to alter the habit of years.

It was the day after Herbert's funeral that Jane had a telephone call from Mr Dunkley of Mercer and Dunkley, asking her to call and see him.

'I'm sure you will already know the terms of your late father-in-law's will, Mrs Gower. For her lifetime everything comes to his widow, thereafter the house and personal monies to pass to his granddaughter Elizabeth Jane and the business to his grandson Richard Herbert. Very straightforward. However, some weeks ago my client asked me to visit him at home and it was then that he gave me this letter, to be passed to you after his death.'

'Jane my dear, I wish I could tell you what it has meant to me to have you working with me. You have a feeling for the business, the same as I have myself. When I'm gone everything will belong to Em as long as she lives. Talk to her, Jane, do it for my sake, make her see that in your hands everything will be safe. You know what we make – see to it that you have a fair reward. Perhaps one day Richard will have had enough of the sea. Let tomorrow worry about itself.'

From the solicitor's office Jane drove out to see Emily. Why was it that between these two women, both of them

166

loving the same people, both of them loved by the same people, lay only mistrust and contempt.

'You!' Hardly a promising beginning when Emily opened the door to her.

'Yes, me. I've just come from Mercer and Dunkley's. Dad wrote a letter, left it for me with Mr Dunkley.'

'You'd better come in if that's what he wants. He left a note for me too. About the business. Says that you will be looking after it – taking a salary out of it.' In her mind she heard what else he'd said: 'Trust Jane, Em.'

'That's what he asked. But I won't do it unless you guarantee to give me a free hand. You must decide.'

How could Emily trust her? She couldn't even like her! But if that was what Father wanted, then let her try her hand at it. With this wretched war on there was little chance of getting a man worth his salt.

'It's what Father wanted. As long as you play fair, I shan't interfere.'

Whatever else their relationship lacked, they each understood all that went unsaid.

'That Meg's off out again, I see.' Mrs Sid found Jane writing at the kitchen table. 'It's not right, you know, Mrs G. You work all day then come home and have Benny for the night so that she can go gallivanting. Not that he's naughty, I'm not saying he is. It's just not right. Did you see who it was tonight? Not even one of our own. A Pole! They say they're cutting quite a dash, these Poles. Well, if there's a dash to be cut, that Meg'll be in the midst of it.'

'Mrs Sid, Meg is one of us, she's part of Denby now.' Jane smiled at her old friend. 'Anyway, Ben's no trouble. And Greta likes helping get him off to bed. Says it's her job.'

'That's as may be! It still doesn't make it your place to have to listen out for him in the evening.'

'What are you suggesting?' Jane laughed. 'That I find myself one of the dashing Poles and hit the high spots of Kingsbridge or Totnes or wherever she's gone?'

167

'Plenty else you could do. I'm not blind. There's that Mr Carlisle, he'd be pleased enough to have a bit more of your company.' And if Mrs Sid could be said to give an arch look, that's what she did now.

'Nonsense! John's down at the Home Guard post just as surely as Sid is.'

'Not every night. Don't you waste yourself, there every day working with a lot of dirty nuts and bolts and such. And look at you! Was a different thing dressing like you do when this was a farm, a working farm. You're a good-looking woman but it won't last forever – and the way you go on, decked up in those nasty dungaree things, it won't last at all. Put a pretty dress on, and when he asks you to go out, you just go. Remember you're a woman still. If you ask me, Mr Carlisle might be quite keen – serious keen, I mean. Now would that be such a bad thing? The children are off making lives for themselves. That Meg . . . well, one of these days someone might take her off your hands – I can't see who would, who's going to buy a book when he can borrow it from the library? – and I reckon in her case it's getting to be a bit shop soiled by now. Still, nothing as silly as a man when a pretty girl sets her cap at him, and I suppose she's pretty. Leastways, she doesn't go about dressed like some farmer's boy.'

Jane laughed. 'I don't worry about Meg. She'll sort herself out when she's ready. And you're not going to persuade me into one of my few decent dresses to clamber about up ladders in the stores. Don't you fret about me, Mrs Sid.' She put down her pen and turned to face her old friend. They both knew that what she said now mattered. 'It's no good saying I don't worry about the children, about things going right for them. I do, of course I do. But for myself, I'm learning how to knock my own life into some sort of shape. It's me,' she tapped her finger on her chest, '*me*, who runs the show. I don't have to sit back and see what happens. It's up to me.'

With her hands under the edge of the table she crossed her fingers and tapped on wood.

Across the desk John watched her. There was nothing altered about Jane's appearance, except perhaps that nowadays her dungarees were more faded and the elbows of her work-a-day sweaters strengthened with leather patches. In that though she wasn't so different from anyone else; even he had the cuffs of his tweed jacket edged with durable leather. The same clothes, patched and strengthened. Ah, now wasn't that perhaps a hint to the change in her that he could sense rather than see? Not like John to be philosophical and even now his thoughts were easily thrown off course when the post girl brought the second delivery of mail.

'Thanks, Ellie.' Jane took the envelope. 'Everything all right?'

The young woman had been doing this round for months; she liked delivering to Herbert Gower and Son. Even if they were busy Mrs Gower always had time for a smile and a thank you. She knew what it was like having someone away at sea too. On a not so busy day a few months ago when Ellie had been worried about Jerry, her husband, they'd even sat and had a cigarette together, just two women.

'Fine. Had a letter yesterday. And you?'

For answer Jane crossed her fingers and knocked the desk top. The exchange had taken no longer than it did to hand the envelope over, yet Ellie went off with a lighter step.

'Women in business.' John smiled at Jane. 'It should have happened before, you know.'

'Why do you say that? But you're right. And I'll tell you another thing, John. After this war, it's not going to be like last time. Women won't get pushed back into the kitchen and the nursery the second time round.'

'That's not how you see your life before the war, Jane.'

'Me! No, of course I don't!'

169

They both laughed, at the trap he'd set for her and the way she'd tumbled into it.

'Look at this, John – an Advice Note – three Fordson tractors on their way. Thank God for Lend Lease. Amen.'

'And for the men who get the stuff over here for us. I'll say Amen to that. Surely he's due home again soon, Jane?' Neither of them needed to give a name. 'The men who get the stuff over here' included Richard.

'I hope so.'

'What power you've got over us poor farmers!' He smiled, watching her check her order book. 'Who are the three lucky ones to be? I suppose none of them has my name on?'

Sometimes John surprised her. His name was on the list; he had given her an order for a new tractor but he already had the one from Denby, one other and a third, with caterpillar tracks, for the hilly areas.

'It's not for me to play God and decide who shall get them. I offer to whoever has been waiting longest. And that, I'm afraid, isn't Keyhaven.'

'Well, if anyone turns the offer down, I'll give one a good home.' And she knew he'd do more than that: he'd give her the cash for it. There would be no helping him fill in his forms for a loan, no waiting for the cheque to come through from the money lenders. 'In the meantime, Jane, I'll collect a new set of plugs for the International and be grateful. And while I'm here, can I just read up anything you've got on this new water pump? Have you a full specification?'

She gave him what he wanted then put through telephone calls to the three farmers who topped her waiting list.

Joshua Grimble was one of these and, that same afternoon, he came to see her. He had never been one of her favourite customers, yet it was hard to pinpoint why she was uneasy with him. Was it because there was always about him a smell of sour milk that she instinctively moved back a step from him, or was it because he stood nearer to

170

her than was necessary? And when she served him, did she imagine that his hand purposely touched hers? Would she not even have noticed had she not been on her guard with him? He and his brother, Archie, had neighbouring farms a few miles further inland. Archie was a round, jolly man, with a round, jolly wife. Joshua was tall, loosely put together, with huge hands and feet – his boots invariably covered with mud and worse. This afternoon he kicked some of it off in the stores before he tracked her down in the office.

'I've come to have a word about this tractor you've got coming for me.' He pushed his hat to the back of his head, an indication that he'd come to stay.

'It'll probably be ten days to a fortnight before it arrives, Mr Grimble. Will you need to sort the finance out? I've got some forms if you want to get the money from Maker and Dinsdale's.'

'Money lenders! Never borrowed a penny.' Then, pulling up a chair by the side of her desk and giving her a knowing wink: 'Get a rake-off from them, do you?'

'From the money lenders? No, I certainly don't. You're paying cash then?'

'Now, there I go, I've said the wrong thing and upset you. Never meant to do that. Here, just you smoke a cigarette with me, eh? And we'll talk about the pounds, shillings and pence.'

The packet he took from his pocket wasn't much cleaner than anything else about him. She would rather have said no to his cigarette, but couldn't without giving offence. So she took it and opened her drawer to find her lighter.

'Here, I've got a light.' He leant across the desk, holding her wrist in his great hand. 'Puff, go on give it a puff.' Hurriedly she did, glad to pull away again. He chuckled, showing teeth as uncared for as the rest of him. 'You know what you put me in mind of? I'll tell you. A frightened colt! Frightened? Of me?'

'What nonsense! Of course I'm not. If I seem to be in a hurry, Mr Grimble, it's because I'm a busy woman.

You were wanting to sort out about the tractor.'

'Busy. Ah, no doubt you are. Plenty going on in the agricultural world these days, and I bet I'm not the only farmer likes to come talking and hindering you.' This time his wink was accompanied by a leer. 'I'm not much of a man of words, but – well, busy woman or no, you're a pretty one.' He settled more comfortably on the wooden chair, stretching out his long legs. She had the impression that he felt his remark had moved their relationship forward, put him in favour with her.

'You want to pay cash, you say. Under the terms of the agreement the machine has to be paid for before it's delivered, you realize that?'

'It's the price I'm coming to. If it's cash, how much will I be getting off? The figure is high you know, more than I'm prepared to run to.'

'The price is nothing to do with me. I'm sorry, I can't take anything off. But I'll help you fill in the form if you want to use hire purchase.'

'I'm a man of principles. Never borrowed a penny, I told you. But I haven't got the sort of money you're after. Three hundred and seventy-five pounds! Two hundred I can put my hands on, perhaps a bit more at a pinch. Profiteering, that's what it is!'

'These tractors have had to be brought from America, brought across the Atlantic.'

'Your boy, he's in one of those ships, isn't he? Fine lad. The old gentleman introduced me to him. If I had the money I'd buy it. Lads like him risking their skins to bring the stuff in . . . oh, I'd like well enough to take the goods. But it looks as though I'll have to stick with the old horses. Not likely these days anyone'll get rid of a tractor unless it's fit just for the scrapyard.'

'Then, Mr Grimble, if you're quite sure, I'll have to offer it to someone else on my waiting list.'

Still making no effort to move, he nodded his agreement. And, thinking to show him the interview was over and just how busy she was, she picked up the telephone.

'Can you get me Shelcoombe 216, please.'

She offered the tractor to John.

It was some weeks later that Joshua Grimble came in one morning to get a replacement disc for his drill.

'And I wanted to be sure and thank 'ee for giving the tip that I was wanting a good tractor.' Boots thick with mud, he followed her into her office. 'A real friendly thing to do.' His great hand landed fair and square on her shoulder.

'How do you mean?'

'Mr Carlisle, him from Keyhaven, came over to see me. Said he understood I was looking for a good second hand machine; told me he'd been offered the new one you were getting in from America. Right beauty it is. A hundred and ninety-five I gave Mr Carlisle, paid him in cash the way I like to do business. Tip top condition. Efficiency, that's what it is we're after, isn't that what the WARAG wants from us? The speed I can get through a field – wonderful, ah, right wonderful. I like to give thanks where they're due. A real friendly act it was, telling him what I was after.'

Certainly Jane had told John. As the great hand left her shoulder, managing to squeeze her elbow in passing, she almost wished she hadn't. His drill disc on the passenger seat of his ancient car, and she on her way to the workshop, there was nothing to keep Joshua. He drove off, leaving her puzzled – but not about him. The more she believed she knew John, the more he surprised her.

The war was dragging on. After so long things like blackout, rationing, queues for everything from the cinema to a packet of cigarettes, were part of the way of life, not even worth a mention. Somewhere at the end of the tunnel there must be light, but by 1943 no one expected it to be within sight. There could be no end until the troops that had been driven out of France went back in again, liberating all that Hitler's armies had conquered. The eyes of the world were on Russia's heroic fight and, in England, everyone was asking: 'When's the Second Front coming?' The country was seething with servicemen, British,

Canadian, Polish and now Americans too; surely, in these men, lay the answer.

Meg was enjoying life. And if her war effort was to see that lonely men, far from their own lands, were doing the same, then she wasn't failing. By the autumn of 1943 Ben was almost five. A seat on the back of Meg's bicycle was his transport to Shelcoombe to school. It was some time since Jane's first advertisement for 'farm cottage holidays'; by word of mouth recommendations had passed, people who stayed once often returned. And then there were troops from overseas, not all of whom wanted the bright lights of the cities. Peace and home comforts, plus Meg's ever eager companionship were much more to the liking of many a homesick serviceman.

It was the 10th November, a day like so many at that season of damp mist, the lanes covered with fallen leaves lying rotting, the air still.

'Jane, I must talk to you.'

She'd never before seen John looking as though he'd been knocked off balance. Even now she wasn't sure how it was that she knew something was wrong; perhaps the way he closed the door firmly behind him as he strode into her office at the stores.

CHAPTER NINE

'Has something happened?'

Clearly, it had. She could tell it by his movements, the way he put his tweed hat down on top of the filing cabinet, the way he fumbled in his pocket for that ever ready gold cigarette case. (How was it, even now she wondered, that while the rest of them were glad to buy any make they could get, John never failed to produce a case full of Passing Cloud?)

'Something at Keyhaven?' she prompted, taking a cigarette and settling herself to listen.

'Keyhaven, Denby, here, Shelcoombe, Torcross, Slapton, Strete –'

'What in the world are you talking about?' A year or two ago she would have known straight away; he would have been telling her the invasion had come. But today the fear was only in the backs of their minds. With the trouble Hitler was having from Russia on the Eastern Front, it hardly seemed the time for him to embark on conquering England!

'I can't believe what I have to tell you. I had a telephone call from Reverend Humphreys – would I call and talk to him?'

'Oh, it's about the Home Guard . . .' For she knew the local platoon met in the Church Hall.

'That's what I expected. Jane, it seems he'd had to go to an emergency meeting – all the clergy from round here were summoned by the Regional Commissioner. None of this is known yet, not in the community. In a day or two we shall be notified officially.'

'None of what? John, I'm lost.'

'It's this: Jane, we've got to clear out. You, me, all of us. Lock, stock and barrel, we've got to vacate the whole district. Furniture, machinery, animals . . . anything that can be moved must be moved. It seems that the Americans are taking over the area as a training ground.'

'Oh, don't talk rubbish! Reverend Humphreys must have got it wrong. He's old, he gets muddled –'

'We have six weeks, Jane. By the 20th December the whole area – six parishes, from Strete along the bay to Torcross, west beyond East Allington. There's to be a meeting the day after tomorrow in East Allington Church. The Lord Lieutenant is going to address it. Then he's going on to another in Stokenchurch. The next day the Chairman of the County Council is coming, he'll speak at Blackawton. Every area is to have it explained. But the important thing is – speed. Six weeks, six winter weeks.'

'And here – East Rimford – that's in the area?'

'Just inside the zone. You'll have to evacuate. They say it may only be for a few months, they can't tell us more than that. Just till the Allies invade Europe. But don't spread that about. The whole thing is to be kept in low key. Denby, Keyhaven . . . do you know, Jane, there are a hundred and seventy farms in that area.'

Silently they both digested what he'd been saying.

'It's knowing where to start . . .' After a while she spoke for both of them.

'And on a farm, Jane, how can you say "just a few months". Think of the damage they'll do. They're to use live ammunition, they're not playing games. And neither must we. We've got to make sure we get everything out that we don't want destroyed.'

'But, John, they're our Allies. They won't be coming in to plunder.'

'Not purposely. But it's inevitable that there'll be damage – particularly, I imagine in the area of the beach. But nowhere will be safe. They can't aim their grenades being careful of properties.'

'It's knowing where to start,' she repeated.

'The Government will pay all expenses entailed by the removals. They'll give all help in finding temporary

176

accommodation – although God knows what that's supposed to mean, how they're supposed to do anything we can't do ourselves. They'll pay our rent, and for storage – and when it's time they'll pay for reinstating everyone, restoring damage. So there you are, Jane, my dear. I've told you the whole thing as it was given to me. Of course, it won't be shouted abroad. In a couple of days all the locals will know but the last thing that's wanted is for the newspapers to get hold of the story. If Jerry got to hear what's going on, he'd do us more harm than the Yanks will.'

A last draw on her Passing Cloud and Jane stubbed it out.

'Well, I'll tell you what,' she sat up straight, 'if that's the way it is, then I'm not going to give the Yanks or anyone else the satisfaction of seeing me make hard work of it!'

'As for the Yanks, I doubt if our paths will cross. They'll come in as we go out, I expect.'

'Well, anyway, I'm not letting them think we won't make the effort willingly. All the other people who take part in the war, people like Richard, Hartley, all the lads, they don't have the chance of saying, "No I don't like the look of . . ." whatever it is they have to do. So, John, neither must we.'

'I've told you before – you're a nice woman.'

'That's just what I'm not! Inside I'm angry, resentful. If the Yanks have to practise throwing grenades at each other, why can't they do it on Dartmoor or Exmoor? Miles of barren land, yet they have to come here and take what's ours. It's pride that makes me determined I'll not let them know I mind clearing out. I'm not nice at all, John. Isn't pride supposed to be a sin? Especially when it's all mixed up with anger. If it were our own boys, English soldiers, turning us out, I wouldn't feel nearly as angry about it. They'd know what it meant to the people; they'd look on the cottages as someone's home. But this swaggering lot, with their brown shoes and their posh uniform – they're not like any of the others; money in their pockets so that they can impress the girls – and the married women half the time – chocolate and chewing gum to hand out to the children . . . ' Her light blue eyes were swimming in tears.

John reached across the desk and took both her hands in his.

'Yes, you are, you're a very nice woman.'

She closed her eyes, but not before one tear managed to escape and roll down her cheek.

'. . . just that it was a shock . . . never thought of anything like that . . . not here . . . '

'No.' This time he put two cigarettes between his lips, lit them both then passed one to her. 'No, I believe we all thought that here we'd jog on through the war, back to peacetime one of these days, season after season. Jane, we're being shaken out of our rut. Wherever we land, why not let it be together?'

'I don't know, John.'

'Ah,' this time he smiled, 'now that at least is a step in the right direction. You told me once that you'd been married to Tim for too long to come next door to look for happiness. Next door? God knows where we shall be, any of us. And if we're out of Shelcoombe too long, who's to say if we *shall* come back? You can't shut the door on a farm, then open up again like you can a house. Farming and planning must go hand in hand. What if we move away, start afresh? Jane, I know you don't feel for me what you did for Tim – still do, I dare say. You were young together, you grew into each other. I may not have much knowledge of these things, but I can't believe that happens more than once in any life. What we'd bring to a partnership would be different – but it could be good.'

'I'm not sure. I know what you say is true. I know I'm fond of you, very fond. I know I'm lonely – you don't have to tell me that – so what is it that stops me?' She'd never come as close as this.

'What stops you today may be the immediate hurdle of what to do with the business, where to find a temporary

178

home for it. That done, you could always put in a chap to run things for you – if you and I were somewhere else.' Then with a sudden grin and closing one eye in an un-Johnlike wink: 'Better with me than with Mother-in-law, wouldn't you say? She's bound to offer you temporary shelter. She's safely out of the evacuation zone.'

Jane laughed, the unlikely prospect of her living under Emily Gower's roof somehow relaxing the tension between them and putting them safely on their familiar footing. Their talk went back to the evacuation, where to go, what to do, where to start. As she talked she busied herself putting papers away in the filing cabinet. It wasn't until he stood up to leave that their minds leapfrogged back to where they'd been before.

'Would it be so bad, Jane? I know my life would be better for having you in it.' His hands were firm on her shoulders as he turned her to face him. 'And yours?'

She didn't answer. She wasn't even thinking coherently as she felt his arms round her, holding her so tightly that the breath seemed forced out of her in a sound like a whimper. When his mouth found hers she clung to him. Every pulse in her body drove her. In that moment he wasn't John, the dear friend she tottered on the brink of marrying, he was a man as hungry for love as she was herself.

'We'd make a good life,' he whispered as he released her. 'Say yes, Jane.'

In the seconds before she answered him, thoughts shot into her mind from all angles. She'd never fall in love again. That glorious madness that had filled her heart had been for Tim, it had been part of being young. And wasn't that what John had said? John – he'd danced well, that had surprised her – and now, when he'd kissed her? She leant against him. A minute ago she'd felt herself sinking, willingly she'd surrendered.

Now she surprised herself when again she said: 'I don't know, John.'

'We'll wait, get all this other business out of the way

179

first. But don't run away from it. Thee and me could go well in harness.' She knew he was trying to put their feet gently on the ground, shying from an emotion that was running away with both of them and yet not leading him where he wanted.

She nodded. 'Six weeks. I'm glad you shared your secret with me. At least I've got two days' headstart, time to pull my thoughts into place.'

'If I hear anywhere where you can store all this stuff, I'll tell you, Jane. I'll keep my ear to the ground.'

She listened to him going out through the stores, heard his car start up. Who would have thought that five minutes ago he'd been kissing her, giving her a hint of what marriage to him could be? Elbows on the desk, head in her hands, she sought in her heart to find the answer. She wasn't in love with him, but at their ages one couldn't expect the sort of all-consuming passion she'd known at nineteen. And yet when he'd held her so close, what had she wanted of him? More? Less? She'd wanted what she'd wanted all these lonely years. But was that reason enough for marriage?

'I don't know . . .' Even to herself she said it.

She'd refused him the farm – and like an angler playing a fish he'd given her time until he'd landed what he'd wanted. And now? She'd refused him right from the start – but wasn't the truth that she'd taken the bait and was only thrashing in the water, tiring of the battle before surrendering?

It was quiet in the stores. A wet November afternoon was hardly the time to expect visiting farmers. They all had to watch the miles they travelled; visits to Herbert Gower and Son were fitted in with trips further on to town, or to the Cattle Market. She decided to leave Raymond Truggs, a bright lad who'd come to learn the trade in the workshop (probably with an eye to being kept in a reserved occupation), to serve anyone who might need it, and to go home in time to collect Greta and Ben from school. First a phone call to Mrs Sid to ask her to tell Meg not to bother to cycle to the village, then she was off. In the summer the clocks had been put forward two hours from Greenwich Mean Time – Double British Summer Time, it had been called; when the days had been at their longest it had been eleven o'clock before dusk gave way to night. Now, in November, one of those hours had been lost. Now it was British Summer Time, one hour ahead of Greenwich; although the mornings were dark, twilight lasted into the early evening. But not today. All day there had been a fine drizzle, the clouds low and grey. By half-past three it was dusk. She was running short of fuel. Before she fetched the children she'd call at Ted Maddiford's and fill the tank. Most cars were laid up until after the war but with an essential job to do she was allowed a petrol ration.

The doors of the garage were closed, but that didn't surprise her. Once it started to get dark Ted always kept them shut so that no light shone out. So she drew up by the petrol pump and sounded her horn to let him know he had a customer.

Looking out of the door of her grocery shop, Madge Tozer recognized the car and came hurrying up the slope to the garage.

'No good you waiting for Ted. Closed up. Won't be opening for a few days, you may be sure of that.'

'Hasn't his petrol delivery come in?' It seemed that nothing could be taken for granted any longer.

'I saw the tanker out there yesterday. Not the petrol that the trouble is. His wife – do you know Evie Maddiford, dear soul, always was. Went off last week to have a few days with their Mary.'

'In Southampton. Ted told me.'

'Not actually Southampton – although near enough for them to have worried about her when Southampton was getting a bashing. Seemed quiet enough though, and Mary asked her mother to stay a bit with her. Just her and the children, after her husband was called up back in the summer.'

'So Ted's gone off.to stay there too, has he?'

181

'This morning it was. He had a telephone call from a neighbour of Mary's. Never seen a man so knocked out. Well, and no wonder! Last night – a stray bomber, must have had just one left it hadn't dropped. On its way across the channel and didn't want to waste it. Makes you wonder if there isn't some truth in what folk say about "if your name's on it then it'll get you". Reckon this had their name on. Direct hit on Mary's house and all of them asleep in their beds. Evie, Mary, and the two little ones. Wiped out. Ted's gone there, of course, but what is there for him when he gets there? A bunch of strangers, a mass of ruins. His son-in-law will have been sent for, I suppose. A quiet little garage here in Shelcoombe . . . this wicked war reaches out to every corner.

'There's my shop doorbell, I must run. Oh, yes, one thing more – I should be getting a few tins of peaches tomorrow if you've got the points left in your book to spare for them. Wholesaler promised they'd be here this week. Nice to have a tin of something put by in case one of them manages to get home unexpectedly, isn't it?' And she was gone, scurrying back down to her waiting customer.

Tomorrow Meg would take their ration books when she cycled to the village to collect Ben from school . . . excitement would come to Shelcoombe in the shape of tinned peaches! And the next day? Already a notice had been pinned on the board outside the Village Hall notifying people of a meeting to be held on the 12th November when the Lord Lieutenant would be making an important announcement. Jane had a momentary picture of Denby's crates and boxes being packed with all her worldly goods and topped with a tin of peaches in readiness for a Red Letter Day. Shopkeepers, cottagers, all of them would soon know what was ahead. And Ted? She looked up the sloping street to the garage, the rooms above it the home he and Evie had made. Like Madge Tozer said, the war reached out to every corner.

'I've heard the news from Meg.' Even on the telephone,

Jane recognized the bristle of displeasure in Emily Gower's voice. 'Didn't it occur to you that I should have been told that Father's business had to find a new home?'

'I've been busy. The stock here can't be bundled into a few suitcases, you know. Did you meet Meg in Kingsbridge?'

'She often finds the time to cycle on that bit further and give me a visit. There's always a welcome waiting for Meg. She never has a word of complaint for the hard blow life's struck her. A sign of breeding. A girl with a good background. You can tell she was never reared to some pokey cottage, earning what she can from lodgers.'

'So now you know what's happening, Mother. You can imagine, there's a lot to sort out, here and at home too.'

'Oh, you won't be too put out by it. Meg tells me the Government will bear the cost. You'll have your things put safely into storage. You'd think there were better places for them to play their war games than good farmland.'

'That was the first thing I said – Exmoor, Dartmoor . . .'

'It's no good you thinking you know better than the authorities, they must have their reasons! I must say though, Jane, this has shown me just how little you concern yourself with my feelings. When Meg mentioned it, of course she expected you'd have told me all about it – Father was always so set on you looking after things. What he'd say if he knew you hadn't so much as bothered to tell me what –'

'Mother, I'm sorry if you're hurt. Talking about what I have to do isn't going to get it done. As soon as I can find somewhere to move into. I'll tell you.'

She meant somewhere to move the business. Too late she realized that surely Emily must now make that offer John had talked about? But no, silence.

'One thing,' Emily said at last, 'at Denby you've only got yourself to think about. You and that Cockney child you took in. Sid Collyer has a brother somewhere Totnes way, I believe. And I'd better tell you myself, I've suggested Meg and her poor little Benjamin come to me.' Surprise robbed Jane of an answer. 'Are you still there? Did you hear me?'

'Yes. That's good of you, Mother.'

'A charming girl. And it seems she's very keen to volunteer her services for the Red Cross Canteen for a few evenings each week. I shall thoroughly enjoy having Benjamin to see off to bed and read a story to. Seldom I had the opportunity with my own grandchildren. Not that I blame them – children go where they're sent.'

Jane blessed the privacy afforded by the telephone. If Emily could have seen the twinkle in her eyes, the way her mouth twitched into a silent laugh, the rift between them would have widened even further. Meg had scored again!

'No let up, day after day it goes on.' Jane knew that Ted Maddiford referred to more than the rain. The grey cheerless weather was in tune with his own low spirits.

'Doesn't make things any easier, does it Ted?' This wasn't the first time she'd stopped to talk to him over this last week or two, seeing him standing idly just inside the garage. 'I suppose you just have to run your fuel low now. They won't put any more in your tanks until we all come back again, will they?'

'All come back!' He shook his head. She knew just what he meant but didn't say. Where, for him, was the 'all'?

'Don't stand our there in the rain. Hop in the dry for five minutes.' She opened the passenger door for him. In the enclosed intimacy of the car it might be easier for him to uncork his bottled up worries. 'What'll you do, Ted? The same as me, I suppose. Find somewhere to live until you can come back into the zone again.'

Still he shook his head. 'If our Mary had come here . . . it was what we wanted, you know. As long as the family could be together, she wouldn't budge. Bob was called up a couple of months ago. Evie made up her mind that now, even though the troubles round that way seemed over, she'd persuade Mary to come down here with the children. She was all set to bring them back with her. We'd

184

got it all planned, even bought an extra bed at the auction room so the children wouldn't have to share. All in there.' He pointed to the rooms above the garage. 'I walk around, see it set out ready just the way Evie did it . . .'

What could Jane say? She reached out one small capable hand and rested it on his arm. For all the sympathy she felt for Ted she knew she had no way of reaching him, she could no more bare her own soul to him than he could to her. Instead she took the other path that carried them towards the practicalities of finding somewhere to go.

'Quite a few people seem to have sorted out their things and gone already. Do you know Tilly Griffiths? Scottish girl. Her husband used to do the milk round for Keyhaven until he went in the Army, then she took it over.' Jane spoke more cheerfully than she felt, seeing the way Ted sat gazing into nothing. 'She didn't waste any time. The Government will pay to send you wherever you want to go – Tilly comes from Inverness and that's where she's gone back to. She'd been trying to save her fare for ages. So there's one silver lining to the cloud.'

'Pay your passage anywhere . . . can't buy a ticket to where I'd like to be.' The grey and uncared for handkerchief he took out to wipe across his eyes told its own story.

'Things'll get better, Ted. This, on top of everything else, no wonder you feel like you do.'

'I ought to have closed the garage, gone with Evie. That's what she wanted. "Not much going on here," she said, "put a notice up that you're away. Let's go together, give Mary a surprise." Time heals, that's what they all say, that's as good as what you were saying just then. Ah, well,' he sniffed, 'we'll just have to see. Now then, was it petrol you wanted?'

'No, I'm all right for a few days. I just stopped to say hello. I'm collecting the children on the way home, the bell's just about due.'

'Oh, just killing time. Well, I'll get back inside and let you get on.'

She'd made a special effort to have the time to kill, but today if she'd told Ted that he probably wouldn't have heard her. Without a backward glance he got out of the car, leaving her to close the door, then ambled back into the empty workshop.

Almost back to Denby she had to jam on her brakes, bringing them to a violent halt in the churned up mud of the lane. Towards them was coming a high sided wagon pulled by a tractor.

'There go the people from the chicken farm. You know, Aunt Jane, along the lane beyond Keyhaven? You'll have to back all the way to the crossroads, won't you?' They did, with the tractor almost pushing them on their way. Jane didn't know the lad who drove. The elderly couple from the chicken farm she knew by sight, they were almost neighbours, a mile or two distant is nothing when they're country miles.

'You'll soon be back,' she wound down her window and called to them as she reversed around the corner to let them pass.

'That's what I tell them,' came the cheery reply from a woman in the green uniform of the Women's Volunteer Service. She was surrounded by cardboard boxes that held anything that hadn't already gone to store. 'Before they have time to get settled, I'll be helping them unpack again.'

Jo Biggs' words in the Village Hall the day she'd collected Greta and Eddie came back to Jane: 'You people have no conception of the machinery of organization . . .'

Many of the people were finding shelter with relatives, some local and some distant – although Tilly of the milk round retained the record. Farm workers found plenty of work available on land outside the zone and Jane suspected the farmers who were now suffering evacuation would be the ones to find themselves short of labour when they were allowed home.

But Jane had more on her mind than to worry about other people's problems. What she needed was a warehouse where she could house the stock with space for a workshop. Had she been the only person hunting for space it might have been easier.

Wanted to Rent: Space for Storage.
Have you any barns lying unused? Have you any space where stock could be stored or where repairs could be carried out? Please help us to stay in business so that we are able to help you!

She wrote her notice in bold lettering on a board which was attached to the door of the stores. Everyone who came in or out read it, but Jane saw it only as an introduction to her direct requests.

'If I have to, I'll divide the stock, put some in one place and some in another. What I don't want is to have to crate it up and put it into store. That way it's no use to anyone.'

'We'd help you if we had the room, my dear. Try Geroge Hookins at Highmoor Farm . . .'

And George Hookins was equally full of regrets. He would have had some space but he'd promised to take the machinery from Hanley Farm in the zone. Had she spoken to Tom Hawkes from Iffley Down? And so it went on. Jane wasn't easily cast down, but day followed day and her enquiries got her nowhere. She would lie awake at night, her mind refusing to relax. What if she couldn't find anywhere? But of course she would. She asked every farmer who came in; the men kept their eyes open when they were out doing repair work; John was trying to find somewhere . . . John . . . and here her mind would veer off out of control. What was it stopped her agreeing to marry him? What if he were here now, sharing a bed with her? Was that what she was running away from? Her eyes wide open, she stared up at the darkness. The truth, she must have the truth. No, it wasn't what she was running from; on the contrary.

'Do I want to sleep with him? Not sleep, make love? Do I? Does he attract me? Forget whether or not I love him, even whether I like him, just do I want to be in bed with him?' So clearly she knew the answer, and what she knew frightened her.

It wasn't John she wanted, it was love. It was to put out her hand in the dark and feel the warmth of him. From all sides worries pressed in on her: where to find a place for the business, where to find a home for herself and Greta. There was one way of escaping, and tonight looking for the truth of her feelings for John she knew she would follow that one way. Always it had been Tim she'd strained towards as she sought to find relief from her loneliness. Even tonight as she made the first conscious move it still was of Tim; then she tried to imagine John, almost as if to test whether her body would reject her fantasies. Tim, John, soon both of them were wiped from her mind. There was nothing but a physical response to a physical need. And at the end of it she was still lying, wide-eyed, the problems of tomorrow chasing away any hope of sleep.

Little did she know that that very evening a solution was already being found.

'Good morning, Mr Grimble. Can I help you with something?'

'Not this time. Reckon this time boot's on the other foot – 'tis me who's come to do the helping. I've driven over 'specially so we can have a chat.' His stained teeth showed in that leer he took to be a smile. 'Best I shut the door, then no one will bother us, eh?' Then out came the crumpled Woodbine packet.

'No, I won't take yours this time. Here, have one of mine.' Without giving offence it saved her from the unsavoury offering he'd pulled out of the pocket it shared with a handkerchief-cum-duster. There was no avoiding the way he held his face too close to hers as he lit it for her. A good many of her customers were equally as mud-caked; he wasn't the only one to carry the stale smell of the milking sheds. It was what she read in those leering glances she cringed from.

'Now, it's like this. Me and my brother – he farms just above me, I dare say you know his place? – we had a talk about you. I told him just how keen I am to be able to help you out of the hole you're in. We've come up with this for an idea: we'll double up together. I can get my gear up to his barns easy. Tell you the truth, half the time the stuff's knocking about in the yard. Archie can find me all the room I need. We're outside the area they're clearing.'

'You mean I can rent your barns? I really am grateful to you and your brother.' And so she was, but how much better if Archie had moved his things down to Joshua! 'I'll pay a fair rent, of course.'

'Ah, they say that Government sees there's money for rent, so I shan't feel bad about making a good charge. I went up to see Archie, put it to him. I like to think you and me are friends. Reckon I fancy the chance of having you about the place.' Again his great paw moved across the desk, but she kept out of its reach.

'Are they Dutch barns?' she asked in a businesslike voice.

'Bless you, no. Proper walls and doors. Got the electric light in one of them. Well, you'll see for yourself. You'll want to take a ride out and let me show you round, won't you?'

'Of course. Can I drive over tomorrow and see you, then we'll fix a fair rent? And, Mr Grimble,' she made an effort to sound as friendly as the situation merited, 'you don't know what a relief it is to know we have somewhere to go.'

'Well, if we can't help one another out in times like these, it'd be a rum world. I suppose over there in America they don't understand about war and fighting. I suppose that's why they have to bring their chaps over here and then teach them their job. Wouldn't you think, though, all the room they must have in that great country, they could manage without kicking people who are trying to do their bit out of their homes?' The business settled, he stretched out his legs. It seemed he was here to stay. 'You'll be opening shop out at my place, making my old Chugford Farm your trading post? Just a few weeks and you maybe wouldn't bother, but who's to say how long the war's going on for. Maybe another year or two before they've done with teaching that lot to be soldiers. What's it to be? A batch at a time learning their shooting, or what?'

'They don't tell us anything,' Jane said, remembering what John had warned her. The less people who guessed the training had anything to do with a Second Front the better. 'You'll have read the notices, I suppose? The Admiralty are handling everything, and officially the land was all requisitioned a fortnight ago, on the 16th November. If they have to, they can come in at any time, but they're trying to give us until the 20th December to be gone, so that we have time to shift everything.'

At last he went. And that same day Jane started boxing up the thousands of bits of ironmongery, working much as Greta had that first summer of the war, counting, sorting, labelling. She had less than three weeks left and her mind had been so taken up with the greater challenge of shifting the business that, except for putting in a request that her furniture should be taken into store on the 16th December, she'd given little constructive thought to the exodus from Denby. Now, with renewed vigour and a heart lighter than it had been for weeks, she turned her attention to finding a home for Greta, Mufti, and herself. Just as Emily had supposed, the Sids were going to his brother near Totnes and they were taking Simpkins, the tabby cat, with them.

'I'll spare her my butter ration to put on her paws if I have to,' Mrs Sid insisted, 'but with us she'll be less likely to wander off and try and get home. No good you having her and then being out all day long. Mufti sleeps most of the time, he's getting old, he won't be so put out.'

There was no chance of finding somewhere one liked; houses were like gold dust. Jane found one to rent furnished, two bedrooms and the third turned into a bathroom with a geyser that looked anything but friendly; downstairs two rooms and a scullery. The rent was exorbitant. The couple who owned it might have been old but they were still quick to recognize the chance of making a few pounds. If the Government was paying the rent, then make it worth having! They went to stay with a son on the Welsh borders. If the Americans were to be in the area until the end of the war, that suited them very nicely and represented a steady income.

Even after the first two or three weeks the area was already beginning to wear a mantle of neglect, made worse by day after day of rain. Those who were storing their furniture and going to live with friends or relatives had nothing to wait for. With Christmas so near, it was better to get settled. Uncurtained windows looked on to the village street; garden gates that had been left unlatched rattled and slammed in the wind.

'After this week you'll have to get your ration from wherever you register in the new place, Mrs Gower,' Oswald Peatty told her when she collected the saucer-sized joint. 'We're off on Wednesday. I've had my last delivery until we come back in. Never heard such a daft idea, turning honest people from their homes – and not to keep them safe from Jerry, but so that the Yanks can wreck the place! Gor blimey, sometimes I think there's none as soft as the English! I thought so this morning in town. Raining cats and dogs, and what did I see? A queue of people waiting good as gold. Ah, what are they after? I wondered. Thought I might be missing out on something. And you know what it was? Paying their bloody rates, that's what they were lining up for. The final demand was in the local paper at the weekend. No wonder they talk about mad dogs and Englishmen. Well, happy landings wherever you go for these next months. I'll be glad to be hanging my sign out again and being back in business.'

'I see Ted's closed up. I suppose he's out of petrol now.'

'That's it. Tanks have gone dry. Had a word with him yesterday, he seemed very down. By the time we're back

191

and they fill his tanks again, I dare say he'll have bucked up. Clearing out like this couldn't have come at a worse time for him.'

Ted was on her mind as she drove home. He was still on her mind as she went into the kitchen to be assailed by a smell of baking.

'Cakes? How did you manage that, Mrs Sid?'

'Mr Carlisle brought over a lovely big piece of butter, his swan song he called it. Looking at it in the larder, I thought, well, just this once, let's remember what it was like to do a proper bake.'

On the table was a Dundee cake, a large Madeira cake and a small one. It was the small one that triggered Jane's idea.

'Poor Ted has been closed down. His petrol's finished. Mrs Sid, what about if I take that small cake and drop it in to him on my way in the morning? We can spare it, can't we?'

'And if we couldn't, we ought to be ashamed of ourselves. Not much cheer to give the poor man.'

Next morning followed the pattern of this wet winter. The rain fell in thin needles, the dull grey sky showed not a glimmer of hope that as the day went on it might ease. It had become almost routine that Jane dropped Greta off at school to save her arriving drenched. Already there were fewer children at the school as, one by one, the families found somewhere else to go.

'Doesn't it look empty, Aunt Jane?' Greta said as they drew up by the gate. 'The houses look sort of sad, don't they? And the shops. Nearly everyone's gone. When do you reckon we'll all leave Denby?'

'Pretty soon. And before we do I know one thing – you and I have to work jolly hard to get our things packed.'

Greta brightened, her confidence restored. Then, the satchel containing last night's homework on her shoulder, she got out of the car.

She was right, the village street had already taken on the look of a ghost town.

Pulling into the forecourt of Ted's garage, Jane expected him to come out to her. There was no petrol, but a car arriving meant a visitor, something he never could resist. Today though there was no movement. He must be upstairs. She believed the 'front door' to the living quarters was round at the side, so she'd go and ring the bell and give him his cake. No reply. The curtains were still hanging at the windows. He surely wouldn't have gone away and left his furniture behind. Or would he? What harm could come to upstairs rooms? But he couldn't have gone, Oswald Peatty would have known. She rang the bell a second time. Still no one answered her.

With rain running down her face she gazed upward at the windows. The blackout curtains weren't pulled at any of the windows. He couldn't still be in bed. What prompted her to walk right round to the back of the building she didn't know, nor yet what she expected to see when, by standing on her toes, she could just look into a small window that served the tiny office at the end of the workshop.

'No!' she breathed. 'Oh, God, no!' Looking upwards towards the roof of the room she could see the rafters, she could see a rope – Ted's tow rope, something so familiar – flung over it. Ted knew all about knots. Looking at it now, memories flooded into her mind of how he used to teach Richard and Hartley knots. The rope was taut, the weight at the end of it heavy. Ted . . . Oh no, please God, don't let it be too late. But she knew there was no hope. One look at him was enough to end all doubt.

Only a few minutes ago she'd thought of it as a ghost town. Suddenly in those next few minutes it came to life. Oswald Peatty telephoned the police and called for an ambulance. Authority took over when hope had given up the fight. Jane didn't wait to see Ted carried out of his garage. But how difficult it is to see to drive through tears.

'Ted, Ted, I'm sorry. It's our fault, my fault, all of us, somehow we let you down,' she sniffed, speaking aloud in the privacy of the car. 'It's the damned, damned war! If you hadn't had to move, you would have battled through. If you hadn't lost Evie you wouldn't have minded moving. If . . . if . . . But there aren't any ifs . . . we have to take what we get. Ted, poor Ted.'

A day's work was the best antidote for the shock of the morning. By the time she met Greta there wasn't a soul in Shelcoombe who hadn't heard. Word had spread like a bush fire, even through the classrooms.

'Tell you one thing, Aunt Jane,' Greta spoke with the simple trust of her years, 'bet those others, his wife and Mary – wasn't that what he called her? – and her kids, bet they're jolly pleased. Don't know much about how it works, but I often thought about it, Aunt Jane – because of Dad, and – ' she added with less confidence and a wary look at Jane ' – 'cos of Uncle Tim too. Seems to me heaven can't be much of a place for them if they see the people they've left behind being all sad. And Mrs Maddiford and Mary – well, how could they have been feeling? Why, clear as anything, he was miserable. And just imagine if he'd had to go off to some strange place, no one he knew to stop for a natter. He'll be all right now, though, won't he?'

'I expect you're right, Greta.'

'We're lucky, aren't we, you and me?' She didn't elaborate.

'Reckon we are, Greta.' Jane understood her thought processes.

'Jane, they sent me to find you in here. Can I come in?' Without waiting for an answer, John came into the mushroom shed.

'You know, John, of all of it, what I hate most is leaving these. I can't move them, they need special conditions.'

'You've put in for compensation? Not just for what you lose now, Jane, but for the regular income you derive from then – and, of course, for starting up again.' He paused. 'If you do.'

'It would never be the same. I remember when I first read up all about mushrooms, Tim and I sorted the sheds

194

out ready. Each day we used to check the temperature in here making sure it was steady before I even started. No, I doubt if I'll ever do it again.'

'I came to tell you, Keyhaven has no herd. The last went under the hammer today. Prices were rock bottom too. What can you expect? The place is flooded with unwanted stock.'

'John, I'm sorry.'

'It's not just the money. It's seeing something you've built up, something you've worked at – gone. We're lucky, of course we are. Funny thing, though, Jane,' he gave her a sheepish grin, 'I don't feel particularly lucky today. And neither, I think, do you.'

'In here where no one can hear us we'll be honest. No, when you arrived I was feeling sorry for myself. But once we get outside, there in the big world, never let it be said!'

'There's a way we could be luckier, could make our own beginning. Have you decided . . . ? I'm going north on the 14th, joining up with the stock I sent on by rail to my cousin. What about it, Jane? We'd get a hill farm of our own, there in the Lake District. It's beautiful. Have you ever seen the lakes?'

'No, I shall miss you. I hope you won't decide to stay. But, no, John, I can't. All along I've not been sure. Now, the 14th, only a week away, there's no more time to put off deciding. And now I know quite clearly, no, I can't marry you. I shan't marry anyone.' Here in a place she and Tim had built together she was sure.

He didn't speak. She wanted to reach out to him, she hated to see that look of disappointment.

'And that, I imagine,' he said at last, 'goes for both of us. What a waste.' Then he put the conversation firmly behind them. 'How's the move going in the yard? If you like, I can give you a hand for a couple of days. Mrs Wainwright is putting herself in charge of my household stuff that's going into store, and I'm really at a loose end – so if I can be any use?'

'I'm sure you can. Returning a compliment you once paid me: you're a nice man, John.'

Her first encounter with American troops in the evacuation zone was the very next day. Often enough she'd come face to face with an oncoming vehicle in the lane; sometimes petrol driven, sometimes horse drawn, but never before one like this. A large uncovered lorry, camouflaged in the greeny-grey of the US Army, emblazoned with its white star, and aboard it soldiers in battle dress and wearing the rounded steel helmets so different from their British brothers. And something else set them apart: every one of them was coloured. About twenty dark faces and forty rows of gleaming white teeth as they yelled their ribald approval of the encounter. They had less distance to back into a turning space than she had, but their hearty enthusiasm that here they were face to face with one of the fairer sex decided her to take the easy way out. After all, these lanes were home to her, she knew every bend and bump. So into reverse gear she went, then foot off the clutch in her customary way expecting the car to obey her command. But no! The wheels started to spin, the more she revved the engine the more deeply embedded in the mud she became – and the louder the men cheered.

On the back seat she had a piece of sacking. If she jammed it under one of the back wheels she'd get a grip. On her own she would have persevered until she succeeded. Just for a second she gripped the steering wheel, embarrassed and ashamed that she'd let herself get stuck. It wasn't the first time it had happened to her, that's why she carried the sack. But shame soon gave way to anger.

Opening the car door, she shouted: 'Instead of laughing like a lot of half-witted schoolboys, what's wrong with getting down and giving me a shove? Or would it dirty your shoes?'

'Okay, okay, ma'am, I's comin',' one of them called.

'Hold still, Bud, don't you run backwards. I's climbin' out to help the lady.'

'Sure, you do that. Just give her a forward push. I'll go on back into that side path we passed. Joe'll soon get you goin' ma'am. What a road! Reckon back home our sidewalks are wider.'

If she'd guessed there to be twenty dark faces and forty rows of white teeth, she now made it twenty-two and forty-four, the driver and his mate grinning at her just as broadly. At their good humour she forgot she'd been angry. But once past them, as they all waved and cheered her on her way, she knew a sense of loss. This was only the beginning. Dear, peaceful Devon, its gentle country and unchanging pattern . . . Bud, Joe and their mates would soon put an end to all that!

CHAPTER TEN

By Friday, when the paper was published bearing a notice that for the foreseeable future Herbert Gower and Son would be trading from Chugford Farm, Mannerby, the move was completed. And by then, too, John had driven away from Keyhaven also for the foreseeable future.

Jane's anger had melted as quickly as it had come on that day she'd come face to face with their 'invaders'. But the thaw proved itself temporary as the days of December passed. Over these last few years the one thing she'd clung to had been Denby. Now as she cleared the books from the shelves, and the pictures from the walls, each one awakened another memory. Photographs of the children looking uncomfortably smart in their new uniforms on the day they went off to school; of the cream flannelled local cricket club, Tim sitting in the front row; of the Sids outside their cottage; of Jane herself, looking remarkably well-groomed in new jodhpurs astride Honey, long since gone. The Gowers of Denby – and here she was stripping the old house, packing into tea chests the story of the years they'd spent here.

'What about this, Aunt Jane? Ought I to wrap it in something, a pillowcase maybe?' Busy helping, Greta held up a figurine of a very elderly and obviously country couple.

Jane sat back on her heels, holding out her hand for it.

'No, we'll put that in the box we're taking.' As clearly as if it had been yesterday she remembered when she and Tim had bought it. Married only two days, they'd been so sure that nothing would ever part them.

'You and me, Lady Jane, sixty years on . . .' A cheap

little ornament, the first thing they'd bought together to grace their sitting room mantelpiece.

Greta didn't ask her about it, but later when an empty shoe box was going to be thrown out she retrieved it and filled it with straw.

'This'll keep that lady and gentleman safe, Aunt Jane.' She hadn't asked if it was special – but then, Greta could usually see below the surface where Jane was concerned.

Cupboards were cleared, drawers were emptied. Denby took on the same uncared for appearance that was apparent all around. The chicken houses stood empty now. Sid had taken the hens to market, except for three which Greta had made herself responsible for to be kept at the end of the tiny garden of their rented home, No. 4 Shalbury Hill.

At last they were as ready as ever they'd be: rugs were rolled, curtains were down. It was the 16th December. Looking out of her bedroom window, Jane heard the motor of the pantechnicon approaching, saw it turn with difficulty from the narrow lane into the entrance to the yard. She closed her eyes, leaning her head against the cold window pane; she tried to conjure up a picture of the yard as it used to be, alive with activity, the farm implements, the men . . . Tim. The Welsh lilt in the voices of the removal men was strange in her ears. For this evacuation the man in charge of transport had had to know every road and lane, had had to organize the exodus so that no two lorries would pass on the same narrow route at the same time. And more than that, he'd had to call on removal firms from all over the country to take and store the contents of the houses. The voices with an accent so unfamiliar to her ears brought Jane back to the present. She opened her eyes. Cardiff. The furniture from Denby was to be taken to Cardiff to be stored! For one frantic moment she thought of those tea chests, tried to remember what was in them and reassure herself that everything she and Greta would need was in the trunk that was to be taken to Shalbury Hill.

Heavy footsteps on the stairs told her that work had started. First they went to the old nursery; then to Richard's room, then Liz's, then along to Hartley's, Greta's. It seemed her own was to be left until last. And still she tried to call up the spirit of yesterday. 'It won't be for long. A few months and we'll be back, putting the pictures on the wall, re-hanging the curtains . . .' Of course they would.

'This room next, ma'am,' a voice cut in on her daydreams, 'all this lot to go to the store or are you wanting any of it?'

While they stripped her bedroom she wandered through the other rooms. How shabby the walls looked now that no furniture stood against them. The paper was faded, the paintwork chipped. The rooms looked unfamiliar. There was nothing of themselves left behind, nothing of the twins, nothing of Hartley . . . nothing of all those years with Tim.

From outside in the yard came the sound of Mrs Sid's voice, overseeing the loading of her few things that were to be stored. A local van had arrived to take her belongings to Sid's brother. And still the air was wet, half rain and half mist. When they looked back to those weeks of the evacuation, surely paramount in their memories must be the constant rain, the mud?

Greta was out in the chicken run conversing with the three hens who'd come into her care and whom she'd put into wire cages ready for their journey. The Sids were busy with their own affairs. A green-clad lady from the Women's Volunteer Service had already collected Meg and Ben. There was no one to notice where Jane went.

Pulling on her overcoat, she crossed the yard and went into the office, closing the door behind her. Even the old oil heater had gone. There was nothing here now except the sloping desk top. But that had ever been her favourite seat so, as she had hundreds of times before, she hoisted herself to sit on it. Surely in here there would be something? Always before she'd sat with her feet on a stool; now the stool had gone, her legs dangled. But the wooden desk felt as it always had under her palms.

'Here, lady, move your behind, you're sitting on my milk returns . . .' A smile touched the corners of her mouth. Tim. Silently she shaped the word. Just for those seconds she was the girl she'd been through all those years, the girl who would forever be Tim's 'lady'. Then the moment was gone, gone just as surely as the years she'd been trying to bring alive. Outside the men were slamming the tailboard of the lorry closed.

Not many minutes after it had trundled away, an Austin Seven arrived driven by yet another WVS lady. Jane wondered how this evacuation could ever have come about without the never flagging energy and kindness of these women. Now it was the Sids' turn to go. How lost they looked, both dressed in their best, prepared to do as they were told in a way quite uncharacteristic of them and somehow bringing it home to Jane just how out of their depth they were. Once settled with Sid's brother, she didn't doubt Mrs Sid would have the household dancing to her tune in no time. But today it hurt to look at them, she with a gallant dab of rouge on each cheek and red on her lips, he in his best bowler hat that hadn't come out of its box since Tim's funeral.

'You look nice, Mrs Sid.' She hugged her bent little friend.

'Many a year since I could be said to have looked nice. But I'm not having those Yankees think they can get the better of us at Denby. And I hope you've remembered to keep a tidy frock out ready to put on before you go off. Now mind what I say – you're doing it for Denby. Not having them think we're a lot of peasants to be turned out at a word from them.'

'We'll soon be back. Imagine the excitement that'll be.'

Mrs Sid blinked hard and held her lips firmly together.

'You make sure you ride out to see us sometimes, Greta ducky.' Sid spoke for both of them, he knew he had to. If his Alice disgraced herself and shed tears, she'd never forgive herself, or him either.

'In we get then,' the portly WVS lady took her arm, 'both of us in the back.'

Nothing could have put metal into Mrs Sid quicker. No one was going to speak to Sid and her as if they were half-wits, and get away with it!

'Both of us? I thought you were supposed to be driving?'

The WVS lady laughed that bit too loudly, the Sids piled into the back of the car with Simpkins in her basket, and she into the front. And it was over. They'd gone, the sound of the engine fading in the still winter air. When the planners had sat around their table, somewhere miles away, selecting the area they were to commandeer, could they have had any idea of the heartache? Six parishes in a district largely agricultural; how simple it must have sounded.

Now only Jane and Greta – plus Mufti and three hens – were left. Jane looked around the muddy yard. Denby, empty . . . Tim's office, empty . . . the chicken runs, empty . . . mushroom sheds, the crop picked this morning and divided, some for the Sids, some for Meg, some for herself. Now it was dark in there. The blue light had been turned off and the heating too.

In the damp winter air Jane shivered. For a day or two the mushrooms would try to grow, then they'd die, they'd wither . . . Ted, hanging with a tow rope around his neck . . . Keyhaven empty . . . The barns empty . . . Ted, carried out, the rooms above the garage just as his Evie had arranged them ready for Mary and the family . . . The school, empty . . . Milking time and the cattle stalls that used to belong to Denby, empty . . . The lanes a quagmire of churned-up mud where the lorries ploughed back and forth . . .

And, as if to add background colour to her fancies, past the gates roared a jeep, jolting, rocking, riding the ruts as if they'd been put there as part of the fun and sending up a spray of thick mud.

Nothing to wait for now. Greta and Mufti were getting in the car, the hen cages tied securely to the back. The moment had come. Jane pressed her face against the kitchen window. The heart of the house, yet now it stared back at her, just an empty room. Panic gripped her, here in the desolate yard that had been the hub of the farm for so long. She was standing in a rivulet from the overflowing water butt; the only sound was the steady drip from a blocked guttering. As dusk gathered, already it seemed to bring with it stagnation and neglect.

'Chin up, Lady Jane.' Her vision misted, her panic melted as suddenly as it had come. Memories weren't in bricks and mortar.

That evening Jane and Greta ate their first supper together in their tiny new home: fish and chips, this time on a plate. Tomorrow was soon enough to try and make the house into a home.

No light shone out from the hospital. Even the most diligent Air Raid Wardens wouldn't have been able to find cause for complaint about the blackout. But Hartley had waited long enough for his eyes to have become used to the moonless night; and in any case he was sure he would have recognized Liz's quick step anywhere.

Hearing the door close he moved forward towards the bottom of the steps.

'Liz!'

'Hartley? Where are you? I can't see you.'

'Here.'

Coming from the brightly lit hospital it was familiarity that brought her unerringly down the flight of steps. Hartley was only a voice, not so much as a dark shape. As she felt his hold on her she melted into his embrace. Work was forgotten; Denby and the move was forgotten.

'I wasn't expecting you. Hartley, there's nothing wrong?'

'Nothing. I've got a forty-eight hours. I'd been trying to

get leave so that I could go and give Aunt Jane a hand with the move. It's been tough for her with all of us away just when she could have used us. But what I finally wangled was just a forty-eight hours and too late to be any good. She's packed up and moved by now.'

Liz laughed, hugging his arm to her. 'So I'm second best!' Then, before he had a chance to answer, 'Forty-eight hours. I'm on lates again tomorrow, I go on duty at two o'clock.'

'What about Rita? Is she getting up at the crack of dawn? Will she mind me dossing down on your sofa? I came straight to the hospital, I've not looked for a bed anywhere.'

'That's fine,' she said. 'We'll go straight home, shall we? It's too late to find anywhere open to get any supper. We'll make toast – and I think there's a tin of beans or something. Not very grand.'

'Sounds like a feast.'

By now they were outside the hospital grounds. Arms around each other's waist they started to walk, at first purposefully, then gradually slowing until, surrounded by the darkness of the sleeping city, they stopped. Silently they turned and clung to each other. There were no words, or if there were they didn't know them. Overhead was the heavy throbbing of tonight's batch of bombers setting off on their mission. The sound made them even more aware of the unexpected joy of their being together, but she could tell from something in the way he was suddenly so still that for him it did more than that.

'Don't listen.' She covered his ears with her hands.

'I don't need to listen.' She could hear the fear in his voice. 'All the time, I hear it.' Holding his head up he peered into the black sky as if he could see the wave after wave of laden planes. 'Liz, I'm an awful coward. Here in the night I can say it.'

'No, Hartley, you're not. Don't you read the papers, what they're saying about the bravery of all of you?'

He seemed not even to have heard her.

'Taxiing to take off . . . the feeling when the wheels go up . . . then you're on your own. You're there to bring hell to the people in the target area, people who are someone else's families, nurses perhaps, people like us. If you're lucky the searchlights won't pick you out. You'll get the crew home. Well done! Knocked hell out of Hamburg, Dresden, Berlin. Oh, God, Liz, what are we doing? Those chaps up there – for some of them it'll be their last night. How many won't get back? When the planes are counted in, how many will be gone?'

She'd never heard him talk like this. The noise of the engines was fading. She was thankful.

'But you've always loved flying. I remember how you used to write to me from Canada when you were training –'

'Flying! Yes, flying's great. And over there – well, I've told you enough times, it was just terrific. But then, the war and all we were learning to fly for was so far removed it hardly seemed real at all.' For a while neither of them spoke. Then he went on: 'One of these days, Liz, when all this is over, I'll take you there. It's the future, you know, in a country the size of Canada. Flying, I mean. Imagine if I could get a job flying for a civilian company – it must be the transport of the future.'

The fear had gone from his voice. He sounded like himself again. She rubbed her cheek against his shoulder and felt his lips on her hair.

'Take me anywhere you like, Hartley – only promise you'll never go without me.'

'I couldn't, Liz. If I hadn't got you, there would be nothing.'

It was as she put her key in the lock of the flat she shared with a fellow nurse that she told him: 'We don't need to creep. Rita isn't in.'

'You mean she's on nights?'

She shook her head. 'I mean she's on leave. Wait there by the light switch while I do the blackout.'

A minute later light flooded the room. The small flat was

their world. Here no one and nothing could disturb them.

'A pity the cottage hasn't a telephone,' Liz said. 'It would be nice to ring up and find how Mum's move went. She's having a telephone put temporarily into Mr Grimble's barn, but she hasn't got it yet, so for a bit we'll just have to rely on letters.' With all the hours of night ahead of them she talked, like a child keeping its favourite sweet until last.

'Liz – just you and me – ' Hartley could see no further than that.

With domesticity they were on familiar ground. Often enough even as children they'd made toast together by the fire at Denby, yet tonight had a feeling of its own. In the tiny kitchen she heated the beans while, kneeling in front of the gas fire, he made the toast. Then she pulled the gateleg table near the fire and set their places each with a knife, a fork, and a Woolworth's wine glass.

'Wine glasses? That's being over optimistic, isn't it?' he laughed. Even beer was hard to come by. More often than not the public houses were closed with a sign on the door 'Beer Sold Out Until . . .' and then the date the next delivery was expected.

'Elderberry. Mrs Sid gave me a bottle to bring back. She said it was for a special occasion, so we'll open it tonight. Drink to Mum soon being able to go back to Denby.'

They did. To both of them having her there represented stability. Then, with Jane slotted comfortably into the background, they forgot her and concentrated on themselves.

'Now we'll drink to us, Liz. To you and me. To the life we'll make.' He reached across the table and took hold of her hand. 'You know something? We've known for so long that one day we'll be together that I've never done the romantic bit – gone down on one knee and asked you to marry me.'

'Perhaps it's the elderberry wine, but – ask me, Hartley. I want to hear you say it.'

With all his natural grace he came to the side of her chair and went down on one knee.

'Liz, my only love,' even when she giggled at his flowery words, he looked at her solemnly, 'my life could never be complete without you. As long as I live, I live just for you. My darling Liz, marry me. Promise me you'll marry me.'

High-faluting words, said with all the passion of a ham actor. Yet both of them knew the underlying truth. Instead of entering into the scene, offering her hand, Liz slipped to her own knees.

'We'll have to wait 'til Richard gets home. I can't get engaged until he knows. But I don't care about rings and all that sort of thing.'

'But you promise me . . . ?'

'You know I do.' Still kneeling, they clung to each other. 'Those planes this evening . . . When you're not here, I listen to them . . . Hartley, I'm frightened too! There's Richard. From day to day we don't know what's happening to him; Denby being made a battleground; Mum in some rotten cottage . . . it's as if nothing is sure.'

'Darling, one thing I swear is sure. Liz, you;re crying! Don't cry, sweetheart.' He held her chin up. 'One thing will always be sure, and that's that I love you.'

'I know. Me too. Silly to cry when I'm happy. Must be the wine.' But they both knew it wasn't. It was the echo of those bombers, planes that even now might have searchlights trained on them, guns firing at them.

'You take the bathroom first, I'll wash the dishes.'

'Can you manage the geyser?'

'Do you want to borrow a towel?'

Such everyday things, he might have been a brother. He might have been, but he wasn't. And while they both tried to hang on to the normality of preparing for the night, yet they couldn't pretend even to themselves that this night was like any other. Nothing unusual in them facing each other in pyjamas and dressing gowns; nothing unusual in

207

him holding her in his arms as he said goodnight. On the sofa she'd put a pillow, two blankets and an eiderdown.

'Don't let's go properly to bed yet. Hartley, come in and talk to me. Let's make plans, talk about what we'll do when we go to Canada. Tell me more about it.'

'You hop into bed then, don't get cold.'

'Okay. You can come under my eiderdown.'

Even that wasn't the first time. Wasn't that how they'd opened their stockings on Christmas morning when they'd been children? For a while it satisfied both of them, his head by the side of hers on the pillow, arms around each other.

'It's lovely and warm in here. Come inside the bed, Hartley. It can't do any harm – just for a while. Leave the light on.' Somehow lying in the dark would have made her feel that what she was doing was wrong. As long as the light was on she wasn't actually sleeping with him, simply lying close to him.

'Liz, I can't. We mustn't.'

'Please, Hartley. Just hold me, that's all. I want to feel us close together, not just arms but all the way down. Right to our feet.'

'Liz, I love you.'

Right to their feet she'd said. And so they lay, his body against hers, each of them buttoned into their pyjamas. It had sounded so easy but in those first minutes they realized how little they'd understood.

'You know what'll happen if I stay here. I must go. But I can't. I can't leave you.' He seemed to be talking half to himself. She was excited by his voice, by his body and by her own. It was her fingers that undid the buttons on their jackets and the waistcord on his trousers.

'I want us to know each other, to touch each other. We belong together, we've said so. When you think about me I want you to know what I look like – and I want to see the real *you*, not just a good-looking RAF officer the same as anyone else can see.'

208

'How can I look at you when I feel like this? Liz, can't you see . . . I must go back in the other room.'

But he didn't.

There was a mixed bag of houses in Shalbury Hill. No. 4 was at the lower end, workmen's cottages with front doors on to the footpath and between them a narrow alleyway leading to a patch of ground that had been turned into allotments. Climbing the hill standards improved with small front gardens which until a year or so back had had iron railings – all gone into the melting pot to be turned into guns by this time; then up again to one or two larger detached properties, and finally to Hillcot House which had a noticeboard on it proclaiming it to be a US Servicemen's Officers' Club.

Greta looked forward to the one great advantage of living in town: pavements. She had a pair of roller skates, inherited from one of the twins (or shared by both of them) but hitherto had been restricted to the yard. On the first morning in Shalbury Hill she practised in the alleyway; by mid-day, her confidence growing, she progressed to the roads in the lower part of town; finally, by the afternoon of that same day and as a feat of daring, she took off from the top of the hill.

Jane had spent her day trying to make someone else's house feel like home. She'd hung her own pictures, put out her own ornaments, put down her own fireside rug.

'What do you think, Mufti? Eh, boy?' In front of the small fireplace she knelt down and was rewarded by a paw on each shoulder and a lick on her nose. Their tête-à-tête was shattered by a hammering on the front door, sending him scampering into the passage with her close behind. Fearing that he might run out in the road she picked him up before finding out who her visitor was.

'The little girl – someone says she's just moved in here?'

'Greta, yes. What about her?'

'Just round the corner. On her roller skates. Was one of

these American jeep things that frightened her . . . she fell down with such a crash . . .'

Mufti found himself pushed back into the passageway and the door slammed shut on him. Just lower than No. 4, Shalbury Hill curved to meet the junction with St Agnes Road. It was here that Jane found the gathering of people around a jeep. As she ran towards them they made a path for her to get through to where Greta lay. How still she was, lying with her arms thrown out before her and one of her skates torn loose, its strap broken.

'Is she badly hurt?' What a stupid thing to ask. How could this American soldier know any more than she did? She knelt on one side of Greta, he on the other.

'I'm pretty sure she isn't.' As if to prove him right, Greta opened her eyes. 'It's okay, your mom's here. Take your time, we'll get you home.'

At the sight of Jane, Greta's efforts to be brave collapsed. She started to cry.

'Aunt Jane . . . hurt my ankle.'

'You said she wasn't hurt.' Jane glowered at the American. 'We mustn't move her until the doctor's looked at her. You've done enough damage already.'

A second American was standing by the vehicle, looking uncomfortable.

'It wasn't the Major, ma'am. I'm the driver. But the kid came at us round the corner. I jammed on the brakes. The jeep didn't touch her, I swear it didn't.'

From his kneeling position American No. 1, whom she now saw was a major, took Greta in his arms. Holding her securely, he stood up.

'You shouldn't move her. She must be examined!' Jane jumped up too. In the crowd were mutterings about 'Yankee hooligans', 'madcap drivers', 'Americans coming here as if they own the place'.

'You comfortable, honey?' he asked Greta.

She nodded. She wished she could stop crying. All these people looking at her – they'd think she was a baby. And her tummy was shaking. She could really feel it as if inside her everything was twitching and she couldn't stop it.

'My skates . . . my skate got broken,' she snorted.

'No bones broken but I want to take a better look at her ankle,' the Major told Jane. 'You live around here, or do we need the jeep?'

'Just around the bend.' Her answer gave no hint of her anger. At this moment only one thing mattered; getting Greta home and sending for the doctor.

'It's okay, ma'am,' American No. 2 put in, 'the Major's a doctor. If he can look after great guys like us, I guess your little girl's safe enough with him.'

Jane's feelings were pulled in so many ways: anger and resentment towards these 'invaders' who weren't satisfied with putting them out of their home but now had frightened and hurt Greta; worry and concern for the child lying in this stranger's arms, a lump that promised to reach the size of a golf ball already swelling on her forehead and her precious skate as much victim as she was herself; yet the third feeling was one of relief that the softly spoken major was a medical man.

The crowd watched them go and then turned to each other prepared to spend an extra few minutes on holding a post-mortem.

These days there were many who were firmly of the mind that the sooner Uncle Sam's sons got taken down a peg or two the better; if the Americans had worn the same coarse battledress as the British or the Canadians, if they'd had less money to spend, then they would have been accepted much more easily by this category. Then there were those who saw the warriors from across the Atlantic as their ticket to some sort of Utopia they'd come to know in the cinema; and others who welcomed them as temporary and affluent escorts. Today's gathering of shoppers mostly came from the first group.

Poor soldier No. 2 climbed back into the jeep. He couldn't hear what was being said; he didn't need to.

211

Once at the cottage an examination proved the only damage to be a badly twisted ankle.

'I tried to stop quickly, jammed my toes together like you should, but I tripped. My foot got caught. That's how the strap broke and my skate came in two.'

Their visitor was examining the metal roller skate – and Jane found herself examining him. He didn't fit into the picture of the typical 'invader' she had built in her mind. A man of about forty, not one of these six-foot heavyweights, he was of average height and slimly built. His features were even, his smile showed good white teeth. The one thing that to her gave him the stamp of an American was that he wore rimless glasses; now, that was something one didn't see on an Englishman.

He must have sensed her scrutiny.

'I ought to tell you who I am. My name's Grant, Grant Holgate. We've just moved into the area.'

'I'm Jane Gower and this is Greta. We've just moved out of our area.'

'You mean you're one of those families who've been shifted? Gee Mrs Gower, that makes me feel rotten.'

She shrugged. She could almost hear Mrs Sid whispering in her ear not to let those Yankees see they'd been able to upset her.

'Would you like a cup of tea?' This seemed to be her day for surprising herself.

'That sounds great. And, Mrs Gower, thank you for taking it like you have. Here, Greta, how about getting your teeth into this?' A bar of American chocolate was produced from his tunic pocket.

'Phew! Thanks.' She turned her first smile of the incident on him. 'Would you like a piece? And you, Aunt Jane. Have a piece of choc?' When they both declined, she tore the end of the package and proceeded to nibble at it, mouse fashion, savouring each tiny piece.

Did these GIs always carry a spare bar of chocolate for

just such an emergency? A bubble of laughter welled up in Jane.

His tea drunk, Grant stood up to leave.

'I'd like to put a better bandage on that ankle.' For all Jane had been able to supply had been strips of a torn up pillow case. 'I don't want to intrude, perhaps you've got company, but it would be a good thing if I could do it before Greta goes to bed. I'm only up the hill at the Club. May I come in this evening, bring a proper dressing?'

'You must be very busy – with everything that's happening just now. I can always ask the local doctor to make a call.'

'If you prefer, of course, but I'd be sorry. And I'm not that busy. This part of the war isn't what I'm wanted for. I'm not so much a soldier, more a back-up man.' He seemed to accept that Jane had agreed to his coming back. 'Hey, Greta, there's a guy at the Club I reckon might be able to fix that skate for you. Can I take it along with me, see what he can do? You won't be using it for a few days, that's for sure.'

Returning from seeing him out, Jane glanced at the clock. Just twenty-four hours ago she had been driving away from Denby.

Jane helped Greta to hop to the car and settled her to sit with her leg resting along the back seat. Then they drove to Mannerby.

'I've been watching out for you these past days.' Joshua's greeting was accompanied by his yellow-toothed leer. 'Now, what about you coming along indoors, making yourself at home? There's a good fire burning in the kitchen. No sense in your staying out in those cold barns.'

'Actually, Mr Grimble, I'm not staying. But in any case, when I do come, I come to work not to sit by the fire! Greta has a sprained ankle. I shall be at home for a few days. I just want a word with the men – I want to make sure they can deal with the stores. And the telephone people are supposed to be coming to install a temporary phone for me.'

'You know, if it's a telephone you're wanting, then I have one in the house. Just you walk in any time, free as if it's your own place.' And his great hand rubbed itself up and down her forearm.

'You're very kind. But I'd rather we didn't confuse our arrangement with telephone charges. They promised to come within a day or two. I'll just go and speak to the men. You stay where you are, Greta, I won't be two minutes.'

As seasons go, this was the quietest. The men were quite happy to look after things without her. She'd come back on Saturday to pay the wages and then take the Day Book home for the weekend so that she could do the book-keeping. Coming out of the barn and seeing Joshua still hanging around the car, she was glad to have the chance to escape for a few days.

'Now I've got a better idea. Just been putting it to the little lassie. I'll bring my sofa into the kitchen from the parlour – she'll be comfortable enough on that. That way, you can be watching the business and her at the same time.' This time his paw landed on her shoulder in a pat that became a squeeze. She shrugged it off, but her movement didn't seem to put him out at all. 'We're friends now, aren't we? I was saying to Archie just last night when I ran my iron steed up to his shed, there's no doubt you're glad to have a place for your business; and friends like we've become, you'll be wanting to let me have a bit of your company. One kindness deserves another, eh? Always enjoyed looking in for a jaw. Don't see why it should be so different for you to come inside with me. Got a nice drop of Archie's parsnip wine. Any time you've got five minutes –'

'Mr Grimble, of course I'm grateful to you for having us here. But one thing I haven't got is time to spare. When I'm here, I shall be working.'

'All work and no play, that's no way for a pretty woman.' He treated her to a gust of sour breath as he leaned close. Then, still smiling: 'Of course, we've nothing written down – about your being here. No contract . . .' Was it a threat?

'I've been thinking about that. I would like to get the solicitor to draw up a document, keep it all legal.'

'Ah, I dare say you would. But what Joshua Grimble does is done for a friend, you understand me. Now don't you get me wrong, I've never been better pleased to do a kindness than over this affair. No, Joshua Grimble isn't a man for written documents, solicitors, all that nonsense. Two friends do a deal, that's sufficient.'

'And that's what we did, Mr Grimble. You agreed the rent and I'm grateful that you have us here. That's the arrangement.' She met his eyes unflinchingly. 'Just that.'

'Don't you upset yourself. I've not suggested going back on our agreement, now have I? A bit of pleasantness doesn't cost anything.'

She opened the door of the car, aware that Greta was watching them, missing nothing. The hand reached out and scored one more squeeze before she managed to slam it shut.

'Nice to be going home, Aunt Jane,' Greta said as they drove out of the yard of Chugford Farm. 'I won't have to go and sit in his house like he said, will I? Aren't his hands horrid? His fingers are so huge and the nails are full of dirt. Not just ordinary dirt like the men get when they're working – it looks as if it's lived there for years.'

'No, I'm certainly not taking you to his house. Let's forget him, dirty nails and all.' Over her shoulder she grinned at Greta. It sounded simple enough but it wasn't possible. In the short time since they'd moved to Chugford, she'd split her time between there and Denby until the move and after that had been at home with Greta. Joshua had had fewer opportunities of getting her to himself than he'd hoped. She wasn't actually scared of him, although he was a big man. Rather, she was repelled. Of course she'd been thankful to find a place to evacuate to, but why, oh why, hadn't it been anyone's farm but his!

There was nowhere to keep a car at No. 4 Shalbury Hill.

So, having seen Greta indoors, she drove to Ashcombe's Garage in St Agnes Road where she rented an undercover parking space. She was nearly home again, rounding the bend in Shalbury Hill, when a telegraph boy raced past her on his bicycle.

'No! Please, no.' It was her instinctive reaction, hers and so many more beside her. Richard . . . Hartley . . . even Liz in Oxford . . . He wouldn't be coming to her, of course he wouldn't. He was pedalling hard like that to get a running start on the hill. 'No. Oh, no. Please, no . . .'

But the lad stopped with a screech of his brakes, and stood his bicycle up against the kerb outside No. 4. Too far away to hear him, yet she could see the urgency with which he pounded the knocker.

CHAPTER ELEVEN

Fumbling to get her key into the lock, she heard Greta hopping to open the door.

'I was standing watching for you at the window. I saw the telegraph boy.' Greta said the first thing that came into her mind. She had to break the silence.

'The telegram . . .'

'Shall I open it for you, Aunt Jane?'

But Jane didn't hand it over. This was something she must do herself. Richard? Hartley? In that moment she knew just how frightened she'd been through these years. Now there was no hiding from it. She sat on the bottom stair and haggled the envelope open.

'Arriving tomorrow, Thursday. Richard.'

'What is it, Aunt Jane. What are you laughing for?' Was she laughing though, or was she crying? 'Can I read what it says?'

'It's Richard. He's coming tomorrow. He's home.'

Greta took the slip of paper out of her hand, reading it for herself. Then she took the envelope, saw the address, 'Denby House, Shelcoombe', crossed out and in pencil '4 Shalbury Hill' written at the side.

'Why does it have yesterday's date on it? Look, handed in at 7.45 p.m. yesterday!'

'Thursday! That's today! Richard's coming home today!' Jane's relief and excitement had to find an outlet and where better than Greta? She hugged her. 'I must go out and find something special for supper. I'll buy candles to put on the table. We've got our week's cheese. Fancy having to make a festive supper of macaroni and about enough cheese for a couple of mousetraps.' Yet still she laughed. What did it matter? What did any of it matter? Richard was safe; he was coming home.

'Shall I give him my room? I can be quite comfy on the settee, I'm the smallest.'

'You, my sweet, will cuddle in with me. Yes, give Richard your room. Oh, Greta, he's home!' It might not have meant as much to Greta as it did to Jane, but she returned the hug with all her strength. And silently she said: 'Thank you for the telegram not being something awful.' For Jane's sake she said it.

'I must go to the shops, see if I can find anything that seems a bit special. I'll dash. Won't be long.'

Already Greta was working her way up the narrow flight of stairs, one step at a time on her bottom.

'And I'll take my nightie and things into your room, ready.'

'I never thought I'd see the day when the only way I could trace my mother would be through the "nick",' Richard laughed. 'Even now, I don't understand what you're doing here. The chap in the taxi had some cock and bull tale that the district had been cleared. So he drove me to the Police Station to see if they knew where you'd gone. Even then it wasn't plain sailing, but finally they told me where I'd find you. Not that I could get any sense out of them. Is it true? That everyone's been moved out. But why? Is it unexploded land mines or what?'

No wonder he couldn't take it in. As soon as he'd landed, he'd put through a call to Denby. 'Number unobtainable' he'd been told. Hence the telegram. But even that, addressed to Denby, had taken until mid-day today to arrive at Shalbury Hill. Now Jane explained how they came to be in their new, cramped, surroundings. His reaction was much the same as most other people's: with miles of moor the Americans could have used, why destroy good high production farmland?

'You're all right here, Mum? Bit of a come down, isn't it?'

'Not such a come down as some people have had to face. It's small – but, Richard, what does that matter? You're home for Christmas! The first time for so long.'

Greta's daytime hours had to be spent on the settee, resting her swollen ankle. From some 'under the counter' source Jane had acquired two packets of coloured strips of paper to be linked and stuck into lengths of paper chains.

'Making decorations?' he asked with surprise.

'My fault. I didn't attempt to clear the loft – and of course that's where the box of paper chains is. I forgot all about them. Too late now, we can't get back in the zone. But Greta's working hard. We're going to look festive.'

'Remember the old Christmases, Mum?' Richard said, watching Greta working. 'The tree in the sitting room, Liz and me getting the holly. We knew just where to find the best bushes, used to cycle miles with our sacks and secateurs.'

'And Hartley, he was there too.'

'There was holly in the shop in the Square. I saw it when I was roller skating – I didn't fall over straight away, I went all round the streets.' Greta wasn't going to have him run away with the idea she couldn't skate just because she'd had one fall! 'But these are going to look great. You just wait 'til you see them.' Her fingers didn't stop, the snake of decoration grew steadily longer. Already in her mind she saw the room festooned with its coloured glory.

'I'd better doss down here on the settee, Mum.' Richard changed the subject.

'You certainly won't! Greta's moved her things into my room already.' Jane believed she must have imagined that just for a second his expression clouded; after all, what was more natural than that Greta should move in with her?

'No chance of Liz getting home, I suppose?' he asked.

'She's not suggested it. Nor Hartley.'

'She never mentions him when she writes. I thought perhaps – are they still as matey?'

'I used to think it was just puppy love, in fact I used to worry for Hartley's sake. But I think I may have been wrong.'

'You can't know, can you? It was different in the days we

were all at home. Now how can you know what matters and what doesn't in our lives?' She felt that he said it purposely, wanting to lash out and hurt.

Still pressing her gluey strips together, Greta looked from one to the other of them. Then, to Jane, her brown eyes sent a silent message of affinity. The moment passed. As if to make up for what he'd said, Richard unpacked his kitbag and produced two pairs of silk stockings he'd bought in the States, some dried banana, dried apricots, and a tinned fruit cake. Christmas fare indeed! And if the stockings had really been bought with Liz in mind, he didn't say so.

'I've got some snaps here. Places I went to when I had shore leave. This one was in New York. See the Empire State Building?' Jane heard the ring of pride in his voice and heard too a ghost from yesterday: she was back again at the Red Lion with John warning her against 'turning him into a farmer, spending his life on the same few acres where he was born and bred'. And John had been right. Richard was a man now, he was his own person. And with that thought came another: if Richard had come a long way, so had she. Not in distance, but in learning to steer her own course. Dear John . . . how much harder her years would have been without him. Now that he'd left his own familiar acres, would he ever return?

'And where's this one, Richard?'

'I don't remember just where. I hired a car, really covered the ground in that ten days I was ashore. It was an old homestead, a hundred years or more old.' He chuckled. 'This was the kitchen. It had been done up like a museum piece. That's why I took the picture. I bet our Denby is twice the age, eh?' And when he'd taken it, he'd imagined himself back home, all of them gathered around the scrubbed wooden table looking at it . . . Mum, Liz, the Sids, Greta, Meg and Ben. Even Hartley had come uninvited into the scene.

No. 4 Shalbury Hill was but the first of his surprises. The second came an hour or so later when he went to answer a knock on the door and was confronted by a major of the US Army.

'Good evening?' His mother hadn't been here a week yet, the visitor must be looking for whoever had moved out.

'One roller skate, returned as good as new.'

And a shout from the sitting room: 'Is that you, Grant? Come in.'

The skate in one hand, a bottle of Californian wine in the other, Grant did as she said, Richard following behind with a puzzled look on his face.

'Here it is at last, Greta. My buddy fixed it for you, it's safely soldered and bolted.'

'And a new strap too! Gosh, thanks, doctor.'

'Just Grant'll do me. But while I'm here I'd better see how that ankle of yours is getting along, hadn't I?'

'She's doing well. Today I can see quite a difference. The swelling is really starting to go down. What do you think?'

'I think, get Christmas over and she'll be zipping around on those skates as good as new. But not down the hill, Greta.'

She shook her head.

'I thought you could make use of this.' Grant handed Jane the bottle.

'What wonderful timing! Thank you. Why don't you stay and eat supper with us? The food may not be up to the standard you'd get at the Club, but it's not every day you'll get the chance of sharing in this sort of celebration.'

'Isn't someone going to introduce me? Or have you forgotten I'm here?' Richard put in.

'Hardly, when you're the reason for the celebration. Grant, this is my son, home from the sea; home from your country. And this, Richard, is Major Grant Holgate. He was there when Greta fell, and he's been looking after her.'

'Oh, I see.' Richard held out his hand. 'Glad to know you, Major.' He was pleased with the expression. Not 'How do you do?' or 'I'm pleased to meet you.' To his ears

'Glad to know you' had the sound of a seasoned traveller, someone familiar with the Major's own country.

'And you, Richard. Cut the Major. Just Grant's fine. So you're home for Christmas? No wonder your mother looks as though the moon and stars had dropped at her feet, eh?'

'Poor old Mum.' How many times had he said it and always the expression had managed to dampen her spirits. Now, though, she noticed the way Grant's lips twitched, and his eyebrows shot up as he looked at her. It was a joke, a joke they shared. If she was 'poor old Mum', what would he be? In Richard's eyes, the people who mattered were the youth; tomorrow's world belonged to them. Not that he fought authority; that was something he'd been trained to take from parents, teachers, senior officers, the 'old codgers'. Ah, that's what Grant would be. Now it was the turn of her lips to twitch. Poor old codger.

'You will stay, Grant?' she urged.

'I ought to say no. You people have tight enough rationing without feeding me twice in one week.' His words weren't lost on Richard. 'But I'm not going to say no. Instead, I'll rustle up something for the larder. How would that be?'

'You're welcome anyway. It's fish, and that's not even rationed.' And a tin of peaches, put by for just such a Red Letter Day! From peaches it was only a short jump to Madge Tozer and from her an even shorter one to Ted . . . No more than seconds ago Jane had been conscious of a feeling of pure, unclouded happiness; those two short jumps stripped her of it. If life deals you a blow, then you have to wrestle with it, knock it into shape. Hadn't that been her motto? Yet she was ashamed that it had brought her to a point where she could forget everything but awareness of her own well-being. It was a reminder that one could be sure of nothing beyond the moment. Looking at the scene in the tiny sitting room she wanted to imprint it on her memory, something to hold and keep.

Fish, not even rationed, she'd told them. In fact she'd queued for three-quarters of an hour for her locally caught salmon. The hard electric light was turned off, the gentle glow from four candles gave their warm illumination, that and a flickering fire in the small grate. Greta was settled at the table first, then Grant, while Richard helped her carry in the dishes. It must have been those tongues of golden flame that cast the spell.

Leaning as near to her as she could, Greta whispered to Jane: 'Sort of magic, isn't it?'

She nodded, and wondered about that feeling of shame she'd had. Surely the greater sin would be to be given an evening like this – Richard safe, home, grown to be a man – and not to appreciate it with her whole heart?

'You pour the wine, Grant.' And somehow, she told herself, even having an American here with them in this little house that wasn't their home, a stranger in a strange land, wasn't that all part of the spirit of this 'almost Christmas' celebration?

'Sure I will. But, excuse me one second if you will.' With a nod of his head in Jane's direction he stood up. 'I nearly forgot something I brought for my friend Greta.' He disappeared to feel in his coat pocket, then returned with a bottle of Coke. 'Now then, the wine.'

Richard looked on. He saw his mother's eyes shining in the candlelight; heard the merry ring in Greta's laugh; remembered other mealtimes, his father carving. Did she remember? Mum, in her dungarees, that's how it had always been. Now here she was tonight dressed in a blue dress that made her look different, younger. But it was for *him* she'd got herself dressed up, because *he'd* come home. The Yank just happened to be here.

'I had a smashing shore leave in the States.' He turned to their visitor with a smile.

He knew he'd felt out of sorts with his homecoming, first with the unexpectedness of finding that Denby and all the old haunts were a prohibited area and then because he'd seemed like a visitor in this tiny house that belonged to his mother and young Greta. Now, in doing his best to make the occasion an enjoyable one, his own spirits lifted. Before the peaches and custard were finished, he found himself much more in tune with life.

'I won't bother with coffee, Mum. I thought I'd give Liz a ring. Suppose there's no phone here?'

'Now, would there be?' she laughed. 'There's a kiosk quite close. Just down the hill and round the bend into St Agnes Road. It's on the right hand side. There's a torch on the scullery table, you'll need it to see to use the phone. Give Liz my love. Ask her if she's got the parcel safely and tell her to be strong willed and not open it until Christmas morning. We're keeping ours until then.'

Ordinary, easy, family talk. Grant thought of the days leading up to Christmas at home, brightly lit trees in the windows, garlands and fairy lights on the front doors. His mind wandered back to other times, to Zara, her eyes wide in wonder that was tinged with fright as he carried her to make her first acquaintance with Santa Claus in his grotto. The feel of her sturdy little body . . . the sound of her chuckle as he'd pushed her on the swing in the garden . . . the feeling of her tears wet on his cheek as he'd held her . . . passing her back to Margaret . . . the sight of her in the hospital cot . . .

'. . . in the sitting room.'

'Jane, I'm sorry. What were you saying?'

'Just that if you go into the sitting room I'll bring our coffee in there by the fire. And for you, Greta my love, it's more than time for bed.'

'Point me to the kitchen,' Grant offered, 'I'm a great coffee maker. Please.'

She knew he wanted to be occupied, that somewhere in his mind the devils were chasing him. There was no hiding it from her, it had happened to her too often for that.

'You won't be impressed by what you find,' she warned him. 'The scullery here hardly compares with one of your New World kitchens.'

'The scullery here, as you call it, managed to produce

the best meal I've had in a long time. So let's see what I can do with the coffee.'

She stacked the dishes, he ground her last precious coffee beans, making a mental note that they might go on the list of 'unobtainables' he had in mind to bring her courtesy of Uncle Sam, and Greta made her way to bed, stair by stair on her bottom.

Each with a cup of aromatic coffee and a Camel cigarette, Jane and Grant settled by the fire.

'Greta's decorations,' Grant said, looking at the paper chains left draped across the back of the settee, 'a reminder of what Christmas ought to be. Tell me what it used to be like here, Jane, before the world went dark.'

'I don't think bright lights have that much to do with it. What it used to be like . . . the excited voices, the sound of footsteps in the yard when they came home with the tree – Tim and the children always went to choose the tree – the silent stillness of Christmas Eve after they'd gone to bed. We always used to open the back door, go out into the yard. What was the difference between that evening and all the others of the year?' Her blue eyes were suddenly swimming. He knew that fetching an ash tray was only an excuse to turn her back on him. Why should they need an ash tray when they were by the side of a perfectly good fire?

'Guess you were the same as the kids, Jane, hearing the sleigh bells,' he laughed, helping her over the moment.

'Sometimes I think I hate it all, the season of goodwill. It's fine when it's – well, when it's like it used to be. But there's no time like it for rubbing salt in the wound. You must feel that, this year, your first away.' By now she was mistress of herself again. She re-filled their cups and sat down. 'Now it's your turn. You tell me about how it is at home for you. Have you a family, Grant? People who'll be thinking of you especially much over these days?'

'No. There's no one.' Silence. The sort of silence she couldn't find a way to break. Then, leaning back in the armchair, he went on: 'I had a wife, but it's over now. We were divorced more years ago than our marriage lasted.

We both knew that we were making a mess of it. My fault just as much as hers. No one can expect marriage to survive when it plays second fiddle to a career – not just in my life, in hers too. Margaret's a researcher, a scientist, a very clever woman. Not that she didn't care about Zara, she did.'

'Zara?'

'We had a daughter. When we were divorced Margaret was given custody. That's customary, I guess, even when the mother is as absorbed in a career as Margaret, but what was rare was the way we sorted things out between ourselves. Zara moved from one to the other. I doubt if she realized things were any different – a family occasion had been a rare enough event in our household. Clara, her nursemaid, gave her any continuity she'd ever known. She was only three when we split up.' He reached for his wallet and took out a much handled picture of a little girl. 'There she is.' The child couldn't have been more than three or four years old.

'But what about now? You said all this was years ago?'

He threw his half smoked cigarette into the fire. 'She'd be about Greta's age. It happened so quickly – meningitis. There was no chance, nothing any of us could do, nothing even the best in the field could do. It was just a week before her fourth birthday.'

'Saying I'm sorry – it sounds like nothing. Grant, to lose a child –'

He took off the glasses that marked him as American, polishing them on his handkerchief with more concentration than the job merited. Putting them on again seemed to give him a mental shake. The wall between him and his memories was firmly back in place.

'Christmases at home, you asked. Well, the world is like one huge glittering light, every shop window, every house, I guess I've been lucky. I've never been without friends even if I don't have family. It's a season of festivity. That way one doesn't have too much time to think, to remember –'

'Not remember! Oh, but Grant, you've got to remember, you must never run away from the hurt of it. You've got to be able to shut your eyes and – and – smell the sweet baby smell of her, feel what it was like lifting her to sit on your knee or in her high chair – all the special moments that belonged just to you and to her. Didn't she sometimes climb in bed with you for a cuddle? You've got to remember all of it. In that short time, not quite four years, she gave you something that will always be just yours.'

She knelt down on the hearth rug, her instinct to reach out to him. But instead she took the tongs and put more coal on the fire. Her impassioned outburst seemed to hang in the air between them, neither of them sure where to go from here.

But they were saved. It was just at that moment that there came a knock on the front door.

'That must be Richard.' She didn't know whether to be pleased or sorry. They'd rushed headlong into emotions far too deep for two comparative strangers. They'd been hurtling towards a relationship beyond anything they knew of each other; both of them had reached towards it, driving with one foot on the accelerator and the other on the brake.

Jane went to answer the door.

'Surprise, surprise!'

'Liz!'

'I'm off until the 27th, what about that!'

'So Richard didn't get through to you – no, of course he didn't. Liz, you're *both* home. He came this afternoon. He went to the call box to try and speak to you. I can't believe it. Where's Hartley? Are you suddenly going to produce him from behind a lamp-post?'

But she wasn't; Liz was alone. The next few moments were full of noise and excitement. Greta, hearing Liz's voice, descended the narrow staircase in the same way as she'd gone up it. The introductions over, Grant looked on. If one thing was geared to put his conversation with Jane to the back of his mind it must be this. It seemed that the three of them possessed that singularly female talent of all talking at the same time, hearing everything and jumping from one subject to the next with never a stumble.

'I ought to go, leave you to your family.'

'No, don't run away. Not unless you've had enough of us.'

And, put like that, it was much more comfortable to stay where he was, legs crossed, taking his ease by the fireside.

The phone box was only just around the corner yet already it was over an hour since Richard had gone out. Could it be because there was a visitor in the house? The idea niggled at Jane, but more than that it irritated her. Another indication how far she'd travelled almost without being aware of it in these last few years on her own.

By the time his knock came on the door Greta was back in bed, Liz had taken her case to the second bedroom and Richard's kitbag had been put on the small landing.

'You answer it, Mum. Don't tell him I'm here!'

After switching off the light in the hallway, Jane let him in. Only as they came back into the sitting room did she see how disgruntled he looked.

'Couldn't get Liz,' he growled, 'so I had a walk.' As anyone would, coming in from the cold night, he went towards the fire, his back to the scullery. Neither Jane nor Grant gave any hint that someone was creeping towards him. 'At the hospital they said she's off duty for Christmas. Got better things to do, I suppose –'

From behind him Liz covered his eyes with her hands. 'Guess who!'

'Liz!' Turning he grasped her in a bear-like hug. Watching them Jane felt her eyes sting with tears. Happiness? Thankfulness? Both of these things, and so much more besides.

'And this time I really am going.' Grant stood up. 'It's been an evening I shall remember.' And looking at Jane, 'Shall make sure I do remember.' A few words that left so much unspoken; but Jane understood.

Liz and Richard watched them go into the tiny hallway,

228

then looked at one another, each hoping to find some simple explanation for what it was they didn't understand and didn't like. Nothing was the same as it used to be. Their own lives were proof enough of it, but that was different. They were young, caught up in the sort of situations that Mum couldn't know anything about. Rations, queues, Home Guard, perhaps the odd stray bomb that would set people talking for days – that was Devon as they thought of it and, amongst it, 'home' something that was always there to come back to. Not that she could help it that she'd had to get out of Denby – a place where they had liked to think she would always be waiting, as sure as the seasons of the year. Was it because they'd arrived when she wasn't expecting them that they'd caught her out? Their thoughts moved on the same lines as, silently, they looked at each other. It was a mean and horrible way to think about her, but what was she doing entertaining some middle-aged American?

That was on the 21st December. The last unwilling couple had given up the struggle and been shifted out of the evacuation zone and already a series of huts had been erected to house the soldiers.

Greta would love to have climbed up to put the drawing pins into the picture rail, but with strict instructions to rest her foot on the settee all she could do was give directions to the twins. Her paper chains were secured, four strips in each room, stretching from the rose in the centre of the ceiling to the corners.

'Phew!' Her big brown eyes shone with the wonder of it all. 'Can't wait for Aunt Jane to get home and see. What do you think?' she added, confident of their praise.

'Smashing.' Richard didn't fail her. 'Next thing, Liz and I are going to see if there's any holly left in the shops. Jolly funny Christmas, us going out to try and buy holly. I wish Mum hadn't stored the bikes. We'd soon have gone out and found enough to tart up this little place.'

'It's going to be a gorgeous Christmas.' Already, in her

mind, Greta saw festoons of greenery around the pictures. 'Wouldn't it be lovely if a knock came on the door and it was Hartley?'

'That won't happen. He's on duty,' Liz told her.

'As well he is. He'd be sleeping in the bath if he came here,' was Richard's comment, his tone somehow putting an end to the idea.

'Would you like some of my popcorn?' Always sensitive to atmosphere, Greta held out her bag to him.

'No thanks, you eat it. A present from the Yankee doctor? He seems very at home here. How well do you and Mum know him?' His question was casual, but Greta gave it her full attention.

'He picked me up and brought me home when I fell and hurt my foot. That was only last week. So if you said how long have we known him, I'd say "not long".' Over her head Richard caught Liz's twinkling glance and shook his head with a sigh. Greta was putting her mind to the question and when she did that there was no hope of pushing her into taking a short cut. 'But you said "how well". Oh, we know him very well, I'm sure we do. I mean, I don't know anything about where he comes from, 'cept it's America, if he's got sons and daughters, all that stuff. Don't know if Aunt Jane does. Shouldn't think so. But we just *know* him. You can feel it when you know a person, can't you? Are you sure you don't want a lump of this? It's really scrumptious!'

'Go on, then, twist my arm,' Richard held out his hand and was rewarded by a sticky lump of toffeed corn.

'Isn't it funny, about knowing people?' She nibbled delicately around the edges, savouring each sweet morsel. 'Mr Carlisle was often about, for years I've been used to him. But I wouldn't say I really *know* him, not at all. Or Mrs Gower, Grandma Gower. Just not at all. Some people you can talk to for hours and hours, find out all about where they live, if they've got kids, all that sort of stuff. But they don't give you even a tiny bit of themselves – same as you don't them.'

'The trouble with having a poorly ankle, Greta my sweet,' Liz laughed, 'is that the only energy you can use is in your brainbox. Come on, clever clogs, you've still got a few of these coloured papers left. What about a strip to put across the doorway into the scullery.'

''course I will. Good idea.'

The days went all too fast. Together Liz and Richard visited the Sids and went to see Emily.

'Meg's fallen on her feet,' Liz reported with much the same affectionate laugh that Tim had used when he'd spoken of his mother, 'she adds a touch of class to the establishment, does our Meg.'

Then it was all over. On the morning of the 27th, Liz went back to Oxford and Richard with her.

'I'll wait and see the New Year in with Liz, then I'll come back on the 1st January,' he told Jane. 'That still gives me three days. I want to see the sort of hovel she calls home.'

'You mind your manners, my fine fellow,' Liz whacked his behind with her handbag, 'or you'll find yourself on the first train back to Totnes.'

Jane watched them. How good these few days had been; all the tensions she used to detect between them seemed to have vanished. It was because they were adults now. They'd outgrown the difficult adjustment of adolescence . . . she thought she understood it all. It wasn't until they'd gone and she was looking back on the bright patch of those few days that she realized something that cast a cloud: Hartley. Liz had talked about him – to her, and only when Richard hadn't been there; Richard hadn't talked about him at all.

As long as Liz had been training she'd had to live in the Nurses' Home. Even though, newly qualified, she and Rita Turnbull had shared these rooms now for four months she was still conscious of a thrill of independence when she put her key in the front door. It was evening by the time she and Richard came out of the railway station at Oxford. Arm in arm they walked to the tree-lined road where she lived, on the north side of the city. She led the way up the linoleum-covered stairs to the first floor, then took her key from her purse, proud to be bringing Richard to her own home.

'I can't remember what shift Rita's on this week. Just wait out here for a second while I go and tell her you've come – make sure she's decent.'

'Oh, tell her not to worry about that!' He chuckled, winking broadly, more than willing to enter into the spirit of this new freedom.

'Shan't be a tick.' And she was gone, the door closed on him. 'Rita, I'm home, are you – ?' The sentence was left hanging unfinished in the air.

Richard frowned, listening. He stood with his ear almost to the door. Yes, there was a voice. Rita? No, surely it was a man's voice. Outside the door he waited, forgotten.

'Hey, Liz.' To him it had seemed far more than seconds since she'd left him. 'Is this the way to bring home a visitor?' He opened the door.

Pulling away from Hartley, Liz turned to him, her eyes telling their own happy story.

'I didn't say anything, not until Hartley was there too. He and I –'

'So I see.'

'You don't mind the thought of me for a brother-in-law, do you?' Hartley grinned his pleasure at seeing Richard, and at so much more besides.

'Come off it, Hartley. You and Liz! Don't talk so bloody daft! Damn it, you were brought up like our brother. Why, it's pretty well incest!' His eyes were cold as steel.

Hartley had been so sure that Richard would welcome their news. Looking at him Liz could feel his hurt, his bewilderment. She took his hand, her face flushing with anger.

'Incest? What would *Hartley* know about incest?'

Clearly nothing, any more than he could follow the undercurrents now.

232

'I promise you I don't feel a bit like a brother to Liz.' He could hardly have said anything less likely to make Richard feel happier with the situation. 'I'm sure Aunt Jane won't put any obstacles in the way. She knows how we feel about each other. Liz wanted us to wait until you were home though before we made anything official. Now the first chance we have, we'll go down and see her.'

'You mean you're serious? You really want to tie yourselves up together? It's daft, bloody daft. Have either of you ever known anyone else? No. Christ, Hartley –'

'Don't talk like that, Richard,' Liz interrupted him, 'it's just not you.' She might as well not have spoken for all the notice he took of her.

'Mum used to shove us in the bath together – first you then me at the plug end while Liz sat it out with both of us; Christmas, Mum and Dad used to fill your stocking the same as they did ours; it was Liz who used to pull your leg when your voice was breaking, remember? How embarrassed you used to be. We went swimming together, all three of us,' his mouth turned down at the corners, 'that year when you were cocky because you'd got a few hairs in your armpits.'

'I remember all of it.' Hartley's voice was quiet and composed.

'Shut up, Richard.' Liz felt sick.

'I wonder what you have to show off to her now, eh? Good God above! Why can't you find yourself a bird somewhere else, one you haven't ogled ever since she was a kid? Anyway, you're not giving her a chance. How does she know if she wants to be stuck with you all her days, if she's never been out with anyone else?'

'Richard, I *do* know. Anyway, I've worked with student doctors. I've met other people.'

Again she might as well not have spoken.

'I might have been jealous of you, you know.' There was a change in Richard's voice. He was trying a different tactic. Liz bit her lip. inside her felt knotted up and miserable. The two people she loved best in all the world –

why did it have to be like this? 'I hardly remember when you first got brought to Denby. Mum used to fetch you to play, didn't she? Then when we had you dumped on us, our parents had to belong to you too. Fair enough. Liz and I never tried to put you down.'

'Don't be beastly, Richard. Hartley knows it was never like that.'

'Yes, it was, Liz.' Hartley put his arm around her shoulders. 'Richard's right. I've never taken any of it for granted, neither you two, nor your parents. I'm not sure where it was that gratitude got taken over by affection –'

'Ah, there you are! What did I tell you? Oh, come on Hartley, don't be daft. Liz is like a sister to you. One of these days you'll fall hook line and sinker for some cracker of a WAAF or something. And where's that going to leave Liz?'

'That's not true, Richard. But let's not argue about it.'

Probably Richard believed that he'd sown the seeds of doubt, and that later his words would come back to Hartley – and to Liz too. Probably Hartley took it all at face value and thought the warning had come from genuine concern. Only Liz knew the whole story; no wonder of the three it was she who found it hardest to put the scene from her mind.

Fate took a hand in seeing there was no repeat performance. Another hour or so and Hartley had to return to his base. On the following three nights he was flying. A bomber pilot on duty would have no time for New Year celebrations. His only contact with Liz was a call to the hospital each morning to say 'Good morning, I'm back.' This week she was on the shift known as 'earlies', leaving the house just after six o'clock and returning at teatime. Rita's path hardly crossed Richard's at all, for she worked from one o'clock until eleven at night and he made sure that by the time she surfaced in the morning he'd vacated the chesterfield where he spent his nights and gone out. Wandering the streets and towpaths of Oxford at the turn of the year was a solitary way to spend his leave, but the evenings made it worthwhile. He and Liz went to the New Theatre and laughed as uproariously at this year's pantomime dame as they had at any in their childhood; the next evening they made do with a quick snack so that they'd be in time for the evening performance of 'Gone With The Wind'; and the one after that they sat sipping in a pub, the smoke from their own cigarettes adding to the foggy atmosphere. Then came his last night, New Year's Eve. Tomorrow he'd be on the train. He took her out to dinner, both of them dressed in their best and enjoying an experience that was new; not new to eat out, for her not new to go to the best hotel in the city either, she and Hartley often came here; and as for Richard, in these last years he'd been in eating houses from Aberdeen to Harlem. Not new for them to have a meal out together either, from Saturday treats in Kingsbridge or Totnes to working lunches at the Milk Bar before he'd been old enough to go to sea, they'd faced each other across many a table. But never before had they shared a meal in the 'grown up' world, Richard holding her chair for her to take her seat, the waiter (only a war could have kept him on his feet so long!) addressing them as 'sir' and 'madam' with all the deference he showed to the bristly colonel and his lady at the next table.

And through those evenings no mention was made of her engagement to Hartley. This evening, their last together, she knew it couldn't be put off any longer. Somehow she had to make Richard understand. What surprised her was that it was he who brought it up.

'I shall remember this, Liz. All our time together here in Oxford. I'm sorry if I made a scene the other day. He wouldn't understand,' he held her gaze, 'no one would understand except you and me.'

'Richard, it must happen. One day we'll both marry, of course we will, we'll have children – imagine them, not just ordinary cousins, special cousins.'

'I know we will. But all that sort of thing's way ahead in the future. It's the war, Liz, everyone's doing it, getting

235

hitched because they have this need to belong to someone. I see it with the chaps on the ship. I hear the way they talk too. I'm sure it never used to be like it. Promiscuity is bred from loneliness and the blackout.' He looked at her keenly as if he'd be able to see into her mind. 'They don't call it that, they call it love. Probably even believe it is.'

'You're talking about other people, Richard, people who get thrown together because they're miles from all that really matters to them.' She waited while the soup was put down in front of them and, with the air of a man of the world, Richard asked for the wine list. It was only when they were back in their isolated tête-à-tête that she picked up the conversation where they'd dropped it. 'Miles away from home. Like that American we found at Mum's.' There was the hint of a question in her voice.

What was she suggesting?

'Oh, come off it, Liz.' Richard's mantle of suavity was dislodged. 'Don't talk daft. Can you imagine Mum with a boyfriend?'

'She was twenty years old, our age, when we were born. That makes her forty. My ward sister is older than that and she's just got engaged to one of the senior consultants. On the ward she's a bit of a dragon, but I saw them walking by the river the other day and it really shook me. She was smart, attractive, glamorous. It didn't look at all wrong for them to be hand in hand.'

'I don't know anything about her, she may be all you say. But, Mum – damn it all, it's mean even to imagine it! As if she would want to go chasing after some other bloke – after Dad, I mean.'

'Mum's a lot prettier than Sister Blake – and she's never a dragon. When you go home – or whatever that cottage is – just take a good look at her. I'll tell you what's done her the world of good: the business. She's using her full potential –'

'I do declare, the lady's a regular Pankhurst!' he laughed. 'Here's the wine coming.'

The wine waiter stood by whilst Richard took a sip, a

wise and knowledgeable expression firmly on his face as he approved it. Jane, with or without the attentions of a member of the invasion force who'd turned them out of Denby, was forgotten.

Coming out of the hotel into the night they were blanketed in darkness, the moon riding high behind a thick curtain of cloud.

'You must eat a lot of carrots, the way you stride along in this lot!' He laughed, grabbing her arm. 'Wait for me!'

'Sorry,' She linked her arm through his, an easy companionable movement. 'We often come here, I know the path with my eyes closed.' She was testing her weight on thin ice and she knew it.

'We? You and Rita? On nurses' pay?'

'No, of course not Rita! Hartley and I –'

'Oh, damn him, Liz! Even this, even tonight, he has to push in and spoil it!'

She stopped walking and turned to face him. Not that they could see each other except for a dark shape.

'I don't understand you. You come home bragging about the places you've been to – you've even thrown in a 'bird' or two, as you call them. What do you expect me to be doing? Sitting by the fireside on my own, waiting for my brother to come home?' He didn't answer. 'Richard?' she prompted softly.

'Let's walk. I'm used to the dark now.'

There was too much left unsaid. Tomorrow he'd be gone. Surely he must know how important it was that he understood?

'Say something, Richard!'

'When we were kids, there were always the three of us. There was us, you and me and there was him. We were a family. He might have been our elder brother. Isn't that right?'

'Yes.'

'Three's a rotten number, it's always two and one. So now it's you and him and I'm the odd one. But, Liz, that's got to be all it is between you. Just that he's been nearby

237

while I've been oceans away.' He could tell from her silence that he wasn't making headway. 'And there's another thing,' he tried again, 'he's no age, only a year more than me. Of course I've chatted up the birds when I've been ashore – and that's what he ought to have been doing too. If you anchor him at twenty-one, give him a year or two and he'll meet some woman and realize that what he'd felt for you was what I was talking about earlier – the war, the need to have someone waiting. Promise me, Liz, just promise me you'll not rush off and get married without me.'

It would have been so easy to say what he wanted to hear. But Liz was too honest for that.

'Of course I don't want to get married without you being there. But I can't promise a thing like that. Anyway it's nonsense, this odd one out you talk about.' Overhead they heard the drone of heavy laden bombers, setting off on their last mission of the Old Year, or their first of the New. And just as she did every time she heard the throbbing of their engines, she remembered Hartley's words: '. . . taxiing . . . the wheels going up . . .' and thought of him isolated in his own fear, him and each member of every crew in that airborne armada. Another wave of bombers went over. Was he up there, lost in the deep black sky? Loving Hartley didn't change anything for Richard and her. Somehow she had to make him understand.

'We've only got tonight, Liz, let's not spoil it arguing.'

'Nothing's spoilt. If you and Hartley didn't get on it would be different. But then if you and Hartley were the sort not to get on, I'd never love him, would I?'

New Year's Eve and on the streets were a few parties of revellers. They painted a backdrop, they and the blanket of darkness, the sound of a piano from the public bar of some side street pub, the baleful cry of a tom cat calling its mate, the clatter of a dustbin lid as a dog – or cat, it was impossible to see what sort of animal it was – sniffed after a smell that held the promise of supper. From a distance they heard a clock strike midnight.

'Happy New Year, Liz.' Richard turned her to face him. 'To me that's the most important thing there is – that you're happy. Stay like you are, Liz. I couldn't bear it if I came home and you were different, belonged to someone else.'

'And you, Richard. Happy New Year to you. Keep safe.' She shut her eyes tight when she said it. 'All of you, keep safe. And whether I'm actually married to him or not – it doesn't make any difference. You know what I'm saying?'

'Not sure. To us? Or you and him? What are you telling me?'

'Both. I'm telling you that I've made love with Hartley.' She heard his sharp intake of breath; he sounded as though he'd hurt himself, a sudden cut or burn. 'But it's not made any difference to us, you and me.' Silence. Still they were facing each other, neither making any move. 'Say something.'

'I can't. All the years, I've seen the way he's watched you. You weren't his. Damn him! We had to take him into our home, but you're mine, you've always been mine. Liz, don't you feel it? Who was the first person to touch you? Who did you tell when your periods started? Who knew you as you changed from a child to –?'

'Stop it, Richard. We were children, curious children.'

'I knew you – yes, and you knew me, too. Used you to look at him, wonder how he measured up?'

'Please, don't spoil everything. Tomorrow you go away. Whatever we used to be, can't you see that was all part of growing up? It'll all happen to you, it'll be just as good for you when you meet the right person. Don't let's spoil what's ahead of us by saying things we shall regret.' She reached out to him, holding her face to his in the dark. 'Let's just say Happy New Year. Let's just wish that 1944 will make everything come right.'

She wasn't prepared for the way he held her, so close that she could hardly breathe.

When they reached the flat it was in darkness. On the table was a note from Rita:

239

'I came home to change, now I've gone to a New Year knees up at Mary's. Am staying night, so won't disturb you. Happy New Year to both. R.'

The bottle of Mrs Sid's elderberry wine was still three-quarters full. Surely wine made from the trees at Denby would prevent any new and unnecessary barrier, would show him that nothing in her had altered? So many shared memories were pulled out of the shadows as they sat before the gas fire, glasses in their hands. Liz could almost persuade herself that she'd imagined his angry hurt.

'Nearly two o'clock! I'm off to bed. Oh, dearie, dearie.' She rocked on her feet as she stood up. It was an exaggerated movement, but even so a little four-year-old elderberry wine goes a long way and she'd had more than a little. They both had; the empty bottle was evidence of that.

Richard stood up too, pulling her to him and kissing her forehead.

'It's been so good, Liz, you and me, these last few evenings. When I'm out there being blown to bits in the Atlantic gales, I'll think of Oxford, of you.'

She nodded. Neither of them mentioned Hartley or what she'd told him. Yet surely he must have been there at the back of both their minds?

A busy day's work, an over emotional evening, a late night and too much elderberry wine all combined to put Liz quickly to sleep, even if the bed did rock gently. On her own she always slept with her window open and the curtains undrawn. Half waking she heard the door of her room open – or was she dreaming? Her mind was suspended between rational thought and oblivion, it seemed not to belong to her at all. Yet she didn't question who it was coming towards the bed. Even before she heard the sob catch in his throat she knew.

'Don't, Richard.' She threw back the covers and tried to pull herself up to go to him. But he was already at her side, sitting on the edge of the bed. In the dark she could see the outline of his form, his head bent. She knew he was crying.

'Is it so awful? Oh, I wish you weren't going.' And into her mind came that memory of Hartley . . . how many of them wouldn't come back tonight? So it was like that for Richard too. For all of them perhaps.

Sitting up she pulled him into her arms, cradling his head against her. Or was it a dream? If only the room would stay still, if only the bed wouldn't sway so. A dream? A nightmare. Part of the guilt that had hammered at the back of her mind since early adolescence, guilt that in loving Hartley she'd almost forgotten, guilt that tonight Richard had rekindled. It couldn't be happening, Richard never cried. She gave up the fight. Real or a dream, he was unhappy, he was frightened. She wasn't quite sure how he got from the side of the bed to be lying next to her, but she didn't question, just held him close.

It was only as the nightmare became reality that she started to fight.

CHAPTER TWELVE

'Last day of the year. I said to Sid when we got up this morning, "I'm off to see Mrs G. and Greta – and Richard too if he's back from his trip to Liz. Can't have the sun go down on 1943 without wishing them a better year to come." Back home again before too many months of it have passed, let's all wish each other that!'

'But you're settling, Mrs Sid? If only we could have got somewhere a big bigger, we could have all stayed together.'

'To be truthful, my dear, it would have upset Sid's brother Clem if we'd not turned to him for a roof. Since Maudie died he's all alone. He says he hasn't had such a happy time as this Christmas has been since he lost her. So there you are. Sometimes things get thrown into place where we least expect. Sid's started going to Home Guard again – joined in with Clem's lot – platoon or some such name they call themselves. Not so bad for me, I've got plenty to do with the two of them to cook and do for. But it's harder on a man. Joining the Home Guard there has settled Sid better than anything else could. Anyway, that's enough about us. It's you I came to hear about.'

And she was still hearing – from the accident on roller skates, with Greta hopping to get the mended one to show her how 'good as new' it was, right through the unexpectedly festive Christmas – when a knock came on the front door.

Thoroughly proficient now on one leg Greta sprang across the little room to the passage to see who it was while, in the scullery, Jane lit the gas under the kettle to make the cup of tea she knew Mrs Sid wanted.

'It's a man's voice. You got a visitor, Mrs G. No one I

recognize.' All this in a stage whisper as Greta brought the visitor in.

Jane recognized it though and watched Mrs Sid's face closely as she heard the accent and realized the caller was one of the Americans who'd turned them out of Denby. Not a flicker of expression. But there wouldn't be! Mrs Sid wasn't going to 'have those Yankees thinking they'd got the better of us at Denby'. She didn't have to say it for Jane to know what was in her mind.

'Come in, Grant,' Jane welcomed him. 'Come and meet Mrs Sid.'

'So you're Mrs Sid. I sure am glad I dropped by and had the chance to meet you. Although from Greta's talk about you, to be honest I feel I know you already.'

'Well now, fancy that.' Forgetting her pre-conceived ideas she smiled – Jane could almost see the ice melting! – her prune like face lighting up and giving a hint of the pretty young woman she used to be. Today, whether to finish the year on a high or simply because she was coming to town, her cheeks were pink and her lips carefully painted.

''course we talk about you, Mrs Sid. It was rotten luck hurting my ankle before Christmas. If I hadn't, I would have been out to see you. My bike's covered up behind the chicken run. As soon as Grant says I can pedal, I'll come.'

'Always got room for you, duckie. More room at Clem's than you have here in this rabbit hutch! A spare bed always made up. Well, it seems they're not going to tell me your name?' Again the smile was turned on the visitor. American invader or not, she liked his soft voice, and it seemed he was taking good care of young Greta.

'My name's Grant. Grant Holgate. You've come specially to talk with Jane, here. I didn't mean to barge in.'

'Rubbish,' Jane laughed. 'I'm making a pot of tea – or you can have coffee if you'd rather?'

'Neither, Jane. I'm on my way down to the base. I just

243

called by to see if there was any chance of your coming to the New Year's dance? It's only just up the hill, you know, at the Club.'

'It would be too late to keep Greta out and I'd not leave her.'

'Come for supper then. Bring her unless you think it's time she ought to be tucked up.'

'You just do as he says and go, Mrs G. I've been telling her for ages, Mr Holgate, it's quite time she put on a pretty frock and went out.'

Jane could feel the silent laughter bubbling up. Oh, Mrs Sid, if you were twenty years younger I'd say you were flirting. This was a side of her old friend she'd never seen. Mrs Sid, practical, bustling, always ready to jump in with a word of criticism: yet here she was only one stage short of fluttering her eye lashes at Grant! There must be something about these Americans!

'Now, Greta? You'd like to come wouldn't you?'

'If Aunt Jane wants us to.' She'd do most things for Jane, but the idea of being the only child at a dance for grown-ups made her feel uncomfortable.

'I've got a better idea. That spare bed, all ready for you, Greta love. How would it be if you rolled up your nightie and put it in my basket and came home with me? Could you hop to the bus stop? Back home it'll pull up by the gate for us to get out. You'd give her an arm down the hill, wouldn't you, Mrs G.?'

Clearly Greta liked the idea. Jane's petrol ration was for essential use. But it wasn't such a big cheat for her to drive them out to Clem Collyer's cottage.

It wasn't Glenn Miller's Band, but it was a good imitation. 'In The Mood', a tune so familiar, yet tonight there was a magic about it as she swayed to its rhythm. She didn't want to talk, she just wanted to absorb the atmosphere, the almost feverish reaching out for enjoyment she was aware of all around her. The other day there had been a man outside the park gates, trying to attract the shoppers, shouting that like him they could be born again Christians. The expression must have made more impression on her than she'd realized. Born again. Suddenly that was how she felt, a born again woman. Dancing with Grant was but part of it. She was herself, Jane, a complete person, not Mum, not Mrs G., not the dungareed storekeeper and general factotum of an agricultural engineering business. Perhaps partly the euphoria stemmed from knowing just how much it must be meaning to the twins tonight to be starting out on a new year together; perhaps from having found that the Sids were settled and she needn't worry about them; perhaps because this invasion of Americans and all they were training to do must mean that the end of the war was nearer; whatever the reason, Jane was 'In The Mood', she felt like a debutante at her first ball, she felt pretty, she felt young. And, if any of that came from being with Grant, she didn't realize it.

As the music came to an end he steered her to an empty table.

'I'll rustle us up some food,' he told her. 'You'll be all right if I leave you while I get it?'

'Oh, yes,' she laughed, 'no one'll steal me.'

'I wouldn't blame them. What was it Mrs Sid told you about putting on a pretty frock? She'd sure be pleased if she could see you tonight. Honey . . . that's what you remind me of, Jane. Pure, golden honey.'

She smiled her pleasure. It had been Christmas Eve when the new dress had called out to her from the window of an expensive and exclusive shop, its colour a deep gold that accentuated the glints that still shone in her hair. She'd never paid so much for a frock in her life and, added to that, reason told her there were more sensible ways of using her clothing coupons. Where, in her life, was there the need for it? Necessity had made her listen to reason for so long that it had become a habit, but this time she'd turned a deaf ear. And now she was glad.

A cold buffet was set out on a long table in the

adjoining room and he moved off to join the line collecting food.

'You must be the mother of the child Grant's been taking care of. Can I sit with you while he gets your supper?'

Suddenly Jane didn't feel quite as pretty. The girl who spoke to her was dressed in the olive green uniform of the US Army. She was slim, groomed to perfection from the top of her smooth dark shining hair to the tips of her polished uniform court shoes; her face was beautifully made-up, but no make-up could give that smoothness of skin, the lack of lines, the youth.

'Of course you can. Yes, Greta belongs to me. She's almost better now.'

'I expect Grant's talked about me?' The girl sat down and crossed her slim, silk-stockinged legs. 'Carol – Carol Roughton. What do I call you?'

'Jane Gower. No,' and she found herself unreasonably glad to be able to say it, 'he's not mentioned you. You're stationed here?'

'Why, sure. Back home I was his nurse. I worked for him – with him – both really! A doctor's office has a nurse, I was the nurse in his. When he was coming in the Army – well, it was just natural to come too. We've been together a long time. You sort of get bonded.' Carol ran her hand over her immaculate hair as if to reassure herself that it was as it should be. She seemed to look at Jane's short 'do as they pleased' curls as she did it. 'The child who fell over – Gladys, is it?'

'No, Greta.'

'Greta – is she your only child? You're lucky to have found someone to stay and look after her on New Year's Eve. Or are you going to be like Cinderella and run away before the party ends?'

'No one's at home with her, she's staying with friends. All my family are away. My daughter is a nurse too. Her twin brother is in the Merchant Navy.'

'Fancy! A nurse, the same as me.' Carol seemed to be

246

sizing her up. 'Talking with you, hearing you say that, makes me think of my own mom. Wonder what she's doing back home. I suppose you're used to this war – you've had the Canadians, the Free French, now it's us Americans. For us, it's all pretty new. For Grant and me it's the first New Year we've not been with our proper friends. Here he comes. Well, it's been nice talking with you. Enjoy your evening. I'm glad you've not got to hurry home like Cinderella before the fun's over. Hi, Grant. I've just been getting acquainted with the little girl's mother. Now, if you'll excuse me, I see Bobby's signalling me.'

The supper was lovely; the music just as gay; Grant as softly spoken, as friendly. So where had the magic gone? When they stood up to dance again he looked at her with the same appreciation as he had before. Yet now she didn't want to meet his gaze, she was frightened that what she'd see was courtesy, kindness that stemmed from the hospitality she'd given to him in his first days here. Like her mom . . . and another echo 'Poor old Mum.'

'Carol kept me company,' she said as they quick-stepped. 'She tells me you and she have worked together for years? How good that you were able to arrange to stay together.'

'Sure, Carol's been with me since she finished her training. At my next move, we shall part company.'

'You'll be sorry. Perhaps not for long though, Grant. Soon, let's hope, you'll be picking up where you left off at home again.'

'Left off?' He laughed. 'I don't know that I'd put it quite like that.' The music came to an end but he kept his arm around her, waiting for the next dance. Around them partners were being changed. Across the floor she saw Meg, two young officers vying for her favours.

The band struck up again. The hokey-cokey.

'Shall we put our right leg out and shake it all about – or shall we let them get on with it and have another drink?'

247

It was tantamount to telling her that this was for the youngsters! Jane's chin went up.

'Let's dance. The hokey-cokey's fun.'

'Yes, ma'am,' he laughed. Before she'd talked to Carol, it would have been fun. Now, though, as they shook their arms and legs, twisted and turned, she felt he was humouring her.

'Hi!' Meg called as they came close. 'What a surprise!'

Jane tried to reach out to Tim, she tried to reach out towards John. She found neither. Here she was in this noisy throng, the room thick with cigarette smoke, an outsider to the revelry that grew ever rowdier. But she wasn't going to let it get the better of her. Her mouth twitched into a semblance of a smile as she thought of Mrs Sid. Over the years some of that battling spirit must have rubbed off on her.

'Auld Lang Syne' was sung. A Happy New Year was wished, over and over, to all and sundry, friend and stranger.

'I think I'll go home, Grant. Thank you for bringing me, it's been fun.'

'Good. I'm glad you've had enough.'

She felt the hot colour rush to her face, even to her neck. Had he been wanting her gone? Looking forward to joining in the fun with Carol and their friends?

'I'll get my coat. Don't you come out. It's no distance down the hill and I know the path well. The dark never bothers me, truly. You stay here and make the most of the rest of the party.'

He raised his brows.

'Not my idea of a good time. Too noisy. But I'm glad you've enjoyed it, Jane.'

Coming from the brilliant light of the Club, night enveloped them. With Grant's arm around her shoulders, they shuffled their first few steps. On down the hill, they quickly adjusted to the darkness but he didn't let go his hold on her.

248

'Are you going to ask me in? What about brewing up our first coffee of the year?'

'The fire will be out. Dead ashes aren't very inviting.'

'Then we'll keep our coats on. What is it, Jane? You seem on edge. If you're scared the neighbours will get the wrong idea, then just say so and I'll go.'

'As if I care a jot about the neighbours! Grant, you've got a lot of friends back there at the Club, you've given up all your evening to me. Go on back, make the most of what's left of welcoming in New Year, this special year.'

'Reckon I feel it's pretty special right here.'

Fumbling for the keyhole she managed to open the door. It was easier than answering him. Then, with the lights switched on, they were on familiar and safer ground. She went to the scullery to see to the coffee; he knelt in front of the dying embers trying to stab some life back into them.

'Change places,' she called to him. 'Something tells me you're not used to coal fires, stirring it from the top like that. You do the coffee, that's your forte.'

Soon small flames were lapping around the edge of the half burnt coals while from the kitchen came the smell of coffee.

'Tomorrow – or rather today – you've got Richard coming home. You won't want me about the place with him here.'

'Greta must be more or less better. You've been very good to her – to both of us, Grant. Taking me there this evening too. You'll probably laugh, but I don't think I've ever seen the year in at a party.'

'If you enjoyed it, then I'm glad. But those sort of evenings aren't really my taste. There's something forced about a party that's geared to build up to a climax like that.' He was standing in front of the fire, his coffee cup on the mantelpiece. She was sitting back on her heels on the hearthrug.

'Starting on a new year is a bit like standing on a bridge,' she mused, 'being able to see both ways. Not that we really can see – only backwards. But we look forward too, we know the shape we mean to make of what's ahead of us. It's scarey, isn't it? We know what we hope, yet even to imagine it is like tempting fate. I always feel we should tap on wood – yet I'm frightened to admit to superstition. It's pagan.'

'And what do you hope for this brave new year, Jane?'

'The same as all of us. I hope it will see the end of the war, I hope it will see Richard home – well, it won't because he'll still be at sea, but I hope the U-boats will have finished chasing him – I hope it'll see Hartley home. And you, Grant, you and all your friends – I hope all that for you too, that you'll be safe and back where you want to be.'

She hardly realized that he held his hands out to her, or that she stood up. Somehow she was facing him.

'Right now, Jane, this is where I want to be.'

What am I doing? she cried silently. Three weeks ago I didn't know him. This is crazy. Falling in love belonged to youth, isn't that what John had said, what she'd believed? So why was her heart hammering, her pulses racing, why did she want to sing for joy? And when his mouth closed over hers, why was her mind swept clean of everything except that she too was where she wanted to be?

'Tell me again what you hope for me,' he whispered.

'That I'll be gone from you? I don't want to believe it.'

'I don't even want to look that far.'

This time he kissed her tenderly, rubbing his chin against her tousled hair.

'I'm going, Jane, while I've still got the willpower. At twenty I might have expected to fall in love at the sight of a pretty girl. I'm forty-four! What have you done to me? It's fourteen days since we came face to face, kneeling there on the sidewalk with Greta. Every hour since, you've been in my mind. Say something, Jane.'

'Two weeks. It's nothing.'

'Two minutes – two weeks – how long does it take?'

Still he held her. She moved her mouth against his chin.

'And you? Tell me the truth,' he whispered.

'I feel like a seventeen-year-old falling in love for the first time. That's what frightens me. Perhaps the truth is that I'm looking for romantic dalliance. That's what Tim used to call it. Is that what's the matter with me?' This time she did pull away from him, just far enough to look at him with a serious, puzzled expression. 'I'm forty years old. Some people say that's the dangerous age. A woman is looking for a last fling.'

'Jane, I love you,' he laughed. 'You're a gem.' He kissed her lightly on the top of her head and then picked up his hat. 'If I stay here, I shan't be responsible for my actions. Especially with the temptation of that romantic dalliance.' His voice teased, but his eyes were serious.

He saw the way she stood straight. She seemed to square her shoulders, look at him very directly.

'Don't run away.' She couldn't bear him to leave her.

There wasn't a sound. His Adam's apple seemed to stick in his throat.

'Are you saying . . . ?'

She nodded. She'd never thought to feel like this. It was more than the frustration of her lonely years. John had offered her an escape from that. Now she knew what it was that had held her back.

Grant put his hands on her shoulders and drew her nearer. 'We can't sleep together, however much we might want to. We both know we can't. I meant what I said just now. I do love you, Jane. That's why I must go. It's too big a risk.'

'You're a doctor, you understand better than I do. I'm due tomorrow and I'm regular. Doesn't that make it safe?' Leaning against him she could feel the beating of his heart. In the room above was her bed. She imagined his head on the pillow next to hers. If he said he was going, she couldn't bear it. But he didn't.

Sleep was a million miles away as she lay gazing into the

251

darkness. Two weeks ago he'd been a stranger; now he was her lover, lying at her side, his deep breathing telling its own story. She had no regrets. What they'd done had been right. In her mind, the word she used was 'beautiful'. Gently she moved her hands down her body, the action recalling the years on her own, then carrying her thoughts to Tim. A smile played around her mouth. She had found a new peace and only now realized that always, only half acknowledged, had been the fear that in giving herself to another man she would have been drawing away from Tim. But it wasn't true. Loving Grant, sharing her body with him, hadn't taken away anything from Tim, nor from the woman who'd been his – who would always be his. In his sleep Grant turned over. She put her arm across his body. No, what she'd done hadn't touched what she and Tim had shared. With her eyes closed she could see him smiling at her, at the woman she'd been, the happy, carefree woman who'd been his and who always would be.

She'd like to go to sleep so that in the morning she could wake and find Grant by her side. Yet she wanted to stay awake, not to waste a precious moment. Tonight she was aware of a contentment that she'd forgotten existed. A satisfied body? Yes, but more than that. A new year. 'Their year.' She wouldn't look beyond.

Even the memory of that good-looking nursing officer held no power to dent her euphoria. Born again. Once more Jane remembered the words as she drifted towards sleep.

'Hartley! I'm home.' He woke to the sound of Liz's call as she bounded up the stairs and rammed her key into the door of the flat. 'I just missed the bus. I ran all the way. Rita said she'd left you here.'

By now he was on his feet. For the last four hours he'd been dead to everything, stretched out on the sofa.

'Happy New Year, Liz.'

She nodded. 'And you. Happy New Year sounds so –

so trite – like saying "How are you?" to someone, never expecting to be told.'

'Not the way I mean it, it doesn't. Not to you, not for us.'

They moved to each other, standing locked in an easy embrace.

'No, I know. Nor me. I just want you to stay safe, always to come back to me . . .'

'I thought of you at midnight. I thought of you all night.'

She'd plunged into a busy day's work, trying to run away from her jumbled memories. Now there was nowhere to run.

'Richard went this morning,' she told him.

'Did you make him understand, Liz? Poor old Richard! I thought he'd realized how we felt for ages. I didn't expect it to hit him like that. But it'll work out, darling. I've thought a lot about it, tried to see things from his angle. He was probably hurt that we'd not told him sooner. He was all right in the end?'

'He wanted me to promise I'd not get married while he was away.'

'Well, it would be much better if he were here. You'd want him to be the one to give you away. Let's hope he gets leave again before long. We'll go down and talk to Aunt Jane as soon as we can get time off together.'

She didn't look at him. She kept her arms around him, her head buried against his shoulder.

'Hartley – don't let's go out. Rita's on duty. I want to be just with you. Please.' As if she needed to beg him! Hours on their own here were precious. They both knew where they would lead. His hold on her tightened.

Last night haunted her. No matter how she'd tried to put it out of her mind, always it was there. She still seemed to hear the sound of Richard crying. It made her flesh tingle to think of it. Her memory had as many holes as a colander. How was it that one moment he'd been sitting on the edge of her bed, the next he'd been lying by her side? She must have drawn him in. Of course she had. 'Is it so awful?' Yes, clearly she remembered saying that. Yet even as she'd asked him she'd know in her heart that his tears had nothing to do with the war. Only one person could help Richard . . . so, of course, she must have pulled him to her side. Thus far she could let her mind explore. It was after that had come what she was frightened to think about; and yet she could think about nothing else. His hands like a vice on her shoulders. He was so strong – so heavy. Purposely he'd forced his full weight on her. She'd thrashed from side to side, she remembered digging her teeth into his shoulder, she'd crossed her ankles. Yes, that much was clear. His tears – or by now had they been hers? – as he'd forced her knees apart. 'Damn him, you're mine. You don't need him.' He'd not sounded sane. It was as if he'd been driven by a devil. Some of it was vivid in her mind; some of it she couldn't be sure of. All her struggling had only made him more and more powerful with every movement until he'd reached his moment of climax and whatever else was lost to her, she must always remember how at that second as his strength had ebbed she'd managed to throw him off her at the same time tumbling out of the bed. There'd been heartbreak in the sound of his crying, but all she'd wanted had been to get away.

'Oh, God, what have I done?' he'd sobbed.

Now, her head against Hartley's shoulder, the whole scene flashed before her; all that she was sure of and all that was heightened by fear and imagination. Even after a hot bath she'd felt soiled. She still did.

'I thought of you all night,' Hartley had just said.

She longed to be purged of what haunted her. Hartley loved her utterly, the fun-loving companion he'd grown up with and the sensuous woman known to no one but him. This evening she was insatiable. But only she knew what it was that was driving her.

It must have been the thought of going back to sea that

made Richard so glum, or so Jane supposed. And the thought made his going even harder for her than it would have been.

'Do you ever wish we'd kept the farm, Richard? I know we'd have had to evacuate now the same as everyone else – but you could have worked somewhere on the land until we are let back in. It's always worried me. You seemed so happy on the farm with Tim.'

He looked at her blankly, as if he hadn't followed the reasoning of what she'd said.

'Do you?'

'Don't know why you keep on about the farm. I've told you times enough.'

They were in the stores, he was spending his last day there. Greta had gone off in the lorry with Ted Hiles to deliver a plough.

'I know you have. But you seemed quiet. I was worried, thought it might be that you wished you'd never gone to sea.'

'What do you want me to do? Keep yakking all the time? We're not at some old women's tea party.'

'No, we're certainly not.' And this time she spoke briskly, her tone calling him to order. Folding her arms she stood in front of him, pulled to her full height. 'And if you were, I hope you'd produce some better manners than you seem to think you need for me.'

'I didn't mean to be rotten to you, Mum.'

'Rotten to me, indeed. What you sounded was ill-mannered, and I don't like it.' It was just as she might have spoken to him ten years ago. Her expression softened. 'If it's nothing to do with going back to sea, then it must be something else bugging you. Can't you share it?'

'Did you know Liz and Hartley want to get hitched? I think it's bloody daft. I told him so.'

'He's always loved Liz, you know he has.'

'He's never known anyone else – and neither's she. I told them!'

'I bet they loved that!' She laughed, then to take the sting out, she hugged him.

'Have you got to call and say goodbye to your grandmother? If you'd like to deliver some ploughshares for me to Millbrook Farm, you can take the car and come back for me later. If we wait until I finish here it makes us late. Anyway, she'd rather have you to herself.'

'Yes, okay. Any message for her?'

'Tell her I phoned to wish her a Happy New Year but she wasn't in. Tell her we're managing to keep going in our new surroundings.'

'Pity you and Gran don't get on better. She likes having Meg there – and Meg seems fond of her. Have you heard what she and Ben call her? "Grandem" – mixture of Grandmother and Emily. When they say it you can see she's tickled pink. Poor old Gran! She really just needs to feel people are fond of her. The trouble is you've always been a bit in awe of her, I suppose, Gran having come from what she calls a "better stable".'

'I may not be a thoroughbred, but I'm the only foreman she's got. I can't be working here and paying social visits too. But you're right, of course. Isn't it what we all want – affection?' There was a cheerfulness in her voice that seemed to him not to fit the words. 'Here are the car keys. Catch! Come back in good time. We want to be able to make the most of your last evening.'

A minute later she heard him drive away.

'Glad you're in here.' It was Joshua, his large frame between her and daylight. 'What I want is a bracket. It's sheared off the riddle – reckon you can find me one? Can't quite read the number. Clogged up with mud, that's the trouble.' He started to pick at the embossed number, adding to the accumulation of dirt already behind his thumbnail. 'Here, Mrs Gower – Jane. Quite time we were Jane and Joshua, friends like we are – you see if your eyes are sharper than mine. You'll need to hold it here in the light.'

Calling him nothing, and in her most businesslike

manner, she took the old bracket and carried it to the daylight.

'S.213, that's clear enough. I'll see if we have it.'

'There's a good lass.' And the large, fat-fingered hand landed on her bottom as she sidled round him. From the way she ignored him he knew she was annoyed. He lolled against the door jamb watching as she propped the ladder against the fitment where the spares were housed. The cubbyhole she was making for wasn't very high, she didn't realize that he'd come to hold the ladder steady, standing on the bottom rung. With the old bracket tucked into the bib of her dungarees and the new one in her hand she started down. Joshua stood quite still, his thick lips parted as, without looking backwards, she hurried down.

Startled, she cried out involuntarily as she felt someone behind her. She lost her balance, he lost his, the ladder started to slide. There was no stopping it, no stopping themselves either, as they came to rest in a heap on the stone floor.

'What a good job I was there! Might have broken your neck.'

'How was I to know you were behind me! Here's your bracket.'

''course I was behind you. Steadying the ladder. Are you fit to stand up?' He pulled her to her feet then, taking her unawares. Both his great paws got busy brushing her down.

'I can manage.'

'Now then, Jane, you've nothing to fear from me. A fall like that could shake a lady up. Just you come across to the house and let's see you have a good sweet drink of tea.'

'I know you mean to be kind.' (What a liar I am. Kind! He's a lecherous old humbug. But I daren't fall out with him. Better to play cat and mouse than that.) 'But I didn't hurt myself, and I really do have things to do. Any minute Richard will be back.' She lied there too.

'Not yet he won't. Gone to see his gran. He told me so himself. No one'll be coming out here buying any bits, not this time o' day. And, anyway, from my kitchen you can see. Just you and me.' He licked his thick lips. 'Here on my own, I've often thought of a lady like you keeping me company. Pretty woman, you are.'

Jane wasn't easily frightened, but there was something about this big man, the way he stood just in front of her, stooping towards her, the way he panted. Probably because the fall had shaken him, that's all it was. None of the men were expected back for at least half an hour. She knew very well what was on Joshua's mind. Well, he'd come to the wrong woman! But what if he decided otherwise? No one would hear her, no matter how hard she shouted.

'Anyone home?'

They'd been standing facing each other like two statues, each waiting for the other one's next move. Now they sprang to life, Joshua stooping to pick up the ladder and Jane leaning back against the fitment of cubbyholes.

'Grant!'

'Are you having trouble?' He might have meant just the fallen ladder but she didn't think so.

'Just trying to help her up. She had a nasty fall, the ladder slipped. I was trying to persuade her that she ought to take a sweet drink.'

'Sure you were. I heard you.' There was no smile in Grant's voice. Of the two men Joshua was taller, bigger built. But there was no doubt who was on top of the situation.

'Are you a customer? Come on an errand for someone?'

'No,' Jane answered for Grant, 'he's a friend of mine.'

The farmer looked from one to the other, his wet lips apart.

'Damn furriners!' was what it sounded like. Then he'd gone, the flop-flop of his muddy wellingtons fading as he crossed the yard.

'I called at the house to say goodbye to Richard. No one was in so we drove on over here.'

'We? You mean Carol's with you?'

He looked puzzled.

'Buzz. Buzz Wilkie. He was driving the day Greta got hurt. He's waiting in the jeep down the lane. I came to find out whether this was the place. Are all your customers like that?'

'No. He's unique, thank God. Anyway, he's not a customer. It's his farm I'm on – without a written contract, as he's quick to tell me.'

'You shouldn't be out here with no one except a man like that.' He studied her carefully. 'So this is my working Jane.'

'Well, how do you expect me to dress, clambering around in here? It may not be elegant, but it's functional.'

'From where I stand it looks great. Tell you something – if I hadn't already fallen for a honey gold lady, I might be tempted to make a pass at you!'

'Try me. We needn't tell your lady friend.'

For answer he drew her into his arms.

By the next morning Richard had gone. For a fortnight Jane had been free of that constant fear of where he was, whether he was battling with storms – actually to let thoughts of torpedoes or U-boats form in her mind was like tempting fate. So she said storms.

She discovered that worrying and caring about him – and about Hartley – was in-built in her, something that went on whatever else happened. And what had happened was Grant and a new fullness to her life. The joy in her seemed to overspill on to those around her; Mufti's tail thumped the floor with that extra excitement at the sight of her, and if Greta had had a tail so would hers have too.

Moving into town, of course, she'd had to change schools. It was on her eleventh birthday that Jane talked to her about her future.

'You know Liz went away to school, Greta? Would you like to go where she did? A good education, that's what you used to say you wanted. You'd get it there.'

'Boarding school? Me go off and leave you all by yourself? Oh, I wouldn't want to do that, Aunt Jane. But I mean to get a good education, like I said. I've never forgotten. I sort of made a promise – to myself and in a way to Dad too.' She was watching Jane to see if she remembered.

'I know. The day you got put on to long division. A long time ago, Greta. You mustn't worry about me. I just want what's best for you.'

'There's the Grammar School, Aunt Jane. I'd get a good education at a grammar school and I could live at home. Even when we go home again, I could cycle if I started early. And from here it's easy as pie.'

'I'll find out about it, if that's honestly what you want.'
But Greta had other ideas.

'Seems to me, Aunt Jane, better than you just buying a place for me there, paying fees each term, I could try and get a scholarship. It's not that I'm not grateful that you want to send me there, it's that I want to get on because I've worked hard. Made up my mind ages ago that I'm not going to be beaten. Getting a free place seems a part of that. Does to me anyway. Is that all right, Aunt Jane. You can see what I mean?'

Jane nodded. She reached out and touched Greta's short, straight hair. She couldn't help it.

'There's the afternoon post come through the door!' Greta ran to pick it up off the mat. What eleven-year-old wouldn't on her birthday! 'There are two, Aunt Jane. Both from Liz. One for you and the other for me.' Hers was a card with a ten shilling note inside it.

Jane's letter was quite short. Liz and Hartley both had some leave. They had something very important to talk about. They would be coming the following Tuesday. That 'something important' was hardly a mystery – they must be wanting to get engaged. She smiled to herself as she imagined them arriving, so sure that no one had any inkling of their secret. That evening she told Grant they were coming, made him promise to be with them for supper on Tuesday evening. The born again woman saw it all in her mind's eye: two happy couples, and Greta who was dear to all of them. Had she not been living in a romantic wonderland of her own, she might have realized that nothing ever works out as one imagines.

It was late on Monday night. Greta was asleep, Grant had gone back to the base, Jane was already upstairs getting ready for bed. Was that the door? Turning out her light she pulled back the curtains and opened the window to lean out.

'Who is it?' she stage-whispered into the night.

'Mum. It's me, Liz.'

And already she could see clearly enough to know that Liz was on her own. No. Please, please, no! Her legs had no more substance than cotton wool as she went down the stairs.

CHAPTER THIRTEEN

Feeling her way in the dark, Jane hurried down to open the door.

'What's happened? Where's Hartley?' Her voice was hardly more than a whisper. Was it because she was afraid of what she would hear, or had it something to do with the silence of the night-time street?

'I managed to switch my shift. I came off duty at midday. His leave doesn't start until tomorrow.'

In a flood of relief Jane led the way in, closing the door and switching on the lights.

'Oh, Liz, what a way to welcome you!' She hugged her as she spoke. 'It was just that I was frightened something was wrong – I mean, I was frightened he'd not managed to get his leave.'

Liz must have known that wasn't what she'd meant. But all she answered was: 'He may only get seventy-two hours.'

Into Jane's memory came a picture of the last time Liz had come. Just like tonight, it had been unexpected. But how different. If the trouble wasn't Hartley, then what was it? Had there been air raids? Perhaps broken nights had left their mark?

'Let's dig some life into the fire. Nice to have you to myself for a while anyway. You look tired, Liz. Was the journey awful?'

She shrugged. 'Pretty beastly. Packed like cattle, I sat on my case in the corridor. I hate trains in the dark. There's not a breath of air with the blinds all down, and those nasty blue lights make everyone look as if they've just risen from the dead! All shrouded in smoke from cigarettes.'

So that's all the matter was. In her relief Jane

262

laughed, giving her a bear-like hug.

'Poor Liz. If you'd waited for Hartley you could have come in daylight and had him for company. But I'm glad you didn't. Is he coping? Each day we read of the raids . . . there . . . here . . . But not tonight. We won't talk about that tonight.'

'Mum,' Liz sat very straight on the edge of one of the fireside chairs, staring at the opposite wall, anywhere but at Jane, 'we'd planned to come as soon as we could. I expect you've guessed what Hartley wants to say to you?'

'I bet a pound to a penny that I have!' she laughed. 'Liz?' Coming home to get engaged to the person she loved . . . it didn't match up with her evasive manner. 'It's what you want, isn't it? I never doubted . . .'

'That American you had here when I came down at Christmas. The doctor. Does he still come?'

'Yes.' Was this what was bothering her? Did she resent it that her mother might be caring for another man? The born again Jane's eyes lighted into a smile this time. 'Yes, he comes. Liz, I want you to know him, to like him.'

'The thing is – Mum, you're not going to like this – I'm pregnant.' Now she *did* look Jane straight in the eyes. 'Will he help me? Can you persuade him? I daren't ask anyone at the hospital. If I told someone, I couldn't be sure Hartley wouldn't get to hear. Please, Mum. You understand. You're the only one I can ask. And I'm not going to have it!' As she'd talked, she'd become more and more aggressive, ready to argue.

'I felt as if the stuffing had been knocked out of me.' How often Jane had heard it said. And it was true. Shock was a physical thing, affecting arms, legs, stomach. In those seconds as she looked at Liz's pale face, the shadows of tiredness under her eyes, so much else flashed through her memory. The happy, confident little girl . . . the first signs of adolescence . . . three youngsters home from school . . . now this.

'But of course Hartley has to know! How late are you?'

'Mum, you've got to help me. I haven't had a period

since the beginning of December. Hartley? No – I just said. He mustn't know. Often he can't get to Oxford for days at a time. He won't have given it a thought.'

'You can't do that to him. You probably can't do it at all. Liz, babies don't shift that easily.'

'But the American – Grant – for you, if you asked him? Mum, I won't have it. I'll do anything.' She was crying, loud gulping sobs. Then, as she wiped the back of her hands across her face, fear seemed to be replaced by something else. Cunning? 'It's such a slur. Not just on me, on all of us. Grandma would be ashamed – she'd see it as a reflection on Dad.'

'More likely on me! Don't you worry about your grandmother.'

'But for Dad's sake. He was so respected – loved. People delight in scandal.'

'Liz, love, it may not be the way you and Hartley had planned to start. But if you love each other – damn the scandalmongers! While they're talking about us, they'll be giving someone else a break. If Tim could, he'd tell you the same, I know he would.'

'So you're not going to help? I can't believe it. These last days, waiting for my leave, I was so sure. Get home and tell Mum, she'll make things right. Always we've come to you when things go wrong . . . Mum'll help. I even believed it was fate that you'd met up with this doctor.'

'I think perhaps it was. But we'll talk about him another time. For tonight, try and feel better about it. Coming home and telling me is one hurdle over. When Hartley comes tomorrow, talk to him, let him believe he's the first you've told. We'll forget tonight, take it from there tomorrow. And you'll feel different about it, once the fear has gone. Another year and you'll have wiped that part of it right out. Babies bring so much love.'

'Stop it!' Liz rammed her fists against her ears. 'I'm not listening. Didn't you understand? I *won't* have it. I'll get rid of it somehow. I swear – on my heart – on Dad's memory –'

'No, Liz, don't talk like that.' She knelt down, taking Liz's hands from her ears and holding them. 'I'll speak to Grant. Perhaps he can give me something you can take. But I can't promise. It's against all the ethics.'

'He'd do it for you, Mum. Wouldn't he?' It hurt Jane to look at her. Never had she seen such slyness in Liz's eyes. 'If he thought it was you who needed it, he'd have to help you, wouldn't he?'

Her words hung between them, the innuendo both asking a question and assuming the answer; and in doing so, bracketing Jane's newfound love with the liaisons of the good time girls of the town.

'If it were me, I wouldn't ask for anything. Neither would he want me to.' Blue eyes met blue.

Liz turned away and Jane's moment of anger passed.

'Oh, Mum, I'm in such a mess . . . such a mess. Don't tell Hartley . . . he'll say he wants me to have it. I won't. I can't!'

The tiny house was bursting at the seams. After one night on the sofa, Liz was taking Greta's bedroom, she moving in with Jane and, in the little dining room, a camp bed had been put up for Hartley.

By daylight Liz looked more like her normal self. It might have cost her an effort to chatter at breakfast with Greta, but she managed it. It was as if last night's scene hadn't happened.

'After school, I'm not coming straight home today. Phyllis Maynard – that's a new friend, she lives near the top of the hill and she's in my form at school – she's asked me back to tea. We shall do our prep together.' Streets to roller skate on had been one advantage to moving to town; living near to school friends was another.

'Make sure you've got your pocket torch for coming home, Greta, and leave Phyllis's at eight o'clock, won't you?'

'Right you are, Aunt Jane.' With a cheeky wink she burst into song:

> 'There was a lover and his lass,
> With a hey and a ho and a hey nonny no . . .'

'Good of me to give you a clear field, Liz.' Then, still grinning, she picked up her satchel.

Jane gave Liz a clear field too. Although she didn't make any reference to what they'd talked about last night, she hoped that the seed had been sown. She'd go in to the stores later in the morning, be out when Hartley actually arrived. She looked forward every bit as much to his coming as she would to the twins', her every inclination was to be here waiting for him. But if she stayed, Liz would keep her secret hidden. Leave them together, that was the right thing to do. If Liz decided to brave it out, to tell Hartley and let the scandalmongers have their moment of fun, then she'd be sure to do it straight away. If, on the other hand, she said nothing, then Jane would look ahead to the next hurdle. Ought she to tell him herself? Ought she to ask Grant if there was anything he could give her? She wouldn't think about it. Not yet. She'd not look as far as that hurdle unless she had to.

The barn at Chugford Farm was cold. With the doors open there was nowhere to get away from the easterly wind. Dungarees, two sweaters, a duffel coat, wellington boots, mittens, and still Jane's fingers and toes ached with cold. When the telephone, newly attached to the wall, rang, it was as much as she could do to lift the receiver in her stiff hand.

'Herbert Gower and Son.'

'I want to speak to Mrs Gower. I'm speaking for Seatrack Shipping Company.'

'Something's happened! Yes, this is Mrs Gower. What's happened?'

'Your son gave me your telephone number –'

'Yes? Yes?'

'He's quite all right. He'll tell you himself about the incident.' Whoever the messenger was, he had a small precise voice, his sentences were short. 'He asked me to speak to you. He's on his way home. He'll be sent for in due course.'

'He's not been hurt?'

'Rest assured. A wetting. Not nice in February. A night in hospital and this morning he was released. Well on his way by now. He didn't want me to send a telegram. Nasty things, telegrams.'

Richard . . . incident . . . a wetting. Richard coming home! Just like he had at Christmas, arriving at the same time as Liz. She couldn't wipe the grin from her face as she put the receiver back on the stand. Whatever Liz's problems were, if Richard was there he would sort things out for her. They'd have no secrets from each other. She felt that a weight had been lifted. Richard would persuade her to tell Hartley, they'd talk about it together, the three of them.

'Hi. You there, Jane?'

'Grant! What are you doing here on a cold Tuesday morning? Don't you chaps ever have any work to do?' But she laughed as she said it, the grin seemed to have taken up permanent residence.

'Yep. It's about that I've come to talk to you. Jane, I've got to go to London. My first visit to your big city. I'll be staying at an American Club near Leicester Square. Couple of meetings, a visit to another base . . . altogether I reckon I can't get back here for ten days or so. I'll be working out of London – staying at the Club and travelling out each day.'

'You mean, they've just dropped this on you? Can they do that?'

'Oh, boy, can they just! I'm in the Army, remember? I like to keep a low profile, let them forget about me. As I see it, my job's to pick up the pieces after they make the mess.'

'Haven't they medics up there already?'

'I guess they've got wind that I'm kicking my heels here with no pieces to pick up. That's the telephone number – not that you've got a telephone but I like to know you can get me if you need to. I'll be there each night. I'll call you here during the day.'

It would be ten days before he came back. For Liz, ten days was a long time. This was her chance. Alone here, she must tell him. She'd explain how, once Hartley knew, she was sure Liz would see the whole thing differently. If Grant gave her some sort of medicine, she probably would never even have to use it. In a minute she'd think of the best way of putting it to him. But it was Richard who was at the front of her mind. So she told him about her phone call.

'So that explains why you looked as though a fortune had just dropped at your feet when I came in! And I thought it was the sight of me.'

So once again Liz and her problems were shelved. Jane left him in no doubt that, compared with him, any fortune would come a poor second.

'And it's today the others come too. You'd think Uncle Sam fixed it purposely, sending me out of the way.'

'Liz has already arrived. Remember at Christmas, Grant,' climbing backwards up the ladder she settled into her favourite perch, 'how she hid in the scullery? Richard didn't know. He doesn't know she's there now either – and I shan't tell her he's coming.' She chuckled.

'Wish I could be there to see it.'

'I wish it too. When the bell rings, I'll make sure she goes to the door. I won't tell any of them he's on his way.' Such pictures she had in her mind! And although she didn't actually work out how it could happen, she was sure that once they all got together, looked at the 'problem' – if problem it was – Liz would learn to accept it. Of Hartley's reaction she had no doubt at all. And somewhere, muddled in with this feeling that Richard coming home was the answer to it all, was something else. Spiritually the twins were almost one. Why, last night when Liz had been at rock bottom, hadn't it been more than coincidence that at that very same time Richard must have been struggling to survive in the February-cold sea?

'Remember me? I'm the guy who's driven out here to talk with you!'

'Sorry. I was miles away. Well, not miles, I was back home. Grant, I don't know how to start saying this so I'll dive right in. Liz is pregnant. There, I've said it! Hartley doesn't even know. She's adamant she wants to get rid of it, not tell him. She loves him right enough – and as for him, it's always frightened me how his world has revolved round Liz. She wants a clean start, no baby on the way, but to get married quickly. She cried so, it was awful. Liz never cries but last night – oh, Grant, it tore me to bits to hear her.'

'I don't honestly see any problem. They want to be married. They're a healthy young couple. They're not the only ones, especially in wartime, that this happens to. To my mind, the sad couples are those who want children and can't have them.'

Jane was getting nowhere.

'It's a bad start. Liz loves nursing. His future – well, he's flying –'

'I think, Jane honey, you're worrying more than you should. And if, as you say, the future is uncertain, don't you think her grief would be all the greater if she'd lost his child?'

'It's not a fair start, though. To know people are whispering, counting how long they've been married. And her grandmother – she'll look on it as a dreadful disgrace. Grant, can't you see what I'm asking you? You're a doctor. If you care about me, then surely you'll give me something? I won't tell her where I got it from. I won't drop you into trouble. But you must know of something. Please, for me.'

Grant put two cigarettes in his mouth, lit them both,

then passed one to her. She waited, it seemed for ages before he spoke.

'To my way of thinking, it's a pretty fair start. For all the reasons I said just now. If I could give you some magic potion, in Liz and Hartley's circumstances I wouldn't do it. Good marriages take the rough and the smooth in one go. That's what makes them strong. You should know that, you had a good marriage. And another thing – you say the future is uncertain. It is, everyone's is, and not just because of the war. Supposing she aborted this child and couldn't have any more for one reason or another? Supposing in time he came to hear of it? Think about it, Jane honey. You'll ride the gossip. I'd have thought people had more to worry about these days.' He looked at her curiously. She knew she'd disappointed him by acting in a way he hadn't expected; she'd let him down and herself too.

A few minutes later he left. On the surface nothing had changed but she was frightened to dig for fear of what she'd find.

Keeping some semblance of order amongst the stock took most of her time at the stores. Of course there were customers, but most of them preferred not to waste their petrol on a journey. A telephone call: 'Can you order a . . . for me, have it delivered direct', or 'When you've got a chap this way put . . . in the van for me, will you.' So it was today. A couple of metal pieces, neither of them easy to pack, had to be put ready for her to post on the way home; a bundle of electric fencing stowed in the car so that from the post office she could go on to the carrier; various other orders labelled and left ready to be loaded on board the van or lorry for the first journey in the appropriate area. Apart from wanting to get home in time for Richard's arrival, she had no intention of being here by herself as daylight faded. Joshua had drooled after her from a distance since the day Grant had walked in on them; he'd probably seen him here this morning too. She hoped he had. That might frighten him off.

Just after four o'clock she closed the first of the big doors and bolted it to the ground – and at that very moment the station lorry turned into the yard, with a delivery from the railway. Two dozen coils of barbed wire – something she always found particularly heavy because they were so difficult to handle. By the time the lorry went and the doors were locked, it was after half-past four.

Back in town, her errands done, she went straight to Ashcombe's Garage in St Agnes Road to leave the car. It all took time but if she parked outside they'd know she was home. This way they wouldn't notice her coming. If she hadn't been there to see the excitement of Richard's arrival, at least she'd be able to walk in on them, catch a glimpse of them without their knowing it. It wasn't that they hid things from her, it was like a game she played for her own pleasure.

Quietly she turned the key in the lock and opened the front door. But there was no need to creep! Come in as noisily as she liked and they'd not have heard her. Rooted to the spot, she listened. Silently she slumped to sit at the foot of the stairs.

It started before Jane reached home. Probably about the same time as she was queuing up with the parcels in the sub-post office, Richard's knock came on the door. It was Hartley who answered it. In that first sight of each other they were drawn together by common experience that had nothing to do with Liz – and everything to do with a fear that she couldn't possibly understand.

'We copped it. Last night. Fishing boat hauled me out. Bloody cold.'

The way they reached out to each other, the firm grip of their hands – if anything could wipe out the memory of their last meeting it must be this. The feeling was intense, but it didn't last. As soon as Richard saw Liz was here too he knew why. They'd come to celebrate their engagement. Hartley and Liz, always it would be Hartley and Liz . . .

'So, what does Mum think? Same as me, that you've neither of you looked around to know what you're talking about?'

Ignoring his remark, Hartley said: 'Never mind us. You're not hurt? How long have you got?'

'Until they send for me. After a ducking in the drink there's always leave anyway.' Civil enough words, but not matched by his unsmiling countenance. Even Mufti sensed all wasn't as it should be. He came to Richard's side, sitting on his hind legs and tapping him with his paw. 'Hello, old fellow. There's a good chap.' Glaring at Hartley was easy enough, speaking to Mufti less so. Richard found he wasn't quite the man he'd thought himself to be. Down on his knees he ruffled the little dog's fur, rubbed his face against him, anything to gain time while he got the upper hand again.

Hartley was speaking to Liz: 'Think of what I've been saying, Liz. Doesn't what happened to Richard prove me right? Supposing – of course it won't happen – but supposing I – ?'

'No, it won't happen. It's just asking for trouble even talking about it.'

'We none of us can be sure what's ahead – not you, not Richard, not me – not even Aunt Jane. There've been plenty of casualties on the ground. We can't afford to wait for tomorrow. Liz, let me get a special licence. I know you don't want to be married without Richard, but he's here now.'

'No! I can't, Hartley. Not now, not like that,' she panicked.

'Does it honestly matter if you don't wear white and have all the fripperies most women care about? You're not like that.' He seemed to have forgotten Richard. 'Liz, to know you were my wife . . . ' He spoke so quietly, yet her fingers were crushed in his grip. 'It's not the same, whatever we might try and think, it's not the same. I

272

want you, but I want a wedding, a marriage. I'd still be scared half out of my mind, yet there'd be something of you with me, I'd never feel isolated.'

'Not now. Not like this. Oh, shut up about it, can't you?'

Hartley took hold of her shoulders. 'How do you mean – "like this"?' She could almost feel the workings of his mind. With his back to Richard he whispered: 'If you mean what I think you mean – oh, Liz, why didn't you tell me? I've thought about it, wondered, but often we've not been together for days at a time. I supposed . . .' He drew her into his arms and she leant against him. For a minute she let herself put everything else out of her mind, believe that it was all as straightforward as this.

'What's she telling you? That she's expecting? Christ, Liz, you can't be!' It was just then that Jane stepped into the passageway, something in Richard's voice riveting her. 'Whose is it? Christ, Liz, what are we going to do?'

'Steady, Richard, just mind how you're talking to her. What the hell's got into you? Shout at me if you want to shout, but if Liz expects support from anyone, then it's you.'

'Liz, you've got to get rid of it. Yes, I'll support her. We got into this together, we'll get out of it together.'

'I don't understand –'

But Richard cut him short. Listening Jane felt sick. She was cold as ice, or thought she was, yet she could feel the sticky sweat above her lip.

'You don't. Of course you don't bloody understand! I'll tell you whose baby it is – it's mine. Now don't you see why she's got to get rid of it?'

'Liz, what's he saying? It's not true. Say something, Liz.'

'I don't know. No, it's ours. It *must* be. But I don't know. I can't remember . . .'

'Then I'll remind you.' Richard spoke more slowly now, hammering each word home. 'Perhaps it's old Mrs Sid's wine that's dulled your memory. I was sitting on the side of your bed – yes, you remember. *On* the bed, then *in* the bed. And who pulled me into it? Yes, you remember.'

'Stop it.' That must have been what Liz was trying to say, but she was choking on her tears. She sounded demented. 'I didn't want it – pushed – I don't know if – can't remember – fought – oh God, I wish I could be dead.'

'Don't say that!' Again it was Richard's voice.

Jane leant her head against the bannisters. Her world was falling apart. Richard and Liz . . . oh God, please, no! Make it not be happening.

'Get away from her. Keep your hands off her.' This time it was Hartley, his voice cold with hate.

'Leave me alone, both of you! I shan't have the baby, not this one, not any.' The wild crying had given way to a sound that was worse, hardly a sound at all in her weeping, no spirit, nothing but hopelessness. 'Now you know why I can't marry you, Hartley. It may be yours – ours – but it's never going to have any life. Don't know how to do it. But I will. Got to.'

Just as quietly as Jane had come in, so she went out again, shutting the door with her key so that no one would hear. For more than an hour she walked. With dusk giving way to darkness she sat alone on a bench in the park. No need to worry about the gates being locked, they'd been taken, the same as the railings had, to be melted down and turned into guns. Just like her life. Once it had been as sound as the iron railings; she'd thought it would last forever. She felt the hot sting of tears. She blinked, then kept her eyes tight shut. She mustn't cry. The children would notice. They mustn't know she'd heard. 'That's a good lady.'

Oh, Tim, why didn't we see? Our little people. So close. Understood each other – we knew that – grew up so close – we knew that too. But this!

Her mind held on to Tim as part of that yesterday, part of the time when the children had been young, when she'd been happy and secure. Now, today there was no way of sharing this with him. How cold it was! She pulled the hood of her duffel coat over her head, sinking into it. The church clock struck seven.

Pull yourself together, they'll wonder what in the world you're doing. You're no help to any of them skulking here. Think of an excuse for being late. Come on, buck your ideas up. See what sort of an actress you are.

At a quick pace she walked home, this time opening the door and calling out at the same time.

'Did you think I was lost? Has he come? Is Richard home? Has Hartley come?' Still smiling she went into the living room. 'Today of all days, when I wanted to be early.'

She hugged Richard. Her heart sent up a silent thank you that he was safe, and another silent and only half formed plea for understanding: Why? Where did we go wrong?

'Where are Liz and Hartley? Who got here first?'

'Hartley didn't come. His leave was cancelled. Liz has gone to lie down, she had a stomach ache or something.'

'I'm not surprised. Disappointment, I expect. I know how much this leave meant to her – to both of them. They're so right for each other.' She knew it would hurt, she wanted it to. Then she pictured him only twenty-four hours ago, perhaps less, waiting to be pulled out of the cold Atlantic. Holding him close, she buried her head against him. Was it her fault? Was it something she and Tim had done wrong? Other people had children who were close, twins who cared about each other, ordinary happy people.

Next morning at breakfast she surprised them all by announcing: 'This is a good opportunity for me to get away for a day or two. You'll see to things in the house, won't you, Liz? And, Richard, I'm sure you'll keep your eye on what's going on at Chugford Farm. If I go today I'll be home again by the weekend.'

'Away?' Richard looked at her as if she'd taken leave of her senses.

'Yes, to London. Grant has to be there for a week or two. I didn't think I'd be free, but why not? You're all quite capable of coping without me.'

'You mean, you're joining this American bloke? But, Mum – I mean, well, he's a nice enough guy, but – where are we supposed to tell people you are?'

'The same as I've told you three: London. People are hardly going to ask you.'

'I mean people like Grandma. We can't say you've gone off to have a few days with some Yank.'

'Oh, your grandmother. There are no "people like her", she's one on her own. Anyway, cheer up, Richard. Grant is staying at an American Club, I shall book in at a hotel. So you needn't let it upset your sensibilities.'

He gave her a curious look but said nothing; Liz looked at her plate, and Greta from one to the other, out of her depth yet unsure why she should be.

'Be funny here without you, Aunt Jane. Fancy you going to London! Are you sure it's safe? They've been having a lot of air raids. I wish you could be going somewhere else. But I'll take Mufti out while you're gone – and see to the chickens.'

'I know I can trust you.' For one sinking moment she wondered about the other two. 'I trust all of you.' Saying it she made a discovery about herself, one that didn't please her. Even more than disappointment, worry, sadness, she was filled with anger at them. Tim's children and hers! She felt cheated. She felt stained; ashamed for them and for herself too. 'I'll leave the car keys with you, Richard. Not for joy riding. You'll have to keep a log of the petrol you use.'

Upstairs, she was packing her case when Liz came into the bedroom.

'You will persuade him, Mum? Somehow you'll manage to make him say yes. Promise me.'

'It's up to him. I haven't much hope, I know his views.

276

Liz, I want the truth. Why isn't Hartley here? Richard said his leave was cancelled.'

'Hartley came. I told him I don't want to get married. Not to him. Not to anyone. He went off . . .'

Jane sat on the edge of the bed, her best honey gold frock half folded by her side.

'Liz, what have you done to him?' Dear, gentle Hartley.

'I'd have thought it would be me you'd be concerned for. It's me who's in this mess.'

Turning her back, Jane put the dress in her case then fastened the clasp.

Luckier than Liz had been, Jane got a seat in a compartment. The countryside flashed by, desolate in its winter bareness. But as the miles slipped by her spirits lifted. What sort of a mother was she that she could feel this way? Everything she'd thought solid in her life had been knocked from under her – and here she was looking ahead with shameless anticipation to being with Grant! Yesterday out of duty to Liz she'd asked for his help, and today she was honest enough to admit that had he agreed without question, just for the sake of helping them avoid gossip, she would have been disappointed in him. A smile played at the corners of her mouth. She wished the train would hurry.

Long before it puffed its way into Paddington the city stretched out to meet them, drab and battered. Reminding her of ungainly elephants, the barrage balloons laid a trap for low flying aircraft. She shivered. There was something eerie about the sight. How long ago it was that she'd last been in London. As a young child, when her father had been alive, London had been home to her. Now she was a stranger, as countrified as Mrs Sid! Again the smile threatened to take control. There was nothing of Mrs Sid in the Jane who pulled her case from the string-net luggage rack as, with a final puff, the engine shuddered to a halt.

CHAPTER FOURTEEN

Jane's memories of London were hazy. Her early childhood in Highgate had left an impression of activity, of people on the move, but not of a populace jostling and shoving as they did as they crowded off the train. Paddington station . . . it seemed to her as she stood with her case in her hand that everyone knew where they were going – and that they should have been there half an hour ago! – except her. Swept with the tide she made her way past the ticket barrier. Amidst all the noise one soldier sprawled full-length on a seat, his kitbag for a pillow, dead to the world. Under the clock various people waited, each one watching the seething mass with a look of expectancy. So many uniforms, every service, every allied nationality, everyone hurrying somewhere. A tea trolley; some customers waiting in an orderly queue, others elbowing their way to the front. Like a colony of ants the human race rushed on its way, and she with them. It did cross her mind as she stepped purposefully on to the escalator that other people might be looking at her, believ ng that she knew where she was going and how to get there. She knew neither. Grant had said something about Leicester Square. The Club must be near there. So she joined the queue, bought a ticket, and then schooled herself to work out her route from the charts on the underground wall.

Chugford Farm, Shalbury Hill . . . they belonged to a different world. Caught up in the excitement of her surroundings she pushed the reason for her journey to the back of her mind. The capital of war torn Britain. Down here in these tunnels people slept, mattresses still lying at the back of the platform a daytime reminder.

Proud of her success she came out into the late

afternoon daylight and, still moving with the throng, turned towards Leicester Square. A newsvendor was shouting something unintelligible, the placard by his side declaring 'RAF Bomb Berlin'. Her thoughts jumped to Hartley. Where had he gone for his seventy-two hour leave? At least he hadn't been in last night's raid. Another placard told her 'Another night of fire for London'. Soon it would be dark. There was no longer any hiding from the purpose of her mission. She'd never felt so utterly alone. Some way ahead of her she could see, taller than the rest, a policeman's helmet. She'd catch up with him. He'd tell her what she needed to know.

It can't be happening. Me, in Leicester Square. It's Wednesday, one of the days of their leave we'd looked forward to. Liz, Hartley . . . please help them, whatever they've done, all of them, please help them. Take care of Hartley, make it come right.

The policeman didn't fail her. He told her just how to walk to the American Club and even gave her the name of an hotel not far from it, adding his advice that she should check in soon. Her spirits bounced back up again. Chin up, best foot forward, she followed his direction.

The young American on the reception desk had perfected the art of grinning, speaking and chewing all at the same time.

'I'm looking for Major Holgate. He arrived here yesterday. Is he in the building, do you know?'

'Take yourself a seat, ma'am, while I find out for you.'

She wouldn't have been human if she hadn't peered into the looking glass, flicked her fingers through her curly hair, generally tried to make herself appear less travel-soiled. In a minute Grant would walk down the corridor. Already there was a glimmer of light on her horizon.

'Mrs Gower! Grant hadn't mentioned that you were in London.' A model of uniformed elegance, it was Carol.

'Nor me that you were,' Jane retaliated.

'He wasn't expecting you, of course. He's not here.

He's gone to – oh, but I mustn't divulge service secrets. "Careless talk costs lives",' she smiled, 'isn't that what your posters warn us?'

'I shall still be here tomorrow.'

'He'll be sorry to have to miss you. But he'll be away then too and, as far as I remember, he said Friday as well. Is there any message for when I see him?'

Jane shook her head. 'Just tell him I was here.'

'Sure, I'll do that for you.'

Just as Jane's spirits had bounced up, so now they slumped. It wasn't Carol's fault that he was away, yet she was sure the girl had enjoyed being able to tell her so. She turned from the reception area into a shuttered porch and from there into the London dusk. Coming from the bright light it seemed dark already out here, that might have been what made her blunder into a uniformed figure just coming in.

'Sorry,' she mumbled, not looking at him. And if she had, she wouldn't have recognized him. On New Year's Eve, except for Grant, one olive-clad figure had looked much the same as another to her. But her honey gold charm hadn't gone unnoticed.

'Say, I know you! You were with Grant for New Year. It was your little girl's skate I mended.'

Back bounced her spirits.

'And I never met you to thank you!'

'He didn't tell me you were to be in town.'

'Something cropped up. It was sudden. I thought, being so close, I'd surprise him. But he's not going to be here, Carol told me. Never mind, I just thought it would be fun – ' Jane was turning into quite a play actor.

'Sure. You're staying somewhere nearby? It's no fun on the tube trains at this time of evening, or so I understand.'

'Just round the corner.' She told him the name of the hotel. 'If my business gets done – and as there's no chance of surprising Grant with the sight of a country cousin come to town – then I'll probably go home tomorrow.'

'How's the roller skating going?' He changed the subject.

'Fine – thanks to you. Like so much more, skates are luxuries most children have to do without these days.'

Yes, she'd go home tomorrow. She pictured the way Greta's eyes would light up at the sight of her arriving a day early. Then she pictured Liz . . . Richard. There was nowhere to turn. But she must. 'Get home and tell Mum,' came the echo of Liz's frightened words, 'she'll make things right. We've always come to you . . . Mum'll help.' But how? Where could she turn?

Once in her hotel bedroom she closed the door and slumped on the bed. She was hungry, her stomach rumbled loudly with its message of how long it was since breakfast. After a wash she'd feel better. She'd get tidy and go down to dinner. The honey gold dress, carefully folded in her case, was a reminder if she'd needed one of what she'd imagined her evening would be. No use leaving it there to crease. She hung it up, then with determination but no touch of eagerness got ready for the evening before her. Her skirt and jumper would have to do, she wasn't going to waste the dress on her solitary meal; but neither was she going to be put down by the glamorous Carol, so she did better than her best with her face, then went down to the dining room.

Brown Windsor soup and a bread roll quietened the hunger pangs. She was waiting for her pigeon pie when she saw him come in.

'Vince told me. He was in the vestibule watching out for me when I got back,' he greeted her, pulling out a chair and sitting opposite her at the small table.

'Vince? The roller skate man? But you were away, they said.'

'Sure, I've been out of London all day. I told you I would be. And again tomorrow. Jane, what brings you?'

281

'I can't talk here. But I've got to talk, just to be able to tell someone – '

'Here comes your dinner.' Then to the waiter: 'Can you bring me the same? Just – whatever it is – I'll skip the soup.'

With her spirits leaping to new heights Jane decided against explaining 'whatever it was'. Better to eat and ask no questions. A taste for pigeon pie had grown out of four years of rationing!

'Talk, you say,' he prompted as they finally finished their meal. 'Nowhere at the Club, and I hardly think they'd encourage you to take a man to your bedroom here.' He laughed. 'Run and get your coat, Jane. Nothing for it but the cold night air.'

A seat to themselves on the grassy patch in the centre of Leicester Square, the only privacy that of being surrounded by strangers – mostly couples who were no more than voices in the dark, positioned by the glow of cigarette tips or the occasional raucous laugh. In the glare of the lights of the half empty dining room what few people there'd been had intruded on them. Here, their world began and ended on a park bench.

'You *must* tell someone, that's what you said. Is it something to do with what we talked of yesterday? Jane, you'll look back on it all, and you'll know I'm right – '

'Of course you were right. It's what I believed too. I just did it for Liz, that's why I asked you.'

'I love you, Jane.' To her it seemed to have no connection with what she was saying.

'Don't say it, Grant. Not 'til you hear. You won't want to love me then. It must be my fault. I ought to have seen, I ought to have suspected – oh God, what a dreadful word, suspect!'

'Darling, maybe they haven't been wise, but there's no sin in what they've done.'

'You don't know. I didn't know, not when I spoke to you. It was when I got home . . .' And so she told him, her words tumbling out in a hushed monotone. Almost word for word she re-lived what she'd heard: 'Richard shouted . . .', 'then it was Hartley, he said . . .', right to the end. 'I couldn't let them know I'd heard. I crept out and walked, went over and over it. Where had we gone wrong? I'd always known they'd loved each other. I'd been happy, proud, they were two halves of one whole. I'd encouraged them to stay close. Me! Now what's going to happen? "Babies bring love", that's what I said to her. But a brother and sister – some sort of a living monster!'

Silence. Please help me. Perhaps he's sickened, revolted. 'I love you, Jane,' he said . . .

He pulled her gently towards him. She felt his lips on her forehead.

'Grant?' she prompted. 'Tell me the truth. How do you feel now?'

'Right now, this second, I feel like I've been given a million dollars.'

'I don't understand.'

'Yesterday – heck, Jane, it was like finding I didn't really know you. To think you weren't prepared to ride out a storm of gossiping neighbours! It wasn't the Jane I knew. Then I got to thinking about it – I even tried to imagine how I'd have felt if Zara had grown up, if she'd come to me for help. I began to see it wasn't the way I'd thought, there in the barn.'

'But that was yesterday. Now – now that you know the whole sickening story?' But she didn't wait for an answer. Sitting up straight, turning towards him, she gripped his hands. Still her voice was quiet, yet it was full of suppressed emotion. 'I don't even know how I ought to feel. I'm angry, disgusted, ashamed, frightened, all those things, but at me as well as them. I can see them all the time, two little children, always turning to each other; then getting bigger, they had no secrets. As they grew up I knew they were as familiar as they'd always been. I was glad. I was proud. When she was falling in love with Hartley, I knew Richard felt put out by it. So why didn't I see? How could I have been so blind, so – so smug?'

For answer he carried her hand to his lips.

'I love you, Jane.'

All her pent up emotion found release. Holding her to him, he let her cry.

That night London slept quietly and the next morning, promptly at 8.30 when the nearest post office opened, Jane handed in a telegram addressed to Elizabeth Gower, 4 Shalbury Hill. 'Will telephone stores this afternoon. Be there. Mum.'

Then she went back to breakfast, checked out of the hotel and into another, taking a double room for one night only.

'My husband can't be here until quite late this evening. Can I sign for us now? Make sure it doesn't get overlooked.'

'By all means, madam.' And, as she wrote, the elderly man on the reception desk casually glanced at the name: Major and Mrs G. Holgate, Denby, Shelcoombe, Devon. Fact blended with fiction, but more than that it was a link between past and future. For this one night they would have just each other. No one would know where she was. In London, untraceable, belonging nowhere. A few hours that for both of them would be an oasis. Troubles would come again, fears for the boys' safety, the battle to come to terms with what she'd learnt, anxiety for Grant, the misery of helplessness as Liz tried to pick up the threads. But for this one night her mind had room for none of those things.

Even a traveller who isn't parched with thirst, weary with his journey, must take refreshment when he comes upon an oasis. Not to would be to abuse what nature provides. On that bench in the middle of Leicester Square, Jane had known the relief of tears that had been bottled up far longer than these last days. As Grant held her in his arms she'd loosened the hold she'd schooled herself to keep on her emotions. 'Mum', the one they brought their troubles to; 'Mrs Gower', who kept the

284

business going; 'Mrs G.', the cornerstone of Denby; 'Aunt Jane' who'd become mother and father to Greta – and to Hartley.

The oasis was no mirage. She would drink deeply, bathe in its cool waters. She was thinking on these lines as she put through her call to Liz.

'But, Mum, I'm on leave until next Wednesday. Why have I got to drag all the way to Oxford to collect whatever he's got for me? Can't you just bring it?'

'He wants to give it to you himself.' Stupid girl! Doesn't she realize that Mrs Chudzey at Mannerby Post Office will be listening to every word! 'Surprises have to be secret. If you ask me anything else I shall put the phone down. Just meet us outside your flat at seven o'clock tomorrow evening, we'll take it from there. And tell Richard that if our party goes on too late for a train home, we'll come on Saturday. Tell him he's to look after Greta. There go the pips. Time's up.'

And before Liz had time to say a word, the receiver was replaced.

This evening she knew she looked her best. And so she ought. Her bath salts had been highly perfumed even if under their coloured exterior they'd been no more than household soda. Out of character perhaps for Mrs G., or Mum either, but what more natural than that as she'd stepped like a nymph from the warm water Jane should have wiped the steam from the long mirror, stretched tall, standing on her toes, feet apart, arms spreadeagled? Her body had glistened wet in the glare of the electric light. The pose had fitted her mood, it had been part of a freedom that had come from being suspended between what was gone and what was still hidden in the future. Satisfied with the reflection, she and the woman in the looking glass had given each other a quick smile then she'd wrapped a hotel towel around her and gone into the bedroom. The luxury of having time to pamper herself was almost unknown. But then everything about the gift of this evening was touched with wonder.

Even being consciously slow, by eight o'clock she was dressed, her honey gold frock every bit as flattering as she remembered, her face made up with care, her hair brushed and shining. Another quarter of an hour and a tap came on her door. In an instant the bubble burst. It must be a message; he wasn't coming!

'Mrs Holgate?'

She never remembered crossing the room nor yet flinging open the door, but she must have. How else could she have been held in such a bear-like embrace. Joy flooded back.

A good start for their time out of place, the beginning of an evening that held them on a high peak. Their hotel had no cabaret so they went out to one that did. They danced through the end of that day and the beginning of the next. A lighted sign told them 'Alert Sounded', but the band was noisy, the room alive with movement. Lately it had been a rarity for there not to be a nightly alert in London so, like the rest of the crowd, they ignored it.

Later, stepping out into the night was like stepping into a different world. Noisy still, but now with the drone of bombers, the heavy barrage of guns. Buildings were silhouetted against a sky that brought to mind Dante's Inferno. The leafless trees around the square looked eerie, evil. This was the London they'd read about, they were living through it, they were part of the blitz. Or so they both supposed.

'Copping it out to the south-west.' The night porter put down his fountain pen and his evening paper and found Grant their key. 'Sounds like Hammersmith way to me. Unless we get a stray one, I'd say Jerry'll leave our neck of the woods alone tonight. 'night, sir, 'night, madam.' Then, back to his crossword puzzle.

So perhaps they hadn't been part of the blitz after all. Was this what happened to people? Did they become so conditioned that they could hang on to normality while hell broke loose around them? For Jane and Grant it couldn't be like that. Passions and emotions were heightened, fear made them ever more aware of the moment. It seemed to say to them, 'If you have nothing more, you'll have had this.'

As a time for sleep and refreshment the night was a non-starter. They heard the 'All-Clear', to be followed some time later by another 'Alert' but no aircraft and shortly after that another 'All-Clear'. About six o'clock in the morning they dressed and went out, walking in the cold morning air, neither of them sure of the roads except that they must be heading towards the river. And when they got there, standing on Westminster Bridge, they looked upstream to where the sky still glowed red.

'"Earth has not anything to show more fair . . ."' she whispered, not wanting to explain, not expecting him to understand.

'"This city doth, like a garment, wear the beauty of the morning".' He spoke softly, slowly. They both knew that what they saw would stay with them always.

Last night they'd thought themselves part of it all, only to find from a blitz-hardened local that they'd been wrong. This morning no one, nothing, could take from them the oneness they felt with the city.

'I didn't expect you to know Wordsworth,' she said as they finally turned away.

'Guess I went through the age of poetic idealism, somewhere way back in my youth. What would he think of it today, I wonder?'

'The city? Oh, still "touching in its majesty", Grant.' Then, somehow frightened of any more emotion, 'but hardly "bright and glittering in the smokeless air".' She shivered. 'Hammersmith? Is that where the porter said he thought it was? Ordinary people, ordinary houses, children with their pets . . .'

'I know, honey. Makes you realize how lucky you are to wake up in the morning and find it's just another day.'

But of course theirs wasn't. Not today.

'Grant, how will you do it? Liz, I mean?'

'Trust me, Jane. She'll be all right.' She had to accept that was all she'd be told. In silence they walked, the task at Oxford at the front of her mind, and his too she knew when he said: 'I wish it weren't me. She's your daughter. It's hardly a good basis for a relationship. I'll be a constant reminder to her of something better forgotten. As soon as it's done, I shall try and get a late train back to London. She'll probably need to stay where she is for the night. Apart from anything else, emotionally she'll need time to adjust.'

His tone was business-like. It was Grant the doctor speaking. Already they were moving on, their oasis left behind them.

Jane suspected that Rita must have been told at least half the story. At the flat there was no sign of her, but Liz seemed to have no trouble in producing plenty of towels and a rubber sheet – hardly a thing likely to be lurking in the cupboard by chance.

Wearing a US green overall, Grant scrubbed his hands at the sink in the tiny kitchen. Jane tried not to watch. For everyone's sake she wished she weren't there. No, that wasn't true, she corrected herself. For her own sake she couldn't bear not to be. Strangely, at this point neither Richard nor Hartley seemed important. Just Liz. Liz, the little girl . . . Liz, grown to be a woman, discovering the mystery of love. What must she be suffering now as she undressed and got into bed as Grant had told her? There in that same bed where she'd given herself to Hartley. Hard on the heels of that thought came another – Richard.

'Go and wait by the fire.' She felt the pressure of Grant's hand on her shoulder. 'Trust me, Jane.'

She did trust him. But there was room in her heart for nothing but Liz as she knelt in front of the hissing gasfire. At last his work was done. She heard him moving about, running water.

'Grant?' From the kitchen doorway she whispered, 'Is she all right? What have you done?'

288

On the wall facing the door was a mirror. What a moment to come face to face with the tired, middle-aged image that looked back at her!

'She'll be fine.' His overall off, he was putting on his tunic jacket. His voice was devoid of expression. There was a weariness in the way he ran his hand across his hair. The washed-out face in the looking glass watched. The silence seemed to accentuate the sound of the zip on his hold-all where he carried 'the tools of his trade' and he put away his overall and surgical gloves.

This is us, Grant and me. Yesterday we were Major and Mrs Holgate. Where's it all gone to, all the magic? I'm so ashamed. To have dragged him into this, as if last night was given him in exchange – oh, but he can't think that! Look at me, just look at me. Drab, washed out, not even young . . . his golden girl! Damn them, damn, damn, damn them! Go home to Mum, Mum'll put things right. Damn them –

'We won't talk tonight, Jane.' He was ready to go, he was going.

'Grant, I've not even thanked –'

He put his hand against her lips.

'You need a proper night's rest. That sofa won't do you any good.' It was the doctor speaking. Where was the man who'd shared the spirit of crazy happiness with her as, part of the long snake of revellers, they'd congaed their way from yesterday to today; whose adrenalin had flowed fast, just as hers had, as they'd felt themselves to be part of the blitz; who'd stood with her on Westminster Bridge and felt the spirit of the city? She lowered her eyes. She couldn't bear to see his recognition of what she was: tired, middle-aged, colourless, a harassed mother whose family had sapped every bit of hope from her.

Still avoiding his gaze, she opened the door of the flat to let him out.

'Keep safe in London.'

'You understand, Jane? Tonight I just want to get away. It's right that I should.' But he was no happier about it than she was. With his hand under her chin, he forced her to look up at him. 'Last night was ours.' And she was struck by something else. These hours had taken as big a toll on him as they had on her. No wonder he wanted to rush away, put it out of his mind. What he'd done had been unethical, against his principles.

'I'm grateful,' hardly more than a mumble, 'ashamed, thankful –'

'Not tonight, Jane. Go and talk to Liz. Your evening's not done with yet.' Gently he kissed her forehead then turned and left her.

Go and talk to Liz! Half an hour ago all her love, all her understanding, had been with the girl. Now she felt drained. Go and be a mother. Forget the born again woman with stars in her eyes. Stars? Lifeless, red-rimmed, certainly no stars now. She rinsed her face in cold water, rubbed her cheeks hard with the kitchen hand-towel. Then she squared her shoulders and went into the bedroom.

'There's no point in my coming all that way just for a few days,' Liz said next morning. 'Anyway, I don't want to. Let it rest, Mum. What about your American boyfriend? Supposing I bumped into him, how do you think I'd feel?'

'You might at least give him a name.' How easy it was to snap.

'Sorry.' The mumbled apology touched Jane's heart. It was a glimpse of Liz's misery. 'Anyway, you won't have to chase around asking favours for me after this. You know what he did? He fitted me with a coil. How's that for freedom!' Her laugh was harsh, un-Liz-like.

'Would you rather I stayed on for a day or two?'

'No. No, Mum, I'd rather you went. I want to forget the whole sickening business, but I can't if you're here to remind me. I'll be glad when I go back to work.'

'Give it time, Liz. It'll fade. You won't forget, but it'll

slip into place in your mind. It won't always be at the top of your thoughts.'

'For heaven's sake, don't preach! Just because you're my mother you don't have to try and know all the answers. Anyway, you're not likely to know the answer to this one, with a comfortable, snug life like you and Dad had.'

Perhaps she was right. But Jane did understand one thing: that Liz needed to lash out, to be cruel.

She was glad to go.

Three-quarters of an hour on Oxford station waiting for a train that turned out to have been cancelled then, finally, a seat on her suitcase in the corridor of the next. Two changes, one with twenty minutes in a cold waiting room, the second with twenty-five in a station buffet with a fruit bun in which she counted only four currants and a surprisingly good cup of tea; then the last lap of the journey and the station taxi home.

When Mufti heard her key in the lock, his excitement knew no bounds. Greta was at the bottom of the narrow garden cleaning the henhouse, her regular job.

'Hi, I'm back!'

The straw was dropped, the hens screeched and flapped, Greta raced to Jane. Their hug squeezed the breath out of both of them. Spontaneous, it said more than any words.

'Did you have a lovely time? What did you and Grant do? They said on the wireless there was a raid. Did you hear any bombs? Was the party good? Liz told us you'd phoned to ask her to come up to a party. I bet when she got there she enjoyed herself, didn't she?'

'I think so. Didn't she want to break her leave and come?'

'She didn't say that. But – well, I might have got it wrong – but she didn't seem all excited, not like I would have been. Off to London to something special. Perhaps she was a bit scared. Air-raids and all that.'

'It wasn't worth her coming all the way back. So she's gone straight to Oxford.'

Greta digested this.

'That's what she tells us,' she gave a knowing look, 'not worth the journey, I mean. 'course she's gone back to Oxford. Hartley's not far from there.' Following Jane indoors she perched herself on the arm of the fireside chair. 'You know, I don't believe I'd like this love business.' In her satisfaction at having Jane home again, she settled herself to give her full consideration to her topic. 'Wouldn't you think it would make a person happy? Isn't that the whole idea of falling in love? She was disappointed that his leave got cancelled, I can quite see she would be . . .'

'Did she give you a hard time?' Jane smiled affectionately at Greta's serious expression.

'Not so much that. She was never grouchy with me, no, not at all. But just so glum, all wrapped up in a sort of angry miserableness.'

'And Richard?'

'Until last night I didn't see him.' She looked puzzled. 'He's been staying with Grandma Gower.' It was a statement, yet from the way she said it, it was a question too. 'Liz left a message at Chugford Farm that he had to come back because of me being on my own. Anyway,' she giggled, 'it isn't Richard who's in love with Hartley. Why should he get in a state because of the leave being cancelled? Anyway,' she repeated, this time turning her full attention on Jane and disposing of the others and the anguish of love, 'like I was saying, I don't know that I want the bother of boyfriends, not if it makes you so that you aren't your ordinary self. I'll just stay with you instead. Reckon you could stand that?' Her brown eyes danced.

'Reckon I could.' Willingly Jane responded. She even tried to believe that the root cause of Liz's wretchedness had been fear that Hartley had left her. Now that she was in Oxford they would come together again, they would find a way back. What had happened had put a cloud between herself and Liz. In imagining that what Greta suggested was true, at any rate in her own mind, that cloud started to lift. It was no more than hope, but surely she was entitled to that?

Then there was Richard, still on leave, running away from everyone – and, she suspected, most of all wanting to run away from himself. If a cloud had come between herself and Liz, the barrier that held her away from Richard was much more substantial. She couldn't even begin to understand. She didn't know how to reach out to him and, worse, she recoiled from trying. Her play-acting ability would have to be stretched to the utmost, pretending that she'd heard nothing.

That same Saturday afternoon, when Greta was outside finishing her weekly ministrations to the hen-house, Richard put play-acting right out of question.

'If it's all the same to you, Mum, I shall go to Grandma for a few days. Now you're home you'll be at Chugford every day. I've done my bit there – anyway, there's no room for both of us. Meg's at Grandma's too, so it's much better than kicking about on my own here. In any case, I've already given them my ration card so I can't sponge on you.' He shot his sentences out quickly, not quite looking at her. Then, his manner changing: 'I've been there while you were painting the town red with your boyfriend.' There was such insolence in his tone!

'If you want to go there, then you must do as you like. But I'm not having you speak to me like that.' There was a physical pain in her chest. Face to face with Richard, glaring at each other, in their unhappiness both of them lashing out to hurt. 'Who do you think you are, to stand in judgement?'

'Damn it, Mum, even Grandma had heard about it! She's quite upset – not that that would bother you, it never has. She feels it's a slur on Dad. If you'd set your sights on some chap like ourselves . . . but a Yank, like every tart in town, out with the ones who can give them the best time! You're –'

His words were brought to an abrupt stop as her hand landed across his cheek. All her rage was in the action; at

293

the sight of the red marks left by her fingers it melted. In stunned silence they looked at each other. At that moment the barrier was wavering, almost falling. Instead Richard turned his back and left her. She heard the front door slam.

Halfway through the next week a telegram came from Seatrack Shipping Company recalling him. This time when he joined his ship she was left with the old fears for him and in addition something far harder to bear: the burden of a secret she could share with none of them. They must never know how she'd sat huddled on the stairs, listening. Even if time laid a veneer over what they had done – they? HE? – nothing could be the same, not for her, not for any of them.

Newspapers blazoned the headlines of raids on Germany. By the cold light of day it read like points scored in a contest. Jane remembered an early morning on Westminster Bridge. Hammersmith, Hamburg, Bristol, Bremerhaven . . . points scored. What of the broken lives, the torn nerves? And always as she read, at the front of her mind was Hartley. Gentle, sensitive Hartley was part of it. For months he'd lived through it, but behind him there'd been the security of home and, more important, of Liz.

She intended to send him a brief note, simply saying how disappointed she'd been that his leave had been cancelled, pretending to believe the lie. But between herself and Hartley there had always been honesty. It was late one evening when, alone by the dying fire, she found her pen running away with her. 'Mum'll make things right' Liz had believed. As the words tumbled across the pages she was sure that was what she was doing.

Hartley's reply was a picture postcard of Buckingham Palace, the postmark London. 'Your letter meant a lot to me, thank you for trusting me. One day, later on, I want to come home. H.'

It was another fortnight before she heard from Liz, her first letter since Jane had left her in Oxford. A letter full of what she'd done, where she'd been, who she'd been with. About Hartley, indeed about what had happened, all she said was: 'Hartley came. I just want to forget the whole wretched, sordid affair. You won't understand. You think we were a dewy-eyed pair of innocents. I don't want even to think about it.' Jane read that part twice, angry and ashamed at Liz's inference that Hartley had been part of that sordidness. 'He said he'd had a letter from you. I wish you hadn't interfered. Being my mother doesn't mean you can live my life for me. I intend to look to the future, not the past. Won't you try and accept that's the way I want things? Tonight I'm going with . . .' It seemed that every evening she was going somewhere and usually with someone different. Liz's idea of 'life' had changed.

If only Jane could do as Grant wanted. It sounded simple. How long he'd be here she had no idea, and perhaps he hadn't either, but over those weeks of March she sensed a heightening of military activity. Farmers from around the outside perimeter of the evacuation area talked of it: 'Another noisy night, those Yanks letting off their crackers . . .' 'Practice they call it, you can't tell me none of those chaps get hurt.' Movement of men and weapons, tanks and ammunition, was a constant reminder of what couldn't be far away. When first John had told her that the Americans were coming, that they would be training for the invasion, it had seemed something as remote as that much-used phrase 'when the war is over'. In the four months since then she knew that thousands of soldiers must have been drafted into the practice area, batches at a time, to be familiarized with the terrors of battle. Military vehicles filled the roads, narrow roads never designed for this kind of traffic. Soldiers were drafted in, any spare civilian accommodation commandeered for their use.

As for Grant, he spoke very little about what went on in his life when he wasn't with her. 'I'm not a proper soldier, I'm just here to pick up the pieces,' he'd once said. Now as the weeks went by she was ever more conscious of one thing: to pick up the pieces meant that he would be there with the fighting men when the pieces fell. Wherever, whenever, this invasion came, Grant would be in the midst of it.

'When I move out from here, Jane, it's not going to be to some place else in England. I figured it was for guys like me to join in this fight, guys with no one to leave behind.' He ran his hand gently across her curly hair. 'Now, having you waiting for me to come back is – I suppose it's my purpose for any of it, for everything I do.'

'You know I'll be waiting.'

'It's because of the family? Is that what holds you back?'

'Nothing holds me back from promising to marry you, from wanting to marry you more than I want anything on this earth. Nothing holds me back from knowing it's right for us to be together. Superstition is wicked, I know it is, I tell myself so over and over. But things are such a mess – Liz, Richard, me, and Hartley too – all of us pulling our own separate ways. I know they wouldn't understand. They'd believe I was deserting them. They don't see us like we see ourselves. To them I'm "Mum" – about the only solid thing left in their lives. I can feel their criticism – Liz and Richard's at any rate – not of you, of me. I expect they see me as middle-aged, chasing a lost youth.' Even his raised brows didn't bring a smile to her face. 'At that age they think they know the lot, the world's put here for their benefit.'

'Superstition, you call it? I don't see where that comes into it.'

'Oh, it does. There's something inside me, telling me, warning me. I'm frightened that if I ignore it, then one of these days it'll rebound on you and me. What I said just now about all of us pulling different ways. It's true, yet they've each of them got me, and because of me they've still got each other. That's how I see it. Take me away and they might fall right away from each other. Then I wouldn't deserve happiness. It's tempting fate . . .'

'I love you, Jane.' He said it solemnly, yet she detected a teasing note in his voice.

'I get it all worked out, what's the right thing and then what would be tempting fate,' she went on, 'and then I come up against something else. It's this. I say "no" to getting married, I've explained all that, then I come to the last bit, the bit it all hinges on. Is it for my own sake that I say "no", because I feel we have to earn the right to what we want? Like going through purgatory before we can have a taste of anything better.'

'I guess I'm just a simple soldier. All this philosophy is outside my realm,' he laughed. 'If you find a way to barter with your conscience, then just you let me know.'

'Oh, I will, never doubt it. Meanwhile,' she rubbed her face against his chin, 'you feel very newly shaved. Can I take that to mean this isn't one of your five minute appearances?'

'You can. I'm a free man until the morning. I was going to take you and Greta along to the Club for an early supper.'

They'd been there before, like a family outing, then supper over, back again to the cottage. This evening they played cards for an hour before Greta went to bed, gambling with halfpennies.

Later, as Jane sat on the hearthrug between his knees, they spent the last hour of the day building castles in the air, planning their own 'after the war'. He talked of Arndale, the little town in New England where he practised; he talked of the sort of life she would have, the future waiting there for Greta. And later again, lying close in his arms, it was to Arndale that she let her mind wander. Between now and then were hurdles, but for tonight they didn't exist.

While Jane perched on the fifth rung of the ladder and the representative of a firm who manufactured swill boilers sat uncomfortably atop a carboy of disinfectant, they conducted their business. With her order for four boilers taken, he was glad to stand up, an indent from the screw top in the seat of his trousers.

'One of these days I'll be able to offer you a chair again, Mr Roach.'

'And soon, let's all hope. Oh, don't misunderstand me,' he blustered, 'I've no complaint with your hospitality. Let's hope before long you'll be back to normal.' He picked up his bowler hat from where he'd laid it carefully on a reel of barbed wire, scrutinized it as if he'd never seen it before, then put it on, coming to stand in front of her and raising it. A giggle threatened to erupt from Jane, but she managed to keep her expression as serious as he expected of her.

'I'll see you in three months, Mr Roach.' She had always had a soft spot for the rotund, dark suited little salesman, even if only because he was so out of place in his job.

'And who knows, my dear Mrs Gower, by then you may be on your home ground. No war lasts forever. Three months and those Americans might have said their goodbyes. It must have been a great trial for you, working under these conditions.' Momentarily that soft spot hardened; but Harold Roach was unaware of it. 'Look back on history. Century after century, people just like you and me have had their troubles and their wars. Times of war, then times of peace. History records them all. And soon it'll come full circle. All these strangers will be gone, the country will be our own again. Dear old England. We'll pick up the threads, settle back – not for the first time. Look at your history books. Well, Mrs Gower, I must be making tracks. Perhaps next time, perhaps the time after, but never you doubt it, you'll be back again in that little office your father-in-law made. A fine gentleman was Mr Gower.' Again he raised his bowler, then the stubby little man left her.

A fine gentleman. Yes, so he had been. 'Back in that

office' – the thought of it was like the sound of the prison door crashing shut. She didn't even remember that not so long ago she'd looked on it as freedom. When she moved the business back to its own buildings, where would Grant be? All she knew for certain was that when the Americans moved out of the 'zone', the invasion everyone was clamouring for would have come.

The shrill telephone bell interrupted her black thoughts.

'Henry Gower and Son,' she answered.

'It's a trunk call I've got for you, Mrs Gower. Just hold the line and I'll connect it up for you,' Mrs Chudzey of Mannerby Post Office announced, and Jane could almost hear the silent rider: 'Then we can find out what it's all about.'

'Mum? It's me.' Always Liz's first words.

'A nice surprise. Is everything – ?' She didn't finish the question. Liz was saying something, her words tumbling out, talking, crying, becoming less and less coherent.

CHAPTER FIFTEEN

It wasn't until the next day that the telegram was delivered. It was regretted, Flight Lieutenant H. Ladell failed to return.

Lying sleepless she'd prayed for a miracle, that somehow he would have limped home. It had been so difficult to understand Liz's message, something about a telephone call. She knew that Hartley had always phoned the hospital as soon as he'd been de-briefed – but that had been before all the trouble. So it must mean that things were right between them again. Liz must have been saying that he hadn't made his regular call. But that could have been because the aircraft had been damaged, perhaps he'd taken longer to get home; it could be that he'd come down over the channel and been picked up by a rescue ship. 'Please, please, don't let him be gone. Please!'

Then the telegram came and there was no way to hide from the truth. Because of Greta she clung on to a hope that in her heart she knew had no reason in it.

'Isn't fair, Aunt Jane,' Greta sobbed, 'I hate them, all the rotten lot of them. How could they do that to Hartley? Why do they do it? Silly, stupid, rotten war!' Greta had met death before, but Hartley was her own generation, Hartley was her friend, almost her brother.

'We mustn't give up hope, Greta. Perhaps he baled out – over France where someone would hide him, or perhaps a fishing boat from some other country picked him up. Perhaps – '

'But if it's any of those things,' Greta snorted, 'just think of what it must be like for him, Aunt Jane. Now, this very minute, where can he be? Perhaps he's freezing cold in the water, or perhaps he's starving hungry and hiding, frightened to be seen. It's Hartley, it's not fair!'

Neither was it. But how can you explain to an eleven year old that one thing she shouldn't look for in life is fairness? In those hours Greta grew up a little; Jane grew old a little.

Her letter to Liz must surely have dispersed anything that still remained of the cloud between them. She wrote straight from her heart. And, crossing with hers in the post, came an envelope addressed in Liz's writing.

'It was the shock, that's why I made such a scene. We hear of tragedies all the time, but it's different when it's someone you've always known. Hartley always used to phone the hospital, I think I told you. Of course he hasn't been doing it lately, but Jerry Osborne his Squadron Leader didn't know that. I had met him a few times, so we weren't strangers. He said they'd been coming home, still over Germany – the last he saw of Hartley's plane was an engine on fire. I didn't behave very well when I talked to you. I'm sorry, Mum. You must have been shocked and I didn't make it any easier. You'll get the official notification, but I don't expect that tells you anything but the bare facts.

'I've been thinking – I've decided to join up. I know nursing is nursing wherever you do it, but I think I will anyway. Imagine seeing the plane on fire. We'll never know what happened. Did he know he was burning? Was he conscious? He must have been so frightened.

'I've got three days between shifts at the end of next week. I wish I wanted to come home, but right now I don't think I could – and Denby would be worse. Is it just conscience that makes me feel so wretched when I think about him? I know I hurt him, he didn't deserve it. But I couldn't just go on as if nothing had happened, it was all so beastly. Perhaps one day things would have come right. Now this damned war has spoilt it all.

'Hope you and Greta are okay. Love always, Liz.'

*

301

April was already over a week old. In the narrow back garden the daffodils were over, and in the strip of flower border tulips bloomed amongst the straggling forget-me-nots. Spring was here. A handsome male blackbird was making regular trips backwards and forwards between the hedge and the ground around the chicken run. A lazy fellow this one, all his friends had had their nests made weeks ago; now he was working in a frenzy of haste and with luck on his side, for the fallen pieces of straw gave him a wealth of good building material all within easy reach. It seemed Mrs Blackbird would be safely housed in time to lay her eggs.

Mrs Sid let herself in through the back gate that led to the alleyway. She considered the front door to be for 'visitors'.

'Coo-eee!' Opening the door to the scullery she announced her arrival.

'You're bright and early, Mrs Sid. Did you meet Greta? She'd just gone off to school.'

'Early I might be, bright I'm not – nor you neither, Mrs G., my dear, so it's no use pretending. No news of him?'

Jane shook her head. 'We know the plane was burning . . . what's the use of pretending? And how long do we keep it up for?'

'As long as it takes, that's how long. If that boy were gone, then we'd feel; it, we'd know it.'

Leading the way into the sitting room, Jane planted herself on the arm of the chair.

'I'm not sure that you're right. Have you ever once had the courage to try and reach out to him, to find him, let your mind speak to him? Have you ever opened your heart and given him a chance to be with you? I bet you haven't, any more than I have. To do that would be like admitting that he's never coming home. So we hang on to hope, frightened to look at the truth – '

'Enough of that talk!'

This morning Mrs Sid had put a defiant rub of colour on each cheek. Jane knew her well enough to be sure that

302

make-up on a Tuesday was a sign of bravado. She reached out and took hold of the rough and lined hand.

'Perhaps if we . . .' But whatever Jane said was lost in the roar of traffic rattling past the cottage window. This time it was US Army lorries, next time it might be tanks. So it went on, day after day.

'Take your life in your hands to step off the path!' Mrs Sid grumbled, glowering out of the window as the last vehicle rumbled down the hill. 'Nice little town this used to be, moved at its own pace. Look at it now, swarming with noisy soldiers. Good-natured I dare say, but the way they shout and bawl – oh, not quarrelsome, I'm not suggesting they're that. More like a lot of unruly schoolboys – and forever chewing their nasty gum!'

'Sometimes I think their noise is a cover-up for the fact they must be so frightened.'

Mrs Sid sniffed. 'Ah, very likely you're right. Frightened – and that's how he must have felt, it's in your mind all the time. That poor dear lad . . . wake in the night and think about him . . . and so do you, I know you do.' Her voice croaked, even her war-paint couldn't help her now. It was a relief to cry, for her and for Jane too.

'We've got to face up to it, Mrs Sid,' Jane gulped, 'we've got to be honest.' A memory of Hartley flashed into her mind, kneeling before the toy horse. The relief she'd found in sharing her unhappiness with him, letting him see the misery she'd tried to hide from all the others. Another memory – the letter she'd written to him. She was glad she'd told him how she'd sat rooted to the stairs, listening. Somehow, she felt that she'd travelled with him in honesty and truth as far as his journey had gone.

'That boy isn't gone.' Mrs Sid mopped her face. 'The day will come when you'll find I'm right. There's not much we can do, a couple of silly women blubbing here, but there's one thing: never give up hope, never give up asking that whoever it is sorts out our tickets when the time comes for our last journey just keeps his hold on Hartley's, lets him have a bit of proper life.'

Jane nodded. For her old friend's sake she pretended to believe.

'What brings you to town so early anyway?' she asked with forced cheerfulness.

'Well, you do, of course. I got the first bus, came with the work people. If I'd waited until the streets were aired you'd have gone off to that Chugford Farm. Now I'm here, though, I'd have time for a nice cup of tea if anyone happened to offer it.'

Jane hugged her and went to put the kettle on. Mrs Sid was the last remaining link with the old days. Whatever else changed, she never would.

A jeep passed the window, at the head of six more lorries.

'Don't you let Greta out on the streets on her skates, not with all these great trucks about,' Mrs Sid said as she followed Jane into the scullery. 'Everywhere you go you hear rumours, everyone thinks they know better than the next one when this invasion's coming. One thing's for certain, we shall have good warning of it down here, the place alive with the military like it is. When it's "get set, get ready" they'll have to be moved on along to where the channel is narrower before anyone gives the order to "go". Dover, Folkestone, somewhere along that way. That's what Sid says. They talk together in the Home Guard, you know. He says that's where it'd have to be, Boulogne, Calais – ah, and Dunkirk too. One in the eye for that Hitler, sending our lads back to Dunkirk! That friend of yours, the American, has he moved out yet? Nice enough sort of person but you watch youself, Mrs G., m'dear. Just the same in the last war, men from the other side of the world came here looking for a few home comforts.'

'Grant's still here. I'm glad you like him, Mrs Sid.'

'I didn't say that. Don't know him well enough to like or dislike. Very likely you don't either. That's the way in wartime. People are so different away from their real folk.'

'How's the Home Guard?' Jane changed the subject.

'Lot of nonsense, if you ask my opinion. Hitler's got too much on his hands with the Russians to send his troops here. Oh, the platoon still meets. Three nights a week they get together. A bit of drilling and strutting about, then down to the Black Swan – unless the door's closed and the sign up saying they're out of ale.'

Another five minutes and she picked up her shopping basket.

'Well, it won't keep the farms running smoothly if you're here wasting your time. I'll get off to the shops. Now you just promise me – the first word you get from our boy you'll let me know. You could telephone a message through to Mr Cutler at the Black Swan, he'd slip along and tell me. And one thing more, Mrs G. None of your letting yourself believe he's gone. Time'll prove me right.'

Jane crossed her fingers and knocked on wood. But it's nearly three weeks since his plane came down. How long is hope supposed to be able to live? A sneaking voice in her mind wouldn't be silenced.

Daily the tension seemed to mount. The district had never been so crowded; the accent of America was being picked up by the local children and by the young women too. The place was full of servicemen, most of them GIs.

For some time the only petrol allowed to civilians had been for essential use and even 'small cheats' were a thing of the past. Now came a further restriction: the roads to the coast must be left clear for the movement of service vehicles. Any journey that necessitated travelling on such a route meant obtaining a special permit. Agricultural use was essential, and on her daily journey to Chugford Farm Jane had to turn on to the coast road, drive on it for about a mile, then turn off towards Mannerby.

It was an evening towards the end of April when she was on her way home. Bearing down on her from the opposite direction was a fast moving convoy. That foretaste of spring earlier in the month had given way to the sort of rain they'd all got used to during the winter, day after day of it. For her to pull on to the grass verge would be asking to be left stuck in the mud. She knew the road well. If the convoy stopped, just about level with the leading truck there was a lead-in to a farm gate. She could pull in there and let them pass. So, instead of slowing down, she tried to indicate what she meant to do by putting her foot on the accelerator and speeding forward.

Still the convoy came on at the same relentless speed. She tried to point towards the gateway, but she was too far away from the driver of the lead vehicle to see. Clearly he considered himself King of the Road. She jammed on her brakes and, at the last moment, so did he. But not quite in time. She swung the wheel to the left, careering onto the soft grassy bank and coming to rest with the nose of the car implanted in the hedge and her rear bumper torn loose.

The convoy halted. King of the Road climbed down from his perch.

'What's a dame doing on this road?' she heard the driver of the next vehicle shout.

Instinct and shock combined. Jane was hardly aware of what she did or said as she opened the window and shouted back in a voice she didn't recognize as her own: 'The same as I'll be doing on it tomorrow, and every day!'

It was the only way not to burst into tears. They must see how she was shaking, although she kept her fists clenched tightly and her teeth clamped hard together.

'Jeez – don't you know how to find reverse? Is that the problem?' King of the Road had climbed down from the cabin of the lorry and was grinning at her, his head poked through the open window. Even when he spoke he chewed, the steady movement of his jaw never altering. A roar of mirth went up from the men in the front few lorries who by now were enjoying the whole situation.

'Of course I know how to reverse! Why don't you use your eyes? Couldn't you see there was a passing point right by you? There's nothing behind me for about half a mile.' With her car nosing into the hedge and its wheels, no doubt, skidded well and truly into the mud, Jane felt helpless. Anyway the GI was a huge man, stooping low to peer in at her. Stuck, shaken, with no hope of driving out of her predicament, Jane was at a miserable disadvantage.

'Here, ma'am.' And through the window came a strip of gum.

She wanted to laugh – or rather she didn't want to but she was afraid she would. And if she laughed she wasn't at all sure that she wouldn't cry.

'Come on, you guys, we've got to give the lady a lift.'

'But I'm going the other way!' And in any case, were they allowed civilians on their vehicles when they were travelling in convoy like this?

Her remarks were ignored and a group of giants tumbled out of the trucks, all grinning good-humouredly.

'Better get out, ma'am,' the King ordered.

Ten giants, one small car. First it was bodily lifted to stand straight on the grass verge, facing in the direction it had been travelling. The GIs stayed with it as the convoy rolled on by, then, the road clear, and with a pantomime of muscle flexing before they started, they pushed it easily back on to the tarmac way.

'Reckon we can fix that fender,' one of them suggested to another.

'You folk round these parts, I guess you'll all be glad to get your lanes to yourselves again.' There was no swagger in the King's voice now. Just for a second she'd glimpsed what lay beneath: uncertainty, fear . . .

Her jaws moved a little more vigorously as she chewed, as if to show him she was with them, not against; she was their friend.

'Not as glad as you will be to drive on your own wide highways,' she laughed. Almost visibly the men relaxed. Until then they'd worked at her 'fender' in silence. Now, like children let out to play, they felt free to banter, to whistle, even to make a ribald remark or two to each other – patently designed to attract her attention – about dolly drivers.

And when after ten minutes or so she was back in the driving seat, she went off to a chorus of: 'Watch out for the crazy Yanks, lady,' 'Mind how you go' and even 'See you around'. Smiling to herself, she drove towards home. They were Grant's countrymen and that pushed her more than halfway towards looking on them as her friends.

The days of April saw other changes. When first Grant had come she'd sometimes teased him: 'Don't you chaps have any work to do?' His answer had been that his job was to pick up the pieces. Now, through these April days, all that was changed. She saw far less of him. Even picking up pieces involved training exercises. If his time with her was shorter, with every passing day what was between them was becoming stronger, their only hold on a future that had no other reality. What had happened to Hartley, the constant fear for Richard, the idea of Liz becoming part of the war, all these things were knitted into the emotion that Jane felt for Grant, shared with Grant.

Things were happening. Everyone knew it.

'Those Yanks seem set on keeping us all from our sleep,' one farmer whose land was just outside the perimeter of the evacuation zone told her. 'I climbed up and looked from the top window last night. You'd have thought it was November the Fifth.' And another from further round the coast: 'I wonder my old house is still standing. There on the beach they were – talk about a demolition squad! Thought we'd all end up in Kingdom Come.'

*

Then came an evening when Grant was expected and didn't arrive. No message.

'Don't forget we haven't got a telephone, Aunt Jane,' said the practical Greta. She was busy with her homework, driven by this 'top of the class' business and, even more important, getting to the Grammar School in the autumn on a scholarship.

Jane left her to her work and went up to her bedroom, opening the bottom window and leaning out. How quiet the street was. A group of girls were hanging about at the bottom of the hill; waiting, perhaps, just like she was . . . She could hear the distant rumble of traffic. It must be tanks to make that noise. Yes, down the hill they came, first a jeep then five lorries, followed by ten, eleven, twelve tanks. The girls on the corner were afforded a wave or two and a few cat-calls, then the sound of the convoy grew fainter. Another half hour went by; still no sign of Grant. More than anything, watching out of the window, Jane was conscious that there were no GIs wandering aimlessly, looking for an evening's amusement.

Her mouth was dry with fear. What was happening? Something important. It had never been quite like this before, even though there had been plenty of exercises.

The long night passed, followed by a long day. Night, day, time went on. He'd come if he could, she never doubted that. Commonsense told her Sid must be right. When the invasion happened, the men would cross the channel further to the east. So as long as the Americans were still here, and as long as there was no news of landings, then it must be another exercise that was keeping him away. Even so her mind was uneasy. She went to bed late, sure she wouldn't sleep. She was wrong. Within minutes she was lost to the world.

What woke her? She sat bolt upright and listened. Gunfire! It sounded a long way off, heavy gunfire out at sea. Her heart was thumping. She climbed out of bed and groped in the dark to the window. There it was again!

And flashes lighting up the sky. 'It must be an exercise. Please let it just be that. Just an exercise. It looks a long way away. If it's right out there at sea, how can he pick up the pieces? Please let him be where it's safe.'

There was no more sleep that night. But there was more gunfire. In the daytime she probably wouldn't even have heard it, but lying awake in the silent night every sound was magnified. The next day she found she'd not been alone in her vigil. Customers at Chugford, farmers from east of Dartmough and west of Kingsbridge, some of them had heard gossip of happenings right to Plymouth and beyond. The day brought no word from Grant.

'If you ask me, 'tiz the beginning of the invasion. Germans will be on the look out all along this channel. Hitler's not such a fool as to keep all his sights on the neck of it. He's got his spies about, never you fear. He must know how many troops we've got stationed round these parts.' So said one farmer, organizing the war as he stacked a bundle of cultivator tines into his car.

These last few days had all been long, but none as long as this one. Stop and listen, was that another explosion? What was happening? But explosions on the beaches, explosions in the 'zone' . . . tanks, armoured cars, lorries, all heading inland from the 'zone', making towards Dartmoor . . . proof that it must all be part of another exercise. Another night. Still Grant didn't come.

A consignment of small spare parts, never Jane's favourite job, to sort and put away, each in its allotted space. But today she welcomed something that needed her concentration. She was high up the ladder, B.241 being put into one cubbyhole and MH.27 into another, when a shadow fell across the doorway of the shed. Only a shadow, so how did she know? By the time Grant came from the bright light of afternoon to the shadowy shed, she was on the ground again, then wordlessly she was in his arms.

'I couldn't get a message to you. What did you imagine?'

'That you couldn't get a message to me.' Now that he was here all her fears had melted. With his arms still around her, she held her head back, studying him.

'Not much sleep?' How tired he looked, drawn, somehow older.

'You could say that.' For a second he shut his eyes. She felt he was trying to banish from his mind what the days had been. 'Let's talk about something different. Have you had any news?' She knew he was asking about Hartley and shook her head. That was something else she didn't want to talk about. Not now. Grant was back. That had to be enough, nothing must cloud it.

'Here's the van back.' She recognized the sound as it turned into the yard. 'I'll come home. Ted can keep an eye on things here.'

There was a movement of the kitchen curtain in the farmhouse as they crossed the yard to her car. Grant opened the door for her and purposely, before she got in, she put her arms around him. Let old Joshua take note! Let him tell his cronies! She wanted the world to know.

Tonight he had brought nothing to augment the larder, and tonight they didn't want to go out for supper. Thanks to Greta and her hens there were a few eggs, and no banquet could have been better than the scrambled egg on almost butterless toast. Yet something was different. He'd been on exercises before – not for so long, certainly – but always when he'd come back there had been an air of celebration. This evening what was there in the set of his mouth, the tired lines around his eyes, that told Jane all wasn't well? It must be that he knew more than he could tell her; perhaps he knew the invasion was about to happen; perhaps this was to be the last time he'd come here.

'Shall we play pontoon?' Greta asked hopefully.

'First, you and I will do the washing up. Grant can have a treat and read the newspaper.'

'Call that a treat?' he laughed, glancing at the headline 'US Planes Pound Nazis'. But he stretched out in the chair by the empty fireside, opening the paper.

Ten minutes later the other two came back from the scullery. The paper was on the floor, Grant was asleep.

'Better not wake him,' Greta whispered, a worried frown on her face as she looked at him. Then she mouthed: 'We'll wait and play tomorrow.' Jane envied her. Just to be eleven, not to see the shadow that hung over their tomorrow. 'I'll learn my history in bed,' the whisper went on as Greta held her face up for her goodnight kiss.

It was nearly dark when, with a start and a muffled shout, Grant woke. He seemed to give himself a mental shake, then he sat up straight.

'Jane, was I asleep? We were having supper . . .' Then he remembered. 'Is that the right time? You shouldn't have let me sleep –'

'Have you to get back?'

He shook his head.

'Then you'd sleep much better in bed than in a chair.' She held her hands out to him. 'Something tells me you and your bed haven't been seeing much of each other.'

Again he shook his head, getting to his feet.

'Jane,' he pulled her gently towards him, 'oh, Jane, you just can't know . . .' And whatever it was she couldn't know he left her guessing.

One thing she believed she did know, and that was how to chase the devils from his mind, for she had no doubt something far greater than tiredness was troubling him. She led the way up the narrow stairs, looked in on a sleeping Greta and turned her light out, then followed Grant into the bedroom and closed the door.

The panacea she put her faith in would bring him back to her, would put everything else away from them.

But tonight it didn't work. Lying close against him she caressed him, knowing passion was mounting in him. Yet, even though his body told its own message, he didn't move but lay on his back, quite still. It was as if his body and his mind served different masters. The room was in darkness, the curtains undrawn. From his deep breathing she might almost believe him to be asleep. But she knew he wasn't. She was physically shaken by her intense feeling of love for him, by a need to give, to serve. She raised herself, prepared to move on to him. Then she heard the sudden change in his even breathing; short, stifled gasps. His will-power had snapped; he was crying.

'Grant!' No more than a whisper. 'Grant, darling, tell me.'

He pulled her to him. She could feel how his hands trembled.

'Hush,' she soothed, 'it's over. Whatever happened, it's over, darling, you're safe.'

It seemed interminable as she listened to his fight for control. It was probably no more than a minute. Still he trembled. His breathing was light and shallow, but she knew the spasm of weeping was over. Still she held him close, waiting.

'Can't you talk to me, Grant?' she whispered at last.

'Just an exercise. We've had plenty of them before. Nearest we'd come to the real thing – that's what we were told when we were briefed.' Again a long silence. 'Jane, if it'd been the real thing there might have been some reason for it! A man might die for a cause – but this shambles! The Navy was supposed to give us cover. God knows what went wrong. Men with wives and –'

'Someone was killed?' She was thankful he'd told her. Now she could try and comfort him, help him to forget. Now he'd shared it with her, he wouldn't be so cut off.

'You know what I've been doing?' This time his voice was hard. 'I've been certifying the dead, putting my signature against the names and numbers so that their families can be notified. But what will they tell them? Where's the glory, where's the reason?'

'Men? More than one?'

'Many, many more.' He pulled away from her and sat

313

up. 'Seven hundred and forty-nine men, that's how many. Carried from the recovery vessels and laid in rows. Just boys, some of them.' Just as suddenly he lay down again, staring blindly at the dark ceiling. Then he went on, his voice low again: 'We guys had gone aboard round beyond Dartmouth. We knew the object of the operation. Craft were putting out from harbours all along the coast. All of them, under the protection of the Navy, were to converge down here on the zone. You must have realized something was going on these last days, Jane? The enemy headquarters was taken to be at a place called Okehampton. The first of the landing craft got ashore, took control of the battle zone – '

'Yes, everyone knew something was going on. We didn't know it was Okehampton, but tanks, lorries, they've all gone charging through. Then a few nights ago I heard different firing. It woke me. I looked out, saw great flashes a long way off. They seemed to light the sky – ' Purposely she talked, giving him time to recover.

'Out in the channel the E-Boats broke through, two of our craft went down. We were hit, eight men killed. Vince – you remember Vince?'

'He mended the skate. Yes, I remember.' And, in the only way she knew to show she wanted to share his torment, she gathered him closer to her.

'Then there were the wounded – stretcher cases. But we stayed afloat. After the E-Boats had got away – I think the Navy set up chase – we were towed into port. Days ago now. Seem to have lost track of time.'

And in those days? In speaking it aloud, perhaps he could ease the pain of what had happened.

'The wounded had to be sent off to the hospital. That part of it ran smoothly. Then back to – Jane, the exercise wasn't over, it had to go on. Some of the guys had no idea that anything had gone wrong even. And back there, not so far from Denby, Keyhaven, the fields you've known as home – already by the time I got there the ground was being got ready. More than seven hundred men were dead, most of them brought out of the sea. Each one had to be checked, identified, recorded – then buried. Doctors, chaplains, priests – we've never worked so fast . . . haste and dignity, they don't go together. A mistake had been made. For all the practising we'd been doing, things had gone wrong. Had to destroy the evidence. Isn't that what they do in all the murder movies, hide the body? So that's what we did. Got rid of the missing men – husbands, sons, some of them just kids, Jane. Mustn't let wind of it get out. Not our idea, just do as we're told. That's war for you. Orders from above. Security demands secrecy. So Vince and all the other guys get pushed under the ground without so much as a cross with their names on! If folk got to hear, they'd know things had gone wrong, bad for morale. So it's like Vince and the others had never been here. And back home their wives and kids won't even know yet what's happened.'

For a long time they lay close to each other, not speaking, not moving.

'A long time ago,' she said at last, 'I remember looking at the fields, looking at Tim and the children getting in the harvest, and do you know what I thought? I thought how grateful I was that whatever happened if war came, here in Devon nothing would ever change.'

'There's only one thing that's certain, and that the moment. Tomorrow, next week, next year –'

She put her fingers across his mouth.

'That's not true, Grant. Changes come, the moment passes. But what it leaves with you stays forever. Those wives you talk about back home, they won't be left with nothing any more than I was. There will be sadness – and loneliness – but what they've had will always be theirs.'

She'd believed she knew the way to cleanse his mind of whatever it was that haunted him. It had been no more than half an hour, but in that time they'd been brought close in a way that would bridge time and distance. They both knew it as now they turned to each other. The only thing one's certain of in life is the moment, he'd said.

And this was their moment. It must stay with them no matter what the future held in store.

For a few days the locals talked about the rumours they'd heard, the extra activity they'd seen by the American military. But it was evident that not even the most fertile imagination supposed that it had been anything more than a larger than usual exercise. 'Security demands secrecy.' How bitter Grant had sounded as he'd thought of his fellow countrymen. His secret was safe with her and, in keeping it, she felt a sense of loyalty not just to him but to those whose last resting place was under some field not far from Denby. In the town other interests soon took over: the draper's shop had a sign in the doorway announcing a delivery of fully fashioned stockings; there was one day when not a single pub in the town had any beer. On the farms there was more to think about than soldiers playing war games at this season when hay-making got under way in a brief spell of hot weather.

It was nearly the end of May when Greta's big day came. She put on a freshly starched school blouse and knotted her tie with extra care, then with carefully sharpened pencils, a new 'good luck' pen from Jane, and great determination, she set off to take her scholarship examination.

On such a Red Letter Day Mrs Sid came to town. Jane wanted to mark it as something special too. If Greta didn't get a scholarship place Jane intended to pay fees but she knew that for Greta that wouldn't be the same thing at all. To mark the day as a celebration Jane had taken Greta and Mrs Sid for tea at the Olde Tudor Cafe. Scones with a smear of margarine, rock cakes that tasted of dried egg, buns filled with synthetic cream – more than once Mrs Sid just stopped herself in time from saying what she thought.

'Fancy! Two and threepence each for a bit of tea.' That much she couldn't hold back.

It was for Greta's sake she didn't want to criticize the

feast. The child sat so straight, her eyes so big and bright. Who'd have thought it the day she'd arrived with that blessed beret pulled on her head!

Jane's mind was wandering down memory lane too. How proud George Blake would have been of his Princess.

Mrs Sid had to catch the five o'clock bus home, but until then they were happy to sit over their tea. Greta wanted it to last; this was her moment, it was a treat especially because of her. Back at the cottage the letter box clicked as the post lady made her afternoon delivery, Mufti barked at the closed door, wagged his tail and sniffed at the envelope.

CHAPTER SIXTEEN

'Here's some post,' Greta picked it up, 'it's a funny postmark. It's . . . it looks like . . . look, Aunt Jane!' She followed Jane from the passage into the sitting room.

'It is! That's Hartley's writing!' Side by side they sat on the arm of the sofa. 'We'll read it together.' Jane tore at the envelope.

Each holding the sheet of paper with one hand, heads close, silently they read. Hartley was safe. He was in a prisoner-of-war camp. They weren't to worry, he'd been treated well and was recovering. Recovering from what? He didn't say. But how could he have come from a burning aeroplane and not been hurt? Reading it through once Jane felt it told her all she needed to know. Hartley was alive, he was well, one day he would come back to them. Reading it the second time she realized just how little it said. Perhaps in a POW camp he wasn't allowed to write freely. His letters would be censored. Would other people read what she wrote to him? But he was alive, just hang on to that. None of the rest mattered.

'I've got to take Mufti o.u.t.' As he heard Greta say his name he sat with his head cocked to one side, his tail trembling into its first hopeful wag. Sometimes Jane wondered whether he couldn't spell too! 'Shall I take the twopence and ring Mr Cutler at the Black Swan? Mrs Sid gave me his number to keep in my pencil box – in case the message came when you weren't in, so that when I telephoned to you at Chugford I could ring Mr Cutler at the same time.'

As she ran off, with Mufti forgetting his age and leaping up to try and bite his lead as they went, Jane took her pen and notepaper.

'My dear Hartley, What a Red Letter Day! Now that

we've had your letter I don't know how we ever got through the weeks, waiting, not knowing.' But if it were a Red Letter Day, why was she biting the corners of her mouth to keep them steady, why was her vision misted with hot tears? She blew her nose, sat up straight and picked up her pen again. If other people read his letters then she must be careful. No mention of the Americans, no hint that where she was living wasn't their normal home. If his letter was guarded, so too was hers. It had to be. Liz's new Army address was temporary, but all she told him was that 'Liz is changing hospitals, so her old address won't find her. If you want to write, it might be best if you address her mail here.' The subject of Greta was safe; there was nothing to fear from the censor about her. She imagined Hartley's pleasure in reading that she had sat her scholarship.

Grant arrived just as she sealed the envelope. He'd never met Hartley yet this evening he couldn't help being affected by the joy that radiated from Jane. To her it seemed perfectly in keeping with this special day that he'd brought wine; he'd brought chocolate and Coke too, and, luxury of luxuries, a tin of American ham.

'You'd think it was Christmas!' she laughed. Her face wanted to wear a smile. She looked younger, gayer. 'You must have had a premonition! Or was it because Greta's taken her exam?'

'One oughtn't to have a reason for a celebration. Just being here, all together, isn't that enough?' His voice teased.

'Oh, yes, it's a wonderful reason. But if we celebrated it every day, the feeling of "party" would soon disappear, wouldn't it?' she answered lightly. Still protected by the euphoria of knowing Hartley would come back, it didn't enter her head to dig deeper into what he was saying. There was a feverish enjoyment in their celebration supper, even Greta was aware of it, but with the self-importance of her age, she supposed Grant had brought the festive fare because she'd sat her exam and been able to answer all the questions.

It was much later. Greta was in bed, the wine was drunk, even with Double British Summer Time dusk was starting to fade. The narrow strip of back garden, shared with a chicken run, left a lot to be desired, but the house was too dark now without the lights and lights meant heavy blackout curtains. So Grant and Jane were sitting on the tiny patch of weedy grass.

It was that hour when the world seems to hold its breath, the day almost over, the night not quite come.

'I have to get back tonight, Jane.'

'Won't early morning do?'

Their voices were hardly more than a whisper, partly because they didn't want to disturb the still of the evening and partly because they were conscious that only feet away, on the other side of the hedge and weeding as near to where they sat as she could get, was Mrs Mitchell, a neighbour with a nose for what went on in other people's lives. From out of the dusk a bat swooped low then disappeared.

'Midnight. Like Cinderella.'

Jane looked at him enquiringly. Midnight? Always it had been enough for him to be back at the base by morning.

'Let's go in, shall we?' he suggested. 'Before the "mosquies" have their supper off us.'

An excuse and they both knew it.

Often enough they'd climbed those narrow stairs together, but this was the first time they'd been so aware of the clock hands.

'You know what I wish right now, more than anything?'

'That the clock would stop?' He heard the smile in her voice, but couldn't match it.

'I wish you were my wife. I wish I could leave you, knowing that.'

'But I will be, Grant. It's what I want too. Like we were before, Major and Mrs Holgate, remember?'

His mouth covered hers, his body too. There was an urgency in his lovemaking tonight not entirely due to the minutes that were melting away all too fast. Soon it was over for both of them. And here, too, the pattern was different. Usually in those first moments he would lie relaxed, half awake and half asleep, while she was wide-eyed and content.

'It's no use,' he mumbled, holding her close to his side, 'I can't put if off. Jane, you've probably guessed from my having to be back at base at midnight. Something's in the wind. Another exercise. I hope I'll come tomorrow, but if I don't, you're not to worry. If it's on for tomorrow, I won't be able to phone you. I thought the last was to be just that – the last. I guess because it was such a shambles we've got to go through something again, put up a better show. Reckon I'd be put against the wall and shot if they knew I'd told you.' In the dark she could only imagine his attempt at a grin.

'You'll have to go to sea?'

'I guess I'm one of the lucky ones. One thing I never get bothered with is sea sickness. Some of them are hanging over the side before we've been on the water an hour! No wonder they need to take a doctor along.' He made light of it. But for Jane the wonder of the evening had evaporated.

In the dark she could just see the moving shape as he groped his way into his clothes.

'Don't come downstairs, stay where you are.' He meant to speak casually. It was when he kissed her goodbye the sudden suspicion hit her. An exercise, he'd said. Was that what he really believed? Was it what the men had been told? When the real thing came, would they know in advance or would they go aboard expecting it to be another training operation?

'The wine . . . the special supper . . . all of us together, you said?'

321

'And so we will be again, Jane, my honey,' He ran his fingers through her hair. She knew that when he called her 'honey' it had nothing to do with the easy term of endearment but conjured up memories of his 'honey gold girl', their night in London, their early dawn and the sinister red glow in the westward sky. Everything that bound them was encapsulated in it.

Despite being told to stay where she was, she climbed out of bed and pulled on her dressing gown. Mufti heard them treading quietly down the stairs and came to investigate, doubtless wondering if someone was going o.u.t., if there was anything in it for him. They couldn't see him, but they heard the thump of his tail on the ground as he waited hopefully. He was a wise old fellow, though. He soon sized the situation up as Jane and Grant hovered just inside the closed front door. A second or two later they heard him settling back in his basket. Then Grant was gone, the door closed softly behind him. Leaning against it, Jane listened as he started up the engine of the jeep and heard the sound gradually dying away in the distance.

It was impossible to escape from her premonition. Tomorrow the men would assemble for what they expected to be an exercise. Tomorrow they would set out on what would be the invasion of France. There was no way of escaping the dread of what she was certain was the truth. She turned first one way then the other, she pummelled her pillows and re-settled, she chased sleep every way she could, but still it eluded her. At four o'clock in the morning she drew her blackout curtain and put on the light. How could she let herself give way to her fears? Tonight of all nights, when she ought to be filled with thankfulness. Hartley was alive. She reminded herself of the premonitions she'd had about him too, and how wrong she'd been. And so she would be again! Creeping downstairs she fetched paper and pen, then she sat up in bed and wrote: 'Dear Liz . . .'

322

The next day was Saturday, but during haymaking Saturday was the same as any other day of the week. The stores would be open until evening. In any case, she wanted to be near the telephone in case Grant called her. The men were all out, delivering, repairing, keeping the wheels in motion. It was halfway through the afternoon when the sound of the shrill bell pierced the air.

'Herbert Gower and Son . . .' It *must* be him. Please let it be him.

'Thank God I found someone there. Garside, from Wendover. Mrs Gower, I'm just plain stuck. It's a bit sheared off the mowing machine. If I give you the number can you check if you've got it?'

She did – and she had.

'What's the chance that you could get it to me? Is there anyone there who could bring it out? One thing after another it is! Can't get my car going or I'd have come in to fetch it. The forecast is that storms are brewing, and I've still got cutting to get done.'

She pictured Harold Garside, Wendover hardly more than a smallholding. Haymaking was important to everyone, but this year especially so to him. He and his wife had worked together, scraping a living, never more. Now she was ill. Jane had heard rumours Garside's wife was in a wheelchair, she was on the downward slope . . .

'Don't you worry. I'll get it to you, Mr Garside. I'll come myself, bring it straight away.'

When Greta heard, she suggested she could put the piece Mr Garside wanted in her saddle bag and ride out to Wendover with it. But a few minutes in a car would be an hour's ride on a bicycle, so Jane left her in charge of the store, told her to be careful to write down anything she sold – and, with a thought for Joshua Grimble, to stay outside in the fresh air unless she had a customer.

She was away from Chugford for about half an hour, time enough for Greta to sell six mower knives and be proud of her efforts. But during that time Jane missed the telephone call she'd been hoping for.

'Grant phoned you, Aunt Jane.'

'Is he coming for supper this evening?'

'No, he can't. He said he'd gone into town this afternoon. He thought being Saturday we might have been home. This evening he can't get away. He said to be sure and tell you that he'd get in touch again. He couldn't say when, but as soon as he could.'

Jane's fear lifted a little.

That was on Saturday 27th May. The next day the troops were all given the order to stay in camp. No mail was allowed out of the base and none in – although Jane wasn't to know that.

Disappointment was tempered with relief as the next few days went by and there was no word from him. They must have started on their exercise. Had it been 'the real thing', then there would have been reports of landings by this time. A whole week went by, another Saturday came and went, but still she heard nothing. There was no pretending that something wasn't happening. The town was usually full of those olive green American-uniformed figures; but not now. Surely everyone must be noticing? Nor were there long convoys of military vehicles heading towards the coast. The stillness could mean only one thing – they must all be involved in the exercise. But where? There was no sound of firing.

Those farmers who hadn't already got their hay in were in trouble. That week gales blew from the Atlantic, bringing squally showers. Wherever the military exercise was, she hoped at least that they had their feet on dry land. Sunday the 4th June dawned, the sky high and blue. Some of the old type countrymen might have sniffed the air and prophesied 'dirty weather on the way', but to Jane it was a morning to lift the spirits. Wherever the operation had taken place, she told herself, it must be over by now. After a whole week, surely the troops would be back in base?

Then her mind took another route. Hadn't Sid said that

they'd all know when the invasion was about to take place? The thousands of men stationed down here for training would have to be moved to the South East where the channel was narrow. Was that where they'd gone? Was that why, here, the town seemed shrouded in silence? But if that were the case, what about the thousands of tanks, lorries, armoured cars and jeeps that had been converging on this part of the coast? If they'd moved off again everyone would know. The strategies of war were outside Jane's understanding. Problems and solutions chased each other in her troubled mind.

Pouring over Greta's school atlas she studied the page that showed the north coast of France and, right at the top of the picture, the south coast of England. She didn't know what she expected to learn; all it did was confirm to her that to cross by sea from here would be one stage short of impossible. The Germans must be watching the channel. Any boats on the sea so long would be sitting targets.

But there was much that she couldn't possibly know: that two days ago the first warships had set out from Scapa Flow, from Belfast and the Clyde; that tomorrow the 5th June was planned as D-Day, the day the first troops should set foot on French soil. Nor could she know on that Sunday that started so bright, a day that to her looked full of hope and promise, the meteorologist gave a forecast for the channel so gloomy that General Eisenhower decided to postpone the invasion for twenty-four hours. D-Day would now be Tuesday the 6th June. Gales, fog, heavy rain . . . in the week ahead, nature was determined to send just the weather the Allies didn't want. On Tuesday the 6th a slight break was promised during the daylight hours. If they didn't go in on the 6th, the tides would be wrong and the whole venture would have to be put off for weeks.

As the hours of Sunday went by, Jane had to accept Grant wasn't coming.

'I'm going to take Mufti o.u.t. Aunt Jane, are you

coming?' Then, understanding far more than she was told: 'It's ever so quiet in the town. I think they must be away somewhere.'

'I think you're right, Greta. But I'll stay here. If they're back, if he gets a chance, he'll come. I'd hate him to find us both out.' The listening Mufti sneezed with excitement at the magic word.

'I'll call for Jeannie Jefferson then. She can bring Rover, he and Mufti like to run together. It's horrid watching for someone who doesn't come, isn't it? I'll not be very long.'

This evening it seemed to Jane that something of the pre-war spirit was abroad in the town. With her elbows on the sill of her open bedroom window she watched the people climb the hill to the church, the women in their best hats – probably most of these had been best hats before the war too, and had been re-trimmed with a fresh flower or a new piece of ribbon.

Except for the churchgoers and two young women pushing prams there was no one about. The very sound and smell of the almost empty street belonged to Sunday. For the past hour or two there had been no sun. Now the wind was getting up, and to the west the sky was grey. She shivered. It wasn't that she was cold, it had more to do with the feeling of Sunday, the memories it stirred, the dreams for a future whose only foundation was hope and trust. She picked up the picture of Tim that she kept by her bed. Sundays at Denby . . . all of it over . . . yet so clear in her mind that it could never be over. Putting the photograph back she pulled herself up straight, looking facts squarely in the face. Denby, a large, empty house. Richard and Liz wouldn't be there with her – instinctively she pulled her thoughts up short. She'd not remember the days when they were both at home. The Sids would come back – but would they want to? She had a suspicion that Mrs Sid rather enjoyed having two men to organize! There was no chance of Hartley coming home until after the war. 'After the war' – and here she willingly let her mind wander off at a tangent.

326

By the time darkness fell the rain was lashing against the window, the wind howling down the chimney. The day was over and Grant hadn't come.

Perhaps tomorrow, was her last thought as she drifted into sleep. But before she woke the ships had sailed, starting on their long sea crossing. This was no exercise.

'Soldiers, Sailors, and Airmen of the Allied Expeditionary Force! You are about to embark upon the Great Crusade . . .'

So began the leaflet given to each man, a leaflet that ended: 'Good luck! And let us all beseech the blessing of Almighty God upon this great and noble undertaking.'

For Jane and Greta that Monday started the same as any other. Hope hadn't died yet. As Jane travelled to Chugford she turned on to the coast road and, just as it had been these last few days, it was empty except for her. It was much later when the first rumour came to her. There were ships ploughing through the grey, mountainous sea towards the far horizon; hundreds of ships. Dusk fell early, visibility was poor, and by then the armada had vanished. The hush of Sunday belonged to yesterday; today, here and everywhere near enough to the coast to be aware, there was a difference in the silence. This wasn't something to gossip and speculate about. Anxiously the people waited, each heart travelling with the men at the mercy of the stormy sea even before they had to face the foe on the beaches. In St Agnes Road the Sailors' Rest had had a notice on the door: 'Next deliver of beer Monday 5th.' But on this Monday evening not even the regulars wanted beer and bar skittles. Tonight they were at home waiting by their wireless sets.

Towards dawn came the heavy drone of aircraft. Bombers! The fires they would light would be a beacon for the landing craft. More planes, this time transporters carrying paratroops. In the silence of night every sound was magnified. Planes so distant that in daytime they wouldn't have been heard, seemed to fill the dark sky. To Jane the important thing was to stay awake. It was the one small way she could keep faith. In any case, sleep was impossible. With her eiderdown wrapped around her, she sat on the edge of the bed, listening, imagining. Keep him safe. Last time, remember last time . . . don't let it be like that! But how can it not be? It must be worse, a hundred times more dreadful. Please, please, take care of him. Keep him safe.

So, as history was made, Jane and millions more waited. To land on foreign soil, to come face to face with another human being, to kill or be killed . . . noise, rubble, screams of fear and of pain . . . only there to pick up the pieces . . . dressing wounds, cutting out shrapnel . . . out in the open, there amongst the fighting . . . only there to pick up the pieces.

The scene was before her constantly; as she went about her work in the stores, as she wrote up her books, sent out her accounts, looked ahead to the next season and put in her orders. Somehow the hours became days; the days, weeks.

'Surprise, surprise!'

She looked up with a start at the unexpected sound of Meg's voice.

'How in the world did you come? Not on your bike surely? Is something wrong with Mother?'

'Grandem? No, she's fine. Doesn't even know I'm here. I was in town – there were oranges at Viner's, three allowed against a child's ration book – so I was in the queue there when Billy Janes came by in his car and stopped. You know Billy? His father has Cload Farm. He's on leave. He was wounded the first day of the landings, got sent back to England. He came home from hospital last Friday.'

'Was he coming here?'

'No, he was going to the abattoir with – well, I didn't actually look into the trailer. Didn't want to meet them eye to eye, whatever they were. He had to pass right by here so it seemed an opportunity too good to miss. He was a real sweetie, waited until it was my turn to be served so that Ben wouldn't miss out on his oranges.'

It was a tonic to see Meg. Nothing changed her. Whatever happened, she managed to turn the situation to her own advantage.

'You're looking very smart. New dress?'

'Mmm. Nice, isn't it? I'd seen it in the window of Fullerton's, but – well, you know what it's like. Coupons just melt, and Ben's grown so much that I've had to let him have pretty well all his own just to keep up with real necessities. Anyway, I happened to be walking by the window with Grandem. We stopped to look.' Meg chuckled. 'You know, Jane, she's a dear with her coupons. I suppose she feels that smart clothes are wasted on her these days. Honestly, I think she gets more pleasure in seeing me wear them, and I'm not complaining!'

'Let's go outside and make the most of the sunshine. I can offer you a seat on a triple roller, how's that?'

'And I can offer you a Gold Flake cigarette. The shop next to Viner's let me have two packets of ten. This is nice, Jane. I'm so glad Billy came long. He said he'd be about an hour.'

It was while they were sitting in the sun that she asked: 'How's that American friend of yours, the major I've seen you with? Did he go over with the others?'

Jane nodded.

'Letters are so slow.'

Meg frowned. 'You've not heard yet? I had a note from Buddy Caffey – a tall captain with very red hair, you've probably noticed him at the Club – I heard from him three days ago.'

Jane didn't answer. She could feel Meg looking at her curiously.

'Jane, you were with him a lot, weren't you?' Just for a moment she sounded concerned, then nature took over and with a chuckle, she went on: 'How word travels, I don't know. Not from me. Honestly, I never told her – anyway, she didn't know I'd been at the Club. She imagined my duties dishing out mugs of tea at the Red Cross canteen kept me busy every evening – but our dear Grandem heard all about the gallant major from someone. It wasn't so much what she said as the way her mouth turned down. She had that bad smell under her nose look when she mentioned it!'

'Usually does where I'm concerned, always has. But it doesn't matter, you know. Tim always accepted that's how it was between his mother and me. I've no idea who told her. Does it matter? Not to me, it doesn't.'

'Ah, so do I take it it's serious?'

'I've not heard though, Meg. If he could have got a letter out, he would.'

'No news is good news.' For Meg to use such a cliché was worse than for her to say nothing. She changed the subject. 'They're clearing the "zone", so they say. Before you know it, you'll be thinking of going home again.'

Jane didn't answer.

In the British Sector the battle for Caen raged; in Normandy the Americans had advanced on Cherbourg.

Hitler was retaliating with his 'secret weapon', the flying bomb, a pilotless plane fired from sites across the channel and aimed at London and the south east counties. Once again children were being sent out of the capital as the toll of dead and injured mounted daily.

It was the beginning of July, a Thursday evening. Greta had gone to Guides. Jane was alone, kneeling on a chair, the newspaper on the table in front of her. Today Winston Churchill had spoken in the House of Commons. He believed in giving the people the truth:

'What of the future? Is this attack going to get worse? Will the rocket bomb come? Will more destructive explosions come? Will there be greater ranges? I can give no guarantee that any of these evils will be finally prevented before the time comes when the soil from which these attacks come has been finally liberated.

'London will never be conquered and will never fail.'

Then Jane's glance travelled further down the page. Hand to hand fighting going on in La Haye – places one had never heard of suddenly found themselves on the front pages of the papers, these days with only four pages and printed so small it needed one's full concentration to read them. She certainly gave hers to the short item of news about La Haye. The Red Cross not being respected, stretcher bearers being shot dead as they carried the wounded. Picking up the pieces . . . The battle must be for existence. How could she hope for mail to come out of that?

It was the picture that small news item left in her mind that decided her. She walked up the hill to the Club. Instinctively she knew that Carol was no friend of hers, but perhaps she would know *something*. But when she got there, she was faced with strangers. No, there was no Carol Roughton here. Major Grant Holgate, was that your friend's name? No, never heard of him. She knew just how they saw her. She wasn't the only woman to be hunting for an American who had moved on. Walking out, she could feel their eyes on her, imagine the sniggers.

They heard that the 'zone' was being cleared, combed for unexploded mines and live ammunition. Jane had bought herself a secondhand bicycle, old and rusted and costing far more than its value. Her own was in store and transport of any sort was at a premium. On the next Sunday afternoon she and Greta cycled as near as they could to the area that had been home.

'Sorry, ma'am, I can't let you down the road.'

'Surely the road itself is safe enough? Why, their own transport used it all the time. We're not sightseers, we live just the other side of Shelcoombe.'

331

The coloured GI, wearing battle dress and a white steel helmet, shook his head dolefully.

'Not even if we promise, cross our hearts, to stay right in the middle of the road?' Greta added her persuasion.

'Wish I could let you go by. But first one then another, always wanting to see their homes are all right. I'd be in the glasshouse if I let you in, and what's more you might be – ' He pointed his thumb heavenwards. 'They're working on it, trying to get things right so you folk can get back home.'

Disappointed, they rode on. Presently they stopped at a heavily barbed wired five-bar gate. The fields lay fallow, there was a curious feeling of emptiness; now the only sound of life was the drone of bees in the wild flowers where no more than weeks ago the air had been rent with the blast of exploding ammunition.

'You'd think they'd never even been here.' Greta's mind must have gone the same way as Jane's.

'Not quite. It was never like this before they came. It's peaceful – but just look at it, Greta. Empty, still, neglected – not a bird, not an animal.' There was something in her voice that disturbed Greta. Denby had been her home for almost half her life; her memories of days before that were pinpointed just by highlights, the rest merging into the mist.

'But it won't be like that when we get back, Aunt Jane. We'll get things going again, we'll soon sort it out.'

If only Jane could find the same enthusiasm. Always she'd been determined not to be beaten by circumstances. But that had been before she'd glimpsed those castles in the air, before she and Grant had planned their 'after the war'.

In the first months after she'd lost Tim, what had frightened her had been that the future had had no shape. Now it had a shape, one she couldn't bear to contemplate.

It was the very next morning when, just before half-past

seven, she heard the click of the letter box, the heavy plop of envelopes landing on the doormat. Greta was on her way down the stairs. She raced to the bottom.

'We've got letters, Aunt Jane! Look, a whole bunch of letters!'

She said 'we', but this time she didn't come to Jane's side to share in that first eager read. Instead she watched and waited, wide-eyed.

'Is he all right?' A reminder that she was here.

Jane nodded.

'Five letters, Greta. All this time we watched and they must have been somewhere on their way. Five all coming together!' She wasn't complaining, there was wonder in her voice. One after the other she tore open the envelopes. The letters were brief, hardly more than notes. They told her nothing, no hint of where he was or what his life was like – and yet they told her everything. He was safe.

'He says to say "Hi" to Greta.'

'Does he say he's had any letters from us?'

'No. They probably take ages. Just like his.'

Up to this point 'after the war' had been something she and Grant had shared with no one.

'Greta, you've heard Grant talk about Arndale, the place he comes from . . .'

'Yes, he showed us some pictures, don't you remember?'

'You know what he wants? What we both want?'

Did she imagine that sudden look of fear in Greta's dark eyes?

'He wants us to be part of his life there.'

'How do you mean, us?'

'You and me?'

'Phew!'

'Somehow this morning, now that letters are starting to come through, it feels safe to look ahead again. The invasion was like a barrier. We had to get through that. If I'd told you before it would have felt like tempting fate.'

'Phew!' For a girl hoping for a scholarship to the Grammar School, she seemed to have a remarkably small vocabulary!

'Is that supposed to sound like approval?' Jane laughed.

'You and Grant and me . . . gosh! Yes, of course it is, Aunt Jane. Phew! But what about Liz and Richard? What about Hartley – and Mr and Mrs Sid – and the stores, who'll look after things there? And Denby, Aunt Jane? That's their home. Will you just leave Mrs Sid to see to things there? And Mufti – can we take Mufti?'

Greta was acknowledging the hurdles that Jane had jumped without so much as a glance. Of course they would have to be faced, each one in its turn. Greta had been the first to be told, but then she presented no problem.

'Now that I know Grant is safe, I shall tell the others. They'll understand, of course they will.' She wished she could feel as confident as she sounded.

'Anyway, today can I cycle to Mrs Sid after school? I want to tell her we've had letters.' Then with that understanding that Jane had learnt to take for granted: 'I won't say more than that. Just how worried we'd been and now everything's all right.'

There was little that went on in Shalbury Hill that Clara Mitchell didn't know about. Living next door to her, Jane had soon found this out. On the day that Grant's first letters arrived, neither Jane nor Greta looked up towards the bedroom window of No. 2 as, with Mufti doing his lead-biting performance, they hurried down the hill to the town and the Post Office. But Clara missed nothing. Carrying envelopes, there was no doubt what the rush was.

Another ten minutes and the post will have gone. No wonder they're running! And just look at that silly dog. Nine years old, I know he is, the child told me so herself. Acting up like a puppy! She took up her knitting again as they disappeared. Not like it was when those Yankeedoodle boys were about the place. Ah, and I'd bet a pound to a penny that's what madam next door thinks too, goings on like I wouldn't mind betting there were next door – and her with a child in the house! Can't tell me he spent the hours he did in there and all he got was his late night cocoa! Now who's that coming up the path from the allotments? Bob Hawkes – got a bundle of – looks for all the world like runner beans. Early for runners. Still, when I walked down to see how things were doing, I did notice his were forming. Wouldn't hurt him to offer me a boiling. But no, not him. Wouldn't give away the drippings from his long nose. Remember when I asked him for a few sprigs of mint – Now, wait a minute, who's this I see?

She didn't wait to answer her silent question. Instead, she flung up her bottom window and leant out.

'Nice to see you home, Mr Gower.'

'Good evening, Mrs Mitchell. Thank you,' Richard called back as he hammered on the door of No. 4.

'You've only just missed them. Your mother and Greta. I happened to look up as they went down the road. You could leave your bag with me and walk to meet them, if you like? They've only gone to the Post Ofice and to take the dog for a run.'

'Don't worry. I'll go and get half a pint while I wait. They'll be home by then. If you see them come back, don't say I'm here. I like to surprise them.'

Now that was a pity. It would have been a chance for a few words with them. With an extra mouth to feed perhaps they might have wanted to borrow a drop of milk or half a loaf. I might have popped round with it, seen some of the fun and excitement. Not once have they asked me inside their door.

She saw Jane and Greta return; she watched for Richard to come back up the hill. Then she rolled away her knitting and hurried down the stairs. At the bottom was a small table where she kept a tumbler handy, an empty one. Putting it against the wall she pressed her ear to it. Clearly she heard the sound of the door knocker, of Jane's shout to Greta to answer it. After that it was hard to pick out what was being said, just an excited clamour. And once they moved away from the passage into the sitting room she could hardly hear at all. She sat on the stairs, her glass hard against her ear; she perked up when there were footsteps on the corresponding flight just through the wall, then she heard Greta run back down, saying that she'd moved her things and put Richard's in her room. But after that the distant voices only emphasized the silence in her own house. Better to have stayed upstairs and got on with her knitting.

She put the glass back on the table and went upstairs again. She'd get to bed before she had to fix the blackout.

What a mistake! If she'd stayed at her post she would have heard something to give her plenty to think about!

'Nice to be home, Mum. After last time I decided not to come. I've been in Liverpool all the week. Then this morning I imagined how you must be watching the post, wondering when I'd get home.'

Richard stretched out in the armchair before the empty grate, the newspaper open and unread on his lap. It was the last hour of the day. Greta was in bed. 'Last time – well, if I was beastly to you, Mum, I'm sorry.'

'About Grant? Let's forget it, Richard. You shouldn't have spoken as you did and I shouldn't have lashed out. So let's forget any of it ever happened.'

'The landlord at the Royal Oak tells me the Yanks have all gone from the evacuation area now that we've invaded. I bet they've left a good many broken hearts behind – and worse.'

'It's like fate, your coming home today. I'd just written to you, to each of you – you, Liz and Hartley. I know the letters won't all arrive at the same time but at least I felt that that's how I told you.'

'Told us what? Let me guess. Something to do with

Denby? Some scheme you're hatching up for when you go back there. I bet you're going to do what Grandma suggested, turn it into a guest house. Am I right?' He sounded like the old Richard, cheerful and affectionate.

'In a way it's about Denby. I'm not going back there. For the time being, Greta and I are managing here.'

'But you can't stay in this rabbit hutch of a place, Mum! I know it's convenient for Greta when she goes to the Grammar School, but have a heart! What about when the stuff comes out of store?' He folded the paper and sat up straighter. His indulgent smile seemed to say that it was time he took her in hand and sorted things out for her.

'I shan't get the furniture out of store. That's to say – I shan't keep it – well, I may get some of it. I don't know. I haven't thought about that sort of thing.' That was yet another hurdle, this time one that even Greta had missed. 'Listen, Richard – and don't interrupt. This is what I told you in my letter. When the war's over, or before if he can get back to England for leave, I'm going to marry Grant.'

The smile vanished.

'You're kidding. You've got to be kidding. Mum, it's bloody daft! How long have you known the man? A few months, a few wartime months.'

'It's nothing to do with being wartime. You said much the same to Liz.' Her voice cut like a knife. 'You managed to wreck their happiness but you're not going to wreck ours.'

'That's a rotten thing to say! Them, you, your Yank, blokes I go to sea with – can't any of you just hang on to the things that matter? Look back to what it used to be like, solid, permanent. Then the blasted war knocks it all from under our feet and you all go chasing rainbows.'

'Richard, I'm not some teenage girl. Remember me? I'm your mother. I know just what we had before the war. Oh, and I thought it was safe, ours forever. But nothing's like that.'

'So you want to throw away all that you and Dad had,

for some bloke you have a wartime affair with? Anyway, if you *were* a teenage girl it wouldn't be so – so unbelievable. Grandma says women were just the same in the last war, and lots of them lived to regret it. Anyway, you're not just *any* woman, you're our mother! You and Dad were super. Nothing at home ever changed. Even when we were kids, we knew how good it all was. When we used to come home from school we knew exactly how it would all be. Surely you can't have forgotten all that, Mum? If you don't care about us then think of Dad. Imagine the old biddies gossiping in Shelcoombe. What a slap in the face for Dad.'

'I'm not going to justify what I do to you. Why should I?'

'Doesn't that just show how you've changed! We used to be a family. Now we're nothing. Bloody nothing!' Standing up, he threw the newspaper to the floor. 'I'm going for a walk. In the morning I'll move over to Grandma's.'

Mufti was out of his basket and making for the door. The magic word hadn't gone unnoticed.

'If you're going out, take the spare key. I shall be in bed.' Not a family! Bloody nothing! Why couldn't he try to understand. Being a family had nothing to do with an unchanging home, meals on the table at the same hour, shirts ironed. '. . . not just *any* woman, you're our mother'.

She heard the front door slam.

If he hadn't heard a lorry rumbling along in the same direction as he was heading, a walk was all it would have been. It wasn't until that moment that the idea came to him and in the moonlight he waved a handkerchief to attract the driver to pull up.

'Any chance of a lift? Where are you heading?'

'Dartmouth. Any use to you?'

'Sure. I'm making for the Ash area. You could drop me off at the fork in the road if you would.'

'Ash, you say. Just missed being turned out then. They tell me the ground is being cleared, but there are still plenty of sentries with road blocks. Mate of mine got through, though. Snared a couple of good rabbits.'

The West Country voice had a soothing effect on Richard. In the dark here he could almost imagine things were as they used to be. He was hitching a lift back home. As if to reassure him, Mufti washed his left ear.

Once he'd been put off at the fork of the road, Richard knew every lane and by-way. A mile or so on was a right turn; but that would probably have a guard. Between here and there were barbed wire fences, signs that by daylight he would read as warnings that it was a 'Restricted Area'. Lying almost flat on the ground he slithered under the wire, he and Mufti too.

For half an hour or more he walked, wondering what all the fuss about mines was for. This was just like it used to be. He skirted the edge of the field, knowing that when he reached the lane he could walk it blindfold. Home, that's what he wanted, what they all wanted. Mum would see things differently once she got home to Denby. All their yesterdays would be waiting there. He quickened his pace, Mufti rushing ahead, then back every minute or so to make sure he was coming.

In his mind he could see Denby so clearly, knew just how it would look in the moonlight, the yard, the barns and sheds, all of it as he'd seen it thousands of times. He'd thought of it so often, remembered the huge old kitchen, the clucking of the chickens out in the yard, the vaguely tobacco smell of Dad's 'office'. Liz with a hamper of food on her luggage grid, Liz in the yard bent so that he could leap-frog over her, Liz helping turn the drying corn, the sound of her laugh, Liz on roller skates, Liz cleaning the henhouse . . . whatever he thought of, always it was Liz. What a bloody fool he'd been! His mother talked about him wrecking Liz's happiness with Hartley, as if that was all that mattered. None of them thought about him, about what he and Liz had always shared.

Out of the dark an animal rushed across their track. A fox looking for a rabbit supper.

They were a long way from the nearest sentry who, in any case, had his mind on other things. A few weeks ago guard duty would have been a solitary affair. Tonight Sergeant Mick O'Mallory had company in the form of a plump and promising blonde, her bicycle propped against the hedge and her mackintosh spread out to protect her from insects, twigs and stinging nettles. Those few weeks had made a difference in other ways too. Now there was a silence in the night not to be known then. Already well after midnight, no one was likely to try and pass down the road now. The sergeant took off his steel helmet and his jacket, then joined her on the mackintosh. He pulled off his tie . . . and at that very second they heard it! Some way away, but certainly within the zone, a muffled explosion.

'Never thought I'd have to trace my mother through the nick.' Richard's words echoed in Jane's memory as she sat in the back of the police car.

'You're sure he's not hurt?'

'Gave him a fright he won't forget in a hurry, ma'am, you may be sure of that. If the little dog hadn't been in trouble, I doubt if the Snowdrop would have tracked him down. He'd probably have gone out the way he'd come in – across the fields and under the wires, I'd bet. But as it was he had to carry the little fellow carefully, had to keep to the road. So that's how they picked him up. He's not the first to have got in there. That's the problem, you see. They all think because they know the lay of the land they can look after themselves. Officialdom, that's the way they see the barriers. Never think they're there for safety's sake.'

'But, Constable, if he's not hurt, and he couldn't have been doing anyone's land any harm – '

'Not the point. Out of bounds is out of bounds. It's time folk saw someone taken to task. Perhaps that might make them think the odd rabbit isn't worth the risk.'

'Richard wasn't after rabbits, I'm sure he wasn't. He only arrived on leave yesterday. We'd been talking about home. He must have wanted to make sure it was still there. Is that such a crime?'

'Out of bounds is out of bounds. I'm sorry, ma'am, for you I mean, just when you're welcoming him home. But we've all got our duty to do. Between ourselves I'll tell you that he was given a good breakfast down at the station. It's safety of others as much as anything, that's why we have to make a case of it. Before we know it, it'll be a poacher not a fox gets his ticket to Kingdom Come.'

In the yard of the Police Station another constable opened the car door for her. Inside, from behind the counter, a police sergeant smiled a welcome.

'You'll be Mrs Gower, ma'am. Mr Squires, the vet, has collected the little dog. His place is in Russell Street.'

'Is Mufti badly hurt?'

'Couldn't seem to stand up. Nice little chap. Never lost his rag with us even though you could see he was hurting.'

'And Richard? Can I see him?'

'Just now he's been taken through to the Magistrate's Court. He told us he'd just come on leave. We did our best to get things moving. Mr Hoskins came in specially for ten o'clock. Won't be many minutes, ma'am. All pretty cut and dried, I expect. Can we get you a cup of tea while you wait?'

It wasn't a bit the sort of reception she'd seen at police stations in the cinema. She declined the cup of tea. While she sat and waited the sergeant and the constable appeared to have forgotten all about her. She found herself thinking how Mrs Mitchell would have enjoyed waiting here. It was impossible not to listen to the two men chattering about their allotments, the size of a fish the sergeant had caught on his last day off, everyday things to while away the time – and always the chance that a villain might be brought in to add extra colour!

The nearest to a villain was Richard, sheepishly avoiding his mother's eyes. On payment of five pounds bail he was allowed home, to present himself again in court on Friday morning.

'From here to Russell Street. Mr Squires is looking after Mufti.' She made no reference to last night.

'Mum, you must have wondered why I didn't come home last night. I've made a right fool of myself.'

She didn't tell him what she'd imagined – that he'd gone to his grandmother.

'Not a fool, Richard. I can understand your wanting to go to Denby. But we can't hold our memories safe in bricks and mortar. The lives we had, everything that we were at Denby, all that's part of each one of us. Children or grown up, whatever we do with our lives builds, today is built on all our yesterdays. You didn't want to farm Denby, does that mean that your years there meant nothing? No, of course it doesn't.'

'I never said that. My years there meant everything. It's you who want to throw it all away.'

'I don't! And even if I did, I couldn't. It's part of you, part of Liz, Hartley, Greta. Part of me, and it always will be.'

'Easy enough to say, then walk off and wash your hands of it all. Can you imagine someone else living there? Probably pulling down Dad's office, putting a garage where you had the henhouse?'

She stopped walking. In the middle of the path, in the middle of the morning, he turned to look at her.

'Well, can you? Or don't you care?'

'I'm not going to imagine it. Oh, Richard, I can't teach you, you have to learn for yourself.' They walked on in an uncomfortable silence. 'For someone who's spent the night in the nick, you don't sound too chastened,' she laughed, trying to put them on an easier footing. 'And, most important, what do you think is the matter with our poor little Mufti?'

'It was some damned fox that triggered the thing off, a hell of a bang. Put an end to his hunting days, no doubt about that. We were some way away, but Mufti had seen it and set up chase so he was closer than I was. He got hurled a long way. I thought he was a gonner when I picked him up. Don't know what he'd done, maybe no more than been knocked senseless. But I told the copper I insisted on a vet. They called old Squires out and he carted him off, but I was kept in the cooler. I didn't get a chance to talk to him.'

'Serves you right, my lad.' Then, mimicking the constable: 'Out of bounds is out of bounds.'

'So the bobby kept telling me. Bloody little Hitler.'

Mufti was still sedated, Mr Squires wanted to keep him until the evening. But there was nothing seriously wrong with him. A dislocated joint had been manipulated back into place and sleep would be his healer.

When, in the afternoon, Richard offered to ride Jane's bicycle to Chugford Farm and collect the car, gladly she agreed. With him out of the way she might better be able to think about what he'd done last night, to put herself in his place. But always her thoughts brought her back to Liz. It wasn't just to Denby that Richard clung. If that dreadful affair hadn't happened, then he and Liz would neither of them have been hurt at the thought of her making a life for herself. But it had happened; nothing could turn the clock back. She was the one thing that held them together. Was that why he was so frightened of her going? Daydreaming, she let her mind wander back down the years, saw the two of them at play, almost heard their voices.

But they're not children any longer. Liz is trying to sort her life out. Richard must learn to do the same. I can't do it for him. I can't do it for either of them. I'm not going to think about it today. I'll leave it, think about it tomorrow . . . Supposing he'd been walking that bit further

343

forward, supposing he'd stepped where the fox did? Was it my fault? Did I drive him to it? To be welcomed home, given a good leave, made to feel how much he matters – is that so much to ask? He gets spiteful because he's hurt, frightened, I know that's what it is. But it's not fair. No, I'll leave it, it may look different by tomorrow. Liz could make things right for him. Yet how could she, after what happened?

CHAPTER SEVENTEEN

Farms were given priority. John Carlisle had wasted no time in applying for a permit to visit to assess the damage. Keyhaven and the fields that had belonged to Denby were amongst the first to be checked, and his permit granted, not yet to move back, but to inspect and have any necessary work put in hand. He told Jane none of this; he wanted to surprise her. It was the day after Richard's arrival that John caught a train from Carlisle just after five o'clock in the morning, taking the station taxi on to Keyhaven. At the road barrier he showed his permit. The 'Snowdrop' on duty let him through, with a warning not to stray beyond the limits of his own boundary. He knew exactly what he meant to do: he would take a good look around his property, then climb the gate that divided the lower fields from the yard at Denby. He'd be able to give Jane a report of how things were there. No longer a farm, it might be many weeks before she was given a permit to look around for herself and he'd hardly trip over live ammunition in the yard there in broad daylight.

The taxi driver stayed in his vehicle. He wasn't going to risk wandering off the road in an area like this! Stories were rife of live ammunition, perhaps even landmines. John carried a notebook and pen. He intended to list everything he found and make sure he put in for repairs. From the attic to the cellar he checked. There was no doubt the house had been used; there were ashes from a wood fire in the sitting room grate, a dart board left hanging on his study wall. But it had been used carefully, the board had even been attached to a wooden backshield. As far as he could see one minute crack in the corner of the hall window was the only damage. And outside the story was the same. One or two patches of oil on the ground, a huge metal container full to overflowing with empty bottles; whoever had made free with Keyhaven hadn't gone short of refreshment! For an hour or so he walked, skirting the fields, the lower ones once part of Tim's farm. Then he climbed the gate and started his examination of Denby.

The day Jane had moved out, the guttering had been blocked and overflowing. Weeks of heavy rain had taken their toll. By the time John saw it it had fallen to lie on the ground. He tried the back door expecting it to be locked. Not so. In he went, his tour of inspection just as thorough here as it had been at Keyhaven. Denby, the farm cottages, the barn extension that had called itself an office, Jane's mushroom sheds . . . everything was in order. He climbed back over the gate, still secured by its lock and chain. When they'd left home they'd all locked their doors, but that hadn't kept their American cousins out. Yet no one had tampered with the padlock that divided a field from a farmyard. Stopping to brush the dirt from his trousers, he smiled to himself, imagining them probably taking it at one neat vault.

When he finally got back to the waiting taxi the driver was asleep in the afternoon sunshine, still behind the steering wheel, mouth open, arms folded. Waking with a snort, he pulled himself together.

'Much trouble down there, Guv?'

'Everything looks in very good shape. Now I'd like you to take me to Chugford Farm, Mannerby.'

He hadn't told Jane when he was coming. Part of the pleasure had been to imagine her expression when she looked up expecting a customer – and there he was! If, deep in his heart, he hoped she'd missed him more than she'd expected over these months, if some of that might show in the smile she'd turn on him, he didn't acknowledge it even to himself.

As they pulled up in the yard of Chugford it was Joshua who came out to greet him.

'Well, dang me if it's not Mr Carlisle! You that let me take over your iron steed. Are they letting you back to your own place again then, Mr Carlisle? Mrs Gower hasn't said anything to me about shifting off yet awhile.'

'No, I've only had permission to check things over. I see Mrs Gower's car's over there. Where does she operate from?'

'From over yonder in those barns. Comfortable enough they are in there, had the electric on and the telephone put through. Many a time I've said to her that I was glad to be able to help her out. Don't know where she would have been with all that clobber to find a home for if it hadn't been for my brother and me. Still, what else are friends for?'

'I'll go and surprise her.'

'Not in my barns, you won't, not this afternoon. Ted Hiles is all you'll find in there, and he doesn't know any more than I do what's up. She turned in as usual this morning – and thinking back to it now, I'd say she didn't look in her best good humour. Not ten minutes later comes this black car and out gets a bobby.'

'A police car?'

'That's what I said. Out she came with the constable and he drove her off. I called out to her, asked her what the trouble was. Behaved just as if I hadn't spoken. That was about half-past nine this morning and there's been not a sign of her since.'

That afternoon Jane would have welcomed any kind of diversion from her thoughts. If John had been hoping for pleasure in her expression, he wasn't disappointed.

'You've actually got your permit?' she said as he told her where he'd been. 'Are you sure it's safe?'

'Here I am as living proof of it. Then, after I'd made a thorough check of Keyhaven, I walked across the fields and down into Denby.'

'But, John, there might have been booby traps, ammunition!'

'I'd say that our American cousins have treated our properties well. As far as I could see – and I went through every room at Denby – there had been no damage at all. In fact, there was no sign there that it had been used, except that the back door had been left unbolted. It opened with the latch. So I suppose someone had picked the front door lock.'

'We used to be able to turn that lock with a sixpence. I bet that's what they did, then unbolted the back. So I take it you'll be coming back soon?'

'What about you, Jane?'

'Do you remember just before we moved out, we were talking about the mushrooms, I said I didn't think I could start up again? No, John, for the present I shall stay here. Anyway,' she heard the defiance in her voice, 'Richard's at sea, Liz in the Army, Hartley a prisoner. Just Greta and me in a house full of ghosts.'

'Keyhaven looked uninvitingly empty too. A bachelor home has no ghosts. It takes living people to leave their spirits behind. Keyhaven is waiting to be lived in. I don't know, Jane, whether to come back or make a fresh start. I talked to you before about buying a hill farm up there.' She heard the question in his words, but chose to ignore it.

She thought of Denby, its rooms full of emptiness; then of Keyhaven, John gone and not coming back. Her mind jumped again, taking her by surprise: Arndale. In her imagination she could see it so clearly, the tree-lined street, the wooden houses, neat and bright. The surgery – the doctor's office – the school where Greta would go. The Junior High, that's what Grant had called it. Happiness bubbled inside her. Her mouth couldn't help smiling.

'I went to Chugford first,' John was saying, 'they said you'd been fetched away.'

'That was a polite way of putting it,' she laughed. 'Richard spent the night in the cells. Unlike you, he didn't wait for a permit. He got in where he shouldn't.'

'You mean he'd already been to Denby?'

'No, he didn't get that far. My son and heir is out on bail at the moment, his case will be heard on Friday.' But still she smiled. There was a gaiety about her than John liked to believe had to do with his unexpected appearance. He didn't probe any deeper, had no intention of pushing her. He was adept at biding his time.

His business in Shelcoombe was done so the next day he returned to the North, leaving behind that veiled hint that he'd dropped and she'd failed to pick up.

Although the incident in the 'zone' had glossed over the scene between Jane and Richard, he still moved on to Emily as he'd said. 'She likes to have me there', '. . . more room', 'don't like putting Greta out of her bedroom'. His departure was wrapped in plausible excuses, his manner unfailingly polite; it drove the wedge between them deeper. A week later he went back to his ship, the twenty pound fine he'd paid into the Court standing as a warning to other locals with an eye on trespass.

Halfway through August came the looked-for letter offering Greta her scholarship place at the Grammar School. They snatched at the interest it gave them, the challenge of fitting her out in her new uniform. Jane thought of what Meg had said about Emily not using her coupons. She telephone from Chugford to tell her mother-in-law that Greta had won a place. She even hoped an offer might be made, at least enough to use on a gymslip or a couple of blouses.

'I've no doubt some people would think it highly commendable,' Jane could imagine her tight-lipped expression, 'but sometimes I do wonder what the country is coming to. The Grammar School for a child from the slums! That's what she was and there's no denying it. If I had a daugher there – sent there properly, paying fees as one should – I'd not want these free places handed out to all and sundry. Jack's as good as his master, that's the way they're all fancying themselves these days!'

'In Greta's case, Mother, Jack's a good deal better. I just thought you might have been interested. Anyway, will you be sure and tell Meg?' She hung up the receiver without waiting for Emily's reply.

The list of necessary uniform was long – at least, long by wartime standards. At the bottom of the printed sheet was a recommendation that there was an 'Exchange Shop' where used clothes could be obtained. But she wasn't having that! She remembered the off-white pillowcase and made up her mind that somehow Greta's elevation to the Grammar School, even if it wasn't to be for long, deserved the best she could buy. For herself, she could manage. Greta had eleven coupons, she had ten and a half . . . In the end it was the Sids who made a complete outfit possible, handing over their coupons with as much pride as if Greta had been their grand-daughter.

So passed August. Allied forces landed on the Southern coast of France; in the northern provinces the push went on; Paris was liberated; Americans pressed on towards the German border; the British freed Antwerp and Brussels. And at home the precise and, by now, familiar tones of the BBC announcers brought word into the living rooms; cold facts, figures. For Jane and for millions more who waited, news meant just one thing – the click of the letterbox, the handwriting that mattered on an envelope. Sometimes almost each day a letter would come; other times a week, even two, would go by and then a heavy plop on the doormat and three or four would arrive together. Allied forces entered Germany; in France a link-up was made between forces from the north and from the south; the Red Army entered Warsaw. And at home with the ending of Double British Summer Time the blackout regulations were lifted; compulsory Home Guard duties were abolished; Greta went proudly to the Grammar School. Yet all that was but a background. Life still revolved around the click of the letterbox.

Each night, sitting up in bed, Jane wrote. She and

Grant had had such a short time together if time can be measured in weeks and months. But it can't. Even in those winter days when first he'd become part of her life, she'd recognized that time had nothing to do with the affinity that drew them to each other.

He never wrote of where he was – and, if he had, there was always the chance that censorship would have struck it out. Normally his writing was neat ('Not like a doctor!' she'd once told him), but there were times when the envelope contained no more than a scribbled single sheet: 'I think of you always, my darling honey gold girl. More than anything right now what I want is to lie close in your arms – and sleep.' And reading it, that was what she wanted too. Just to hold him, to comfort and try and take away from him the memories this war was inflicting. Then there was a day late in September when he wrote: 'Imagine, Jane, at home it's fall. Please God next year we'll be there together to see it. Shattered lives, broken bodies, helplessness, hopelessness – sometimes I look around and I'm plain scared, for *us* I'm scared. Why should we expect to be different from all these others? What right have we to the sort of vision I see for us? The nearest to that vision is your letters. But we must never doubt, we must hold on to the tomorrow that will come one day. Many years ahead, when we're old, we'll sit on the verandah and remember all this. It'll be no more than one link in the chain that has made our lives together.' How could she help looking at that ornament of the elderly country couple? 'You and me, Lady Jane, when we've grown old together.'

For all John's talk of a hill farm, by the end of September he was living at Keyhaven. Moving back involved much more organization than moving out had done. Then it had been a question of selling stock, taking the best price the market could offer. Now the stock had to be replaced, an opportunity for farmers from outside the 'zone' to off-load livestock, knowing that with demand high so too would be prices. Another problem was staff. They might not have wanted to shift out, but nine months later most of them were settled and not at all keen on moving back. Of course there were exceptions, but Jane knew from other farmers she talked to as well as from John that all the problems of the return wouldn't be covered by the Government's guarantee that expenses would be met and any damage made good.

Main items of machinery had been stored, but much had been discarded; items like half used reels of wire, opened boxes of electric fence insulators, half used drums of disinfectant.

John passed Jane his neatly written list.

'No great panic with any of it, I've a long way to go before I'm back in business. I imagine you'll get the go ahead at Denby pretty soon now.'

'I'm not going back to Denby. I told you, John – it's like the mushrooms, I'm not starting it again.'

'You mean . . . ?' Too late she realized he'd misunderstood her.

'These months have altered things.'

'You've thought about it, about us?'

'No, not us, John. I've hardly seen you – on our own, I mean. I want to tell you – '

'I met Mrs Gower, Tim's mother. Full of gossip as always.'

On the surface it had no connection with what they'd been saying, but rake that surface and it was as clear as if he'd asked her a direct question.

'She told you about Grant?' So now Jane too told him. 'When we were evacuated, I said I would never marry again, remember? I honestly believed it. He wanted it to be before the invasion – I did, too, but because of the children I wouldn't. Sounds silly, when they're grown up and gone away, but they hardly knew him. I wanted everyone to be happy about what I was doing – so I said I wanted to wait.'

'He's a lucky man, Jane. And Richard and Liz? What do

they think about you going away? Or is he staying here when the fighting's done?'

'Richard thinks I'm making a laughing stock of myself.' She sounded aggressive, her blue eyes defying him to agree. 'Liz says very little. Or rather, writes very little. She hasn't been home for months. Not since Hartley was shot down. I've heard from him. You never have to spell things out to Hartley.'

He opened that ever ready gold cigarette case and passed it to her. How was it he still managed to smoke Passing Cloud? She smiled to herself, but John didn't notice. What of his own future? Strangers at Denby, no Jane to drive to town with, to take to lunch at the Red Lion, to try to persuade to marry him.

Sitting on the triple roller that had to double as a garden seat for her at Chugford, enjoying the autumn sunshine, she smoked in silence. Behind them in the barn came the hammering of metal being shaped on the anvil, the sound of it all part of the country peace.

'You didn't say. Are you staying here or is he taking you away?'

'Away, John.' And try as she might she couldn't keep the smile out of her voice. 'It really looks as if things are on the last downhill run, doesn't it? Here and in Europe too. You back at Keyhaven; I've been to check Gower's stores and workshops. There's a bit of damage but we'll soon be shifting back. Street lights on again. Suddenly we don't feel frightened to hope any more.'

'A brave new world waiting for us tomorrow. Well, Jane, my dear, you deserve it. I hope I meet Grant. Mostly I hope he'll make you as happy as you deserve to be.'

Her eyes were bright with tears.

'Dear John.' He never failed her; he never had.

'See who's coming.' He was the first to notice. 'The girl who lived with you at Denby? Meg, isn't that her name?'

How could Meg pedal more than four miles and arrive looking like this? As she free-wheeled into the yard the other two got up to meet her. What John's thoughts were Jane couldn't know, but her reaction was to be conscious of her own untidiness. In a cool-looking, green and white checked dress with a wide white belt, her pageboy hair smoothly secured in a white net snood, white wedge-heeled sandals and bare legs. Meg looked fresh, young, yet with a sophistication that was in-built. Looking at her own worn dungarees, washed until the blue was faded, the knees covered with ingrained dirt from where she'd been kneeling to sort out the bottom cubbyholes, Jane couldn't help hearing an echo of Mrs Sid's warnings. 'Looks don't last forever, and they won't last at all if you always get yourself up like some farmer's boy.'

'Oh, good, you don't look desperately busy.' Meg propped her bike against a tractor that had been in for repair. 'I've only come to waste your time. Ben had the lad from Rylands to tea yesterday – you know it, a mile or so back up the lane. Silly creature left his blazer behind so I just dropped it home for him.' Then to John, and with the smile that made men her willing slaves: 'Hello, Grandem told me she'd met you. Nice to see people coming back where they belong. Can I share your roller or am I disturbing private business talk?'

'Neither private nor business. Come and join us.' Jane moved along. 'Here, sit where I've been. I'll have rubbed the worst of the grubbiness off already. You look crisp and clean.'

'I'm kidding myself it's still summer. Any day the autumn winds will blow and away will have to go the summer dresses. Oh, bother, it looks as though you've got a customer.' A van turned into the yard. 'Is there anyone else in there to serve him?'

'No, I'd better go. Don't run away, I'll be back.'

But she didn't hurry. Old Joseph Bucknall looked on five minutes' chatter as part of the service. If a man had to use his petrol ration to get here, he expected full value! Looking out at the two on the roller, she could see they were doing well enough without her. They must have

354

half known each other for years, known each other without the interest to go beyond a nodding acquaintance. This morning was remedying that. Then, as Joseph Bucknall said goodbye, the railway delivery lorry drew up, followed closely by a muddied tractor driver with a broken casting in his hand and a worried look on his face. By the time she was free again, Meg was already standing up, a four mile ride facing her.

'I'm not letting you ride all that way.' John stood up too. 'Let's see if we can find a piece of rope and tie your cycle on the car, shall we? Let me take you back to town.'

'What a lovely idea! And you can tell me all your plans for opening up Keyhaven again.'

Jane hadn't wanted to hurt John. But watching them drive away without a backward glance, no wonder she thought again of Mrs Sid's dire warning about what happened to women who don't make the best of themselves!

A week or so later it was Mrs Sid herself who mentioned to Jane that she'd seen Meg and John together, coming out of the George.

'I hope you know what you're doing, Mrs G., my dear, you and this American major you're set on marrying. I would have staked all my savings on Mr Carlisle being serious sweet on you, didn't I tell you so? Now, you just see if I'm not right, that young minx'll get him on the rebound.'

'Mrs Sid, you're an old romantic. John and I are very good friends. We're fond of each other, that's all. Anyway, he's old enough to be Meg's father.'

'Nothing as silly as a man gone beyond his prime, especially a man who's a mite conceited of himself. Not that I've anything against Mr Carlisle, a better neighbour we couldn't have had. But fond of his looks, always was, even as a young man. Now that Meg, she's shared herself around over these years when there've been plenty of takers. But before we know it, peace will be here again, the men gone back where they belong. The likes of Meg have a thin time then. Maybe it's just a sugar daddy she's after – ah, and maybe it isn't. More likely it's a meal ticket for life. Before you let her push your nose right out of joint, Mrs G., you just be sure you know what you're doing. Come peacetime and all the strangers go back where they fit in, it could be you'd find yourself a square peg in a round hole out there in a strange land.'

But Jane was so sure. No words could hurt her.

'Peace nearly here. Suddenly everything seems to be falling into place. We've taken more than half the stock back to the stores. Another day or two and we can say goodbye to Chugford Farm.'

'And what about Denby?'

'I've not been in yet. John looked over it, I told you, he says it's in good condition.' She was watching her old friend closely. 'Tell me the truth, Mrs Sid. How do you both feel about it being sold?'

'The truth . . . well, the honest truth is, we're managing on our bit of pension, it's time we gave up working. And we fit in very snug where we are. I'm not saying I shan't be sad to see Denby go, many happy years we had there together. Ah, and many happy memories we're left with. Just you make sure when you get out there you and Greta don't forget us. Letters can make the high spots in a body's life – that's something we've all come to know.'

That was in October. The talk of peace being almost here was on everyone's lips. A few days ago the newspaper had given almost a full page to details of the plans for demobilization. It was impossible not to be infected with the fever of optimism, and after more than five years of war people were eager to believe.

On her own Jane took her permit and drove to Denby. Shelcoombe was coming to life again. Oswald Peatty had a notice on his empty window 'Opening November – Our Sausages will still be the Best in the West'. There was no smell of baking yet from Harold Batty's bakehouse, but Madge Tozer had hopefully opened up even though only one or two of the cottages were occupied. Like a memorial to all their yesterdays stood Ted Maddiford's Garage. Jane was glad to leave the village behind her and drive on down the familiar lane. Denby. As she rounded the bend it came into sight. Instinctively she jammed on her brakes. But this was crazy! John had been round it, he had told her nothing had been damaged. The windows were broken, the guttering down. She drove into the yard and climbed slowly out of the car, frightened of what she'd see next. Instead of going into the house, she walked across to Tim's office. At least there the window was intact. Before she looked around she'd go in there, shut the door, climb to sit on the bench; it was as if that way she'd re-charge her batteries, find the strength to look further.

'Oh, no. But why? Damn them, damn them!' The bench was gone, the little room stripped bare. She was consumed with rage. If the Americans had done it, she would have been angry, hurt. But this! Their own people, to come to Denby, to vandalize, steal – believing the Americans would be blamed for the damage that was found. How dare they? Inside the house the story was the same. The copper tank had been taken from the roof, copper piping stripped, brass taps taken, the bathroom basin smashed. Brass doorhandles were gone, even the door itself from the children's den. In the bedroom that had been hers and Tim's the faded patches on the wallpaper told their story of where pictures used to hang; now in the corner the plaster ceiling had been brought down when the tank above it had been taken out by people who didn't know what they were doing and had let water pour through. With her eyes closed she leant against the wall. Closed lids can't hold back tears. She felt them roll down her cheeks. The Gowers of Denby.

'Tim, who'd want to do it?' she gulped. She could feel the embossed wallpaper under her palms. She remembered when they'd had Cyril Ridley decorate it for them. It had been just before the twins had gone away to school. They'd all stood here together admiring it. The Gowers of Denby. Forget what it was today, hang on to the memories. What was the good of standing here snivelling? It was this feeling of guilt the children gave her.

'It's as if all this is some sort of sign, a punishment,' she snorted, speaking aloud in the empty house. 'That's how they'd see it, I know they would. Tim . . . our home . . . just a broken down house. Please, Tim, please understand.'

But would he, any more than they did?

It would have been so easy to accept John's offer that he should go through the house again, note anything that had to be done, put the repairs in hand. But this was something she had to do herself. In her heart she felt she was doing it for Tim.

And so passed October, days that history would remember for the gallantry of the British at Arnhem, and the Americans at Aachen, the relentless air attacks on the Ruhr – and days that were grey or bright depending on whether that looked-for letter had arrived. Weeks ago one of the newspapers had offered a prize of £500 for the best Armistice Day Cartoon. Perhaps November would be the month everyone was waiting for. It came and went, Belgium was freed, Budapest fell to the Russians. And still for the lucky ones the letters came.

The higher one rides on the spirit of hope, the greater the fall. December and the German counter attack, Christmas and the Battle of Ardennes. At home Bing Crosby crooned from every wireless set that he was 'dreaming of a White Christmas'. In Europe Christmas was the whitest and coldest for a quarter of a century. Attack and counter attack. On both sides prisoners taken, on both sides agony and slaughter. So ended 1944.

'A Happy New year, our new year,' Jane and Grant had said at its beginning. And so it had proved. Its last day brought the familiar click of the letterbox. So far apart, yet they were still together.

'Richard wanted me to get some leave when he was in port, Mum. He phoned me, tried to persuade me to arrange to join him. Did he tell you?'

Jane could feel how closely Liz was watching her.

'No. I just had a letter saying it was a quick turn round, he'd not be coming home.'

'He said that?'

'Liz, whatever's wrong between you two, is anything worth what's happening? You avoid being together, you even avoid talking about each other. If Richard held out an olive branch, couldn't you have grasped it? Life goes on a long time.'

'Easy for you, Mum. You don't understand! And even if I could try and explain, you still wouldn't be able to understand. How could you? I've known other twins, twins you think of as two separate people . . . That's how we should have been. Had our own lives, found our own way.'

'But you wouldn't go and see him? Aren't you hurting yourself every bit as much as you are him?'

Liz turned her back and looked out on to Shalbury Hill, the pavement slippery with ice.

'Don't you mean that you want me to kiss and make up with Richard so that you can wash your hands of us with a clear conscience?'

'Is that what you really think?'

Ice outside and ice inside; they both knew it was dangerously thin.

'I try not to think about any of it. But if you had to get another husband after Dad, I wish you'd picked one who hadn't such a knowledge of me.' She was full of resentment.

'You're not being fair, Liz. He helped you and you resent him for it. Anyway, after the life he's had these last months, I hardly think you weigh very heavy on his mind. What was of paramount importance to you was hardly likely to have been to him.' It was a lie and she knew it, but a lie on which they had to build towards a future. 'We were talking about Richard. He's miserable, you're miserable – and Liz, I hate saying this, but not saying it could be even worse – supposing he didn't come home? Supposing after all you've meant to each other, you weren't given the chance to put your differences aside?'

'Shut up, Mum,' Liz croaked. 'Don't even say it! Don't you see I can't, not until things are right again with Hartley.'

Standing by her side, Jane put an arm around her shoulders.

'It'll all come right. For you and Hartley, for Richard, for Grant and me – '

'Why should it? What makes you think we're so different from all the others?'

That was on the 1st of January, a bright day if it was to be measured by the click of the letterbox, although from the date Jane could see that Grant's short note had been written a week before Christmas. As the early days of the new year passed other letters came: the usual bills, a form from the Grammar School for her to sign vouching that Greta hadn't been in contact with any infectious diseases during the holidays, a letter from Hartley, a letter from Richard. But nothing from Grant.

Since before Christmas the Battle of the Bulge had raged. To bolster the public's morale seemed to be the newspapers' task. Facts were there, buried under the headline. 'Two Armies Slug Ahead'; only in small print further down the page was mention made of the thousands killed, taken prisoner, or flooding into the hospitals behind the front. Combat fatigue, trench foot, pneumonia, exhaustion, fighting wounds – the pieces that had to be picked up. But what of him? Was he not as vulnerable as the next, as cold, as exhausted? Each morning she watched for the post woman to cycle up the hill.

CHAPTER EIGHTEEN

No one admitted that the optimism of a couple of months ago had taken a nose dive. But in the shops, at the workshops, on the streets where the shoppers stopped to talk, those magic words 'as soon as it's over' weren't spoken with the same buoyancy as winter held Europe in its grip.

'I saw the post lady go by, Aunt Jane. She didn't bring us anything.'

'I know. I was watching from upstairs.'

That was for the first week or so; next came the 'I expect there'll be a whole batch together' period, lasting about a fortnight and becoming increasingly difficult to say with any ring of conviction; then, even harder, Jane pretended she wasn't listening for the click of the letterbox and Greta that she wasn't watching her anxiously. People talked about the Battle of the Bulge, the Ardennes, and heavy fighting around a town called Bastogne – somewhere Jane had never even heard of until now, yet which was etched on her mind by a newspaper picture of an American soldier, haggard and battle-weary. Looking at that picture she thought of the swagger of the men they'd got used to seeing about the town here, a swagger that they'd come to know as covering a need to be liked. The picture haunted her through those days as she waited for a letter that didn't come.

Greta's life was very full but she still had time to worry about Jane. The exam results at the end of last term had been her encouragement for hard work and much the same sort of inspiration as those long division sums had been in her early days at Shelcoombe village school. But Greta was no swot. She was just as thrilled when she was selected for the first year netball team as when she got the highest mark in algebra. No letters from Grant cast a black cloud, would have done even if she hadn't known in that way she always did just what the silence was doing to Jane.

By this time Herbert Gower and Son had moved back to East Rimford. Jane was working at her ledgers in the office at the back of the stores on a bitterly cold day towards the end of January. She could hear the howl of the wind, buffeting from the north east, and even with two bars of the electric fire on, still her feet and fingers were like ice. Adding up a column of figures, she was interrupted by a tap on her door.

'Come in.' She looked up to see her bowler-hatted friend Harold Roach beaming at her.

'The day I've been looking forward to, Mrs Gower! Back where you belong! Nothing is so bad it lasts forever.' He pulled off his woollen glove and wrung her hand with vigour. 'Not too late to wish you a happy new year, I hope?'

'And you, Mr Roach. Do sit down. A chair this time, not a carboy of disinfectant.'

'Got rid of your American invasion. Back to normal. Ah, yes, and soon we'll be out of the wood altogether. Next visit, perhaps that will be how we find things, eh?'

The rotund little fellow was digging in his case for pamphlets, smiling with delight at the thought of normality waiting just around the corner. He had the sort of unfaltering faith in tomorrow Jane needed. Always at the top of her mind was the daily vigil for the post lady; now, listening to his assurance, she made herself believe it was only a matter of being patient. Letters would come; Grant would come; peace would come.

'And when we find ourselves out of the wood, as you call it, then, Mr Roach, I shan't be here at all.' Hearing herself say it helped to chase the shadows and fears back into perspective. 'I shall be living in New England, a place called Arndale – with one of those American invaders.' Talking to the cheery little man, it was possible to hold doubt at bay.

Grant's last letter had been written on the 18th of December. Now it was the 28th of January. She had no illusions about the fighting. The newspapers worked on their usual principle: good news in large print, bad in small. But Jane read even the smallest; thousands of men killed, wounded, taken prisoner as fighting went on in the Ardennes. And where was Grant? If he could he would have got a letter to her . . . if he could . . . if . . .

All day she tried to cling to that confidence she'd felt as she'd told Harold Roach of her plans. She let herself imagine the sight of letters waiting on the mat at home. She was almost frightened to put her key in the front door.

'I'm first today, Aunt Jane.' Greta's voice was full of excitement. 'I've lit the fire. And look! Look! Three of them, all waiting together!'

Only now as she slit open the first envelope did Jane admit even to herself just how frightened she'd been.

You think it's a pattern for living, you think you're used to it. Yet every time there's this gap it's like the first time all over again. But aloud, as she scanned the short letters, all she said was: 'He's okay. The last one was written on the 24th, so that was quick. He says to give you his love and say he hopes the netball is going well. He says to write and tell him.'

Their world was secure again.

January gave way to February. Peace wasn't here yet, the fighting was still bitter, but the newspapers were prescribing the sort of medicine their readers wanted. At Yalta the Big Three, Roosevelt, Churchill, and Stalin, met to discuss the framework of the terms of peace. A German Foreign Office spokesman declared that that same Yalta declaration released Germany from all moral scruples, and that every citizen was pledged to murder or poison any invader on his native soil; but this was given only a few lines at the bottom of the inside page.

Early March. Today the headline was big and bold: 'Patton's Men Reach the Rhine'; today Jane put an advertisement in a national farming paper offering the post of manager of Herbert Gower and Son, thriving agricultural engineering business in the beautiful and peaceful South Hams; today a letter arrived from Hartley, not from a prison camp but from an American transit centre. As the Allies moved forward, the German Army retreated and the camps were liberated. Hartley had taken the first step towards coming home. Today was a Red Letter Day, the first of all their tomorrows.

There were plenty of military hospitals in the south of England. Fate must have had a hand in sending the repatriated RAF prisoners released from the Oflag where Hartley had been held to the one it did. Arriving at Dover they were carried in waiting coaches, their thoughts already moving ahead of the hospital check they had to go through. Home. Wives, sweethearts, parents, English voices, the scent of an English spring.

'I remember this road.' Sitting next to Hartley, a young Flying Officer spoke – to himself or to anyone with an ear to listen. 'If they dropped me off now, I could cycle home from here. See right over there, Sugar Loaf Hill? Yes, and Caesar's Camp . . . Damned silly, taking us to some hospital! We know the medicine we need. Just to be free of the krauts. Why can't they give out the leave passes and let's get on our way?'

On this coach that was the general view. On some of the others the men had been in prison far longer. They were suffering from malnutrition and digestive disorders. But this lot considered themselves fit men. They even believed that their people would find no change in them.

'Journey's end!' someone shouted. The barrier had been lifted and the coach was passing into the grounds of a military hospital. Hartley was as keen as any of them to get through the medical examination and be on his way.

And then he saw the painted board and realized where they were. In that second all that coming back meant was brought home to him. Perhaps in a minute, perhaps in an hour, he'd see Liz. With a hand that was far from steady, he felt in his pocket for a packet of Lucky Strike, a gift from the American centre.

His medical went without a hitch. A year of captivity, short and far from nutritious rations, had cost him over two stone in weight. Twelve months ago he'd been well built and slim; now he was thin, and there were lines etched down his cheeks that belied his age. But considering the life he'd had, he was in good shape and was sent on to the Admin. block where he was issued with a leave pass for thirty-six days and a First Class Railway Warrant to take him to Totnes.

Enquiries here about Liz got him nowhere. She was a name on a register, a number on a payslip, nothing more as far as the administrators were concerned. So he decided to go to one of the wards, make enquiries of the nursing staff. A letter in advance, an arrangement of where and when they'd meet, these things would have given them time to prepare. As he came out of the Admin. block, he saw her hurrying across the quadrangle. Even at this distance there was no doubt. He could never mistake her.

'Liz!' His shout was spontaneous, just as it was to start to run towards her.

Normally to hear her name called would have made her turn to answer; to hear it called in *this* voice stopped her in her tracks. She was frightened to look round, frightened that it couldn't be true.

She heard his steps on the tarmac as he ran. Yes, it was, it must be! Not only did she turn, she ran to meet him. They neither of them thought beyond these seconds as they clung to each other. Feeling his arms around her was like coming home. How breathless he was after such a short sprint! That was her first coherent thought. Then, pulling back and looking at him, came another: life had left its mark on him.

The last time they'd been together had been that dreadful day with Richard. It crowded back on her. And on him too? Was that why his hands were shaking, why he couldn't control the nervous tic in his cheek?

'I'd no idea the men coming through were from your camp. Have you been checked?' She tried to sound nurse-like. It was the shelter she hid behind.

'Yes. I've got thirty-six days' leave. Five weeks, Liz!'

'The way things are looking, Hartley, I'd say five weeks' leave might mean that your war's over.'

'It wasn't the war I was thinking of. Liz! Oh, Liz.' He pressed her hands hard against his cheeks. His eyes were closed. For a moment she thought he was going to cry, but he controlled himself. 'When are you free? When can I be with you?'

'I don't know. I'm off duty at five o'clock, but I don't know. Today we're thrown off balance with your coming home. We must be sensible, Hartley. I meant all those things I said.'

He held her chin in his hand and forced her to meet his eyes.

'We've said so many things. We've said we love each other; we've said we always will; I've asked you to be my wife; you've told me that one day you will. And then there were other things. Things that between us we can overcome. Liz, if we meant all we told each other – and before God I swear to you that I meant every precious word – then how can there be anything we can't overcome?' His hands were on her shoulders. Her head was bent and this time he couldn't read her expression. He saw a tear splash on to her starched apron. Now, when he pulled her into his arms, it was a gentle gesture. They rested against each other.

Only then did they seem to realize their surroundings. The middle of the quadrangle, the middle of the day!

'I'll find somewhere to stay, meet you just after five. Liz, I love you so much.'

She nodded, the nearest she could manage to an answer on all counts.

'Here, blow your nose.' He passed her a brand new handkerchief. 'Courtesy of the American centre.' Then he smiled at her. It was a glimpse of the Hartley she'd grown up with. Richard, Hartley and her . . . No, she wouldn't let herself even begin to think.

'Hartley, book in for both of us. I'm not on duty until late tomorrow.' She met his eyes squarely. 'Book in for us together, both of us Ladell. Don't ask me anything. Just do it, Hartley. We can't talk in pubs or on park benches.'

'Liz, I – '

'Don't say anything now. Meet me at five – no, quarter past, that'll give me time to get my things.'

And she was gone.

He booked in at an old coaching house, left his bag in their room and walked; walked through the little town, his consciousness devouring every sound and movement, English voices, women with their shopping baskets, a post lady emptying a familiar red pillar box; walked in freedom. The joy of standing at a junction and deciding which way to go! Out of town he followed a stream then turned into a lane where, through the bare winter hedges, he could see the fields. Coming to a five bar gate, he climbed up to sit on it. Not a soul about, just himself under the clear March sky. How could anyone know if they'd never been held captive, never been herded always with hundreds of other men, just how precious freedom was? He looked around at a view as lovely as he'd dreamed of. His mind had never been so aware of beauty. He'd never heard the song of the birds as clearly.

This evening Liz would be with him. Taking off his cap he ran his fingers through his hair. Just to hold her in his arms, to know that was what she wanted. His throat felt tight with fear. Those nights he'd lain on his hard bunk, the air full of the smell of the spirits they used to kill the lice! Here, in the spring sunshine, he could still seem to smell the filthy stuff. How he'd longed for her . . . ached to be near her. Now, remembering, he pushed his shaking fist to his mouth, feeling his teeth bite. Supposing tonight he was no more able than he had been then? With his eyes closed he seemed to be back in that long hut, shutters closed over the windows; for men living under those conditions there is no privacy.

One night particularly stayed in his memory; somehow it encompassed all that the months had been. In the pitch black of a hot and sticky night he'd fed his mind on thoughts of home, of Liz, of all they'd shared. That last scene had thrust itself to the foreground, but he'd stamped it down. He'd imagined walking the Devon lanes with her, or swimming from a gritty shore; he'd thought of the first time he'd looked down at the white flesh of her lovely body, of loving her, of her warmth. With everything that he was his mind had reached out to her, his body aching with a longing from which there was no release. Movements from a bunk nearby. In the isolation of the black night someone else's dreams and desires had just for a moment unchained his fetters, transported him to where he longed to be. Listening, Hartley had lain there, jealous, filled with shame at his own frailties.

'Imagine it's Liz . . . go on . . . keep going . . . go on.' For a moment he'd believed his body might have weakly been trying to respond, then from the bunk below him had come a sudden movement. Cliff Harnett had been here nearly four years. Any dreams he had once had must long ago have passed from women to food and now to no more than survival. In the dark Cliff had blundered from the bunk, had groped for the bucket. The sound of his retching had been the end of hope for Hartley.

'Sorry, boys,' Cliff had panted when it was over, 'too much rich living.'

'Bloody maggoty soup,' someone from further down the hut had sympathized.

Cliff had shuffled back to his bunk. Now mixed with

he stench of the spirit was the smell of vomit. Hartley had tried to lose himself in Liz, even now his body had wanted her . . . tried . . . tried . . . until at last, hopelessly, he turned to lie on his front, his head buried in the crook of his arm to silence his tears. Twenty-three years old and impotent.

And tonight she'd be with him. It had to be right, like it used to be, or what hope had he?

'We can't talk in pubs or on park benches,' Liz had believed. Was it any easier when they finally got upstairs to the room they were to share? A wardrobe, a small chest of drawers, an armchair, a table to stand their cases on and a double bed, that was the extent of the furnishings. It was the bed that filled most of the room and most of their minds. When they'd met unexpectedly the barriers had been down; but it seemed to Liz that an afternoon apart had been enough to put them on their guard. How could Hartley believe they could ignore what had happened? How could he not condemn her for it? He must do. So she was on the defensive, expecting awkward undercurrents; she was frightened and uncertain.

Hartley was frightened too. It had been so easy to tell her there was nothing they couldn't overcome. But was it true? No one had ever mentioned Richard to him in all these months, except for that one letter from Jane. But he'd been there in Hartley's mind, ready to taunt him with memories of all their years together. Had there always been things he hadn't known about? Even when he and Liz had seemed to hold the whole world as their own, had Richard always held a part of her that could never belong to anyone else? And this evening, was that what she wanted to try to make him understand? Or did she want just to be alone with him, to let them find what they used to know? And if so, what if he were as useless as he feared?

'Who'd have thought, last night . . . ?' she laughed

370

nervously. Then she rushed on, not quite looking at him:
'It was so that we could have time on our own, that's why
I wanted us to come here. We can't gloss over things,
pretend it didn't happen.' Now she forced her eyes to
meet his. 'I got rid of the baby. I expect it was yours. If I'd
been sure of it then I wouldn't have cared about gossip,
all that sort of rot, but there was this other business.
Please, I've got to tell you. Don't interrupt, don't stop me.'
Again her gaze was on some spot on the wall beyond his
shoulder. 'Those days of Richard's leave in Oxford, I
knew how he felt about us. I tried to make him
understand, let him realize that it didn't make him and
me any less close –'

'Liz, that's –'

'No, don't stop me. He wouldn't understand about
you, he wouldn't listen. It's not fair, both of you pulling
at me. I am as I am. I love you both.'

'Are you saying –'

'I'm saying shut up, can't you, and listen.'

He reached out his hand to take hers but she pulled
away.

'All that week Richard and I were together in the
evenings. It was as if he was only complete because I was
there. In a way it was like that for me too; at least it was
with part of me. I told him that one day he'd fall in love,
get married. He knows it, Hartley, but he was frightened.
It was almost as if, until that day comes, he couldn't stand
on his own. Can you understand that? I doubt it. Richard
and I have never been the same as two ordinary separate
people.'

'I can understand all that, Liz. I've known it, I grew up
with it. It was always you and Richard.' He put his hands
on her shoulders and willed her to look at him. 'But that's
not all you are, one half of a relationship you say can't
stand alone. You're living in the past, pretending so that
you can protect a twin brother you love. All that I can
understand. But the baby – you said you couldn't be
sure?'

'It was his last evening . . . ' And so she told him. As she talked he drew her to sit on the edge of the bed. From the moment they came back to the flat in Oxford, through all that was left of Mrs Sid's elderberry wine, to the sound of her door opening, the knowledge that Richard was crying in the dark, to holding him in her arms, to fighting as his emotion, fear and passion gave him a strength she couldn't bear to think of . . . As she talked, her own tears helped wash away some of the shame and misery. He held his arm around her shoulder, drew her towards him.

'It's all behind us, Liz. There's so much that's happened to us we want just to forget.'

'There, you see!' She snorted. 'I knew you wouldn't understand. "I'm all right, Jack" isn't that what they say? When Richard was on leave he wanted me to go to Liverpool to meet him. He wanted to be able to feel that everything was right between us, that he hadn't let that one mistake spoil it all. But I couldn't go. Because of you I couldn't. Now, don't you see, it's the same for us. I can't just brush Richard to one side. If I did it would be a shadow always on us. Once the danger is all over, once I know he's safe . . .'

He seemed to be pondering what she'd told him.

'Yet you wanted us to come here tonight?'

'Tonight belongs just to us. How can that hurt anyone?'

Excitement tugged at him, excitement that at this moment knew no fear.

Their stolen hours in the flat at Oxford had always afforded them a certain amount of privacy. A cramped double bedroom in an old coaching house offered none. Back to back they prepared for the night. If he'd carried her here, swept along on a tide of passion, getting ready for bed would have been easy. If they'd been a married couple, they could have reached out to the past and it would have been easy. As it was, in silence they undressed. It was only March. The warm day had given way to a clear, cold night. The bedroom had no heating. Her nightdress on, she turned to him, running her fingers through her short curls in a nervous gesture. He was sitting on the edge of the bed wearing only his pyjama trousers, pulling on his jacket. His body was evidence of what this past year had been for him and the sight banished every other thought from her mind except thankfulness that he was home. Coming to kneel in front of him, she leant against him.

All his fears returned. Liz, his beloved Liz. With every fibre of his being he wanted to love her. He was useless. The hand that pressed her head against him was unsteady. And in those seconds she knew and understood. It was all part of the sight of his thin body, the shaking hands, the tic in his cheek.

'Liz . . . I want you, I want it to be like it was. I want . . . so ashamed . . .'

'It's cold out here. Let's get into the bed. I want it to be like it was too. So it will be. We've our whole lives ahead of us.' She'd believed herself in love with Hartley since she'd been at school – yet she felt that until this moment she'd never understood its true meaning. As they pulled the covers over them and lay close in each other's arms she tried to find the right words. 'This is our special moment. Nothing has ever made us more one with each other. Hold me close.' And then, a ghost from yesterday. 'I want to know we're together again, right down to our feet.'

When she'd dreamed of being with him again she'd never imagined that they could lie like this, their hearts filled with thankfulness. Both of them wanted a greater expression of their love, but because of these hours the foundations on which they built would be stronger.

She woke in the early hours and reached out to him. Half asleep he knew nothing but the warmth, the nearness, the love of his Liz. Moving on to him she carried him forward. He woke – or was it some wonderful dream?

Hartley was home, his war over.

The Rhine and the Oder had been crossed. The newspapers triumphantly proclaimed that all it would take now was 'One Good, Strong Heave'. But for Jane all the good news was overshadowed by that old fear. Again no letters. 'Germans Crack Up', 'Annihilation is Near at Hand'. Still no letter.

'Hi, Jane, it's me!' She recognized Meg's voice.

'In a car? Who are you with?' Jane shouted in answer.

'No one. It's legitimate business. John lent me his car and gave me an order of things he wants, just to keep it all above board. Can I come in? I want to talk to you.'

'Of course. Anything special, or just a chat? Nice to see you, either way.'

'Leading towards special. Put that nasty ledger away, Jane.' She settled in a chair facing Jane across the desk and dug in her handbag for a packet of nothing less than Passing Cloud. Jane took that as a pointer towards where the conversation would lead. 'John says he talked to you a day or two ago and that you hadn't heard from Grant for ages. What about now? Has anything come through?'

Jane shook her head. 'Things are pretty rough out there. It's happened before that there have been gaps.'

'Last night was my canteen night – well, sort of canteen night.' Meg chuckled. 'In fact I was at the American Club with a lieutenant; he's in administration at the hospital. I gave him Grant's name. This lieutenant, he's called Gavin Boone, he promised to make enquiries, see if anyone had had any contact with him, check the casualty lists. Don't bank on anything Jane. After all, if he's okay it's not likely there'll be anything to report.'

'Thanks, Meg. It's the uncertainty. I keep thinking if only I'd married him, been his next of kin. But as far as the authorities go, I'm nothing.'

Meg seemed to have dispensed with the subject of Grant.

'Here's John's list.' She put a piece of paper down, his

374

neat writing so familiar. 'He said to bring the harrow tines, the rest can wait until the lorry comes Keyhaven way. Jane, you asked me if I wanted to talk about anything special. I'm seriously thinking it might be time Benny and I came to roost somewhere.'

'Staying on for good with Mother, you mean?'

'Come on, Jane!' Meg laughed the suggestion aside.

'With John? John wants you to marry him?'

'Getting warmer. Very warm, in fact. He does want me to. He may not have got around to realizing it, but it's only a matter of time. I suppose you'll tell me I'm a fool. He's more than twice my age, I'll find someone else and regret it . . . all the sensible things that I ought to be weighing up against the positive advantages.'

'Do you love him, Meg?'

'You sound like an Agony Aunt in some dreadful women's mag! I think I could be quite happy living with him. He's not unattractive, likes the same sort of life as I do. And you know, Jane, it's rather nice being a lot younger, something I've not been used to. I've had lots of boyfriends – wouldn't be any good pretending different, not to you – but I've been on the same plane as them. John's a nice guy, he really is, and I can tell he likes me being younger. He's good to Benny too. I thought it would be a wise thing after I marry him if I let him officially adopt Ben, make him his proper father.'

'But you say he hasn't asked you to marry him?'

'Once I've decided, that can soon be remedied. John's dead keen. I know about these things.' She chuckled contentedly.

No agile cat had ever been more adept than Meg at falling safely on her feet! But what about John? Jane had come to know Meg well, good points and bad. Was she really ready to settle down with a husband old enough to be her father or, indeed, a husband of any age?

'On Saturday morning there's a pony sale in the Market. John's suggested taking us. He says Ben could keep a pony at Keyhaven. So on Saturday I may not be able to get in to see you, but if Gavin can tell me anything, I'll give you a ring from Grandem's before we go. It's "canteen" night Friday. Perhaps Gavin will have heard something by then.'

'Meg, you will play fair with John? Does he know you're not at the canteen?'

'What would be the point of telling him? He's much happier in ignorance. "Play fair", you say? Jane, I *always* play fair. If I marry John, I won't sell him short. He'll get good value.'

But Jane had a feeling Meg's idea of value had narrower parameters than the ones she had in mind.

'I'd better collect up those tines. I'm meeting John at the Red Lion for lunch.'

The incident had about it an element of fantasy. Ten minutes ago she'd been stacking a delivery of drill discs. Now here she was sitting in a jeep by the side of the young American lieutenant whom Meg had told her about only yesterday. Her own car was following behind with Meg at the steering wheel.

'I only met Meg the other evening, but when she heard I was based at the hospital she wanted me to ask around, see if any of the guys brought back knew of the whereabouts of this Major Holgate. I promised I would,' he grinned disarmingly, 'once I knew it was for a friend that she was asking. But with all that's been happening over there, I figured I hadn't a hope in hell of finding out anything about him. I guess I'm not the first to fall in and do as Meg wants. Have you any idea of just how many have gotten hurt fighting to get across the Rhine? The Field Hospitals must be overflowing. The tales I've heard these last weeks make your hair stand on end.'

'I've read every word I could lay eyes on. The newspapers look as though they tell you so much, yet they tell you nothing but bare bones with no flesh on, and everything's always wrapped up to make it sound like one happy victory march. I know that's not true. This sergeant you talked to – you say Grant had been looking after him. Did he say when – or where? Didn't he give you any idea at all of what he's going to tell me?' The hope in her held on to the thought: If it were something dreadful, surely it would have been easier for him to send a message, while at the same time fear clamoured: It must be bad. A sergeant Grant tended in a Field Dressing Station . . . why would he ask for me to be brought more than twenty miles to be told just that?

At the fork in the road Meg gave a cheery parp of her horn and turned off towards town, while the jeep continued until they joined the main road. It was a long time since Jane had travelled along here, a route that before the war, before petrol shortages, had been so familiar. She and Tim, a day at Newton Abbot Cattle Market . . . it was like looking at another life. In memory the sun must surely have been shining, at home the children on holiday from school, the four of them together, no shadows, no doubts. Another world. Today as they drove through the little market town, and on to the hospital of prefabricated buildings erected since last she'd passed this way, she made a discovery: it no longer hurt to take the lid off that box of memories, even to let her mind listen to the three young voices as the twins and Hartley had ridden back into the yard from one of their jaunts. Yesterday, all their yesterdays, were safely locked into the making of the woman she was today.

Lieutenant Gavin Boone braked and stopped with a suddenness akin to her own driving, then leapt out and came to open her door.

'I'll take you straight along to Bob – that's his name, Sergeant Bob Mullins. He's this way. When you're ready, you come and fetch me. That's me over there, the Admin. block. Second door along the corridor. Here we go then. And, say, Mrs Gower, I sure hope you'll like what he's got for you.'

Sergeant Bob Mullins wasn't a bit what she expected. A man of about her own age, overweight, with a cheery grin despite being held in a rigid and surely uncomfortable position. He had one leg in traction; his head too, the pulley fixed to an attachment fitted through what looked like a plaster helmet. Both arms were plastered.

'And you can still smile!' Her words were spontaneous.

'Won't feel any better if I cry, ma'am, so what's the use of grizzling?' Then, his smile gone: 'Plenty of my buddies would have liked the chance to be in my place.' She felt it was a warning, a lead-in to what he was going to tell her. 'Draw your chair up, ma'am –'

'Jane, Jane Gower, and you're Sergeant Mullins, the lieutenant told me.'

'Bob. I like just to be Bob. It's the major you want to hear about. If you like, you can pull the curtain along. Best I can offer in the way of private accommodation.'

She did as he said then drew the chair near to his bedside.

'Grant looked after you over there? When was that? You see, I've not heard anything for weeks. And I know I would have. I mean,' she rushed into what she felt she owed it to him to make clear, 'I wasn't – wasn't –'

'Just a pick-up? No. I reckon I can see you wouldn't be.'

A giggle threatened. At any other time it would have been funny. Now nerves and fear combined. To laugh would have been as much of a relief as to cry. But she did neither. Her fat friend hadn't realized his unfortunate choice of words; she mustn't embarrass him. Just wait till I tell Grant! bravado whispered.

'Can't tell you just when it was I saw him. Days of the week didn't mean much out there. Some of the FDSs – that's the dressing stations where the medics were – were set up out in the open ground. Sometimes they'd had time to dig slit trenches to work in, or again sometimes they took themselves a building if there was one still standing. Advancing, nothing's permanent. When I got this packet I don't remember where they took me. Guess I wouldn't have cared too much right then. Anyway,

378

when I came to – I'm not going to lie to you – when I came to, I yelled like a baby. That's when I came face to face with your major. I knew who he was, recognized him straight away from before we went over, when we were training. Funny how you can be so sure. Never a proper night's sleep, never an hour to draw a curtain on it all and rest your mind. No wonder he looked different – couldn't have been a man among us who didn't. We crossed the Rhine, and had it tough. I reckon when a soldier fights on his own soil, he finds extra strength. Jeez, but there was carnage – did your newspapers tell you about that? But I recognized him straight away, dead on his feet or not.

'Jeez, but I went to pieces! Couldn't stop myself. I can't tell you what I said – reckon it wouldn't have been fit for your ears if I could – nor what he said, but I remember him talking to me, I remember his steady voice – real gentle. Hell was going on all round us – there's no way I could make you feel what it was like. We talk of things being hell – Jeez, we don't know the meaning, most of the time. Yet he seemed to put himself between me and all that. Steady as a rock. He gave me a sort of quietness, inside me, I mean, ma'am, I felt safe.' She nodded.

'We were in a building of some sort. I figure, thinking about it now, that it might have been a warehouse. Then there was the most goddam terrible explosion. We all seemed to be thrown apart, that's the only way I can put it, all the wind sucked out of us. I must have gone unconscious. Next thing I knew, half knew, was the stretcher being carried out into the open. The air was thick, dust clogged in your mouth. I saw him again then, the major. The building was hit, like a broken toy in a sea of dust. There was yelling. They were trying to bring out the guys who'd been trapped. There was a sudden quiet. I reckon everything that could fall must have fallen. Then a cry, someone still inside the building. In all that hullabaloo, someone produced a needle and jabbed something into me. But I saw the major go back.

'The building was pretty knocked about. Another shell

was all it took. Like when you build cards into a tower. Just that final one is enough to knock the whole thing down. Must have been just seconds, those jabs soon send you off, but I saw him go inside, saw the front wall come down like a kid's toy.'

There was a pause. On the other side of the curtain, ward life went on; a cat-call to a nurse, badinage between the patients, the clatter of crockery. It must have been tea time. Hospitals were always hours ahead of anywhere else.

Jane ought to say something, she ought to thank him for wanting to tell her.

'If it's any help to know these things, when I look back on what happened, out of it all I shall remember him. He sort of stands out in my mind. In all that – that hell, he was steady, as understanding as my mom used to be when I was a kid. You know what I mean?'

She nodded. 'Yes, Bob, I know just what you mean. It couldn't have been easy for you to have to tell me.'

'Was the best way I could say thank you to him, that's what I figured.'

It was easier not to talk as the young lieutenant took her home. He must have realized that whatever Bob had had to tell her, he'd given her little grounds for hope. Good news doesn't wrap one in a protective shield of silence.

'Shalbury Hill,' she directed as they came into town.'Do you know it?'

'Sure I know it. That's where I met Meg, at the Club.'

The Officers' Club . . . dancing to what was so nearly the Glenn Miller sound . . . suppers taken early so that Greta could come.

'Thank you for taking me.' Her light blue eyes met his; she wasn't hiding from the truth. 'To know *anything* must be better than to be left with nothing – mustn't it?'

In the house Meg and Greta waited, watching the door as she came in.

'Not good?' Meg didn't need to ask.

'A sergeant, dreadfully wounded. Grant had looked after him at a Field Dressing Station. No, not good.'

Greta knew when not to ask and Meg accepted that she was going to hear no more than she knew already, at least for the present.

'I'm really sorry, you know that, Jane. Look, I'm going to get on my way. Grandem was meeting Ben from school and giving him his tea. I'm on duty at six.' Then, with a wink, 'Pouring mugs of tea. I actually am, tonight.'

They saw her out, and smiled. Jane thanked her for trying to help, Greta thanked her for being there after school. Then she was gone, and there was nothing left but the pretence of tea.

'I've got to take Mufti out,' Greta said afterwards. 'You wouldn't like to come, I suppose?'

Jane didn't want to go walking, but then she didn't want to stay at home either. Daylight was fading when, with Mufti playing his usual game of jumping to bite his lead, they made for the park.

'Remember the day you had to tell me about Dad, Aunt Jane? All the things you said to me?' Greta wanted to help but she didn't know how to. 'It was awful, that day was. Like I didn't have anything to hang on to. But I did.' She took hold of Jane's hand.

'Fish and chips, remember?' Jane tried to respond. Later, on her own, she'd let her mind follow where Bob Mullins had led; then, there would be no hiding from it.

'It wasn't the treat of the fish and chips though, it was because you were making me feel safe again, you sort of shared it with me.' Silence. And that's true, Greta told herself, I'm not making it up to make her feel better. But I hope she understands what I'm trying to tell her – about the sharing bit. Good job we've got each other.

They'd come to a bench by the riverside path. With Mufti standing with his head on one side, at a loss to understand what could be holding them up on a cold blustery evening, they sat down.

'There was a sergeant at the hospital, that's who I went to see . . .' And so Jane shared too.

Greta didn't interrupt. Only when Jane finished speaking she said: 'It's not fair. Why do the nice people have to get hurt – the good guys?' She purposely used the American expression, it was her epitaph for Grant.

The last evening that Grant had been at the cottage he'd said they were celebrating 'all of us being together'. All. Greta, her, and himself. Greta might not have shared the making of the plans for their 'after the war' but those castles in the air had housed all three of them. Jane knew there was a void in Greta's life as well as in her own. Neither of them talked about it, they didn't need to; they each put up a show of cheerfulness, but neither of them was fooled.

Hartley was free. He'd phoned Gower's and talked to Jane, his familiar voice and what he told her about spending his leave in Kent to be near Liz filling her with joy. How strange that joy and sorrow can live together in one heart.

'Herbert Gow – '

'Jane, it's me,' Meg's voice cut in. 'Get a piece of paper and a pencil.'

Jane did as she said. She wrote what she was told. She listened.

CHAPTER NINETEEN

She couldn't have heard right! It must have been a major who knew the *name* of Grant Holgate.

'Jane! Are you still there? Did you hear what I said?'

'No. I wrote down the address, but I wasn't sure what it was you said after that.'

'Grant – that's where he is! Gavin telephoned me this morning. He'd been making enquiries, you know. He heard last night that Grant had been brought back. He didn't know much, only that he has head wounds and has been sent to be seen by some high-ranking chappie. I don't remember his name. Jane, can you hear? Is it a bad line or something? You're not saying anything.'

'Can't believe it . . .'

'Gavin said he understood Grant had lost his memory. He phoned this hospital so that he could tell me as much as possible. They're operating either today or tomorrow. Jane, they told him it's a dangerous operation. There's no guarantee which way it could go. It's better to know, isn't it? Even a fifty-fifty chance must be so much better than nothing.'

Jane nodded – not that Meg knew that. 'It's like a miracle.'

'What will you do? I was thinking, if you want to go and see him, Ben and I could move in with Greta for a few days. I wouldn't mind a little while in town, to be honest.'

In just as long as it took to lock her desk drawers and put the ledgers in the cupboard, Jane was on her way home. She threw a few things in a small suitcase, wrote a letter to be left for Greta, then drove to Emily's to collect Meg.

As she drew up outside the house, her mother-in-law

came out to greet her, her expression setting the scene.

'You mean to tell me you're chasing off after this GI you were always about with! If you want my opinion,' and even if she didn't, it was apparent Jane was going to be treated to it, 'it's nothing short of disgraceful. That my son's wife could throw herself at a man's head like that! Where's your sense of shame? If this American you seem so besotted with had wanted you to know where he was, don't you think he would have got a message through to you? As clear as a pikestaff, he'd thought to have shaken the dust of England off his boots.'

'Mother, I've told you before . . . Grant isn't some American good time boyfriend. I'm going to marry him.'

'Stupid woman. And what about your responsibilities to Tim's people – to Richard and Liz, to the business and all you promised his father? The very idea of putting some stranger in to manage Father's business! Throw the whole lot away without a qualm because you don't like the bed to yourself, is that it?'

'Is Meg ready?'

'When she is, she'll come out. I told her I wanted a word with you. Someone's got to speak to you straight. Have you stopped to look at poor young Richard? And Liz, what does she think of the man you want to put in Tim's place?' From Jane's tight-lipped expression she knew she'd gone further than was wise; antagonize her too much and it could rebound, it could find Father's business with no manager engaged and no one to look after things. 'I'm not denying you've had worries, I can quite see you would have been more than ready to fall for a smooth tongue. We none of us can help what we are. Some of us have more strength of character than others, I dare say. Now, take Meg –'

'I'm hoping to. Is she going to be long?'

Ignoring her, Emily went on: 'Such a pretty girl. If she'd been some simpleton ready to fall for the first sweet word, she could have found herself a man before this, working at the canteen pretty well every evening. But she puts her responsibilities first. Between you and me, I can see the way John Carlisle looks at her. Don't they say it's when a man thinks that he is past love, it's then he meets his last love? It gladdens my heart to see it. Meg comes from a good stable, I can recognize it in her. It'll please me to see her mistress of Keyhaven, and what a good start in life for my little Ben!'

'Here she comes now.' Jane leant across to open the door for Meg, a sign to Emily that she was on her way.

'Just you remember what I said. If you haven't any pride for your own sake, then think of Tim and of his children. Chasing after a man who gives no sign of wanting you!'

The car moved off.

'You'd think I'd be worrying about what she says,' Jane mused, as much to herself as to Meg, 'but I'm not. It's one of two reasons that he hasn't got in touch with me. One is that he can't remember. The second is that there's more wrong with him than we know, that he believes he ought not to draw me into it.'

In fact there was yet another reason, one that she hadn't considered.

It was nearly an hour's bus ride from the station to the hospital, a complex of long concrete buildings, metal-framed casement windows and flat roofs. The complex was a blot on the landscape, yet today Jane saw it as beautiful as she hurried up the tarmac driveway.

A notice board on one building declared it to be 'Block A. Admin'. Thinking of helpful Lieutenant Gavin Boone she decided that was where she should go. It was a sergeant who greeted her. He listened to her request, nodding his head as he digested her words. With her heart a hundred per cent on her mission, her mind couldn't help but be fascinated by his slow, steady movements: two chews of the jaw to every one nod of the head.

'You just take a seat in here, ma'am, and I'll go hustle

up the major's whereabouts. If he's in for a head wound, I'd say we'll track him down in Block F. How's about a cup of coffee? Hey, Morg, get the lady a coffee, will ya, while I go find out where this Major Holgate is.'

Her journey had been long and uncomfortably crowded, ending in strap hanging for more than half the distance from Salisbury on the country bus. There was a friendliness about these GIs that warmed her heart. While she waited for the sergeant she drank a cup of coffee such as she hadn't tasted for months. She didn't even try to stop the pictures that formed in her mind as she re-kindled those dreams of what must surely one day be waiting for them in Arndale.

It was some minutes before she heard footsteps, the sergeant, and preceding him along the corridor, a nurse with all the smartness if not all the looks of Carol Roughton.

'You've come to visit Major Holgate? I can take you to see him, but I'm afraid he won't know you.'

'Is there someone who can explain to me what's wrong? What they're doing to him?'

'You'd better come into the office here. I'll read you his historiography.'

She did. To Jane it might have been in a foreign language. Uninvited, there came into her mind the memory of Emily's words, that she was chasing after a man who didn't want her. Probably that's what the nurse thought too. She saw herself as the crisply efficient American girl must see her.

'I can't understand what you've just read – you know I can't.' She was much too worried to be anything but honest. 'If you can't explain it to me, then I want to see someone who can. There must be a doctor I can talk to.' She stood up.

'Of course. I understand. The major's one of my patients.'

'So, in simple plain English, I want to know what happened to him. Why can't he remember? And I was

386

told he was going to have an operation. What will they do to him?' She couldn't bring herself to voice the other question: 'Is he going to get well?' Of course he was. Once she was with him, she'd make him remember. Whatever the barrier was, she'd break through it.

The plain English explanation told her that injuries had been sustained to his head and cervical vertebrae. He'd been sent back from the line to a military hospital in France. From his notes it seemed that on arrival he'd been unconscious for several hours. Afterwards he could remember only spasmodically and suffered frequent complete blackouts. He'd been shipped back to the United Kingdom, to a hospital in Surrey, for tests and examinations. His condition had remained unchanged and that's when he'd been passed on here.

'Colonel Spanswick is here, he's about the best in the field. If anyone can help him, it'll be the Colonel. He's operating tomorrow. He'll take a vein from the leg, then part of it will be used to replace an artery that feeds the brain. It's a long operation. The damage done to the brain may be irrecoverable.' Then she smiled, her expression saying as clearly as any words that she'd had time to change her opinion and that she recognized Jane's right to be concerned. 'It can be no more than a fifty-fifty chance. But any chance is better than none, and he could have no one better than Colonel Spanswick to take care of him. Now, if you like, I'll take you to see him.'

'How long can I stay?'

'I guess, Mrs Gower, it won't make any difference. He's in a room on his own so you won't be disturbing anyone however long you stay.' Then, holding Jane's gaze: 'Not even him.'

The corridor was long, the gunmetal grey heavy duty linoleum gleaming like glass. At the far end they turned to the right. Another corridor. Halfway down it the nurse opened a door and ushered Jane in, leaving her alone with him.

So many emotions pushed into her mind. Love . . . shock . . . tenderness . . . fear. Love.

Bending over the bed, she rested her cheek against his. Did he even know? She tried to believe he did. Surely he must be aware? His eyes were half open, his breathing fast and shallow. As she touched him, as she spoke his name, as minute after minute she talked to him, he gave no sign. His body still had life; it was as if his soul had already gone. He had changed physically too; but then, of course he had! For weeks he'd lain like this, attached to drips to keep him alive; and the months before that had taken a toll just as great. She looked at his thin face, lines deeply etched, eyes sunk into their sockets.

'But you're here, you're alive.' She held his hand to her face as she knelt by the bed. 'Grant darling, it'll be all like we planned. Please, please, let him be better. Please, whatever they do tomorrow, let them make him well.'

It was hard to leave him. Tomorrow she'd come again. But by then the operation with its fifty-fifty chance would be over.

The bus stop was at a road junction about half a mile away. She was on completely strange ground. All she knew was that there was a bus due just after six o'clock and it would take her to Salisbury. Once there she'd have to find somewhere to stay the night.

Walking back to the junction she had to pass a cottage where the large garden had been turned over to growing vegetables. The board on the gate told her there were carrots, parsnips and leeks for sale. This was the only house around – and it was no more than five minutes' walk from the hospital.

A woman of indeterminate age and shape answered her knock.

'All I've got this evening is carrots or parsnips. The hens are laying though, I do have a few eggs.'

'No, it's not vegetables I want. I'm looking for somewhere to sleep for a few nights. My fiancé is in the American hospital up the road. He was brought back

388

from France. It took me an hour from Salisbury on the bus and that's the only place I know. I came there this morning – from Devon.'

'Going to get wed to one of those 'mericans? Well, fancy that. Not easy to take folk in, what with the rationing. Got your book, I take it?'

'Yes, I have – and my Identity Card, so you can see I'm what I say.'

'Best to step inside. I'll have to speak to Will. Don't know what he'll make of the idea. Don't take lodgers, never have. Had a couple pushed on us from Southampton back earlier, billeted you know, not because we wanted them. Still, these are not usual times we're living through and it's no good trying to believe they are.'

'The bus is due in a few minutes. Do you think he'll take long to make his mind up?'

'I'll brivet him along. Look at it out there, here comes the rain again. Thought it was too good to be true, trying to keep fine all day. Will, here's a body wants us to give her a bed.' Then, to Jane: 'You better wait here in the passage, let me talk to him.' And waiting, Jane heard the whispered conversation: 'Looks honest enough. Going to be married to one of the Yanks – no, before you jump in, she's not some flighty girl. Nice enough person.'

'Can't tell by looking,' hissed Will. 'Perhaps she's no such thing? Perhaps she's spying out the land there at the hospital?'

'Oh, you and all your silly spy talk! Those days are behind us. The way Hitler must be feeling right now, he'll be too busy protecting his own skin. Here, just you read the evening paper: "No Halting Monty's Tanks". Well, can I tell her we'll take her for a night and see how we like each other? If I throw her back on the street now she'll have a job to run to the main road in time for the bus back to Salisbury. That's where she was thinking she'd have to go.'

'Bring her in. I'll take a look.'

Jane must have passed the test. Ten minutes later she

had her feet under their kitchen table and a meal to match their own, two boiled eggs apiece.

At any other time Jane would have enjoyed the Stapletons. To sit by their kitchen range while Bertha's knitting needles clicked and Will puzzled over the crossword puzzle was like spending an evening with the Sids. So that they wouldn't feel they had to entertain her with conversation they could do without, she wrote to Greta. Tomorrow she'd add some more; or perhaps tomorrow she would tear up what she wrote tonight. Everything hinged on what the day would bring. Only one thing was harder than to build a picture in her mind of what those hours might bring – and that was to hold her imagination in check.

They plied her with coffee. One after another they looked in at the room where she waited – a reminder from the nurse that there was none better than the Colonel; an offer of his portable wireless set from the sergeant on the desk. She'd never been so aware that each hour is made up of sixty separate minutes and each minute of sixty separate seconds. Today she felt she'd counted each one of them.

But at last the time dragged by and the moment came when she was taken to his room. The start of another vigil, but this time one of hope. No longer did she restlessly look at her watch. Evening had come. The long ward just beyond the cubicle where they'd brought him was quiet, held in that stillness that starts the night.

Please, let him wake. Let him know and understand. Please . . .

Much later, from the other end of the building came a clatter that sounded like a pile of crockery being dropped. Someone must have had an accident in the kitchen. A hoot of laughter, then a door slammed. Perhaps it was the sudden noise that pierced his consciousness.

'Grant?' Did she imagine it or was there a flicker of his eyelids? 'Grant, can you hear me?' She slipped from the chair to kneel at his side, bending close to him. 'Please . . .' For surely this would be the moment? She'd been haunted by the emptiness she'd seen in his eyes yesterday.

Yes, he'd heard her, she was sure he had. 'Grant, darling, you're going to be better. You can hear me.'

His eyes flickered. For a second or two she knew he looked at her. He wanted to smile. The corners of his mouth told her so as his dry tongue reached to lick his cracked lips. She took his hand and felt his fingers bend to hold hers.

The next morning she telephoned John. He would tell Meg, Meg would tell Greta: Grant was on the road back to them.

At the end of the week she went home, knowing that as soon as Colonel Spanswick considered him fit to be moved, Grant would be sent to the hospital at Newton Abbot. Would Sergeant Mullins still be there? she wondered. He'd hardly looked likely to be going anywhere in a hurry!

'Isn't it remarkable, Aunt Jane,' Greta settled comfortably on the arm of the settee, Jane could tell from her expression that she was ready for an 'in-depth' talk, 'how it can seem as if nothing is straightforward, then suddenly everything falls into place? Like when you play patience. You seem quite stuck, can't do anything. Then one of the cards that's holding you up appears and you can start to move the others from one pile to another. And getting that one card can trigger off a whole lot of moves, sometimes get all four suits out. It's like that for us, isn't it? We were so deep in the doldrums when we didn't know what had happened about Grant. Now, suddenly, almost without us having to do more than sit and watch, just look at us!'

'It's no use our sitting and watching, Greta, my sweet. We have a lot to do.'

'Oh, yes, but doing is easy enough. What's so hard is when you don't know *what* to do, when there doesn't seem any pointer to where you're going.'

'We've got that all right,' Jane laughed, looked affectionately at her solemn young friend. 'Doing' wasn't always as easy as Greta imagined, though. It was months since Jane had decided she would never go back to Denby. She'd had the repair work carried out, then she'd put it in the agent's hands. Even that hadn't been easy. Now came the really difficult part. This morning she had received an offer for it. She'd been to see her solicitor, the wheels had been put in motion. Then the next difficult step. All the furniture was still in store. She mustn't be sentimental – and yet every single article in those chests was part of her life with Tim.

'There's Liz and Hartley soon going to be married; and we can stop worrying about Richard now. The war is good as finished, they're all signing treaties and things. Mr Hibbard comes next week to start helping you run the firm; Mr and Mrs Sid are truly pleased with living where they do. So, really, Aunt Jane, our cards have sorted themselves out like I said. Of course it may be a little while before we actually start living in Arndale. I expect I'll have another term or so at the Grammar School, don't you?'

She sounded so matter-of-fact. Yet, was she? Couldn't Jane detect a note of uncertainty at the thought of leaving all she'd worked so hard for and finding a place in a new country?

'Like you say, Greta, it's all working out. And we're lucky, so very lucky. Lots of people aren't.'

'I know. Millicent Proctor's father is a prisoner of war in the Far East. She feels pretty sick about all this talk of celebrating peace. It's so easy because it was the Germans who dropped the bombs here, and because of all the fighting just across the sea, for us to forget the men still out there. That's what she says.'

'That's how all their families must feel.'

'I've been thinking about it, Aunt Jane, about whether it's right for people here to celebrate as if peace has come. And do you know what I think? I think that we ought to. We ought to ring the church bells, put up the flags, cheer like mad. Because, you see, all the men who got themselves killed for this – men who got lost at sea – and remember how frightened we've been for Richard, supposing he'd been one of them – men who got shot down like Hartley – and those others like Dad, just ordinary people at home. Does it sound daft or can you see what I mean? That when we give a big cheer that it's over, it's really a big cheer for them, every one of them.'

Jane felt the sting of tears.

'Doesn't sound daft at all, Greta. It's about the most sensible reason I've heard for any of it.' But if it hadn't been for the war, she would never have known this child who was so dear to her.

After driving through Shelcoombe Jane turned right at the crossroads, drove along the top boundary of Keyhaven, turned left again and so down towards the coast. She knew she was being a coward, but she couldn't bring herself to pass Denby with 'Sold' on the notice board at the entrance to the yard.

'You're all right? These ruts in the lane aren't jarring you too much?' She looked anxiously at Grant.

'Sure I'm all right. Oh boy, am I just! You and me, driving together under a clear blue sky.' Then, as she pulled up behind the beach at Slapton, 'Just look at the sea. Would you ever believe it could turn into the evil grey devil we knew?'

'Let's walk a while, Grant. I want to show you the Leys. Oh, I dare say you've been there already, but not with an experienced hand. This was the children's favourite place, the first place they used to come to in the school holidays.'

'You've not told me much, Jane. Not about then –

about now, I mean. Have they sorted things out between them, all three of them?'

They sat down on a fallen tree trunk.

'Richard is so withdrawn. They were only all here for one weekend. Richard went to his grandmother, Hartley put up at the George and Liz with me. He accepts that Liz and Hartley are to be married – yet in such a surly way that it must spoil what she ought to be feeling. Hasn't she gone through enough, and Hartley too, without Richard behaving like the injured party?'

'Hmm, that's what reason tells us. I guess he can't help how he feels. Does it worry you, leaving them? Don't you think that they've got a grip on each other again now without you having to hold the strings?'

'Yes, I think they have. If all three of them had been unhappy, then there was no hope. But somehow, sometime, they'll find their way. No one can do it for them.'

'You say Richard's withdrawn with them? You've never really told me how he feels about us. He and I got on, I think – and yet you never say.'

'He likes you, as a person. But, darling, he wouldn't like me to marry even the Archangel Gabriel! Hartley loved Tim as dearly as either of them did, yet he can understand. Just give them time.'

'Jane, my honey, does it spoil the start for you? Like you say things are being spoilt for Liz?'

'Nothing could, Grant. When Meg phoned me to say she'd found out you'd been injured and were in that hospital in Hampshire, it was as if I'd been given a way forward. When you believe you've lost someone you love, and suddenly they're brought back to you, you see things clearly and you know –'

'Hampshire? But you knew before that. You say Meg told you?'

Jane laughed. 'Meg has contacts. She asked Lieutenant Boone to make enquiries. See if he could have lists checked for your name, all that sort of thing. He learnt that you'd been wounded –'

'But you knew! Carol wrote to you for me. I watched her write it when I was in the first hospital in France. I don't remember much, just snatches, but that's quite clear.'

'Perhaps it went astray. Perhaps you weren't thinking coherently and gave her the wrong address.'

He didn't answer. And wasn't it proof of her own happiness that she could feel a moment's sympathy for the girl who'd worked for him for so long? Just to look at his face was to tell her that Carol would be seeking fresh employment!

'You're going back a different way,' he remarked as she started up the car for the homeward run.

She nodded. He asked no questions. Neither did she when, a mile or so from the coast, he asked her to pull up. They both got out of the car and alone he walked to lean against the gate, gazing across the sloping fields, fields that were green again, cattle grazing as if nothing had ever disturbed the gentle way of life here in the South Hams. She didn't go with him. This moment was his own, his and those men whose memorial was only in the hearts of those who remembered them.

Some way away a tractor was at work. She closed her eyes and listened. From a branch of an elm tree on the edge of the field a blackbird called. In the far distance a dog barked. The sounds of the countryside – and on the breeze a voice whispered to her: 'All right, lady?' She nodded, opening her eyes and looking up at the high clear sky.

As Grant turned to come back to her she went to meet him, slipping her hand into his. This June day was special in so many ways. In Shelcoombe peace was being celebrated. The village street was on a slope, so the long trestle tables had been set up in Clampet Lane, a turning just beyond the school. A sloping hill couldn't stop them hanging bunting across the road, though, and today as Jane and Grant had driven through they'd seen Shelcoombe dressed overall for celebration. A piano stood on the forecourt outside Harold Batty's Bakery. It seemed a hill wouldn't deter the evening dancers either.

Today was special for another and more personal reason. This was the first time Grant had been allowed out for so long. Jane had collected him at two o'clock and brought him to the 'zone'. Now she was taking him home for tea before delivering him back to the hospital. It meant being less than honest in her petrol return, but she had no scruples about that.

Back in the car they drove on along the lane. The fields that had been Denby's, then Denby itself. Already the old barns were being taken down, Tim's office had gone. Again she drew to a halt, but this time she didn't get out.

'It's silly to care, I'm being sentimental and stupid. It's only a house and I shan't be here to see what goes on. But I do wish it was to be a family home again. Two women running stables for riding holidays! It's such a waste of all the house has to give.'

'Whatever Denby was, was what you were – you, Tim, the family, even the Sids from what I hear. The love you say it gave was only there because you folk made it that way.'

She nodded. 'I wish you and Tim had known each other.'

'I guess that's about the nicest thing you could say to me.'

And looking at Denby, remembering, she knew he was right.

The garden at Shalbury Hill was hardly the place for afternoon tea, but at least Mrs Mitchell wouldn't be finding a little job that needed her attention by the fence. As they'd passed the Institute on the way home, Jane had noticed her going in ready for the weekly Whist Drive.

From the scullery window she looked out. Grant and Greta were in deep conversation. On Greta's face was

396

that serious, thinking, expression. Watching them, Jane smiled to herself. Whatever it was the child found so important, Grant was giving her his whole attention. No need to hurry with the tea. She'd had Grant to herself all the afternoon. This was the first chance Greta had had to talk to him on his own for so long.

The two outside didn't even realize they were being watched.

'I've been thinking, Grant. And before I tell you what I've been thinking, I want you to promise me, honest injun, cross your heart and hope to die, because I do want the truth – I want you to promise not to fall in with what I think just to please me. Will you swear?'

'Solemnly I swear. You'll be truthful with me, so I will be with you, Greta.'

She liked the importance he gave to her deliberations.

'It started a long time ago. You know I was an evacuee, came to Aunt Jane when I was only six? There was just Dad and me in London, then my dad was killed in an air raid. Trying to rescue someone, he was.'

Grant heard the pride in her voice and nodded. For both of them it was an important moment. In that slight movement of his head, in the way she watched to see the effect of her words, they both paid their tribute to George Blake's bravery.

'When Aunt Jane adopted me, made me a proper part of the family, I stayed being Greta Blake. You must have noticed I didn't change to be Greta Gower? I was only a kid, you see, Grant. I thought that if I gave up Dad's name, it would make me less his. Aunt Jane never pushed me. Now, this is what I've been thinking: I've grown up a lot since those days, I've come to understand better. I hope you won't be upset if I talk to you about Uncle Tim? I can't remember him that clearly, I didn't know him for long. I never had time really to give anything of myself to him, nor time to take anything of him to keep for me either; not deep sort of mattering feelings, not like Aunt Jane must have. But Aunt Jane isn't going to be Gower any more, that's what I'm coming to. She's got more sense than I had when I was frightened of not keeping Dad's name.'

Again Grant nodded, a sign that he was following her reasoning.

'So, what I think is this, Grant. If you want us all to be called Holgate, then – well, that's all right with me.'

This time he smiled.

'Cross my heart, Greta, I think it's a splendid thing for us to be.'

'Phew! I was a bit scared. I thought you might think I was trying to take the place of . . .' Perhaps she ought not to have said it? Her voice faded.

'Of Zara? No one will do that, Greta, any more than I'll take the place of your dad in London.'

'Nor of Uncle Tim for Aunt Jane. It's like saying the Gowers who used to live at Denby are all safe in the Denby that used to be. Mrs Sid talks about it all so often. She's not seen what they're doing to Denby now. She says she doesn't want to know. For her Denby belongs to the Gowers, and that's how it will always be.'

'Mrs Sid is a wise lady. You'll miss her, Greta.'

'Sure I will.' The phrase tripped oddly from her lips. It seemed Greta was looking ahead to the next phase. 'Here comes Aunt Jane with the tea tray. Let's tell her what we've decided, shall we?'

Fontana Fiction

Fontana is a leading paperback publisher of fiction.
Below are some recent titles.

- [ ] KRYSALIS John Trenhaile £3.99
- [ ] PRINCES OF SANDASTRE Antony Swithin £2.99
- [ ] NIGHT WATCH Alastair MacNeill £3.50
- [ ] THE MINOTAUR Stephen Coonts £4.50
- [ ] THE QUEEN'S SECRET Jean Plaidy £3.99
- [ ] THE LEMON TREE Helen Forrester £3.99
- [ ] THE THIRTEEN-GUN SALUTE Patrick O'Brian £3.50
- [ ] STONE CITY Mitchell Smith £4.50
- [ ] ONLY YESTERDAY Syrell Leahy £2.99
- [ ] SHARPE'S WATERLOO Bernard Cornwell £3.50
- [ ] BLOOD BROTHER Brian Morrison £3.50
- [ ] THE BROW OF THE GALLOWGATE Doris Davidson £3.50

You can buy Fontana paperbacks at your local bookshop or
newsagent. Or you can order them from Fontana, Cash Sales
Department, Box 29, Douglas, Isle of Man. Please send a
cheque, postal or money order (not currency) worth the
purchase price plus 22p per book for postage (maximum postage
required is £3.00 for orders within the UK).

NAME (Block letters)_____

ADDRESS_____

_____

While every effort is made to keep prices low, it is sometimes necessary to increase them at short
notice. Fontana Paperbacks reserve the right to show new retail prices on covers which may differ
from those previously advertised in the text or elsewhere.